THE DARK TOWER VI
SONG OF SUSANNAH

STEPHEN KING

ILLUSTRATED BY
DARREL ANDERSON

POCKET BOOKS
New York   London   Toronto   Sydney

POCKET BOOKS, a division of Simon & Schuster, Inc.
1230 Avenue of the Americas, New York, NY 10020

This book is a work of fiction. Names, characters, places and incidents are products of the author's imagination or are used fictitiously. Any resemblance to actual events or locales or persons living or dead is entirely coincidental.

Originally published in hardcover in 2004 by Donald M. Grant, Publisher, Inc.

ISBN-13: 978-1-4165-2149-5
ISBN-10:   1-4165-2149-6

This Pocket Books premium edition June 2006

20 19

POCKET and colophon are registered trademarks of Simon & Schuster, Inc.

Cover illustration by Cliff Nielsen/Shannon Associates

Manufactured in the United States of America

For information regarding special discounts for bulk purchases, please contact Simon & Schuster Special Sales at 1-800-456-6798 or business@simonandschuster.com.

For Tabby, who knew when it was done

"Go, then. There are other worlds than these."

> John "Jake" Chambers

"I am a maid of constant sorrow
I've seen trouble all my days
All through the world I'm bound
  to ramble
I have no friends to show my
  way . . ."

> Traditional

"Fair is whatever God wants to do."

> Leif Enger
> *Peace Like a River*

CONTENTS

19

REPRODUCTION

THE DARK TOWER VI
SONG OF SUSANNAH

BEAMQUAKE

1ˢᵗ STANZA

ONE

"How long will the magic stay?"

At first no one answered Roland's question, and so he asked it again, this time looking across the living room of the rectory to where Henchick of the Manni sat with Cantab, who had married one of Henchick's numerous granddaughters. The two men were holding hands, as was the Manni way. The older man had lost a granddaughter that day, but if he grieved, the emotion did not show on his stony, composed face.

Next to Roland, holding no one's hand, silent and dreadfully white, sat Eddie Dean. Beside him, cross-legged on the floor, was Jake Chambers. He had pulled Oy into his lap, a thing Roland had never seen before and would not have believed the billy-bumbler would allow. Both Eddie and Jake were splattered with blood. That on Jake's shirt belonged to his friend Benny Slightman. That on Eddie's belonged to Margaret Eisenhart, once Margaret of Redpath, the lost granddaughter of the old patriarch. Both Eddie and Jake looked as tired as Roland felt, but he was quite sure there would be no rest for them this night. Distant, from town, came the sounds of fireworks and singing and celebration.

There was no celebration here. Benny and Margaret were dead, and Susannah was gone.

"Henchick, tell me, I beg: how long will the magic stay?"

The old man stroked his beard in a distracted fashion. "Gunslinger—*Roland*—I can't say. The magic of the door in that cave is beyond me. As thee must know."

"Tell me what you think. Based on what you *do* know."

Eddie raised his hands. They were dirty, there was blood under the nails, and they trembled. "Tell, Henchick," he said, speaking in a voice, humble and lost, that Roland had never heard before. "Tell, I beg."

Rosalita, Pere Callahan's woman of all work, came in with a tray. There were cups on it, and a carafe of steaming coffee. She, at least, had found time to change out of her bloody, dusty jeans and shirt and into a housedress, but her eyes were still shocked. They peered from her face like small animals from their burrows. She poured the coffee and passed the cups without speaking. Nor had she gotten all the blood, Roland saw as he took one of the cups. There was a streak of it on the back of her right hand. Margaret's or Benny's? He didn't know. Or much care. The Wolves had been defeated. They might or might not come again to Calla Bryn Sturgis. That was ka's business. Theirs was Susannah Dean, who had disappeared in the aftermath, taking Black Thirteen with her.

Henchick said: "Ye ask of kaven?"

"Aye, father," Roland agreed. "The persistence of magic."

Father Callahan took a cup of coffee with a nod and a distracted smile, but no word of thanks. He had spoken little since they'd come back from the cave. In his lap was a book called 'Salem's Lot, by a man of whom he had never heard. It purported to be a work of fiction, but he, Donald Callahan, was in it. He had lived in the town of which it told, had taken part in the events it recounted. He had looked on the back and on the rear flap for the author's photograph, queerly certain that he would see a version of his own face looking back at him (the way he'd looked in 1975, when these events had taken place, most likely), but there had been no picture, just a note about the book's writer that told very little. He lived in the state of Maine. He was married. He'd written one previous book, quite well reviewed, if you believed the quotations on the back.

"The greater the magic, the longer it persists," Cantab said, and then looked at Henchick questioningly.

"Aye," Henchick said. "Magic and glammer, both are one, and they do unroll from the back." He paused. "From the past, do'ee ken."

"This door opened on many places and many times in the world my friends came from," Roland said. "I would open it again, but just on the last two. The most recent two. Can that be done?"

They waited as Henchick and Cantab considered. The Manni were great travelers. If anyone

knew, if anyone could do what Roland wanted—
what they all wanted—it would be these folk.

Cantab leaned deferentially toward the old man,
the dinh of Calla Redpath. He whispered.
Henchick listened, his face expressionless, then
turned Cantab's head with one gnarled old hand
and whispered back.

Eddie shifted, and Roland felt him getting ready
to break loose, perhaps to begin shouting. He put a
restraining hand on Eddie's shoulder, and Eddie
subsided. For the time being, at least.

The whispered consultation went on for perhaps
five minutes while the others waited. The sounds of
celebration in the distance were difficult for Roland
to take; God knew how they must make Eddie feel.

At last Henchick patted Cantab's cheek with his
hand and turned to Roland.

"We think this may be done," he said.

"Thank God," Eddie muttered. Then, louder:
"Thank *God!* Let's go up there. We can meet you on
the East Road—"

Both of the bearded men were shaking their
heads, Henchick with a kind of stern sorrow,
Cantab with a look that was almost horror.

"We'll not go up to the Cave of the Voices in the
dark," Henchick said.

"We *have* to!" Eddie burst out. "You don't understand! It's not just a question of how long the magic
will or won't last, it's a question of time on the other
side! It goes faster over there, and once it's gone, it's
gone! Christ, Susannah could be having that baby
right now, and if it's some kind of cannibal—"

"Listen to me, young fellow," Henchick said,

"and hear me very well, I beg. The day is nigh gone."

This was true. Never in Roland's experience had a day run so quickly through his fingers. There had been the battle with the Wolves early, not long after dawn, then celebration there on the road for the victory and sorrow for their losses (which had been amazingly small, as things had fallen). Then had come the realization that Susannah was gone, the trek to the cave, their discoveries there. By the time they'd gotten back to the East Road battlefield, it had been past noon. Most of the townsfolk had left, bearing their saved children home in triumph. Henchick had agreed willingly enough to this palaver, but by the time they'd gotten back to the rectory, the sun had been on the wrong side of the sky.

We're going to get a night's rest, after all, Roland thought, and didn't know whether to be glad or disappointed. He could use sleep; that much he did know.

"I listen and hear," Eddie said, but Roland's hand was still on his shoulder, and he could feel the younger man trembling.

"Even were we willing to go, we couldn't persuade enough of the others to come wi' us," Henchick said.

"You're their dinh—"

"Aye, so you call it, and so I suppose I am, although it isn't our word, ye ken. In most things they'd follow me, and they know the debt they owe your ka-tet out of this day's work and would say thank ya any way they could. But they wouldn't go up that path and into that haunted place after dark." Henchick was shaking his head slowly and with great certainty. "No—that they will not do.

"Listen, young man. Cantab and I can be back at Redpath Kra-ten well before full dark. There we'll call our menfolk to the Tempa, which is to us as the Meeting Hall is to the forgetful folk." He glanced briefly at Callahan. "Say pardon, Pere, if the term offends ye."

Callahan nodded absently without looking up from the book, which he was turning over and over in his hands. It had been covered in protective plastic, as valuable first editions often are. The price lightly penciled on the flyleaf was $950. Some young man's second novel. He wondered what made it so valuable. If they ran into the book's owner, a man named Calvin Tower, he would surely ask. And that would only be the start of his questioning.

"We'll explain what it is ye want, and ask for volunteers. Of the sixty-eight men of Redpath Kraten, I believe all but four or five will agree to help—to blend their forces together. It will make powerful khef. Is that what ye call it? Khef? The sharing?"

"Yes," Roland said. "The sharing of water, we say."

"You couldn't fit anywhere that number of men in the mouth of that cave," Jake said. "Not even if half of them sat on the other half's shoulders."

"No need," Henchick said. "We'll put the most powerful inside—what we call the senders. The others can line up along the path, linked hand to hand and bob to bob. They'll be there before the sun goes rooftop tomorrow. I set my watch and warrant on it."

"We'll need tonight to gather our mags and bobs, anyway," Cantab said. He was looking at Eddie apologetically, and with some fear. The young man was in terrible pain, that was clear. And he was a gunslinger. A gunslinger might strike out, and when one did, it was never blindly.

"It could be too late," Eddie said, low. He looked at Roland with his hazel eyes. They were now bloodshot and dark with exhaustion. "Tomorrow could be too late even if the magic *hasn't* gone away."

Roland opened his mouth and Eddie raised a finger.

"Don't say ka, Roland. If you say ka one more time, I swear my head'll explode."

Roland closed his mouth.

Eddie turned back to the two bearded men in their dark, Quakerish cloaks. "And you can't be sure the magic will stay, can you? What could be opened tonight could be closed against us forever tomorrow. Not all the magnets and plumb-bobs in Manni creation could open it."

"Aye," Henchick said. "But your woman took the magic ball with her, and whatever'ee may think, Mid-World and the Borderlands are well shed of it."

"I'd sell my soul to have it back, and in my hands," Eddie said clearly.

They all looked shocked at this, even Jake, and Roland felt a deep urge to tell Eddie he must take that back, must unsay it. There were powerful forces working against their quest for the Tower, dark ones, and Black Thirteen was their clearest sigul. What could be used could also be misused, and the bends o' the rainbow had their own malevolent glammer, Thirteen most of all. Was the sum of all, perhaps. Even if they had possessed it, Roland would have fought to keep it out of Eddie Dean's hands. In his current state of sorrowing distraction, the ball would either destroy him or make him its slave in minutes.

"A stone might drink if it had a mouth," Rosa said dryly, startling them all. "Eddie, questions of magic aside, think of the path that goes up there. Then think of five dozen men, many of them nigh as old as Henchick, one or two blind as bats, trying to climb it after dark."

"The boulder," Jake said. "Remember the boulder you have to kind of slide by, with your feet sticking out over the drop?"

Eddie nodded reluctantly. Roland could see him trying to accept what he couldn't change. Groping for sanity.

"Susannah Dean is also a gunslinger," Roland said. "Mayhap she can take care of herself a little while."

"I don't think Susannah's in charge anymore," Eddie replied, "and neither do you. It's Mia's baby, after all, and it'll be Mia at the controls until the baby—the chap—comes."

Roland had an intuition then, and like so many he'd had over the years, it turned out to be true. "She may have been in charge when they left, but she may not be able to stay in charge."

Callahan spoke at last, looking up from the book which had so stunned him. "Why not?"

"Because it's not her world," Roland said. "It's Susannah's. If they can't find a way to work together, they may die together."

TWO

Henchick and Cantab went back to Manni Redpath, first to tell the gathered (and entirely male) elders about the day's work, and then to tell them what payment was required. Roland went with Rosa to her cottage. It stood up the hill from a formerly neat privy which was now mostly in ruins. Within this privy, standing useless sentinel, was what remained of Andy the Messenger Robot (many other functions). Rosalita undressed Roland slowly and completely. When he was mother-naked, she stretched beside him on her bed and rubbed him with special oils: cat-oil for his aches, a creamier, faintly perfumed blend for his most sensitive parts. They made love. They came together (the sort of physical accident fools take for fate), listening to the crackle of firecrackers from the Calla's high street and the boisterous shouts of the *folken,* most of them now well past tipsy, from the sound.

"Sleep," she said. "Tomorrow I see you no more. Not me, not Eisenhart or Overholser, not anyone in the Calla."

"Do you have the sight, then?" Roland asked. He sounded relaxed, even amused, but even when he had been deep in her heat and thrusting, the gnaw of Susannah had never left his mind: one of his ka-tet, and lost. Even if there had been no more than that, it would have been enough to keep him from true rest or ease.

"No," said she, "but I have feelings from time to time, like any other woman, especially about when her man is getting ready to move on."

"Is that what I am to you? Your man?"

Her gaze was both shy and steady. "For the little time ye've been here, aye, I like to think so. Do'ee call me wrong, Roland?"

He shook his head at once. It was good to be some woman's man again, if only for a short time.

She saw he meant it, and her face softened. She stroked his lean cheek. "We were well-met, Roland, were we not? Well-met in the Calla."

"Aye, lady."

She touched the remains of his right hand, then his right hip. "And how are your aches?"

To her he wouldn't lie. "Vile."

She nodded, then took hold of his left hand, which he'd managed to keep away from the lob-strosities. "And this un?"

"Fine," he said, but he felt a deep ache. Lurking. Waiting its time to come out. What Rosalita called the dry twist.

"Roland!" said she.

"Aye?"

Her eyes looked at him calmly. She still had hold of his left hand, touching it, culling out its secrets. "Finish your business as soon as you can."

"Is that your advice?"

"Aye, dearheart. Before your business finishes you."

THREE

Eddie sat on the back porch of the rectory as midnight came and what these folk would ever after call The Day of the East Road Battle passed into history (after which it would pass into myth . . . always assuming the world held together long enough for it to happen). In town the sounds of celebration had grown increasingly loud and feverish, until Eddie seriously began to wonder if they might not set the entire high street afire. And would he mind? Not a whit, say thanks and you're welcome, too. While Roland, Susannah, Jake, Eddie, and three women—Sisters of Oriza, they called themselves—stood against the Wolves, the rest of the Calla-*folken* had either been cowering back in town or in the rice by the riverbank. Yet ten years from now—maybe even five!—they would be telling each other about how they'd bagged their limit one day in autumn, standing shoulder to shoulder with the gunslingers.

It wasn't fair and part of him knew it wasn't fair, but never in his life had he felt so helpless, so lost, and so consequently mean. He would tell himself not to think of Susannah, to wonder where she was or if her demon child had yet been delivered, and find himself thinking of her, anyway. She had gone to New York, of that much he was sure. But when? Were people traveling in hansom cabs by gaslight or jetting around in anti-grav taxis driven by robots from North Central Positronics?

Is she even alive?

He would have shuddered away from this

thought if he could have, but the mind could be so cruel. He kept seeing her in the gutter somewhere down in Alphabet City, with a swastika carved on her forehead, and a placard reading GREETINGS FROM YOUR FRIENDS IN OXFORD TOWN hung around her neck.

Behind him the door from the rectory's kitchen opened. There was the soft padding sound of bare feet (his ears were sharp now, trained like the rest of his killer's equipment), and the click of toenails. Jake and Oy.

The kid sat down next to him in Callahan's rocking chair. He was dressed and wearing his docker's clutch. In it was the Ruger Jake had stolen from his father on the day he had run away from home. Today it had drawn . . . well, not blood. Not yet. Oil? Eddie smiled a little. There was no humor in it.

"Can't sleep, Jake?"

"Ake," Oy agreed, and collapsed at Jake's feet, muzzle resting on the boards between his paws.

"No," Jake said. "I keep thinking about Susannah." He paused, then added: "And Benny."

Eddie knew that was natural, the boy had seen his friend blown apart before his very eyes, of *course* he'd be thinking about him, but Eddie still felt a bitter spurt of jealousy, as if all of Jake's regard should have been saved for Eddie Dean's wife.

"That Tavery kid," Jake said. "It's his fault. Panicked. Got running. Broke his ankle. If not for him, Benny'd still be alive." And very softly—it would have chilled the heart of the boy in question had he heard it, Eddie had no doubt of that—Jake said: "Frank . . . fucking . . . Tavery."

Eddie reached out a hand that did not want to comfort and made it touch the kid's head. His hair was long. Needed a wash. Hell, needed a cut. Needed a mother to make sure the boy under it took care of it. No mother now, though, not for Jake. And a little miracle: giving comfort made Eddie feel better. Not a lot, but a little.

"Let it go," he said. "Done is done."

"Ka," Jake said bitterly.

"Ki-yet, ka," Oy said without raising his muzzle.

"Amen," Jake said, and laughed. It was disturbing in its coldness. Jake took the Ruger from its make-shift holster and looked at it. "This one will go through, because it came from the other side. That's what Roland says. The others may, too, because we won't be going todash. If they don't, Henchick will cache them in the cave and maybe we can come back for them."

"If we wind up in New York," Eddie said, "there'll be plenty of guns. And we'll find them."

"Not like Roland's. I hope like hell they go through. There aren't any guns left in any of the worlds like his. That's what I think."

It was what Eddie thought, too, but he didn't bother saying so. From town there came a rattle of firecrackers, then silence. It was winding down there. Winding down at last. Tomorrow there would undoubtedly be an all-day party on the common, a continuation of today's celebration but a little less drunk and a little more coherent. Roland and his ka-tet would be expected as guests of honor, but if the gods of creation were good and the door opened, they would be gone. Hunting Susannah. Finding her. Never mind hunting. *Finding.*

As if reading his thoughts (and he could do that, he was strong in the touch), Jake said: "She's still alive."

"How can you know that?"

"We would have felt it if she was gone."

"Jake, can you touch her?"

"No, but—"

Before he could finish, a deep rumbling came from the earth. The porch suddenly began to rise and fall like a boat on a heavy sea. They could hear the boards groaning. From the kitchen came the sound of rattling china like chattering teeth. Oy raised his head and whined. His foxy little face was comically startled, his ears laid back along his skull. In Callahan's parlor, something fell over and shattered.

Eddie's first thought, illogical but strong, was that Jake had killed Suze simply by declaring her still alive.

For a moment the shaking intensified. A window shattered as its frame was twisted out of shape. There was a crump from the darkness. Eddie assumed—correctly—that it was the ruined privy, now falling down completely. He was on his feet without realizing it. Jake was standing beside him, gripping his wrist. Eddie had drawn Roland's gun and now they both stood as if ready to begin shooting.

There was a final grumbling from deep in the

earth, and then the porch settled under their feet. At certain key points along the Beam, people were waking up and looking around, dazed. In the streets of one New York when, a few car alarms were going off. The following day's papers would report a minor earthquake: broken windows, no reported casualties. Just a little shake of the fundamentally sound bedrock.

Jake was looking at Eddie, eyes wide. And knowing.

The door opened behind them and Callahan came out onto the porch, dressed in flimsy white underpants that fell to his knees. The only other thing on him was the gold crucifix around his neck.

"It was an earthquake, wasn't it?" he said. "I felt one in northern California once, but never since coming to the Calla."

"It was a hell of a lot more than an earthquake," Eddie said, and pointed. The screened-in porch looked east, and over there the horizon was lit by silent artillery bursts of green lightning. Downhill from the rectory, the door of Rosalita's snug creaked open and then banged shut. She and Roland came up the hill together, she in her chemise and the gunslinger in a pair of jeans, both barefoot in the dew.

Eddie, Jake, and Callahan went down to them. Roland was looking fixedly at the already diminishing flickers of lightning in the east, where the land of Thunderclap waited for them, and the Court of the Crimson King, and, at the end of End-World, the Dark Tower itself.

If, Eddie thought. *If it still stands.*

"Jake was just saying that if Susannah died, we'd know it," Eddie said. "That there'd be what you call a sigul. Then comes this." He pointed to the Pere's lawn, where a new ridge had humped up, peeling the sod apart in one ten-foot line to show the puckered brown lips of the earth. A chorus of dogs was barking in town, but there were no sounds from the *folken,* at least not yet; Eddie supposed a goodly number had slept through the whole thing. The sleep of the drunken victorious. "But it wasn't anything to do with Suze. Was it?"

"Not directly, no."

"And it wasn't ours," Jake put in, "or the damage would have been a lot worse. Don't you think?"

Roland nodded.

Rosa looked at Jake with a mixture of puzzlement and fright. "Wasn't our *what,* boy? What are you talking about? It wasn't an earthquake, sure!"

"No," Roland said, "a *Beam*quake. One of the Beams holding up the Tower—which holds up everything—just let go. Just snapped."

Even in the faint light from the four 'seners flickering on the porch, Eddie saw Rosalita Munoz's face lose its color. She crossed herself. "A *Beam?* One of the *Beams?* Say no! Say not true!"

Eddie found himself thinking of some long-ago baseball scandal. Of some little boy begging, *Say it ain't so, Joe.*

"I can't," Roland told her, "because it is."

"How many of these Beams are there?" Callahan asked.

Roland looked at Jake, and nodded slightly: *Say your lesson, Jake of New York—speak and be true.*

"Six Beams connecting twelve portals," Jake said. "The twelve portals are at the twelve ends of the earth. Roland, Eddie, and Susannah really started their quest from the Portal of the Bear, and picked me up between there and Lud."

"Shardik," Eddie said. He was watching the last flickers of lightning in the east. "That was the bear's name."

"Yes, Shardik," Jake agreed. "So we're on the Beam of the Bear. All the Beams come together at the Dark Tower. Our Beam, on the other side of the Tower . . . ?" He looked at Roland for help. Roland, in turn, looked at Eddie Dean. Even now, it seemed, Roland was not done teaching them the Way of Eld.

Eddie either didn't see the look or chose to ignore it, but Roland would not be put off. "Eddie?" he murmured.

"We're on the Path of the Bear, Way of the Turtle," Eddie said absently. "I don't know why it would ever matter, since the Tower's as far as we're going, but on the other side it's the Path of the Turtle, Way of the Bear." And he recited:

> *"See the TURTLE of enormous girth!*
> *On his shell he holds the earth,*
> *His thought is slow but always kind;*
> *He holds us all within his mind."*

At this point, Rosalita took up the verse

> *"On his back the truth is carried,*
> *And there are love and duty married.*

He loves the earth and loves the sea,
And even loves a child like me."

"Not quite the way I learned it in my cradle and taught it to my friends," Roland said, "but close enough, by watch and by warrant."

"The Great Turtle's name is Maturin," Jake said, and shrugged. "If it matters."

"You have no way of telling which one broke?" Callahan said, studying Roland closely.

Roland shook his head. "All I know is that Jake's right—it wasn't ours. If it had been, nothing within a hundred miles of Calla Bryn Sturgis would be standing." Or maybe within a thousand miles— who could know? "The very birds would have fallen flaming from the sky."

"You speak of Armageddon," Callahan said in a low, troubled voice.

Roland shook his head, but not in disagreement. "I don't know that word, Pere, but I'm speaking of great death and great destruction, sure. And somewhere— along the Beam connecting Fish to Rat, perhaps— that has now happened."

"Are you positive this is true?" Rosa asked, low.

Roland nodded. He had been through this once before, when Gilead fell and civilization as he then understood it had ended. When he had been cast loose to wander with Cuthbert and Alain and Jamie and the few others of their ka-tet. One of the six Beams had broken then, and almost certainly not the first.

"How many Beams remain to hold the Tower?" Callahan asked.

For the first time, Eddie seemed interested in something other than the fate of his lost wife. He was looking at Roland with what was almost attention. And why not? This was, after all, the crucial question. *All things serve the Beam,* they said, and although the actual truth was that all things served the Tower, it was the Beams which held the Tower up. If they snapped—

"Two," Roland said. "There have to be at least two, I'd say. The one running through Calla Bryn Sturgis and another. But God knows how long they'll hold. Even without the Breakers working on them, I doubt they'd hold for long. We have to hurry."

Eddie had stiffened. "If you're suggesting we go on without Suze—"

Roland shook his head impatiently, as if to tell Eddie not to be a fool. "We can't win through to the Tower without her. For all I know, we can't win through without Mia's chap. It's in the hands of ka, and there used to be a saying in my country: 'Ka has no heart or mind.'"

"That one I can agree with," Eddie said.

"We might have another problem," Jake said.

Eddie frowned at him. "We don't *need* another problem."

"I know, but . . . what if the earthquake blocked the mouth of that cave? Or . . ." Jake hesitated, then reluctantly brought out what he was really afraid of. "Or knocked it down completely?"

Eddie reached out, took hold of Jake's shirt, and bundled it into his fist. "Don't say that. Don't you even *think* that."

Now they could hear voices from town. The *folken* would be gathering on the common again, Roland guessed. He further guessed that this day—and now this night—would be remembered in Calla Bryn Sturgis for a thousand years. If the Tower stood, that was.

Eddie let go of Jake's shirt and then pawed at the place he had grabbed, as if to erase the wrinkles. He tried a smile that made him look feeble and old.

Roland turned to Callahan. "Will the Manni still turn up tomorrow? You know this bunch better than I."

Callahan shrugged. "Henchick's a man of his word. Whether he can hold the others to his word after what just happened . . . that, Roland, I don't know."

"He better be able to," Eddie said darkly. "He just better be."

Roland of Gilead said, "Who's for Watch Me?"

Eddie looked at him, unbelieving.

"We're going to be up until morning light," the gunslinger said. "We might as well pass the time."

So they played Watch Me, and Rosalita won hand after hand, adding up their scores on a piece of slate with no smile of triumph—with no expression at all that Jake could read. At least not at first. He was tempted to try the touch, but had decided that to use it for any but the strongest reasons was wrong. Using it to see behind Rosa's poker face would be like watching her undress. Or watching her and Roland make love.

Yet as the game went on and the northeast

finally began to grow lighter, Jake guessed he knew what she was thinking of after all, because it was what *he* was thinking of. On some level of their minds, all of them would be thinking of those last two Beams, from now until the end.

Waiting for one or both of them to snap. Whether it was them trailing Susannah or Rosa cooking her dinner or even Ben Slightman, mourning his dead son out there on Vaughn Eisenhart's ranch, all of them would now be thinking of the same thing: only two left, and the Breakers working against them night and day, eating into them, *killing* them.

How long before everything ended? And *how* would it end? Would they hear the vast rumble of those enormous slate-colored stones as they fell? Would the sky tear open like a flimsy piece of cloth, spilling out the monstrosities that lived in the todash darkness? Would there be time to cry out? Would there be an afterlife, or would even Heaven and Hell be obliterated by the fall of the Dark Tower?

He looked at Roland and sent a thought, as clearly as he could: *Roland, help us.*

And one came back, filling his mind with cold comfort (ah, but comfort served cold was better than no comfort at all): *If I can.*

"Watch Me," said Rosalita, and laid down her cards. She had built Wands, the high run, and the card on top was Madame Death.

STAVE: *Commala-come-come*
There's a young man with a gun.

Young man lost his honey
When she took it on the run.

RESPONSE: *Commala-come-one!*
She took it on the run!
Left her baby lonely but
Her baby ain't done.

THE PERSISTENCE OF MAGIC

2ND STANZA

ONE

They needn't have worried about the Manni-folk showing up. Henchick, dour as ever, appeared at the town common, which had been the designated setting-out point, with forty men. He assured Roland it would be enough to open the Unfound Door, if it could indeed be opened now that what he called "the dark glass" was gone. The old man offered no word of apology for showing up with less than the promised number of men, but he kept tugging on his beard. Sometimes with both hands.

"Why does he do that, Pere, do you know?" Jake asked Callahan. Henchick's troops were rolling eastward in a dozen bucka-waggons. Behind these, drawn by a pair of albino asses with freakishly long ears and fiery pink eyes, was a two-wheeled fly completely covered in white duck. To Jake it looked like a big Jiffy-Pop container on wheels. Henchick rode upon this contraption alone, gloomily yanking at his chin-whiskers.

"I think it means he's embarrassed," Callahan said.

"I don't see why. I'm surprised so many showed up, after the Beamquake and all."

"What he learned when the ground shook is that some of his men were more afraid of that than of him. As far as Henchick's concerned, it adds up to an unkept promise. Not just *any* unkept promise, either, but one he made to your dinh. He's lost face." And, without changing his tone of voice at all, tricking him into an answer he would not otherwise have given, Callahan asked: "Is she still alive, then, your molly?"

"Yes, but in ter—" Jake began, then covered his mouth. He looked at Callahan accusingly. Ahead of them, on the seat of the two-wheeled fly, Henchick looked around, startled, as if they had raised their voices in argument. Callahan wondered if everyone in this damned story had the touch but him.

It's not a story. It's not a story, it's my life!

But it was hard to believe that, wasn't it, when you'd seen yourself set in type as a major character in a book with the word FICTION on the copyright page. Doubleday and Company, 1975. A book about vampires, yet, which everyone *knew* weren't real. Except they had been. And, in at least some of the worlds adjacent to this one, still were.

"Don't treat me like that," Jake said. "Don't *trick* me like that. Not if we're all on the same side, Pere. Okay?"

"I'm sorry," Callahan said. And then: "Cry pardon."

Jake smiled wanly and stroked Oy, who was riding in the front pocket of his poncho.

"Is she—"

The boy shook his head. "I don't want to talk

about her now, Pere. It's best we not even think about her. I have a feeling—I don't know if it's true or not, but it's strong—that something's looking for her. If there is, it's better it not overhear us. And it could."

"Something . . . ?"

Jake reached out and touched the kerchief Callahan wore around his neck, cowboy-style. It was red. Then he put a hand briefly over his left eye. For a moment Callahan didn't understand, and then he did. The red eye. The Eye of the King.

He sat back on the seat of the waggon and said no more. Behind them, not talking, Roland and Eddie rode horseback, side by side. Both were carrying their gunna as well as their guns, and Jake had his own in the waggon behind him. If they came back to Calla Bryn Sturgis after today, it wouldn't be for long.

In terror was what he had started to say, but it was worse than that. Impossibly faint, impossibly distant, but still clear, Jake could hear Susannah screaming. He only hoped Eddie did not.

TWO

So they rode away from a town that mostly slept in emotional exhaustion despite the quake which had struck it. The day was cool enough so that when they started out they could see their breath on the air, and a light scrim of frost coated the dead cornstalks. A mist hung over the Devar-tete Whye like the river's own spent breath. Roland thought: *This is the edge of winter.*

An hour's ride brought them to the arroyo country. There was no sound but the jingle of trace, the squeak of wheels, the clop of horses, an occasional sardonic honk from one of the albino asses pulling the fly, and distant, the call of rusties on the wing. Headed south, perhaps, if they could still find it.

Ten or fifteen minutes after the land began to rise on their right, filling in with bluffs and cliffs and mesas, they returned to the place where, just twenty-four hours before, they had come with the children of the Calla and fought their battle. Here a track split off from the East Road and rambled more or less northwest. In the ditch on the other side of the road was a raw trench of earth. It was the hide where Roland, his ka-tet, and the ladies of the dish had waited for the Wolves.

And, speaking of the Wolves, where were they? When they'd left this place of ambush, it had been littered with bodies. Over sixty, all told, man-shaped creatures who had come riding out of the west wearing gray pants, green cloaks, and snarling wolf-masks.

Roland dismounted and walked up beside Henchick, who was getting down from the two-wheeled fly with the stiff awkwardness of age. Roland made no effort to help him. Henchick wouldn't expect it, might even be offended by it.

The gunslinger let him give his dark cloak a final settling shake, started to ask his question, and then realized he didn't have to. Forty or fifty yards farther along, on the right side of the road, was a vast hill of uprooted corn-plants where no hill had been the day before. It was a funerary heap, Roland saw, one which had been constructed without any degree of respect. He hadn't lost any time or wasted any effort wondering how the *folken* had spent the previous afternoon—before beginning the party they were now undoubtedly sleeping off—but now he saw their work before him. Had they been afraid the Wolves might come back to life? he wondered, and knew that, on some level, that was exactly what they'd feared. And so they'd dragged the heavy, inert bodies (gray horses as well as gray-clad Wolves) off into the corn, stacked them willy-rully, then covered them with uprooted corn-plants. Today they'd turn this bier into a pyre. And if the seminon winds came? Roland guessed they'd light it up anyway, and chance a possible conflagration in the fertile land between road and river. Why not? The growing season was over for the year, and there was nothing like fire for fertilizer, so the old folks did say; besides, the *folken* would not really rest easy until that hill was burned. And even then few of them would like to come out here.

"Roland, look," Eddie said in a voice that trembled somewhere between sorrow and rage. "Ah, goddammit, *look*."

Near the end of the path, where Jake, Benny Slightman, and the Tavery twins had waited before making their final dash for safety across the road, stood a scratched and battered wheelchair, its chrome winking brilliantly in the sun, its seat streaked with dust and blood. The left wheel was bent severely out of true.

"Why do'ee speak in anger?" Henchick inquired. He had been joined by Cantab and half a dozen

elders of what Eddie sometimes referred to as the
Cloak Folk. Two of these elders looked a good deal
older than Henchick himself, and Roland thought
of what Rosalita had said last night: *Many of them
nigh as old as Henchick, trying to climb that path
after dark.* Well, it wasn't dark, but he didn't know
if some of these would be able to walk as far as the
upsy part of the path to Doorway Cave, let alone
the rest of the way to the top.

"They brought your woman's rolling chair back
here to honor her. And you. So why do'ee speak in
anger?"

"Because it's not supposed to be all banged up,
and she's supposed to be in it," Eddie told the old
man. "Do you ken that, Henchick?"

"Anger is the most useless emotion," Henchick
intoned, "destructive to the mind and hurtful of the
heart."

Eddie's lips thinned to no more than a white scar
below his nose, but he managed to hold in a retort.
He walked over to Susannah's scarred chair—it
had rolled hundreds of miles since they'd found it
in Topeka, but its rolling days were done—and
looked down at it moodily. When Callahan
approached him, Eddie waved the Pere back.

Jake was looking at the place on the road where
Benny had been struck and killed. The boy's body
was gone, of course, and someone had covered his
spilled blood with a fresh layer of the oggan, but
Jake found he could see the dark splotches, anyway.
And Benny's severed arm, lying palm-up. Jake
remembered how his friend's Da' had staggered out
of the corn and seen his son lying there. For five sec-

onds or so he had been capable of no sound whatever, and Jake supposed that was time enough for someone to have told sai Slightman they'd gotten off incredibly light: one dead boy, one dead rancher's wife, another boy with a broken ankle. Piece of cake, really. But no one had and then Slightman the Elder had shrieked. Jake thought he would never forget the sound of that shriek, just as he would always see Benny lying here in the dark and bloody dirt with his arm off.

Beside the place where Benny had fallen was something else which had been covered with dirt. Jake could see just a small wink of metal. He dropped to one knee and excavated one of the Wolves' death-balls, things called sneetches. The Harry Potter model, according to what was written on them. Yesterday he'd held a couple of these in his hand and felt them vibrating. Heard their faint, malevolent hum. This one was as dead as a rock. Jake stood up and threw it toward the heap of corn-covered dead Wolves. Threw hard enough to make his arm hurt. That arm would probably be stiff tomorrow, but he didn't care. Didn't care much about Henchick's low opinion of anger, either. Eddie wanted his wife back; Jake wanted his friend. And while Eddie might get what *he* wanted somewhere down the line, Jake Chambers never would. Because dead was the gift that kept on giving. Dead, like diamonds, was forever.

He wanted to get going, wanted this part of the East Road looking at his back. He also wanted not to have to look at Susannah's empty, beat-up chair any longer. But the Manni had formed a ring around the spot where the battle had actually taken place, and Henchick was praying in a high, rapid voice that hurt Jake's ears: it sounded quite a lot like the squeal of a frightened pig. He spoke to something called the Over, asking for safe passage to yon cave and success of endeavor with no loss of life or sanity (Jake found this part of Henchick's prayer especially disturbing, as he'd never thought of sanity as a thing to be prayed for). The boss-man also begged the Over to enliven their mags and bobs. And finally he prayed for kaven, the persistence of magic, a phrase that seemed to have a special power for these people. When he was finished, they all said "Over-sam, Over-kra, Over-can-tah" in unison, and dropped their linked hands. A few went down on their knees to have a little extra palaver with the really *big* boss. Cantab, meanwhile, led four or five of the younger men to the fly. They folded back its snowy white top, revealing a number of large wooden boxes. Plumb-bobs and magnets, Jake guessed, and a lot bigger than the ones they wore around their necks. They'd brought out the heavy artillery for this little adventure. The boxes were covered with designs—stars and moons and odd geometric shapes—that looked cabalistic rather than Christian. But, Jake realized, he had no basis for believing the Manni were Christians. They might *look* like Quakers or Amish with their cloaks and beards and round-crowned black hats, might throw the occasional *thee* or *thou* into their conversation, but so far as Jake knew, neither the Quakers nor the Amish had ever made a hobby of traveling to other worlds.

Long polished wooden rods were pulled from another waggon. They were thrust through metal sleeves on the undersides of the engraved boxes. The boxes were called coffs, Jake learned. The Manni carried them like religious artifacts through the streets of a medieval town. Jake supposed that in a way they *were* religious artifacts.

They started up the path, which was still scattered with hair-ribbons, scraps of cloth, and a few small toys. These had been bait for the Wolves, and the bait had been taken.

When they reached the place where Frank Tavery had gotten his foot caught, Jake heard the voice of the useless git's beautiful sister in his mind: *Help him, please, sai, I beg.* He had, God forgive him. And Benny had died.

Jake looked away, grimacing, then thought *You're a gunslinger now, you gotta do better.* He forced himself to look back.

Pere Callahan's hand dropped onto his shoulder. "Son, are you all right? You're awfully pale."

"I'm okay," Jake said. A lump had risen in his throat, quite a large one, but he forced himself to swallow past it and repeat what he'd just said, telling the lie to himself rather than to the Pere: "Yeah, I'm okay."

Callahan nodded and shifted his own gunna (the halfhearted packsack of a town man who does not, in his heart, believe he's going anywhere) from his left shoulder to his right. "And what's going to happen when we get up to that cave? *If* we can get up to that cave?"

Jake shook his head. He didn't know.

THREE

The path was okay. A good deal of loose rock had shaken down on it, and the going was arduous for the men carrying the coffs, but in one respect their way was easier than before. The quake had dislodged the giant boulder that had almost blocked the path near the top. Eddie peered over and saw it lying far below, shattered into two pieces. There was some sort of lighter, sparkly stuff in its middle, making it look to Eddie like the world's largest hard-boiled egg.

The cave was still there, too, although a large pile of talus now lay in front of its mouth. Eddie joined some of the younger Manni in helping to clear it, tossing handfuls of busted-up shale (garnets gleaming in some of the pieces like drops of blood) over the side. Seeing the cave's mouth eased a band which had been squeezing Eddie's heart, but he didn't like the silence of the cave, which had been damnably chatty on his previous visit. From somewhere deep in its gullet he could hear the grating whine of a draft, but that was all. Where was his brother, Henry? Henry should have been bitching about how Balazar's gentlemen had killed him and it was all Eddie's fault. Where was his Ma, who should have been agreeing with Henry (and in equally dolorous tones)? Where was Margaret Eisenhart, complaining to Henchick, her grandfather, about how she'd been branded forgetful and then abandoned? This had been the Cave of the Voices long before it had been the Doorway Cave, but the voices had fallen silent. And the door looked . . . *stupid* was the word which first came to Eddie's mind. The second was *unimportant*. This cave had once been informed and defined by the voices from below; the door had been rendered awful and mysterious and powerful by the glass ball—Black Thirteen—which had come into the Calla through it.

But now it's left the same way, and it's just an old door that doesn't—

Eddie tried to stifle the thought and couldn't.

—that doesn't go anywhere.

He turned to Henchick, disgusted by the sudden welling of tears in his eyes but unable to stop them. "There's no magic left here," he said. His voice was wretched with despair. "There's nothing behind that fucking door but stale air and fallen rock. You're a fool and I'm another."

There were shocked gasps at this, but Henchick looked at Eddie with eyes that almost seemed to twinkle. "Lewis, Thonnie!" he said, almost jovially. "Bring me the Branni coff."

Two strapping young men with short beards and hair pulled back in long braids stepped forward. Between them they bore an ironwood coff about four feet long, and heavy, from the way they carried the poles. They set it before Henchick.

"Open it, Eddie of New York."

Thonnie and Lewis looked at him, questioning and a little afraid. The older Manni men, Eddie saw, were watching with a kind of greedy interest. He supposed it took a few years to become fully invested in the Manni brand of extravagant weirdness; in time Lewis and Thonnie would get there, but they hadn't made it much past peculiar as yet.

Henchick nodded, a little impatiently. Eddie bent and opened the box. It was easy. There was no lock. Inside was a silk cloth. Henchick removed it with a magician's flourish and disclosed a plumb-bob on a chain. To Eddie it looked like an old-fashioned child's top, and was nowhere near as big as he had expected. It was perhaps eighteen inches long from its pointed tip to its broader top and made of some yellowish wood that looked greasy. It was on a silver chain that had been looped around a crystal plug set in the coff's top.

"Take it out," Henchick said, and when Eddie looked to Roland, the hair over the old man's mouth opened and a set of perfect white teeth displayed themselves in a smile of astounding cynicism. "Why do'ee look to your dinh, young snivelment? The magic's gone out of this place, you said so yourself! And would'ee not know? Why, thee must be all of . . . I don't know . . . twenty-five?"

Snickers from the Manni who were close enough to hear this jape, several of them not yet twenty-five themselves.

Furious with the old bastard—and with himself, as well—Eddie reached into the box. Henchick stayed his hand.

"Touch not the bob itself. Not if thee'd keep thy cream in on one side and thy crap on the other. By the chain, do'ee kennit?"

Eddie almost reached for the bob anyway—he'd already made a fool of himself in front of these people, there was really no reason not to finish the job—but he looked into Jake's grave gray eyes and changed his mind. The wind was blowing hard up here, chilling the sweat of the climb on his skin, making him shiver. Eddie reached forward again, took hold of the chain, and gingerly unwound it from the plug.

"Lift him out," Henchick said.

"What'll happen?"

Henchick nodded, as if Eddie had finally talked some sense. "That's to see. Lift him out."

Eddie did so. Given the obvious effort with which the two young men had been carrying the box, he was astounded at how light the bob was. Lifting it was like lifting a feather which had been attached to a four-foot length of fine-link chain. He looped the chain over the back of his fingers and held his hand in front of his eyes. He looked a little like a man about to make a puppet caper.

Eddie was about to ask Henchick again what the old man expected to happen, but before he could, the bob began to sway back and forth in modest arcs.

"I'm not doing that," Eddie said. "At least, I don't think I am. It must be the wind."

"I don't think it can be," Callahan said. "There are no flukes to—"

"Hush!" Cantab said, and with such a forbidding look that Callahan did hush.

Eddie stood in front of the cave, with all the arroyo country and most of Calla Bryn Sturgis spread out below him. Dreaming blue-gray in the far distance was the forest through which they had come to get here—the last vestige of Mid-World, where they would never go more. The wind gusted, blowing his hair back from his forehead, and suddenly he heard a humming sound.

Except he didn't. The humming was inside the hand in front of his eyes, the one with the chain lying upon the spread fingers. It was in his arm. And most of all, in his head.

At the far end of the chain, at about the height of Eddie's right knee, the bob's swing grew more pronounced and became the arc of a pendulum. Eddie realized a strange thing: each time the bob reached the end of its swing, it grew heavier. It was like holding onto something that was being pulled by some extraordinary centrifugal force.

The arc grew longer, the bob's swings faster, the pull at the end of each swing stronger. And then—

"Eddie!" Jake called, somewhere between concern and delight. "Do you see?"

Of course he did. Now the bob was growing *dim* at the end of each swing. The downward pressure on his arm—the bob's weight—was rapidly growing stronger as this happened. He had to support his right arm with his left hand in order to maintain his grip, and now he was also swaying at the hips with the swing of the bob. Eddie suddenly remembered where he was—roughly seven hundred feet above the ground. This baby would shortly yank him right over the side, if it wasn't stopped. What if he couldn't get the chain off his hand?

The plumb-bob swung to the right, tracing the shape of an invisible smile in the air, gaining weight as it rose toward the end of its arc. All at once the puny piece of wood he'd lifted from its box with such ease seemed to weigh sixty, eighty, a hundred pounds. And as it paused at the end of its arc, momentarily balanced between motion and gravity, he realized he could see the East Road through it, not just clearly but *magnified*. Then the Branni bob started back down again, plummeting, shedding weight. But when it started up again, this time to his left . . .

"Okay, I get the point!" Eddie shouted. "Get it off me, Henchick. At least make it stop!"

Henchick uttered a single word, one so guttural it sounded like something yanked from a mudflat. The bob didn't slow through a series of diminishing arcs but simply quit, again hanging beside Eddie's knee with the tip pointing at his foot. For a moment the humming in his arm and head continued. Then that also quit. When it did, the bob's disquieting sense of weight lifted. The damn thing was once more feather-light.

"Do'ee have something to say to me, Eddie of New York?" Henchick asked.

"Yeah, cry your pardon."

Henchick's teeth once more put in an appearance, gleaming briefly in the wilderness of his beard and then gone. "Thee's not entirely slow, is thee?"

"I hope not," Eddie said, and could not forbear a small sigh of relief as Henchick of the Manni lifted the fine-link silver chain from his hand.

FOUR

Henchick insisted on a dry-run. Eddie understood why, but he hated all this foreplay crap. The passing time now seemed almost to be a physical thing, like a rough piece of cloth slipping beneath the palm of your hand. He kept silent, nevertheless. He'd already pissed off Henchick once, and once was enough.

The old man brought six of his *amigos* (five of them looked older than God to Eddie) into the cave. He passed bobs to three of them and shell-shaped magnets to the other three. The Branni bob, almost certainly the tribe's strongest, he kept for himself.

The seven of them formed a ring at the mouth of the cave.

"Not around the door?" Roland asked.

"Not until we have to," Henchick said.

The old men joined hands, each holding a bob or a mag at the clasping point. As soon as the circle was complete, Eddie heard that humming again. It was as loud as an over-amped stereo speaker. He saw Jake raise his hands to his ears, and Roland's face tighten in a brief grimace.

Eddie looked at the door and saw it had lost that dusty, unimportant look. The hieroglyphs on it once more stood out crisply, some forgotten word that meant UNFOUND. The crystal doorknob glowed, outlining the rose carved there in lines of white light.

Could I open it now? Eddie wondered. *Open it and step through?* He thought not. Not yet, anyway. But he was a hell of a lot more hopeful about this process than he'd been five minutes ago.

Suddenly the voices from deep in the cave came alive, but they did so in a roaring jumble. Eddie could make out Benny Slightman the Younger screaming the word *Dogan,* heard his Ma telling him that now, to top off a career of losing things, he'd lost his *wife,* heard some man (probably Elmer Chambers) telling Jake that Jake had gone crazy, he was *fou,* he was *Monsieur Lunatique.* More voices joined in, and more, and more.

Henchick nodded sharply to his colleagues. Their hands parted. When they did, the voices from below ceased in mid-babble. And, Eddie was not surprised to see, the door immediately regained its look of unremarkable anonymity—it was any door you ever passed on the street without a second look.

"What in God's name was *that?*" Callahan asked, nodding toward the deeper darkness where the floor sloped down. "It wasn't like that before."

"I believe that either the quake or the loss of the magic ball has driven the cave insane," Henchick said calmly. "It doesn't matter to our business here, any-roa'. Our business is with the door." He looked at Callahan's packsack. "Once you were a wandering man."

"So I was."

Henchick's teeth made another brief guest appearance. Eddie decided that, on some level, the old bastard was enjoying this. "From the look of your gunna, sai Callahan, you've lost the knack."

"I suppose it's hard for me to believe that we're really going anywhere," Callahan said, and offered a smile. Compared to Henchick's, it was feeble. "And I'm older now."

Henchick made a rude sound at that—*fah!,* it sounded like.

"Henchick," Roland said, "do you know what caused the ground to shake early this morning?"

The old man's blue eyes were faded but still sharp. He nodded. Outside the cave's mouth, in a line going down the path, almost three dozen Manni men waited patiently. "Beam let go is what we think."

"What I think, too," Roland said. "Our business grows more desperate. I'd have an end to idle talk, if it does ya. Let's have what palaver we must have, and then get on with our business."

Henchick looked at Roland as coldly as he had looked at Eddie, but Roland's eyes never wavered. Henchick's brow furrowed, then smoothed out.

"Aye," he said. "As'ee will, Roland. Thee's rendered us a great service, Manni and forgetful folk alike, and we'd return it now as best we can. The magic's still here, and thick. Wants only a spark. We can make that spark, aye, easy as commala. You may get what'ee want. On the other hand, we all may go to the clearing at the end of the path together. Or into the darkness. Does thee understand?"

Roland nodded.

"Would'ee go ahead?"

Roland stood for a moment with his head lowered and his hand on the butt of his gun. When he looked up, he was wearing his own smile. It was handsome and tired and desperate and dangerous. He twirled his whole left hand twice in the air: *Let's go.*

FIVE

The coffs were set down—carefully, because the path leading up to what the Manni called Kra Kammen was narrow—and the contents were removed. Long-nailed fingers (the Manni were allowed to cut their nails only once a year) tapped the magnets, producing a shrill hum that seemed to slice through Jake's head like a knife. It reminded him of the todash chimes, and he guessed that wasn't surprising; those chimes *were* the kammen.

"What does Kra Kammen mean?" he asked Cantab. "House of Bells?"

"House of Ghosts," he replied without looking up from the chain he was unwinding. "Leave me alone, Jake, this is delicate work."

Jake couldn't see why it would be, but he did as bade. Roland, Eddie, and Callahan were standing just inside the cave's mouth. Jake joined them. Henchick, meanwhile, had placed the oldest members of his group in a semicircle that went around the back of the door. The front side, with its incised hieroglyphs and crystal doorknob, was unguarded, at least for the time being.

The old man went to the mouth of the cave, spoke briefly with Cantab, then motioned for the line of Manni waiting on the path to move up. When the first man in line was just inside the cave, Henchick stopped him and came back to Roland. He squatted, inviting the gunslinger with a gesture to do the same.

The cave's floor was powdery with dust. Some came from rocks, but most of it was the bone residue of small animals unwise enough to wander in here. Using a fingernail, Henchick drew a rectangle, open at the bottom, and then a semicircle around it.

"The door," he said. "And the men of my kra. Do'ee kennit?"

Roland nodded.

"You and your friends will finish the circle," he said, and drew it.

"The boy's strong in the touch," Henchick said, looking at Jake so suddenly that Jake jumped.

"Yes," Roland said.

"We'll put him direct in front of the door, then, but far enough away so that if it opens hard—and it may—it won't clip his head off. Will'ee stand, boy?"

"Yes, until you or Roland says different," Jake replied.

"You'll feel something in your head—like a sucking. It's not nice." He paused. "Ye'd open the door twice."

"Yes," Roland said. "Twim."

Eddie knew the door's second opening was about Calvin Tower, and he'd lost what interest he'd had in the bookstore proprietor. The man wasn't entirely without courage, Eddie supposed, but he was also greedy and stubborn and self-involved: the perfect twentieth-century New York City man, in other words. But the most recent person to use this door had been Suze, and the moment it opened, he intended to dart through. If it opened a second time on the little Maine town where Calvin Tower and his friend, Aaron Deepneau, had gone to earth, fine and dandy. If the rest of them wound up there, trying to protect Tower and gain ownership of a certain vacant lot and a certain wild pink rose, also fine and dandy. Eddie's priority was Susannah. Everything else was secondary to that.

Even the tower.

SIX

Henchick said: "Who would'ee send the first time the door opens?"

Roland thought about this, absently running his hand over the bookcase Calvin Tower had insisted on sending through. The case containing the book which had so upset the Pere. He did not much want to send Eddie, a man who was impulsive to begin with and now all but blinded by his concern and his love, after his wife. Yet would Eddie obey him if Roland ordered him after Tower and Deepneau instead? Roland didn't think so. Which meant—

"Gunslinger?" Henchick prodded.

"The first time the door opens, Eddie and I will go through," Roland said. "The door will shut on its own?"

"Indeed it will," Henchick said. "You must be as quick as the devil's bite, or you'll likely be cut in two, half of you on the floor of this cave and the rest wherever the brown-skinned woman took herself off to."

"We'll be as quick as we can, sure," Roland said.

"Aye, that's best," Henchick said, and put his teeth on display once more. This was a smile

(*what's he not telling? something he knows or only thinks he knows?*)

Roland would have occasion to think of not long hence.

"I'd leave your guns here," Henchick said. "If you try to carry them through, you may lose them."

"I'm going to try and keep mine," Jake said. "It came from the other side, so it should be all right. If it's not, I'll get another one. Somehow."

"I expect mine may travel, as well," Roland said. He'd thought about this carefully, and had decided to try and keep the big revolvers. Henchick shrugged, as if to say *As you will.*

"What about Oy, Jake?" Eddie asked.

Jake's eyes widened and his jaw dropped. Roland realized the boy hadn't considered his bumbler friend until this moment. The gunslinger reflected (not for the first time) how easy it was to forget the most basic truth about John "Jake" Chambers: he was just a kid.

"When we went todash, Oy—" Jake began.

"This ain't that, sugar," Eddie said, and when he heard Susannah's endearment coming out of his mouth, his heart gave a sad cramp. For the first time he admitted to himself that he might never see her again, any more than Jake might see Oy once they left this stinking cave.

"But . . ." Jake began, and then Oy gave a reproachful little bark. Jake had been squeezing him too tightly.

"We'll keep him for you, Jake," Cantab said gently. "Keep him very well, say true. There'll be folk posted here until thee comes back for thy friend and all the rest of thy goods." *If you ever do* was the part he was too kind to state. Roland read it in his eyes, however.

"Roland, are you sure I can't . . . that he can't . . . no. I see. Not todash this time. Okay. No."

Jake reached into the front pocket of the poncho, lifted Oy out, set him on the powdery floor of the cave. He bent down, hands planted just above his knees. Oy looked up, stretching his neck so that their faces almost touched. And Roland now saw something extraordinary: not the tears in Jake's eyes, but those that had begun to well up in Oy's. A billy-bumbler crying. It was the sort of story you might hear in a saloon as the night grew late and drunk—the faithful bumbler who wept for his departing master. You didn't believe such stories but never said so, in order to save brawling (perhaps even shooting). Yet here it was, he was seeing it, and it made Roland feel a bit like crying himself. Was it just more bumbler imitation, or did Oy really understand what was happening? Roland hoped for the former, and with all his heart.

"Oy, you have to stay with Cantab for a little while. You'll be okay. He's a pal."

"Tab!" the bumbler repeated. Tears fell from his muzzle and darkened the powdery surface where he stood in dime-sized drops. Roland found the creature's tears uniquely awful, somehow even worse than a child's might have been. "Ake! *Ake!*"

"No, I gotta split," Jake said, and wiped at his cheeks with the heels of his hands. He left dirty streaks like warpaint all the way up to his temples.

"No! Ake!"

"I gotta. You stay with Cantab. I'll come back for you, Oy—unless I'm dead, I'll come back." He hugged Oy again, then stood up. "Go to Cantab. That's him." Jake pointed. "Go on, now, you mind me."

"Ake! Tab!" The misery in that voice was impossible to deny. For a moment Oy stayed where he was. Then, still weeping—or imitating Jake's tears, Roland still hoped for that—the bumbler turned, trotted to Cantab, and sat between the young man's dusty shor'boots.

Eddie attempted to put an arm around Jake. Jake shook it off and stepped away from him. Eddie looked baffled. Roland kept his Watch Me face, but inside he was grimly delighted. Not thirteen yet, no, but there was no shortage of steel there.

And it was time.

"Henchick?"

"Aye. Would'ee speak a word of prayer first, Roland? To whatever God thee holds?"

"I hold to no God," Roland said. "I hold to the Tower, and won't pray to that."

Several of Henchick's 'migos looked shocked at this, but the old man himself only nodded, as if he had expected no more. He looked at Callahan. "Pere?"

Callahan said, "God, Thy hand, Thy will." He sketched a cross in the air and nodded at Henchick. "If we're goin, let's go."

Henchick stepped forward, touched the Unfound Door's crystal knob, then looked at Roland. His eyes were bright. "Hear me this last time, Roland of Gilead."

"I hear you very well."

"I am Henchick of the Manni Kra Redpath-a-Sturgis. We are far-seers and far travelers. We are sailors on ka's wind. Would thee travel on that wind? Thee and thine?"

"Aye, to where it blows."

Henchick slipped the chain of the Branni bob over the back of his hand and Roland at once felt some power let loose in this chamber. It was small as yet, but it was growing. Blooming, like a rose.

"How many calls would you make?"

Roland held up the remaining fingers of his right hand. "Two. Which is to say *twim* in the Eld."

"Two or twim, both the same," Henchick said. "Commala-come-two." he raised his voice. "Come, Manni! Come-commala, join your force to my force! Come and keep your promise! Come and pay our debt to these gunslingers! Help me send them on their way! *Now!*"

SEVEN

Before any of them could even begin to register the fact that ka had changed their plans, ka had worked its will on them. But at first it seemed that nothing at all would happen.

The Manni Henchick had chosen as senders—six elders, plus Cantab—formed their semicircle behind the door and around to its sides. Eddie took Cantab's hand and laced his fingers through the Manni's. One of the shell-shaped magnets kept their palms apart. Eddie could feel it vibrating like something alive. He supposed it was. Callahan took his other hand and gripped it firmly.

On the other side of the door, Roland took Henchick's hand, weaving the Branni bob's chain between his fingers. Now the circle was complete save for the one spot directly in front of the door. Jake took a deep breath, looked around, saw Oy sitting against the wall of the cave about ten feet behind Cantab, and nodded.

Oy, stay, I'll be back, Jake sent, and then he stepped into his place. He took Callahan's right hand, hesitated, and then took Roland's left.

The humming returned at once. The Branni bob began to move, not in arcs this time but in a small, tight circle. The door brightened and became more *there*—Jake saw this with his own eyes. The lines and circles of the hieroglyphs spelling UNFOUND grew clearer. The rose etched into the doorknob began to glow.

The door, however, remained closed.

(*Concentrate, boy!*)

That was Henchick's voice, so strong in his head that it almost seemed to slosh Jake's brains. He lowered his head and looked at the doorknob. He saw the rose. He saw it very well. He imagined it turning as the knob upon which it had been cast turned. Once not so long ago he had been obsessed by doors and the other world

(*Mid-World*)

he knew must lie behind one of them. This felt like going back to that. He imagined all the doors he'd known in his life—bedroom doors bathroom doors kitchen doors closet doors bowling alley doors cloakroom doors movie theater doors restaurant doors doors marked KEEP OUT doors marked EMPLOYEES ONLY refrigerator doors, yes even those—and then saw them all opening at once.

Open! he thought at the door, feeling absurdly like an Arabian princeling in some ancient story. *Open sesame! Open says me!*

From the cave's belly far below, the voices began to babble once more. There was a whooping, windy sound, the heavy crump of something falling. The cave's floor trembled beneath their feet, as if with another Beamquake. Jake paid no mind. The feeling of live force in this chamber was very strong now—he could feel it plucking at his skin, vibrating in his nose and eyes, teasing the hairs out from his scalp—but the door remained shut. He bore down more strongly on Roland's hand and the Pere's, concentrating on firehouse doors, police station doors, the door to the Principal's Office at Piper, even a science fiction book he'd once read called *The Door into Summer.* The smell of the cave—deep must, ancient bones, distant drafts—seemed suddenly very strong. He felt that brilliant, exuberant uprush of certainty—*Now, it will happen now, I know it will*—yet the door still stayed closed. And now he could smell something else. Not the cave, but the slightly metallic aroma of his own sweat, rolling down his face.

"Henchick, it's not working. I don't think I—"

"Nar, not yet—and never think thee needs to do it all thyself, lad. Feel for something between you and the door . . . something like a hook . . . or a thorn . . ." As he spoke, Henchick nodded at the Manni heading the line of reinforcements. "Hedron, come forward. Thonnie, take hold of Hedron's shoulders. Lewis, take hold of Thonnie's. And on back! Do it!"

The line shuffled forward. Oy barked doubtfully.

"Feel, boy! Feel for that hook! It's between thee and t'door! Feel for it!"

Jake reached out with his mind while his imagination suddenly bloomed with a powerful and terrifying vividness that was beyond even the clearest dreams. He saw Fifth Avenue between Forty-eighth and Sixtieth ("the twelve blocks where my Christmas bonus disappears every January," his father had liked to grumble). He saw every door, on both sides of the street, swinging open at once: Fendi! Tiffany! Bergdorf Goodman! Cartier! Doubleday Books! The Sherry Netherland Hotel! He saw an endless hallway floored with brown linoleum and knew it was in the Pentagon. He saw doors, at least a thousand of them, all swinging open at once and generating a hurricane draft.

Yet the door in front of him, the only one that mattered, remained closed.

Yeah, but—

It was rattling in its frame. He could hear it.

"Go, kid!" Eddie said. The words came from between clamped teeth. "If you can't open it, knock the fucker down!"

"Help me!" Jake shouted. "*Help* me, goddammit! *All of you*!"

The force in the cave seemed to double. The hum

seemed to be vibrating the very bones of Jake's skull. His teeth were rattling. Sweat ran into his eyes, blurring his sight. He saw two Henchicks nodding to someone behind him: Hedron. And behind Hedron, Thonnie. And behind Thonnie, all the rest, snaking out of the cave and down thirty feet of the path.

"Get ready, lad," Henchick said.

Hedron's hand slipped under Jake's shirt and gripped the waistband of his jeans. Jake felt pushed instead of pulled. Something in his head bolted forward, and for a moment he saw all the doors of a thousand, thousand worlds flung wide, generating a draft so great it could almost have blown out the sun.

And then his progress was stopped. There was something . . . something right in front of the door . . .

The hook! It's the hook!

He slipped himself over it as if his mind and lifeforce were some sort of loop. At the same time he felt Hedron and the others pulling him backward. The pain was immediate, enormous, seeming to tear him apart. Then the draining sensation began. It was hideous, like having someone pull his guts out a loop at a time. And always, the manic buzzing in his ears and deep in his brain.

He tried to cry out—*No, stop, let go, it's too much!*—and couldn't. He tried to scream and heard it, but only inside his head. God, he was caught. Caught on the hook and being ripped in two.

One creature *did* hear his scream. Barking furiously, Oy darted forward. And as he did, the Unfound Door sprang open, swinging in a hissing arc just in front of Jake's nose.

"Behold!" Henchick cried in a voice that was at once terrible and exalted. *"Behold, the door opens! Over-sam kammen! Can-tah, can-kavar kammen! Over-can-tah!"*

The others responded, but by then Jake Chambers had already been torn loose from Roland's hand on his right. By then he was flying, but not alone.

Pere Callahan flew with him.

EIGHT

There was just time for Eddie to hear New York, *smell* New York, and to realize what was happening. In a way, that was what made it so awful—he was able to register everything going diabolically counter to what he had expected, but not able to do anything about it.

He saw Jake yanked out of the circle and felt Callahan's hand ripped out of his own; he saw them fly through the air toward the door, actually looping the loop in tandem, like a couple of fucked-up acrobats. Something furry and barking like a motherfucker shot past the side of his head. Oy, doing barrel-rolls, his ears laid back and his terrified eyes seeming to start from his head.

And more. Eddie was aware of dropping Cantab's hand and lunging forward toward the door—*his* door, *his* city, and somewhere in it *his* lost and pregnant wife. He was aware (exquisitely so) of the invisible hand that *pushed him back*, and a voice that spoke, but not in words. What Eddie heard was far more terrible than any words could have been. With words you could argue. This was only an inarticulate negation, and for all he knew, it came from the Dark Tower itself.

Jake and Callahan were shot like bullets from a gun: shot into a darkness filled with the exotic sounds of honking horns and rushing traffic. In the distance but clear, like the voices you heard in dreams, Eddie heard a rapid, rapping, ecstàtic voice streetbopping its message: "Say *Gawd,* brotha, that's right, say *Gawd* on Second Avenue, say *Gawd* on Avenue B, say *Gawd* in the Bronx, I say *Gawd,* I say *Gawd*-bomb, I say *Gawd!*" The voice of an authentic New York crazy if Eddie had ever heard one and it laid his heart open. He saw Oy zip through the door like a piece of newspaper yanked up the street in the wake of a speeding car, and then the door slammed shut, swinging so fast and hard that he had to slit his eyes against the wind it blew into his face, a wind that was gritty with the bone-dust of this rotten cave.

Before he could scream his fury, the door slapped open again. This time he was dazzled by hazy sunshine loaded with birdsong. He smelled pine trees and heard the distant backfiring of what sounded like a big truck. Then he was sucked into that brightness, unable to yell that this was fucked up, assbackw—

Something collided with the side of Eddie's head. For one brief moment he was brilliantly aware of his passage between the worlds. Then the gunfire. Then the killing.

STAVE: *Commala-come-coo*
The wind'll blow ya through.
Ya gotta go where ka's wind blows ya
Cause there's nothin else to do.

RESPONSE: *Commala-come-two!*
Nothin else to do!
Gotta go where ka's wind blows ya
Cause there's nothin else to do.

T R U D Y   A N D   M I A

3RD STANZA

ONE

Until June first of 1999, Trudy Damascus was the sort of hard-headed woman who'd tell you that most UFOs were weather balloons (and those that weren't were probably the fabrications of people who wanted to get on TV), the Shroud of Turin was some fourteenth-century con man's trick, and that ghosts—Jacob Marley's included—were either the perceptions of the mentally ill or caused by indigestion. She was hard-headed, she *prided* herself on being hard-headed, and had nothing even slightly spiritual on her mind as she walked down Second Avenue toward her business (an accounting firm called Guttenberg, Furth, and Patel) with her canvas carry-bag and her purse slung over her shoulder. One of GF&P's clients was a chain of toy stores called KidzPlay, and KidzPlay owed GF&P a goodly sum of money. The fact that they were also tottering on the edge of Chapter Eleven meant el zippo to Trudy. She wanted that $69,211.19, and had spent most of her lunch-hour (in a back booth of Dennis's Waffles and Pancakes, which had been Chew Chew Mama's until 1994) mulling over ways to get it.

During the last two years she had taken several steps toward changing Guttenberg, Furth, and Patel to Guttenberg, Furth, Patel and Damascus; forcing KidzPlay to cough up would be yet another step—a long one—in that direction.

And so, as she crossed Forty-sixth Street toward the large dark glass skyscraper which now stood on the uptown corner of Second and Forty-sixth (where there had once been a certain Artistic Deli and then a certain vacant lot), Trudy wasn't thinking about gods or ghosts or visitations from the spirit world. She was thinking about Richard Goldman, the asshole CEO of a certain toy company, and how—

But that was when Trudy's life changed. At 1:19 P.M., EDT, to be exact. She had just reached the curb on the downtown side of the street. Was, in fact, stepping up. And all at once a woman appeared on the sidewalk in front of her. A wide-eyed African-American woman. There was no shortage of black women in New York City, and God knew there had to be a fair percentage of them with wide eyes, but Trudy had never seen one emerge directly from thin air before, which was what this one did. And there was something else, something even more unbelievable. Ten seconds before, Trudy Damascus would have laughed and said *nothing* could be more unbelievable than a woman flicking into existence in front of her on a Midtown sidewalk, but there was. There definitely was.

And now she knew how all those people who reported seeing flying saucers (not to mention ghosts wrapped in clanking chains) must feel, how they must grow frustrated by the entrenched disbelief of people like . . . well, people like the one Trudy Damascus had been at 1:18 P.M. on that day in June, the one who said goodbye for good on the downtown side of Forty-sixth Street. You could tell people *You don't understand, this REALLY HAPPENED!* and it cut zero ice. They said stuff like *Well, she probably came out from behind the bus shelter and you just didn't notice* or *She probably came out of one of the little stores and you just didn't notice.* You could tell them that there *was* no bus shelter on the downtown side of Second and Forty-sixth (or on the uptown side, for that matter), and it did no good. You could tell them there *were* no little stores in that area, not since 2 Hammarskjöld Plaza went up, and that didn't work, either. Trudy would soon find these things out for herself, and they would drive her close to insanity. She was not used to having her perceptions dismissed as no more than a blob of mustard or a bit of underdone potato.

No bus shelter. No little shops. There were the steps going up to Hammarskjöld Plaza, where a few late lunchers were still sitting with their brown bags, but the ghost-woman hadn't come from there, either. The fact was this: when Trudy Damascus put her sneaker-clad left foot up on the curb, the sidewalk directly ahead of her was completely empty. As she shifted her weight preparatory to lifting her right foot up from the street, a woman appeared.

For just a moment, Trudy could see Second

Avenue through her, and something else, as well, something that looked like the mouth of a cave. Then that was gone and the woman was solidifying. It probably took only a second or two, that was Trudy's estimate; she would later think of that old saying *If you blinked you missed it* and wish she had blinked. Because it wasn't just the materialization.

The black lady grew legs right in front of Trudy Damascus's eyes.

That's right; grew legs.

There was nothing wrong with Trudy's powers of observation, and she would later tell people (fewer and fewer of whom wanted to listen) that every detail of that brief encounter was imprinted on her memory like a tattoo. The apparition was a little over four feet tall. That was a bit on the stumpy side for an ordinary woman, Trudy supposed, but probably not for one who quit at the knees.

The apparition was wearing a white shirt, splattered with either maroon paint or dried blood, and jeans. The jeans were full and round at the thighs, where there *were* legs inside them, but below the knees they trailed out on the sidewalk like the shed skins of weird blue snakes. Then, suddenly, they plumped up. *Plumped up,* the very words sounded insane, but Trudy saw it happen. At the same moment, the woman rose from her nothing-below-the-knee four-feet-four to her all-there height of perhaps five-six or -seven. It was like watching some extraordinary camera trick in a movie, but this was no movie, it was Trudy's *life.*

Over her left shoulder the apparition wore a cloth-lined pouch that looked as if it had been woven of reeds. There appeared to be plates or dishes inside it. In her right hand she clutched a faded red bag with a drawstring top. Something with square sides at the bottom, swinging back and forth. Trudy couldn't make out everything written on the side of the bag, but she thought part of it was MIDTOWN LANES.

Then the woman grabbed Trudy by the arm. "What you got in that bag?" she asked. "You got shoes?"

This caused Trudy to look at the black woman's feet, and she saw another amazing thing when she did: the African-American woman's feet were *white*. As white as her own.

Trudy had heard of people being rendered speechless; now it had happened to her. Her tongue was stuck to the roof of her mouth and wouldn't come down. Still, there was nothing wrong with her eyes. They saw everything. The white feet. More droplets on the black woman's face, almost certainly dried blood. The smell of sweat, as if materializing on Second Avenue like this had only come as the result of tremendous exertion.

"If you got shoes, lady, you best give em to me. I don't want to kill you but I got to get to folks that'll help me with my chap and I can't do that barefoot."

No one on this little piece of Second Avenue. People—a few, anyway—sitting on the steps of 2 Hammarskjöld Plaza, and a couple were looking right at Trudy and the black woman (the *mostly* black woman), but not with any alarm or even interest, what the hell was *wrong* with them, were they blind?

Well, it's not them she's grabbing, for one thing. And it's not them she's threatening to kill, for anoth—

The canvas Borders bag with her office shoes inside it (sensible half-heels, cordovan-colored) was snatched from her shoulder. The black woman peered inside it, then looked up at Trudy again. "What size're these?"

Trudy's tongue finally came unstuck from the roof of her mouth, but that was no help; it promptly fell dead at the bottom.

"Ne'mine, Susannah says you look like about a seven. These'll d—"

The apparition's face suddenly seemed to shimmer. She lifted one hand—it rose in a loose loop with an equally loose fist anchoring the end, as if the woman didn't have very good control of it—and thumped herself on the forehead, right between the eyes. And suddenly her face was different. Trudy had Comedy Central as part of her basic cable deal, and she'd seen stand-up comics who specialized in mimicry change their faces that same way.

When the black woman spoke again, her voice had changed, too. Now it was that of an educated woman. And (Trudy would have sworn it) a frightened one.

"Help me," she said. "My name is Susannah Dean and I . . . I . . . oh dear . . . oh *Christ*—"

This time it was pain that twisted the woman's

face, and she clutched at her belly. She looked
down. When she looked back up again, the first
one had reappeared, the one who had talked of
killing for a pair of shoes. She took a step back on
her bare feet, still holding the bag with Trudy's
nice Ferragamo low-heels and her *New York
Times* inside it.

"Oh Christ," she said. "Oh don't that hurt!
Mama! You got to make it stop. It can't come yet,
not right out here on the street, you got to make it
stop awhile."

Trudy tried to raise her voice and yell for a cop.
Nothing came out but a small, whispering sigh.

The apparition pointed at her. "You want to get
out of here now," she said. "And if you rouse any
constabulary or raise any posse, I'll find you and
cut your breasts off." She took one of the plates
from the reed pouch. Trudy observed that the
plate's curved edge was metal, and as keen as a
butcher's knife, and suddenly found herself in a
struggle to keep from wetting her pants.

Find you and cut your breasts off, and an edge
like the one she was looking at would probably do
the job. Zip-zoop, instant mastectomy, O dear
Lord.

"Good day to you, madam," Trudy heard her
mouth saying. She sounded like someone trying to
talk to the dentist before the Novocain has worn
off. "Enjoy those shoes, wear them in good
health."

Not that the apparition looked particularly
healthy. Not even with her legs on and her fancy
white feet.

Trudy walked. She walked down Second Avenue. She tried to tell herself (with no success at all) that she had *not* seen a woman appear out of thin air in front of 2 Hammarskjöld, the building the folks who worked there jokingly called the Black Tower. She tried to tell herself (also with no success at all) that this was what she got for eating roast beef and fried potatoes. She should have stuck to her usual waffle-and-egg, you went to Dennis's for *waffles,* not for roast beef and potatoes, and if you didn't believe that, look what had just happened to her. Seeing African-American apparitions, and—

And her bag! Her canvas Borders bag! She must have dropped it!

Knowing better. All the time expecting the woman to come after her, shrieking like a head-hunter from the deepest, darkest jungles of Papua. There was a ningly-tumb place on her back (she meant *a tingly-numb place,* but ningly-tumb was how it actually felt, kind of loose and cool and distant) where she knew the crazy woman's plate would bite into her, drinking her blood and then eating one of her kidneys before coming to rest, still quivering, in the live chalk of her spine. She would hear it coming, somehow she knew that, it would make a whistling sound like a child's top before it chunked into her and warm blood went splashing down over her buttocks and the backs of her legs—

She couldn't help it. Her bladder let go, her urine gushed, and the front of her slacks, part of a *très* expensive Norma Kamali suit, went distressingly dark. She was almost at the corner of Second and

Forty-fifth by then. Trudy—never again to be the hard-headed woman she'd once fancied herself—was finally able to stop and turn around. She no longer felt quite so ningly-tumb. Only warm at the crotch.

And the woman, the mad apparition, was gone.

TWO

Trudy kept some softball-practice clothes—tee-shirts and two old pairs of jeans—inside her office storage cabinet. When she got back to Guttenberg, Furth, and Patel, she made changing her first priority. Her second was a call to the police. The cop who took her report turned out to be Officer Paul Antassi.

"My name is Trudy Damascus," she said, "and I was just mugged on Second Avenue."

Officer Antassi was extremely sympathetic on the phone, and Trudy found herself imagining an Italian George Clooney. Not a big stretch, considering Antassi's name and Clooney's dark hair and eyes. Antassi didn't look a bit like Clooney in person, but hey, who expected miracles and movie stars, it was a real world they were living in. Although . . . considering what had happened to her on the corner of Second and Forty-sixth at 1:19 P.M., EDT . . .

Officer Antassi arrived at about three-thirty, and she found herself telling him exactly what had happened to her, *everything,* even the part about feeling ningly-tumb instead of tingly-numb and her weird certainty that the woman was getting ready to throw that dish at her—

"Dish had a sharpened edge, you say?" Antassi asked, jotting on his pad, and when she said yes, he nodded sympathetically. Something about that nod had struck her as familiar, but right then she'd been too involved in telling her tale to chase down the association. Later, though, she wondered how she could possibly have been so dumb. It was every sympathetic nod she'd ever seen in one of those lady-gone-crazy films, from *Girl, Interrupted* with Winona Ryder all the way back to *The Snake Pit,* with Olivia de Havilland.

But right then she'd been too involved. Too busy telling the nice Officer Antassi about how the apparition's jeans had been dragging on the sidewalk from the knees down. And when she was done, she for the first time heard the one about how the black woman had probably come out from behind a bus shelter. Also the one—this'll killya—about how the black woman had probably just stepped out of some little store, there were billions of them in that neighborhood. As for Trudy, she premiered her bit about how there *were* no bus shelters on that corner, not on the downtown side of Forty-sixth, not on the uptown side, either. Also the one about how all the shops were gone on the downtown side since 2 Hammarskjöld went up, that would prove to be one of her most popular routines, would probably get her onstage at Radio Goddam City someday.

She was asked for the first time what she'd had for lunch just before seeing this woman, and realized for the first time that she'd had a twentieth-century version of what Ebenezer Scrooge had eaten shortly before seeing his old (and long-dead) business partner: potatoes and roast beef. Not to mention *several* blots of mustard.

She forgot all about asking Officer Antassi if he'd like to go out to dinner with her.

In fact, she threw him out of her office.

Mitch Guttenberg poked his head in shortly thereafter. "Do they think they'll be able to get your bag back, Tru—"

"Get lost," Trudy said without looking up. "Right now."

Guttenberg assessed her pallid cheeks and set jaw. Then he retired without saying another word.

THREE

Trudy left work at four-forty-five, which was early for her. She walked back to the corner of Second and Forty-sixth, and although that ningly-tumb feeling began to work its way up her legs and into the pit of her stomach again as she approached Hammarskjöld Plaza, she never hesitated. She stood on the corner, ignoring both white WALK and red DON'T WALK. She turned in a tight little circle, almost like a ballet dancer, also ignoring her fellow Second Avenue-ites and being ignored in turn.

"Right here," she said. "It happened right here. I know it did. She asked me what size I was, and before I could answer—I *would* have answered, I would have told her what color my underwear was if she asked, I was in shock—before I could answer, she said . . ."

Ne'mine, Susannah says you look like about a seven. These'll do.

Well, no, she hadn't quite finished that last part, but Trudy was sure that was what the woman had meant to say. Only then her face had changed. Like a comic getting ready to imitate Bill Clinton or Michael Jackson or maybe even George Clooney. And she'd asked for help. Asked for help and said her name was . . . what?

"Susannah Dean," Trudy said. "That was the name. I never told Officer Antassi."

Well, yeah, but fuck Officer Antassi. Officer Antassi with his bus shelters and little stores, just *fuck* him.

That woman—Susannah Dean, Whoopi Goldberg, Coretta Scott King, whoever she was— thought she was pregnant. Thought she was in labor. *I'm almost sure of it. Did she look pregnant to you, Trudes?*

"No," she said.

On the uptown side of Forty-sixth, white WALK once again became red DON'T WALK. Trudy realized she was calming down. Something about just standing here, with 2 Dag Hammarskjöld Plaza on her right, was calming. Like a cool hand on a hot brow, or a soothing word that assured you that there was nothing, absolutely *nothing* to feel ningly-tumb about.

She could hear a humming, she realized. A sweet humming sound.

"That's not humming," she said as red DON'T WALK cycled back to white WALK one more time (she remembered a date in college once telling her the worst karmic disaster he could imagine would be coming back as a traffic light). "That's not humming, that's *singing*."

And then, right beside her—startling her but not frightening her—a man's voice spoke. "That's right," he said. Trudy turned and saw a gentleman who looked to be in his early forties. "I come by here all the time, just to hear it. And I'll tell you something, since we're just ships passing in the night, so to speak—when I was a young man, I had the world's most terrible case of acne. I think coming here cleared it up, somehow."

"You think standing on the corner of Second and Forty-sixth cleared up your acne," she said.

His smile, only a small one but very sweet, faltered a tiny bit. "I know it sounds crazy—"

"I saw a woman appear out of nowhere right here," Trudy said. "Three and a half hours ago, I saw this. When she showed up, she had no legs from the knees down. Then she grew the rest of em. So who's crazy, my friend?"

He was looking at her, wide-eyed, just some anonymous time-server in a suit with his tie pulled down at the end of the work-day. And yes, she could see the pits and shadows of old acne on his cheeks and forehead. "This is true?"

She held up her right hand. "If I'm lyin, I'm dyin. Bitch stole my shoes." She hesitated. "No, she wasn't a bitch. I don't believe she was a bitch. She was scared and she was barefooted and she thought she was in labor. I just wish I'd had time to give her my sneakers instead of my good goddam shoes."

The man was giving her a cautious look, and Trudy Damascus suddenly felt tired. She had an idea this was a look she was going to get used to.

The sign said WALK again, and the man who'd spoken to her started across, swinging his briefcase.

"Mister!"

He didn't stop walking, but did look back over his shoulder.

"What used to be here, back when you used to stop by for acne treatments?"

"Nothing," he said. "It was just a vacant lot behind a fence. I thought it would stop—that nice sound—when they built on the site, but it never did."

He gained the far curb. Walked off up Second Avenue. Trudy stood where she was, lost in thought. *I thought it would stop, but it never did.*

"Now why would that be?" she asked, and turned to look more directly at 2 Hammarskjöld Plaza. The Black Tower. The humming was stronger now that she was concentrating on it. And sweeter. Not just one voice but many of them. Like a choir. Then it was gone. Disappeared as suddenly as the black woman had done the opposite.

No it didn't, Trudy thought. *I just lost the knack of hearing it, that's all. If I stood here long enough, I bet it would come back. Boy, this is nuts. I'm nuts.*

Did she believe that? The truth was that she did not. All at once the world seemed very thin to her, more an idea than an actual thing, and barely there at all. She had never felt less hard-headed in her life. What she felt was weak in her knees and sick to her stomach and on the verge of passing out.

FOUR

There was a little park on the other side of Second Avenue. In it was a fountain; nearby was a metal sculpture of a turtle, its shell gleaming wetly in the fountain's spray. She cared nothing for fountains or sculptures, but there was also a bench.

WALK had come around again. Trudy tottered across Second Avenue, like a woman of eighty-three instead of thirty-eight, and sat down. She began to take long, slow breaths, and after three minutes or so felt a little better.

Beside the bench was a trash receptacle with KEEP LITTER IN ITS PLACE stenciled on the side. Below this, in pink spray-paint, was an odd little graffito: *See the TURTLE of enormous girth.* Trudy saw the turtle, but didn't think much of its girth; the sculpture was quite modest. She saw something else, as well: a copy of the *New York Times,* rolled up as she always rolled hers, if she wanted to keep it a little longer and happened to have a bag to stow it in. Of course there were probably at least a million copies of that day's *Times* floating around Manhattan, but this one was hers. She knew it even before fishing it out of the litter basket and verifying what she knew by turning to the crossword, which she'd mostly completed over lunch, in her distinctive lilac-colored ink.

She returned it to the litter basket and looked across Second Avenue to the place where her idea of how things worked had changed. Maybe forever.

Took my shoes. Crossed the street and sat here by the turtle and put them on. Kept my bag but dumped the Times. *Why'd she want my bag? She didn't have any shoes of her own to put in it.*

Trudy thought she knew. The woman had put her plates in it. A cop who got a look at those sharp edges might be curious about what you served on dishes that could cut your fingers off if you grabbed them in the wrong place.

Okay, but then where did she go?

There was a hotel down at the corner of First and Forty-sixth. Once it had been the U.N. Plaza. Trudy didn't know what its name was now, and didn't care. Nor did she want to go down there and ask if a black woman in jeans and a stained white shirt might have come in a few hours ago. She had a strong intuition that her version of Jacob Marley's ghost had done just that, but here was an intuition she didn't want to follow up on. Better to let it go. The city was full of shoes, but *sanity,* one's *sanity—*

Better to head home, take a shower, and just . . . let it go. Except—

"Something is wrong," she said, and a man walking past on the sidewalk looked at her. She looked back defiantly. "Somewhere something is *very* wrong. It's—"

Tipping was the word that came to mind, but she would not say it. As if to say it would cause the tip to become a topple.

It was a summer of bad dreams for Trudy Damascus. Some were about the woman who first appeared and then *grew.* These were bad, but not the worst. In the worst ones she was in the dark, and terrible chimes were ringing, and she sensed something tipping further and further toward the point of no return.

STAVE: *Commala-come-key*
Can ya tell me what ya see?
Is it ghosts or just the mirror
That makes ya want to flee?

RESPONSE: *Commala-come-three!*
I beg ya, tell me!
Is it ghosts or just your darker self
That makes ya want to flee?

SUSANNAH'S DOGAN

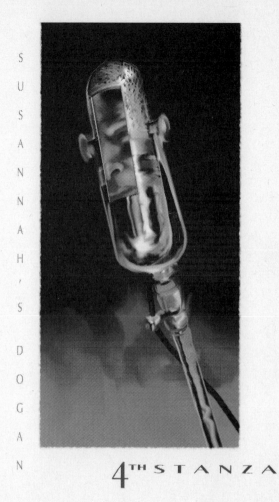

4ᵀᴴSTANZA

ONE

Susannah's memory had become distressingly spotty, unreliable, like the half-stripped transmission of an old car. She remembered the battle with the Wolves, and Mia waiting patiently while it went on . . .

No, that wasn't right. Wasn't fair. Mia had been doing a lot more than waiting patiently. She had been cheering Susannah (and the others) on with her own warrior's heart. Holding the labor in abeyance while her chap's surrogate mother dealt death with her plates. Only the Wolves had turned out to be robots, so could you really say . . .

Yes. Yes, you can. Because they were more than robots, much more, and we killed them. Rose up righteous and killed their asses.

But that was neither here nor there, because it was over. And once it was, she had felt the labor coming back, and strong. She was going to have the kid at the side of the damn road if she didn't look out; and there it would die, because it was hungry, Mia's chap was *hongry,* and . . .

You got to help me!

Mia. And impossible not to respond to that cry. Even while she felt Mia pushing her aside (as Roland had once pushed Detta Walker aside), it was impossible not to respond to that wild mother's cry. Partly, Susannah supposed, because it was *her* body they shared, and the body had declared itself on behalf of the baby. Probably could not do otherwise. And so she had helped. She had done what Mia herself no longer could do, had stopped the labor a bit longer. Although that in itself would become dangerous to the chap (funny how that word insinuated itself into her thoughts, became her word as well as Mia's word) if it was allowed to go on too long. She remembered a story some girl had told during a late-night hen party in the dorm at Columbia, half a dozen of them sitting around in their pj's, smoking cigarettes and passing a bottle of Wild Irish Rose— absolutely *verboten* and therefore twice as sweet. The story had been about a girl their age on a long car-trip, a girl who'd been too embarrassed to tell her friends she needed a pee-stop. According to the story, the girl had suffered a ruptured bladder and died. It was the kind of tale you simultaneously thought was bullshit and believed absolutely. And this thing with the chap . . . the *baby* . . .

But whatever the danger, she'd been able to stop the labor. Because there were switches that could do that. Somewhere.

(*in the Dogan*)

Only the machinery in the Dogan had never been meant to do what she—they—

(*us we*)

were making it do. Eventually it would overload and

(*rupture*)

all the machines would catch fire, burn out. Alarms going off. Control panels and TV screens going dark. How long before that happened? Susannah didn't know.

She had a vague memory of taking her wheelchair out of a bucka-waggon while the rest of them were distracted, celebrating their victory and mourning their dead. Climbing and lifting weren't easy when you were legless from the knees down, but they weren't as hard as some folks might believe, either. Certainly she was used to mundane obstacles—everything from getting on and off the toilet to getting books off a shelf that had once been easily accessible to her (there had been a step-stool for such chores in every room of her New York apartment). In any case, Mia had been insisting—had actually been *driving* her, as a cowboy might drive a stray dogie. And so Susannah had hoisted herself into the bucka, had lowered the wheelchair down, and then had lowered herself neatly into it. Not quite as easy as rolling off a log, but far from the hardest chore she'd ever done since losing her last sixteen inches or so.

The chair had taken her one last mile, maybe a little more (no legs for Mia, daughter of none, not in the Calla). Then it smashed into a spur of granite, spilling her out. Luckily, she had been able to break her fall with her arms, sparing her turbulent and unhappy belly.

She remembered picking herself up—correction, she remembered Mia picking up Susannah Dean's hijacked body—and working her way on up the path. She had only one other clear memory from the Calla side, and that was of trying to stop Mia from taking off the rawhide loop Susannah wore around her neck. A ring hung from it, a beautiful light ring that Eddie had made for her. When he'd seen it was too big (meaning it as a surprise, he hadn't measured her finger), he had been disappointed and told her he'd make her another.

You go on and do just that if you like, she'd said, *but I'll always wear this one.*

She had hung it around her neck, liking the way it felt between her breasts, and now here was this unknown woman, this *bitch,* trying to take it off.

Detta had *come forward,* struggling with Mia. Detta had had absolutely no success in trying to reassert control over Roland, but Mia was no Roland of Gilead. Mia's hands dropped away from the rawhide. Her control wavered. When it did, Susannah felt another of those labor pains sweep through her, making her double over and groan.

It has to come off! Mia shouted. *Otherwise, they'll have* his *scent as well as yours! Your husband's! You don't want that, believe me!*

Who? Susannah had asked. *Who are you talking about?*

Never mind—there's no time. But if he comes after you—and I know you think he'll try—they mustn't have his scent! I'll leave it here, where he'll find it. Later, if ka wills, you may wear it again.

Susannah had thought of telling her they could wash the ring off, wash Eddie's smell off it, but she knew it wasn't just a smell Mia was speaking of. It was a love-ring, and that scent would always remain.

But for whom?

The Wolves, she supposed. The *real* Wolves. The ones in New York. The vampires of whom Callahan had spoken, and the low men. Or was there something else? Something even worse?

Help me! Mia cried, and again Susannah found that cry impossible to resist. The baby might or might not be Mia's, and it might or might not be a monster, but her body wanted to have it. Her eyes wanted to see it, whatever it was, and her ears wanted to hear it cry, even if the cries were really snarls.

She had taken the ring off, kissed it, and then dropped it at the foot of the path, where Eddie would surely see it. Because he would follow her at least this far, she knew it.

Then what? She didn't know. She thought she remembered riding on something most of the way up a steep path, surely the path which led to the Doorway Cave.

Then, blackness.

(*not blackness*)

No, not *complete* blackness. There were blinking lights. The low glow of television screens that were, for the time being, projecting no pictures but only soft gray light. The faint hum of motors; the click of relays. This was

(*the Dogan Jake's Dogan*)

some sort of control room. Maybe a place she had constructed herself, maybe her imagination's version of a Quonset hut Jake had found on the west side of the River Whye.

The next thing she remembered clearly was

being back in New York. Her eyes were windows she looked through as Mia stole some poor terrified woman's shoes.

Susannah *came forward* again, asking for help. She meant to go on, to tell the woman she needed to go to the hospital, needed a doctor, she was going to have a baby and something was wrong with it. Before she could get any of that out, another labor pain washed over her, this one monstrous, deeper than any pain she had ever felt in her life, worse even than the pain she'd felt after the loss of her lower legs. This, though—*this*—

"Oh Christ," she said, but Mia took over again before she could say anything else, telling Susannah that she had to make it stop, and telling the woman that if she whistled for any John Laws, she'd lose a pair of something a lot more valuable to her than shoes.

Mia, listen to me, Susannah told her. *I can stop it again—I think I can—but you have to help. You have to sit down. If you don't settle for awhile, God Himself won't be able to stop your labor from running its course. Do you understand? Do you hear me?*

Mia did. She stayed where she was for a moment, watching the woman from whom she'd stolen the shoes. Then, almost timidly, she asked a question: *Where should I go?*

Susannah sensed that her kidnapper was for the first time becoming aware of the enormous city in which she now found herself, was finally seeing the surging schools of pedestrians, the floods of metal carriages (every third one, it seemed, painted a yellow so bright it almost screamed), and towers so high that on a cloudy day their tops would have been lost to view.

Two women looked at an alien city through one set of eyes. Susannah knew it was *her* city, but in many ways, it no longer was. She'd left New York in 1964. How many years further along was this? Twenty? Thirty? Never mind, let it go. Now was not the time to worry about it.

Their combined gaze settled on the little pocket park across the street. The labor pains had ceased for the time being, and when the sign over there said WALK, Trudy Damascus's black woman (who didn't look particularly pregnant) crossed, walking slowly but steadily.

On the far side was a bench beside a fountain and a metal sculpture. Seeing the turtle comforted Susannah a little; it was as if Roland had left her this sign, what the gunslinger himself would have called a sigul.

He'll come after me, too, she told Mia. *And you should 'ware him, woman. You should 'ware him very well.*

I'll do what I need to do, Mia replied. *You want to see the woman's papers. Why?*

I want to see when this is. The newspaper will say.

Brown hands pulled the rolled-up newspaper from the canvas Borders bag, unrolled it, and held it up to blue eyes that had started that day as brown as the hands. Susannah saw the date—June 1st, 1999—and marveled over it. Not twenty years or even thirty, but thirty-five. Until this moment she hadn't realized how little she'd thought of the world's chances to survive so long. The contemporaries she'd known in her old life—fellow students, civil rights advocates, drinking buddies, and folk-music *aficionados*—would now be edging into late middle age. Some were undoubtedly dead.

Enough, Mia said, and tossed the newspaper back into the trash barrel, where it curled into its former rolled shape. She brushed as much dirt as she could from the soles of her bare feet (because of the dirt, Susannah did not notice they had changed color) and then put on the stolen shoes. They were a little tight, and with no socks she supposed they'd give her blisters if she had to walk very far, but—

What do you care, right? Susannah asked her. *Ain't your feet.* And knew as soon as she'd said it (for this *was* a form of talking; what Roland called palaver) that she might be wrong about that. Certainly her own feet, those which had marched obediently through life below the body of Odetta Holmes (and sometimes Detta Walker), were long gone, rotting or—more likely—burned in some municipal incinerator.

But she did not notice the change in color. Except later she'd think: *You noticed, all right. Noticed it and blocked it right out. Because too much is too much.*

Before she could pursue the question, as much philosophical as it was physical, of whose feet she now wore, another labor pain struck her. It cramped her stomach and turned it to stone even as it loosened her thighs. For the first time she felt the dismaying and terrifying need to *push.*

You have to stop it! Mia cried. *Woman, you have to! For the chap's sake, and for ours, too!*

Yes, all right, but how?

Close your eyes, Susannah told her.

What? Didn't you hear me? You've got to—

I heard you, Susannah said. *Close your eyes.*

The park disappeared. The world went dark. She was a black woman, still young and undoubtedly beautiful, sitting on a park bench beside a fountain and a metal turtle with a wet and gleaming metal shell. She might have been meditating on this warm late-spring afternoon in the year of 1999.

I'm going away for a little while now, Susannah said. *I'll be back. In the meantime, sit where you are. Sit quiet. Don't move. The pain should draw back again, but even if it doesn't at first, sit still. Moving around will only make it worse. Do you understand me?*

Mia might be frightened, and she was certainly determined to have her way, but she wasn't dumb. She asked only a single question.

Where are you going?

Back to the Dogan, Susannah said. *My Dogan. The one inside.*

TWO

The building Jake had found on the far side of the River Whye was some sort of ancient communications-and-surveillance post. The boy had described it to them in some detail, but he still might not have recognized Susannah's imagined version of it, which was based on a technology which had been far out of date only thirteen years later, when Jake had left New York for Mid-World. In Susannah's when, Lyndon Johnson had been President and color TV was still a curiosity. Computers were huge things that filled whole buildings. Yet Susannah had visited the city of Lud and seen some of the wonders there, and so Jake *might* have recognized the place where he had hidden from Ben Slightman and Andy the Messenger Robot, after all.

Certainly he would have recognized the dusty linoleum floor, with its checkerboard pattern of black and red squares, and the rolling chairs along consoles filled with blinking lights and glowing dials. And he would have recognized the skeleton in the corner, grinning above the frayed collar of its ancient uniform shirt.

She crossed the room and sat in one of the chairs. Above her, black-and-white TV screens showed dozens of pictures. Some were of Calla Bryn Sturgis (the town common, Callahan's church, the general store, the road leading east out of town). Some were still pictures like studio photographs: one of Roland, one of a smiling Jake holding Oy in his arms, and one—she could hardly bear to look at it—of Eddie with his hat tipped back cowpoke-style and his whittling knife in one hand.

Another monitor showed the slim black woman sitting on the bench beside the turtle, knees together, hands folded in her lap, eyes closed, a pair of stolen shoes on her feet. She now had three bags: the one she'd stolen from the woman on Second

Avenue, the rush sack with the sharpened Orizas in it . . . and a bowling bag. This one was a faded red, and there was something with square corners inside it. A box. Looking at it in the TV screen made Susannah feel angry—betrayed—but she didn't know why.

The bag was pink on the other side, she thought. *It changed color when we crossed, but only a little.*

The woman's face on the black-and-white screen above the control board grimaced. Susannah felt an echo of the pain Mia was experiencing, only faint and distant.

Got to stop that. And quick.

The question still remained: how?

The way you did on the other side. While she was horsing her freight up to that cave just as fast as she damn could.

But that seemed a long time ago now, in another life. And why not? It *had* been another life, another world, and if she ever hoped to get back there, she had to help right now. So what had she done?

You used this stuff, that's what you did. It's only in your head, anyway—what Professor Overmeyer called "a visualization technique" back in Psych One. Close your eyes.

Susannah did so. Now both sets of eyes were closed, the physical ones that Mia controlled in New York and the ones in her mind.

Visualize.

She did. Or tried.

Open.

She opened her eyes. Now on the panel in front of her there were two large dials and a single toggle-

switch where before there had been rheostats and
flashing lights. The dials looked to be made of Bake-
lite, like the oven-dials on her mother's stove back in
the house where Susannah had grown up. She supposed there was no surprise there; all you imagined,
no matter how wild it might seem, was no more than
a disguised version of what you already knew.

The dial on her left was labeled EMOTIONAL
TEMP. The markings on it ran from 32 to 212 (32 in
blue; 212 in bright red). It was currently set at 160.
The dial in the middle was marked LABOR FORCE.
The numbers around its face went from 0 to 10,
and it was currently turned to 9. The label under
the toggle-switch simply read CHAP, and there were
only two settings: AWAKE and ASLEEP. It was currently set to AWAKE.

Susannah looked up and saw one of the screens
was now showing a baby *in utero*. It was a boy. A
beautiful boy. His tiny penis floated like a strand of
kelp below the lazy curl of his umbilical cord. His
eyes were open, and although the rest of the image
was black and white, those eyes were a piercing
blue. The chap's gaze seemed to go right through
her.

They're Roland's eyes, she thought, feeling stupid with wonder. *How can that be?*

It couldn't, of course. All this was nothing but
the work of her own imagination, a visualization
technique. But if so, why would she imagine
Roland's blue eyes? Why not Eddie's hazel ones?
Why not her husband's hazel eyes?

No time for that now. Do what you have to do.

She reached out to EMOTIONAL TEMP with her

lower lip caught between her teeth (on the monitor showing the park bench, Mia also began biting her lower lip). She hesitated, then dialed it back to 72, exactly as if it was a thermostat. And wasn't it?

Calm immediately filled her. She relaxed in her chair and let her lip escape the grip of her teeth. On the park monitor, the black woman did the same. All right, so far, so good.

She hesitated for a moment with her hand not quite touching the LABOR FORCE dial, then moved on to CHAP instead. She flipped the toggle from AWAKE to ASLEEP. The baby's eyes closed immediately. Susannah found this something of a relief. Those blue eyes were disconcerting.

All right, back to LABOR FORCE. Susannah thought this was the important one, what Eddie would call the Big Casino. She took hold of the old-fashioned dial, applied a little experimental force, and was not exactly surprised to find the clunky thing dully resistant in its socket. It didn't want to turn.

But you will, Susannah thought. *Because we need you to. We* need *you to.*

She grasped it tightly and began turning it slowly counter-clockwise. A pain went through her head and she grimaced. Another momentarily constricted her throat, as if she'd gotten a fishbone stuck in there, but then both pains cleared. To her right an entire bank of lights flashed on, most of them amber, a few bright red.

"WARNING," said a voice that sounded eerily like that of Blaine the Mono. "THIS OPERATION MAY EXCEED SAFETY PARAMETERS."

No shit, Sherlock, Susannah thought. The LABOR FORCE dial was now down to 6. When she turned it past 5, another bank of amber and red lights flashed on, and three of the monitors showing Calla scenes shorted out with sizzling pops. Another pain gripped her head like invisible pressing fingers. From somewhere beneath her came the start-up whine of motors or turbines. Big ones, from the sound. She could feel them thrumming against her feet, which were bare, of course—Mia had gotten the shoes. *Oh well,* she thought, *I didn't have any feet at all before this, so maybe I'm ahead of the game.*

"WARNING," said the mechanical voice. "WHAT YOU'RE DOING IS DANGEROUS, SUSANNAH OF NEW YORK. HEAR ME I BEG. IT'S NOT NICE TO FOOL MOTHER NATURE."

One of Roland's proverbs occurred to her: You do what *you* need to, and I'll do what *I* need to, and we'll see who gets the goose. She wasn't sure what it meant, but it seemed to fit this situation, so she repeated it aloud as she slowly but steadily turned the LABOR FORCE dial past 4, to 3 . . .

She meant to turn the dial all the way back to 1, but the pain which ripped through her head when the absurd thing passed 2 was so huge—so *sickening*—that she dropped her hand.

For a moment the pain continued—intensified, even—and she thought it would kill her. Mia would topple off the bench where she was sitting, and both of them would be dead before their shared body hit the concrete in front of the turtle sculpture. Tomorrow or the next day, her remains would take a quick trip to Potter's Field. And what would go on the death certificate? Stroke? Heart attack? Or maybe that old standby of the medical man in a hurry, natural causes?

But the pain subsided and she was still alive when it did. She sat in front of the console with the two ridiculous dials and the toggle-switch, taking deep breaths and wiping the sweat from her cheeks with both hands. Boy-howdy, when it came to visualization technique, she had to be the champ of the world.

This is more than visualization—you know that, right?

She supposed she did. Something had changed her—had changed all of them. Jake had gotten the touch, which was a kind of telepathy. Eddie had grown (was still growing) into some sort of ability to create powerful, talismanic objects—one of them had already served to open a door between two worlds. And she?

I . . . see. That's all. Except if I see it hard enough, it starts to be real. The way Detta Walker got to be real.

All over this version of the Dogan, amber lights were glowing. Even as she looked, some turned red. Beneath her feet—special guest feet, she thought them—the floor trembled and thrummed. Enough of this and cracks would start to appear in its elderly surface. Cracks that would widen and deepen. Ladies and gentlemen, welcome to the House of Usher.

Susannah got up from the chair and looked

around. She should go back. Was there anything else that needed doing before she did?

One thing occurred to her.

THREE

Susannah closed her eyes and imagined a radio mike. When she opened them the mike was there, standing on the console to the right of the two dials and the toggle-switch. She had imagined a Zenith trademark, right down to the lightning-bolt Z, on the microphone's base, but NORTH CENTRAL POSITRONICS had been stamped there, instead. So something was messing in with her visualization technique. She found that extremely scary.

On the control panel directly behind the microphone was a semicircular, tri-colored readout with the words **SUSANNAH-MIO** printed below it. A needle was moving out of the green and into the yellow. Beyond the yellow segment the dial turned red, and a single word was printed in black: **DANGER.**

Susannah picked up the mike, saw no way to use it, closed her eyes again, and imagined a toggle-switch like the one marked with AWAKE and ASLEEP, only this time on the side of the mike. When she opened her eyes again, the switch was there. She pressed it.

"Eddie," she said. She felt a little foolish, but went on, anyway. "Eddie, if you hear me, I'm okay, at least for the time being. I'm with Mia, in New York. It's June first of 1999, and I'm going to try and help her have the baby. I don't see any other choice. If nothing else, I have to be rid of it myself. Eddie, you take care of yourself. I . . ." Her eyes welled with tears. "I love you, sugar. So much."

The tears spilled down her cheeks. She started to wipe them away and then stopped herself. Didn't she have a right to cry for her man? As much right as any other woman?

She waited for a response, knowing she could make one if she wanted to and resisting the urge. This wasn't a situation where talking to herself in Eddie's voice would do any good.

Suddenly her vision doubled in front of her eyes. She saw the Dogan for the unreal shade that it was. Beyond its walls were not the deserty wastelands on the east side of the Whye but Second Avenue with its rushing traffic.

Mia had opened her eyes. She was feeling fine again—*thanks to me, honeybunch, thanks to me*—and was ready to move on.

Susannah went back.

FOUR

A black woman (who still thought of herself as a Negro woman) was sitting on a bench in New York City in the spring of '99. A black woman with her traveling bags—her gunna—spread around her. One of them was a faded red. NOTHING BUT STRIKES AT MIDTOWN LANES was printed on it. It had been pink on the other side. The color of the rose.

Mia stood up. Susannah promptly *came forward* and made her sit down again.

What did you do that for? Mia asked, surprised.

I don't know, I don't have a clue. But let's us palaver a little. Why don't you start by telling me where you want to go?

I need a telefung. Someone will call.

*Tele*phone, Susannah said. *And by the way, there's blood on our shirt, sugar, Margaret Eisenhart's blood, and sooner or later someone's gonna recognize it for what it is. Then where will you be?*

The response to this was wordless, a swell of smiling contempt. It made Susannah angry. Five minutes ago—or maybe fifteen, it was hard to keep track of time when you were having fun—this hijacking bitch had been screaming for help. And now that she'd gotten it, what her rescuer got was an internal contemptuous smile. What made it worse was that the bitch was right: she could probably stroll around Midtown all day without anyone asking her if that was dried blood on her shirt, or had she maybe just spilled her chocolate egg-cream.

All right, she said, *but even if nobody bothers you about the blood, where are you going to store your goods?* Then another question occurred to her, one that probably should have come to her right away.

Mia, how do you even know what a telephone is? And don't tell me they have em where you came from, either.

No response. Only a kind of watchful silence. But she had wiped the smile off the bitch's face; she'd done that much.

You have friends, don't you? Or at least you think they're friends. Folks you've been talking to behind my back. Folks that'll help you. Or so you think.

Are you *going to help me or not?* Back to that. And angry. But beneath the anger, what? Fright? Probably that was too strong, at least for now. But worry, certainly. *How long have I—have we—got before the labor starts up again?*

Susannah guessed somewhere between six and ten hours—certainly before midnight saw in June second—but tried to keep this to herself.

I don't know. Not all that long.

Then we have to get started. I have to find a tele-fung. Phone. *In a private place.*

Susannah thought there was a hotel at the First Avenue end of Forty-sixth Street, and tried to keep this to herself. Her eyes went back to the bag, once pink, now red, and suddenly she understood. Not everything, but enough to dismay and anger her.

I'll leave it here, Mia had said, speaking of the ring Eddie had made her, *I'll leave it here, where he'll find it. Later, if ka wills, you may wear it again.*

Not a promise, exactly, at least not a direct one, but Mia had certainly *implied*—

Dull anger surged through Susannah's mind. No, she'd not promised. She had simply led Susannah in a certain direction, and Susannah had done the rest.

She didn't cozen me; she let me cozen myself.

Mia stood up again, and once again Susannah *came forward* and made her sit down. Hard, this time.

What? Susannah, you promised! The chap—

I'll help you with the chap, Susannah replied grimly. She bent forward and picked up the red bag. The bag with the box inside it. And inside the box? The ghostwood box with UNFOUND written upon it in runes? She could feel a baleful pulse even through the layer of magical wood and cloth which hid it. Black Thirteen was in the bag. Mia had taken it through the door. And if it was the ball that opened the door, how could Eddie get to her now?

I did what I had to, Mia said nervously. *It's my baby, my chap, and every hand is against me now. Every hand but yours, and you only help me because you have to. Remember what I said . . . if ka wills, I said—*

It was Detta Walker's voice that replied. It was harsh and crude and brooked no argument. "I don't give a shit bout ka," she said, "and you bes be re- memberin dat. You got problems, girl. Got a rug- monkey comin you don't know what it is. Got folks say they'll he'p you and you don't know what *dey* are. Shit, you doan even know what a telephone is or where to find one. Now we goan sit here, and you're goan tell me what happens next. We goan palaver, girl, and if you don't play straight, we still be sittin here with these bags come nightfall and you can have your precious chap on this bench and wash him off in the fuckin fountain."

The woman on the bench bared her teeth in a gruesome smile that was all Detta Walker.

"*You* care bout dat chap . . . and Susannah, she care a *little* bout dat chap . . . but I been mos'ly turned out of this body, and I . . . don't . . . *give* a shit."

A woman pushing a stroller (it looked as divinely lightweight as Susannah's abandoned wheelchair) gave the woman on the bench a nervous glance and then pushed her own baby onward, so fast she was nearly running.

"So!" Detta said brightly. "It's be purty out here, don't you think? Good weather for talkin. You hear me, mamma?"

No reply from Mia, daughter of none and mother of one. Detta wasn't put out of countenance; her grin widened.

"You hear me, all right; you hear me just *fahn*. So let's us have a little chat. Let's us palaver."

> STAVE: *Commala-come-ko*
> *Whatcha doin at my do'?*
> *If you doan tell me now, my friend,*
> *I'll lay ya on de flo'.*

> RESPONSE: *Commala-come fo'!*
> *I can lay ya low!*
> *The things I done to such as you*
> *You never want to know.*

THE TURTLE

5TH STANZA

ONE

Mia said: *Talking will be easier—quicker and clearer, too—if we do it face-to-face.*

How can we? Susannah asked.

We'll have our palaver in the castle, Mia replied promptly. *The Castle on the Abyss. In the banquet room. Do you remember the banquet room?*

Susannah nodded, but hesitantly. Her memories of the banquet room were but recently recovered, and consequently vague. She wasn't sorry, either. Mia's feeding there had been . . . well, enthusiastic, to say the very least. She'd eaten from many plates (mostly with her fingers) and drunk from many glasses and spoken to many phantoms in many borrowed voices. Borrowed? Hell, *stolen* voices. Two of these Susannah had known quite well. One had been Odetta Holmes's nervous—and rather hoity-toity—"social" voice. Another had been Detta's raucous who-gives-a-shit bellow. Mia's thievery had extended to every aspect of Susannah's personality, it seemed, and if Detta Walker was back, pumped up and ready to cut butt, that was in large part this unwelcome stranger's doing.

The gunslinger saw me there, Mia said. *The boy, too.*

There was a pause. Then:

I have met them both before.

Who? Jake and Roland?

Aye, they.

Where? When? How could y—

We can't speak here. Please. Let us go somewhere more private.

Someplace with a phone, isn't that what you mean? So your friends can call you.

I only know a little, Susannah of New York, but what little I know, I think you would hear.

Susannah thought so, too. And although she didn't necessarily want Mia to realize it, she was also anxious to get off Second Avenue. The stuff on her shirt might look like spilled egg-cream or dried coffee to the casual passerby, but Susannah herself was acutely aware of what it was: not just blood, but the blood of a brave woman who had stood true on behalf of her town's children.

And there were the bags spread around her feet. She'd seen plenty of bag-*folken* in New York, aye. Now she felt like one herself, and she didn't like the feeling. She'd been raised to better, as her mother would have said. Each time someone passing on the sidewalk or cutting through the little park gave her a glance, she felt like telling them she wasn't crazy in spite of how she looked: stained shirt, dirty face, hair too long and in disarray, no purse, only those three bags at her feet. Homeless, aye—had anyone ever been as homeless as she, not just out of house but out of time itself?—but in her right mind. She needed to palaver with Mia and get an understanding of what all this was about, that was true. What she *wanted* was much simpler: to wash, to put on fresh clothes, and to be out of public view for at least a little while.

Might as well wish for the moon, sugar, she told herself . . . and Mia, if Mia was listening. *Privacy costs money. You're in a version of New York where a single hamburger might cost as much as a dollar, crazy as that sounds. And you don't have a sou. Just a dozen or so sharpened plates and some kind of black-magic ball. So what are you gonna do?*

Before she could get any further in her thinking, New York was swept away and she was back in the Doorway Cave. She'd been barely aware of her surroundings on her first visit—Mia had been in charge then, and in a hurry to make her getaway through the door—but now they were very clear. Pere Callahan was here. So was Eddie. And Eddie's brother, in a way. Susannah could hear Henry Dean's voice floating up from the cave's depths, both taunting and dismayed: "I'm in hell, bro! I'm in hell and I can't get a fix and *it's all your fault!*"

Susannah's disorientation was nothing to the fury she felt at the sound of that nagging, hectoring voice. "Most of what was wrong with Eddie was *your fault!*" she screamed at him. "You should have done everyone a favor and died young, Henry!"

Those in the cave didn't even look around at her. What was this? Had she come here todash from New York, just to add to the fun? If so, why hadn't she heard the chimes?

Hush. Hush, love. That was Eddie's voice in her mind, clear as day. *Just watch.*

Do you hear him? she asked Mia. *Do you—*

Yes! Now shut up!

"How long will we have to be here, do you think?" Eddie asked Callahan.

"I'm afraid it'll be awhile," Callahan replied, and Susannah understood she was seeing something that had already happened. Eddie and Callahan had gone up to the Doorway Cave to try to locate Calvin Tower and Tower's friend, Deepneau. Just before the showdown with the Wolves, this had been. Callahan was the one who'd gone through the door. Black Thirteen had captured Eddie while the Pere was gone. And almost killed him. Callahan had returned just in time to keep Eddie from hurling himself from the top of the bluff and into the draw far below.

Right now, though, Eddie was dragging the bag—pink, yes, she'd been right about that, on the Calla side it had been pink—out from underneath the troublesome sai Tower's bookcase of first editions. They needed the ball inside the bag for the same reason Mia had needed it: because it opened the Unfound Door.

Eddie lifted it, started to turn, then froze. He was frowning.

"What is it?" Callahan asked.

"There's something in here," Eddie replied.

"The box—"

"No, in the bag. Sewn into the lining. It feels like a little rock, or something." Suddenly he seemed to be looking directly at Susannah, and she was aware that she was sitting on a park bench. It was no longer voices from the depths of the cave she heard, but the watery hiss and plash of the fountain. The cave was fading. Eddie and Callahan were fading. She heard Eddie's last words as if from a great distance: "Maybe there's a secret pocket."

Then he was gone.

TWO

She hadn't gone todash at all, then. Her brief visit to the Doorway Cave had been some kind of vision. Had Eddie sent it to her? And if he had, did it mean he'd gotten the message she'd tried to send him from the Dogan? These were questions Susannah couldn't answer. If she saw him again, she'd ask him. After she'd kissed him a thousand times or so, that was.

Mia picked up the red bag and ran her hands slowly down its sides. There was the shape of the box inside, yes. But halfway down there was something else, a small bulge. And Eddie was right: it felt like a stone.

She—or perhaps it was they, it no longer mattered to her—rolled the bag down, not liking the intensified pulse from the thing hidden inside but setting her mind against it. Here it was, right in here . . . and something that felt like a seam.

She leaned closer and saw not a seam but some kind of a seal. She didn't recognize it, nor would Jake have done, but Eddie would have known Velcro when he saw it. She *had* heard a certain Z.Z. Top tribute to the stuff, a song called "Velcro

Fly." She got a fingernail into the seal and pulled with her fingertip. It came loose with a soft ripping sound, revealing a small pocket on the inside of the bag.

What is it? Mia asked, fascinated in spite of herself.

Well, let's just see.

She reached in and brought out not a stone but a small scrimshaw turtle. Made of ivory, from the look of it. Each detail of the shell was tiny and precisely executed, although it had been marred by one tiny scratch that looked almost like a question-mark. The turtle's head poked halfway out. Its eyes were tiny black dots of some tarry stuff, and looked incredibly alive. She saw another small imperfection in the turtle's beak—not a scratch but a crack.

"It's old," she whispered aloud. "So old."

Yes, Mia whispered back.

Holding it made Susannah feel incredibly good. It made her feel . . . *safe,* somehow.

See the Turtle, she thought. *See the Turtle of enormous girth, on his shell he holds the earth.* Was that how it went? She thought it was at least close. And of course that was the Beam they had been following to the Tower. The Bear at one end— Shardik. The Turtle at the other—Maturin.

She looked from the tiny totem she'd found in the lining of the bag to the one beside the fountain. Barring the difference in materials—the one beside her bench was made of dark metal with brighter coppery glints—they were exactly the same, right down to the scratch on the shell and the tiny wedge-shaped break in the beak. For a moment her breath stopped, and her heart seemed to stop, also. She went along from moment to moment through this adventure—sometimes even from day to day— without thinking much but simply driven by events and what Roland insisted was ka. Then something like this would happen, and she would for a moment glimpse a far bigger picture, one that immobilized her with awe and wonder. She sensed forces beyond her ability to comprehend. Some, like the ball in the ghostwood box, were evil. But this . . . *this* . . .

"Wow," someone said. Almost sighed.

She looked up and saw a businessman—a very successful one, from the look of his suit—standing there by the bench. He'd been cutting through the park, probably on his way to someplace as important as he was, some sort of meeting or a conference, maybe even at the United Nations, which was close by (unless that had changed, too). Now, however, he had come to a dead stop. His expensive briefcase dangled from his right hand. His eyes were large and fixed on the turtle in Susannah-Mia's hand. On his face was a large and rather dopey grin.

Put it away! Mia cried, alarmed. *He'll steal it!*

Like to see him try, Detta Walker replied. Her voice was relaxed and rather amused. The sun was out and she—all parts of she—suddenly realized that, all else aside, this day was beautiful. And precious. And gorgeous.

"Precious and beautiful and gorgeous," said the businessman (or perhaps he was a diplomat), who had forgotten all about his business. Was it the day he was talking about, or the scrimshaw turtle?

It's both, Susannah thought. And suddenly she thought she understood this. Jake would have understood, too—no one better! She laughed. Inside her, Detta and Mia also laughed, Mia a bit against her will. And the businessman or diplomat, he laughed, too.

"Yah, it's both," the businessman said. In his faint Scandinavian accent, *both* came out *boad.* "What a lovely thing you have!" *Whad a loffly thing!*

Yes, it *was* lovely. A lovely little treasure. And once upon a time, not so long ago, Jake Chambers had found something queerly similar. In Calvin Tower's bookshop, Jake had bought a book called *Charlie the Choo-Choo,* by Beryl Evans. Why? Because it had called to him. Later—shortly before Roland's ka-tet had come to Calla Bryn Sturgis, in fact—the author's name had changed to Claudia y Inez Bachman, making her a member of the ever-expanding Ka-Tet of Nineteen. Jake had slipped a key into that book, and Eddie had whittled a double of it in Mid-World. Jake's version of the key had both fascinated the folks who saw it and made them extremely suggestible. Like Jake's key, the scrimshaw turtle had its double; she was sitting beside it. The question was if the turtle was like Jake's key in other ways.

Judging from the fascinated way the Scandinavian businessman was looking at it, Susannah was pretty sure the answer was yes. She thought, *Dad-a-chuck, dad-a-churtle, don't worry, girl, you got the turtle!* It was such a silly rhyme she almost laughed out loud.

To Mia she said, *Let me handle this.*

Handle what? I don't understand—

I know you don't. So let me handle it. Agreed?

She didn't wait for Mia's reply. She turned back to the businessman, smiling brightly, holding the turtle up where he could see it. She floated it from right to left and noted the way his eyes followed it, although his head, with its impressive mane of white hair, never moved.

"What's your name, sai?" Susannah asked.

"Mathiessen van Wyck," he said. His eyes rolled slowly in their sockets, watching the turtle. "I am second assistant to the Swedish Ambassador to the United Nations. My wife has taken a lover. This makes me sad. My bowels are regular once again, the tea the hotel masseuse recommended worked for me, and this makes me happy." A pause. Then: "Your *sköldpadda* makes me happy."

Susannah was fascinated. If she asked this man to drop his trousers and evacuate his newly regularized bowels on the sidewalk, would he do it? Of course he would.

She looked around quickly and saw no one in the immediate vicinity. That was good, but she thought it would still behoove her to transact her business here as quickly as she could. Jake had drawn quite the little crowd with his key. She had no urge to do the same, if she could avoid it.

"Mathiessen," she began, "you mentioned—"

"Mats," he said.

"Beg your pardon?"

"Call me Mats, if you would. I prefer it."

"All right, Mats, you mentioned a—"

"Do you speak Swedish?"

"No," she said.

"Then we will speak English."

"Yes, I'd prefer—"

"I have quite an important position," Mats said. His eyes never left the turtle. "I am meeting many important peoples. I am going to cocktail parties where good-looking women are wearing 'the little black dress.'"

"That must be quite a thrill for you. Mats, I want you to shut your trap and only open it to speak when I ask you a direct question. Will you do that?"

Mats closed his mouth. He even made a comical little zipping gesture across his lips, but his eyes never left the turtle.

"You mentioned a hotel. Do you stay at a hotel?"

"Yah, I am staying at the New York Plaza–Park Hyatt, at the corner of First and Forty-sixth. Soon I am getting the condominium apartment—"

Mats seemed to realize he was saying too much again and shut his mouth.

Susannah thought furiously, holding the turtle in front of her breasts where her new friend could see it very well.

"Mats, listen to me, okay?"

"I listen to hear, mistress-sai, and hear to obey." That gave her a nasty jolt, especially coming out as it did in Mats's cute little Scandihoovian accent.

"Do you have a credit card?"

Mats smiled proudly. "I have many. I have American Express, MasterCard, and Visa. I have the Euro-Gold Card. I have—"

"Good, that's good. I want you to go down to the—" For a moment her mind blanked, and then it came. "—to the Plaza–Park Hotel and rent a room. Rent it for a week. If they ask, tell them it's for a friend of yours, a lady friend." An unpleasant possibility occurred to her. This was New York, the *north,* in the year 1999, and a person liked to believe that things continued to go in the right direction, but it was best to be sure. "Will they make any unpleasantness about me being a Negro?"

"No, of course not." He looked surprised.

"Rent the room in your name and tell the clerk that a woman named Susannah Mia Dean will be using it. Do you understand?"

"Yah, Susannah Mia Dean."

What else? Money, of course. She asked him if he had any. Her new friend removed his wallet and handed it to her. She continued to hold the turtle where he could see it in one hand while she riffled through the wallet, a very nice Lord Buxton, with the other. There was a wad of traveler's checks—no good to her, not with that insanely convoluted signature—and about two hundred dollars in good old American cabbage. She took it and dropped it into the Borders bag which had lately held the pair of shoes. When she looked up she was dismayed to see that a couple of Girl Scouts, maybe fourteen years old and both wearing backpacks, had joined the businessman. They were staring at the turtle with shiny eyes and wet lips. Susannah found herself remembering the girls in the audience on the night Elvis Presley had played *The Ed Sullivan Show.*

"Too *cooool,*" one of them said, almost in a sigh.

"Totally awesome," said the other.

"You girls go on about your business," Susannah said.

Their faces tucked in, assuming identical looks of sorrow. They could almost have been twins from the Calla. "Do we have to?" asked the first.

"*Yes!*" Susannah said.

"Thankee-sai, long days and pleasant nights," said the second. Tears had begun to roll down her cheeks. Her friend was also crying.

"Forget you saw me!" Susannah called as they started away.

She watched them nervously until they reached Second Avenue and headed uptown, then turned her attention back to Mats van Wyck. "You get a wiggle on, too, Mats. Hoss your freight down to that hotel and rent a room. Tell them your friend Susannah will be right along."

"What is this freight-hossing? I do not understand—"

"It means hurry up." She handed back his wallet, minus the cash, wishing she could have gotten a longer look at all those plastic cards, wondering why anyone would need so many. "Once you have the room nailed down, go on to where you were going. Forget you ever saw me."

Now, like the girls in their green uniforms,

Mats began to weep. "Must I also forget the *sköld-padda?*"

"Yes." Susannah remembered a hypnotist she'd once seen performing on some TV variety show, maybe even *Ed Sullivan.* "No turtle, but you're going to feel good the rest of the day, you hear me? You're going to feel like . . ." *A million bucks* might not mean that much to him, and for all she knew a million kroner wouldn't buy a haircut. "You're going to feel like the Swedish Ambassador himself. And you'll stop worrying about your wife's fancy-man. To hell with him, right?"

"Yah, to hell wit *dot* guy!" Mats cried, and although he was still weeping, he was now smiling, too. There was something divinely childish in that smile. It made Susannah feel happy and sad at the same time. She wanted to do something else for Mats van Wyck, if she could.

"And your bowels?"

"Yah?"

"Like clockwork for the rest of your life," Susannah said, holding the turtle up. "What's your usual time, Mats?"

"I am going yust after breakfast."

"Then that's when it'll be. For the rest of your life. Unless you're busy. If you're late for an appointment or something like that, just say . . . um . . . *Maturin,* and the urge'll pass until the next day."

"Maturin."

"Correct. Go on, now."

"May I not take the *sköldpadda?*"

"No, you may not. Go on, now."

He started away, then paused and looked back at her. Although his cheeks were wet, his expression was pixie-ish, a trifle sly. "Perhaps I should take it," he said. "Perhaps it is mine by right."

Like to see you try, honky was Detta's thought, but Susannah—who felt more and more in charge of this wacky triad, at least for the time being—shushed her. "Why would you say that, my friend? Tell, I beg."

The sly look remained. *Don't kid a kidder,* it said. That was what it looked like to Susannah, anyway. "Mats, Maturin," he said. "Maturin, Mats. You see?"

Susannah did. She started to tell him it was just a coincidence and then thought: *Calla, Callahan.*

"I see," she said, "but the *sköldpadda* isn't yours. Nor mine, either."

"Then whose?" Plaintive. *Den hoose?* it sounded like.

And before her conscious mind could stop her (or at least censor her), Susannah spoke the truth her heart and soul knew: "It belongs to the Tower, sai. The Dark Tower. And it's to there I'll return it, ka willing."

"Gods be with you, lady-sai."

"And you, Mats. Long days and pleasant nights."

She watched the Swedish diplomat walk away, then looked down at the scrimshaw turtle and said, "That was pretty amazing, Mats old buddy."

Mia had no interest in the turtle; she had but a single object. *This hotel,* she said. *Will there be a telephone?*

THREE

Susannah-Mia put the turtle into the pocket of her bluejeans and forced herself to wait for twenty minutes on the park bench. She spent much of this time admiring her new lower legs (whoever they belonged to, they were pretty fine) and wiggling her new toes inside her new

(*stolen*)

shoes. Once she closed her eyes and summoned up the control room of the Dogan. More banks of warning lights had gone on there, and the machinery under the floor was throbbing louder than ever, but the needle of the dial marked SUSANNAH-MIO was still just a little way into the yellow. Cracks in the floor had begun to appear, as she had known they would, but so far they didn't look serious. The situation wasn't that great, but she thought they could live with it for now.

What are you waiting for? Mia demanded. *Why are we just sitting here?*

I'm giving the Swede a chance to do his business for us at the hotel and clear out, Susannah replied.

And when she thought enough time had passed for him to have done that, she gathered her bags, got up, crossed Second Avenue, and started down Forty-sixth Street to the Plaza–Park Hotel.

FOUR

The lobby was full of pleasant afternoon light reflected by angles of green glass. Susannah had never seen such a beautiful room—outside of St. Patrick's, that was—but there was something alien about it, too.

Because it's the future, she thought.

God knew there were enough signs of that. The cars looked smaller, and entirely different. Many of the younger women she saw were walking around with their lower bellies exposed and their bra-straps showing. Susannah had to see this latter phenomenon four or five times on her stroll down Forty-sixth Street before she could completely convince herself that it was some sort of bizarre fashion fillip, and not a mistake. In her day, a woman with a bra-strap showing (or an inch of slip, *snowing down south* they used to say) would have ducked into the nearest public restroom to pin it up, and at once. As for the deal with the nude bellies . . .

Would have gotten you arrested anywhere but Coney Island, she thought. *No doubt about it.*

But the thing which made the biggest impression was also the hardest thing to define: the city just seemed *bigger*. It thundered and hummed all around her. It vibrated. Every breath of air was perfumed with its signature smell. The women waiting for taxis outside the hotel (with or without their bra-straps showing) could only be New York women; the doormen (not one but two) flagging cabs could only be New York doormen; the cabbies (she was amazed by how many of them were dark-skinned, and she saw one who was wearing a *turban*) could only be New York cabbies, but they were all . . . different. The world had moved on. It was as if her New York, that of 1964, had been a triple-A ball-club. This was the major leagues.

She paused for a moment just inside the lobby, pulling the scrimshaw turtle out of her pocket and getting her bearings. To her left was a parlor area. Two women were sitting there, chatting, and Susannah stared at them for a moment, hardly able to credit how much leg they were showing under the hems of their skirts (*what* skirts, ha-ha?). And they weren't teenagers or kollege kuties, either; these were women in their thirties, at least (although she supposed they might be in their *sixties,* who knew what scientific advances there might have been over the last thirty-five years).

To the right was a little shop. Somewhere in the shadows behind it a piano was tinkling out something blessedly familiar—"Night and Day"—and Susannah knew if she went toward the sound, she'd find a lot of leather seats, a lot of sparkling bottles, and a gentleman in a white coat who'd be happy to serve her even if it *was* only the middle of the afternoon. All this was a decided relief.

Directly ahead of her was the reception desk, and behind it was the most exotic woman Susannah had ever seen in her life. She appeared to be white, black, and Chinese, all whipped together. In 1964, such a woman would undoubtedly have been called a mongrel, no matter how beautiful she might have been. Here she had been popped into an extremely handsome ladies' suit and put behind the reception desk of a large first-class hotel. The Dark Tower might be increasingly shaky, Susannah thought, and the world might be moving on, but she thought the lovely desk clerk was proof (if any were needed) that not *everything* was falling down or going in the wrong direction. She was talking to a customer who was complaining about his in-room movie bill, whatever that might be.

Never mind, it's the future, Susannah told herself once again. *It's science fiction, like the City of Lud. Best leave it at that.*

I don't care what it is or when, Mia said. *I want to be near a telephone. I want to see to my chap.*

Susannah walked past a sign on a tripod, then turned back and gave it a closer look.

AS OF JULY 1ST, 1999, THE NEW YORK PLAZA–PARK HYATT WILL BECOME THE REGAL U.N. PLAZA HOTEL ANOTHER GREAT *SOMBRA/ NORTH CENTRAL* PROJECT!!

Susannah thought, *Sombra as in Turtle Bay Luxury Condominiums . . . which never got built, from the look of that black-glass needle back on the corner. And North Central as in North Central Positronics. Interesting.*

She felt a sudden twinge of pain go through her head. Twinge? Hell, a bolt. It made her eyes water. And she knew who had sent it. Mia, who had no interest in the Sombra Corporation, North Central

Positronics, or the Dark Tower itself, was becoming impatient. Susannah knew she'd have to change that, or at least try. Mia was focused blindly on her chap, but if she wanted to *keep* the chap, she might have to widen her field of vision a little bit.

She fight you ever' damn step of the way, Detta said. Her voice was shrewd and tough and cheerful. *You know dat too, don't you?*

She did.

Susannah waited until the man with the problem finished explaining how he had ordered some movie called *X-Rated* by accident, and he didn't mind paying as long as it wasn't on his bill, and then she stepped up to the desk herself. Her heart was pounding.

"I believe that my friend, Mathiessen van Wyck, has rented a room for me," she said. She saw the reception clerk looking at her stained shirt with well-bred disapproval, and laughed nervously. "I really can't wait to take a shower and change my clothes. I had a small accident. At lunch."

"Yes, madam. Just let me check." The woman went to what looked like a small TV screen with a typewriter attached. She tapped a few keys, looked at the screen, and then said: "Susannah Mia Dean, is that correct?"

You say true, I say thank ya rose to her lips and she squelched it. "Yes, that's right."

"May I see some identification, please?"

For a moment Susannah was flummoxed. Then she reached into the rush bag and took out an Oriza, being careful to hold it by the blunt curve. She found herself remembering something Roland had said to Wayne Overholser, the Calla's big rancher: *We deal in lead*. The 'Rizas weren't bullets, but surely they were the equivalent. She held the plate up in one hand and the small carved turtle in the other.

"Will this do?" she asked pleasantly.

"What—" the beautiful desk clerk began, then fell silent as her eyes shifted from the plate to the turtle. They grew wide and slightly glassy. Her lips, coated with an interesting pink gloss (it looked more like candy than lipstick to Susannah), parted. A soft sound came from between them: *ohhhh* . . .

"It's my driver's license," Susannah said. "Do you see?" Luckily there was no one else around, not even a bellman. The late-day checkouts were on the sidewalk, fighting for hacks; in here, the lobby was a-doze. From the bar beyond the gift shop, "Night and Day" gave way to a lazy and introspective version of "Stardust."

"Driver's license," the desk clerk agreed in that same sighing, wondering voice.

"Good. Are you supposed to write anything down?"

"No . . . Mr. Van Wyck rented the room . . . all I need is to . . . to check your . . . may I hold the turtle, ma'am?"

"No," Susannah said, and the desk clerk began to weep. Susannah observed this phenomenon with bemusement. She didn't believe she had made so many people cry since her disastrous violin recital (both first and last) at the age of twelve.

"No, I may not hold it," the desk clerk said, weeping freely. "No, no, I may not, may not hold it, ah, Discordia, I may not—"

"Hush up your snivel," Susannah said, and the desk clerk hushed at once. "Give me the room-key, please."

But instead of a key, the Eurasian woman handed her a plastic card in a folder. Written on the inside of the folder—so would-be thieves couldn't easily see it, presumably—was the number 1919. Which didn't surprise Susannah at all. Mia, of course, could not have cared less.

She stumbled on her feet a little. Reeled a little. Had to wave one hand (the one holding her "driver's license") for balance. There was a moment when she thought she might tumble to the floor, and then she was okay again.

"Ma'am?" the desk clerk inquired. Looking remotely—*very* remotely—concerned. "Are you feeling all right?"

"Yeah," Susannah said. "Only . . . lost my balance there for a second or two."

Wondering, *What in the blue hell just happened?* Oh, but she knew the answer. Mia was the one with the legs, *Mia.* Susannah had been driving the bus ever since encountering old Mr. May I Not Take The *Sköldpadda,* and this body was starting to revert to its legless-below-the-knee state. Crazy but true. Her body was going Susannah on her.

Mia, get up here. Take charge.

I can't. Not yet. As soon as we're alone I will.

And dear Christ, Susannah recognized that tone of voice, recognized it very well. The bitch was *shy.*

To the desk clerk, Susannah said, "What's this thing? Is it a key?"

"Why—yes, sai. You use it in the elevator as well

as to open your room. Just push it into the slot in the direction the arrows point. Remove it briskly. When the light on the door turns green, you may enter. I have slightly over eight thousand dollars in my cash drawer. I'll give it all to you for your pretty thing, your turtle, your *sköldpadda,* your *tortuga,* your *kavvit,* your—"

"No," Susannah said, and staggered again. She clutched the edge of the desk. Her equilibrium was shot. "I'm going upstairs now." She'd meant to visit the gift shop first and spend some of Mats's dough on a clean shirt, if they carried such things, but that would have to wait. *Everything* would have to wait.

"Yes, sai." No more *ma'am,* not now. The turtle was working on her. Sanding away the gap between the worlds.

"You just forget you saw me, all right?"

"Yes, sai. Shall I put a do-not-disturb on the phone?"

Mia clamored. Susannah didn't even bother paying attention. "No, don't do that. I'm expecting a call."

"As you like, sai." Eyes on the turtle. Ever on the turtle. "Enjoy the Plaza–Park. Would you like a bellman to assist you with your bags?"

Look like I need help with these three pukey li'l things? Detta thought, but Susannah only shook her head.

"Very well."

Susannah started to turn away, but the desk clerk's next words swung her back in a hurry.

"Soon comes the King, he of the Eye."

Susannah gaped at the woman, her surprise close to shock. She felt gooseflesh crawling up her arms. The desk clerk's beautiful face, meanwhile, remained placid. Dark eyes on the scrimshaw turtle. Lips parted, now damp with spittle as well as gloss. *If I stay here much longer,* Susannah thought, *she'll start to drool.*

Susannah very much wanted to pursue the business of the King and the Eye—it was *her* business—and she could, she was the one up front and driving the bus, but she staggered again and knew she couldn't . . . unless, that was, she wanted to crawl to the elevator on her hands and knees with the empty lower legs of her jeans trailing out behind her. *Maybe later,* she thought, knowing that was unlikely; things were moving too fast now.

She started across the lobby, walking with an educated stagger. The desk clerk spoke after her in a voice expressing pleasant regret, no more than that.

"When the King comes and the Tower falls, sai, all such pretty things as yours will be broken. Then there will be darkness and nothing but the howl of Discordia and the cries of the can toi."

Susannah made no reply, although the gooseflesh was now all the way up the nape of her neck and she could feel her scalp tightening on her very skull. Her legs (*someone's* legs, anyway) were rapidly losing all feeling. If she'd been able to look at her bare skin, would she have seen her fine new legs going transparent? Would she have been able to see the blood flowing through her veins, bright red going down, darker and exhausted heading back up to her heart? The interwoven pigtails of muscle?

She thought yes.

She pushed the UP button and then put the Oriza back into its bag, praying one of the three elevator doors would open before she collapsed. The piano player had switched to "Stormy Weather."

The door of the middle car opened. Susannah-Mia stepped in and pushed 19. The door slid shut but the car went nowhere.

The plastic card, she reminded herself. *You have to use the card.*

She saw the slot and slid the card into it, being careful to push in the direction of the arrows. This time when she pushed 19, the number lit up. A moment later she was shoved rudely aside as Mia *came forward.*

Susannah subsided at the back of her own mind with a kind of tired relief. Yes, let someone else take over, why not? Let someone else drive the bus for awhile. She could feel the strength and substance coming back into her legs, and that was enough for now.

FIVE

Mia might have been a stranger in a strange land, but she was a fast learner. In the nineteenth-floor lobby she located the arrow with 1911–1923 beneath it and walked briskly down the corridor to 1919. The carpet, some thick green stuff that was delightfully soft, whispered beneath her

(*their*)

stolen shoes. She inserted the key-card, opened

the door, and stepped in. There were two beds. She put the bags on one of them, looked around without much interest, then fixed her gaze on the telephone.

Susannah! Impatient.

What?

How do I make it ring?

Susannah laughed with genuine amusement. *Honey, you aren't the first person to ask* that *question, believe me. Or the millionth. It either will or it won't. In its own good time. Meanwhile, why don't you have a look around. See if you can't find a place to store your gunna.*

She expected an argument but didn't get one. Mia prowled the room (not bothering to open the drapes, although Susannah very much wanted to see the city from this height), peeked into the bathroom (palatial, with what looked like a marble basin and mirrors everywhere), then looked into the closet. Here, sitting on a shelf with some plastic bags for dry-cleaning on top, was a safe. There was a sign on it, but Mia couldn't read it. Roland had had similar problems from time to time, but his had been caused by the difference between the English language alphabet and In-World's "great letters." Susannah had an idea that Mia's problems were a lot more basic; although her kidnapper clearly knew numbers, Susannah didn't think the chap's mother could read at all.

Susannah *came forward,* but not all the way. For a moment she was looking through two sets of eyes at two signs, the sensation so peculiar that it made her feel nauseated. Then the images came together and she could read the message:

**THIS SAFE IS PROVIDED FOR YOUR
PERSONAL BELONGINGS THE MANAGEMENT
OF THE PLAZA–PARK HYATT ASSUMES
NO RESPONSIBILITY FOR ITEMS LEFT HERE
CASH AND JEWELRY SHOULD BE DEPOSITED
IN THE HOTEL SAFE DOWNSTAIRS
TO SET CODE, PUNCH IN FOUR NUMBERS
PLUS ENTER TO OPEN, ENTER YOUR
FOUR-NUMBER CODE AND PUSH OPEN**

Susannah retired and let Mia select four numbers. They turned out to be a one and three nines.
It was the current year and might be one of the first
combinations a room burglar would try, but at
least it wasn't quite the room number itself.
Besides, they were the *right* numbers. Numbers of
power. A *sigul*. They both knew it.

Mia tried the safe after programming it, found it
locked tightly, then followed the directions for
opening it. There was a whirring noise from somewhere inside and the door popped ajar. She put in
the faded red MIDTOWN LANES bag—the box inside
just fit on the shelf—and then the bag of Oriza
plates. She closed and locked the safe's door again,
tried the handle, found it tight, and nodded. The
Borders bag was still on the bed. She took the wad
of cash out of it and tucked it into the right front
pocket of her jeans, along with the turtle.

Have to get a clean shirt, Susannah reminded her
unwelcome guest.

Mia, daughter of none, made no reply. She
clearly cared *bupkes* for shirts, clean or dirty. Mia
was looking at the telephone. For the time being,

with her labor on hold, the phone was all she cared about.

Now we palaver, Susannah said. *You promised, and it's a promise you're going to keep. But not in that banquet room.* She shuddered. *Somewhere outside, hear me I beg. I want fresh air. That banqueting hall smelled of death.*

Mia didn't argue. Susannah got a vague sense of the other woman riffling through various files of memory—examining, rejecting, examining, rejecting—and at last finding something that would serve.

How do we go there? Mia asked indifferently.

The black woman who was now two women (again) sat on one of the beds and folded her hands in her lap. *Like on a sled,* the woman's Susannah part said. *I'll push, you steer. And remember, Susannah-Mio, if you want my cooperation, you give me some straight answers.*

I will, the other replied. *Just don't expect to like them. Or even understand them.*

What do you—

Never mind! Gods, I never met anyone *who could ask so many questions! Time is short! When the telephone rings, our palaver ends! So if you'd palaver at all—*

Susannah didn't bother giving her a chance to finish. She closed her eyes and let herself fall back. No bed stopped that fall; she went right through it. She was falling for real, falling through space. She could hear the jangle of the todash chimes, dim and far.

Here I go again, she thought. And: *Eddie, I love you.*

STAVE: *Commala-gin-jive*
Ain't it grand to be alive?
To look out on Discordia
When the Demon Moon arrives.

RESPONSE: *Commala-come-five!*
Even when the shadows rise!
To see the world and walk the world
Makes ya glad to be alive.

THE CASTLE ALLURE

6ᵀᴴ STANZA

ONE

All at once she was falling into her body again and the sensation provoked a memory of blinding brilliance: Odetta Holmes at sixteen, sitting on her bed in her slip, sitting in a brilliant bar of sun and pulling up a silk stocking. For the moment this memory held, she could smell White Shoulders perfume and Pond's Beauty Bar, her mother's soap and her mother's borrowed perfume, so grown-up to be allowed perfume, and she thought: *It's the Spring Hop! I'm going with Nathan Freeman!*

Then it was gone. The sweet smell of Pond's soap was replaced by a clean and cold (but somehow dank) night breeze, and all that remained was that sense, so queer and perfect, of stretching into a new body as if it were a stocking one was pulling up over one's calf and knee.

She opened her eyes. The wind gusted, blowing a fine grit in her face. She squinted against it, grimacing and raising an arm, as if she might have to ward off a blow.

"Over here!" a woman's voice called. It wasn't the voice Susannah would have expected. Not strident, not a triumphant caw. "Over here, out of the wind!"

She looked and saw a tall and comely woman beckoning to her. Susannah's first look at Mia in the flesh astounded her, because the chap's mother was *white*. Apparently Odetta-that-was now had a Caucasian side to her personality, and how that must frost Detta Walker's racially sensitive butt!

She herself was legless again, and sitting in a kind of rude one-person cart. It had been parked at a notch in a low parapet wall. She looked out at the most fearsome, forbidding stretch of countryside she had ever seen in her life. Huge rock formations sawed at the sky and jostled into the distance. They glistened like alien bone beneath the glare of a savage sickle moon. Away from the glare of that lunar grin, a billion stars burned like hot ice. Amid the rocks with their broken edges and gaping crevices, a single narrow path wound into the distance. Looking at it, Susannah thought that a party would have to travel that path in single file. *And bring plenty of supplies. No mushrooms to pick along the way; no pokeberries, either.* And in the distance—dim and baleful, its source somewhere over the horizon—a dark crimson light waxed and waned. *Heart of the rose,* she thought, and then: *No, not that. Forge of the King.* She looked at the pulsing sullen light with helpless, horrified fascination. Flex . . . and loosen. Wax . . . and wane. An infection announcing itself to the sky.

"Come to me now, if you'd come at all, Susannah of New York," said Mia. She was dressed in a heavy serape and what looked like leather pants that stopped just below the knee. Her shins were scabbed and scratched. She wore thick-soled *huaraches* on her feet. "For the King can fascinate, even at a distance. We're on the Discordia side of the Castle. Would you like to end your life on the needles at the foot of this wall? If he fascinates you and tells you to jump, you'll do just that. Your bossy gunslinger-men aren't here to help you now, are they? Nay, nay. You're on your own, so y'are."

Susannah tried to pull her gaze from that steadily pulsing glow and at first couldn't do it. Panic bloomed in her mind

(*if he fascinates you and tells you to jump*)

and she seized it as a tool, compressing it to an edge with which to cut through her frightened immobility. For a moment nothing happened, and then she threw herself backward so violently in the shabby little cart that she had to clutch the edge in order to keep herself from tumbling to the cobbles. The wind gusted again, blowing stone-dust and grit against her face and into her hair, seeming to mock her.

But that pull . . . fascination . . . *glammer* . . . whatever it had been, it was gone.

She looked at the dog-cart (so she thought it, whether that was the right name or not) and saw at once how it worked. Simple enough, too. With no mule to draw it, *she* was the mule. It was miles from the sweet, light little chair they'd found in Topeka, and light-years from being able to walk on the strong legs that had conveyed her from the little park to the hotel. God, she missed having legs. Missed it already.

But you made do.

She seized hold of the cart's wooden wheels, strained, produced no movement, strained harder. Just as she was deciding she'd have to get out of the chair and hop-crawl her ignominious way to where Mia waited, the wheels turned with a groaning, oil-less creak. She rumbled toward Mia, who was standing behind a squat stone pillar. There were a great many of these, marching away into the dark along a curve. Susannah supposed that once upon a time (before the world had moved on), archers would have stood behind them for protection while the assaulting army fired their arrows or red-hot catapults or whatever you called them. Then they'd step into the gaps and fire their own weapons. How long ago had that been? What world *was* this? And how close to the Dark Tower?

Susannah had an idea it might be very close indeed.

She pushed the balky, gawky, protesting cart out of the wind and looked at the woman in the serape, ashamed to be so out of breath after moving less than a dozen yards but unable to help panting. She drew down deep breaths of the dank and somehow stony air. The pillars—she had an idea they were called merlons, or something like that—were on her right. On her left was a circular pool of darkness surrounded by crumbling stone walls. Across the way, two towers rose high above the outer wall, but one had been shattered, as if by lightning or some powerful explosive.

"This where we stand is the allure," Mia said. "The wall-walk of the Castle on the Abyss, once known as Castle Discordia. You said you wanted fresh. air. I hope this does ya, as they say in the Calla. This is far beyond there, Susannah, this is deep in End-World, near the place where your quest ends, for good or for ill." She paused and then said, "For ill, almost surely. Yet I care nothing for that, no, not I. I am Mia, daughter of none, mother of one. I care for my chap and nothing more. Chap be enough for me, aye! Would you palaver? Fine. I'll tell you what I may and be true. Why not? What is it to me, one way or the other?"

Susannah looked around. When she faced in toward the center of the castle—what she supposed was the courtyard—she caught an aroma of ancient rot. Mia saw her wrinkle her nose and smiled.

"Aye, they're long gone, and the machines the later ones left behind are mostly stilled, but the smell of their dying lingers, doesn't it? The smell of death always does. Ask your friend the gunslinger, the *true* gunslinger. He knows, for he's dealt his share of it. He is responsible for much, Susannah of New York. The guilt of worlds hangs around his neck like a rotting corpse. Yet he's gone far enough with his dry and lusty determination to finally draw the eyes of the great. He will be destroyed, aye, and all those who stand with him. I carry his doom in my own belly, and I care not." Her chin jutted forward in the starlight. Beneath the serape her breasts heaved . . . and, Susannah saw, her belly curved. In this world, at least, Mia was very clearly pregnant. Ready to burst, in fact.

"Ask your questions, have at me," Mia said. "Just remember, we exist in the other world, too, the one where we're bound together. We're lying on a bed in the inn, as if asleep . . . but we don't sleep, do we, Susannah? Nay. And when the telephone rings, when my friends call, we leave this place and go to them. If your questions have been asked and answered, fine. If not, that's also fine. Ask. Or . . . are you not a gunslinger?" Her lips curved in a disdainful smile. Susannah thought she was pert, yes, pert indeed. Especially for someone who wouldn't be able to find her way from Forty-sixth Street to Forty-seventh in the world they had to go back to. "So *shoot!* I should say."

Susannah looked once more into the darkened, broken well that was the castle's soft center, where lay its keeps and lists, its barbicans and murder holes, its God-knew-what. She had taken a course in medieval history and knew some of the terms, but that had been long ago. Surely there was a banqueting hall somewhere down there, one that she herself had supplied with food, at least for awhile. But her catering days were done. If Mia tried to push her too hard or too far, she'd find that out for herself.

Meantime, she thought she'd start with something relatively easy.

"If this is the Castle on the Abyss," she said, "where's the Abyss? I don't see anything out that way except for a minefield of rocks. And that red glow on the horizon."

Mia, her shoulder-length black hair flying out behind her (not a bit of kink in that hair, as there was in Susannah's; Mia's was like silk), pointed across the inner chasm below them to the far wall, where the towers rose and the allure continued its curve.

"This is the inner keep," she said. "Beyond it is the village of Fedic, now deserted, all dead of the Red Death a thousand years ago and more. Beyond that—"

"The Red Death?" Susannah asked, startled (also frightened in spite of herself). "*Poe's* Red Death? Like in the story?" And why not? Hadn't they already wandered into—and then back out of—L. Frank Baum's Oz? What came next? The White Rabbit and the Red Queen?

"Lady, I know not. All I can tell you is that beyond the deserted village is the outer wall, and beyond the outer wall is a great crack in the earth filled with monsters that cozen, diddle, increase, and plot to escape. Once there was a bridge across, but it fell long ago. 'In the time before counting,' as 'tis said. They're horrors that might drive an ordinary man or woman mad at a glance."

She favored Susannah with a glance of her own. A decidedly satiric one.

"But not a *gunslinger*. Surely not one such as *thee*."

"Why do you mock me?" Susannah asked quietly.

Mia looked startled, then grim. "Was it my idea to come here? To stand in this miserable cold where the King's Eye dirties the horizon and sullies the very cheek of the moon with its filthy light? Nay, lady! 'Twas you, so harry me not with your tongue!"

Susannah could have responded that it hadn't

been her idea to catch preg with a demon's baby in the first place, but this would be a terrible time to get into one of those yes-you-did, no-I-didn't squabbles.

"I wasn't scolding," Susannah said, "only asking."

Mia made an impatient shooing gesture with her hand as if to say *Don't split hairs,* and half-turned away. Under her breath she said, "I didn't go to Morehouse or *no* house. And in any case I'll bear my chap, do you hear? Whichever way the cards fall. Bear him and feed him!"

All at once Susannah understood a great deal. Mia mocked because she was afraid. In spite of all she knew, so much of her *was* Susannah.

I didn't go to Morehouse or no house, for instance; that was from *Invisible Man,* by Ralph Ellison. When Mia had bought into Susannah, she had purchased at least two personalities for the price of one. It was Mia, after all, who'd brought Detta out of retirement (or perhaps deep hibernation), and it was Detta who was particularly fond of that line, which expressed so much of the Negro's deep-held disdain for and suspicion of what was sometimes called "the finer postwar Negro education." Not to Morehouse or *no* house; I know what I know, in other words, I heard it through the grapevine, I got it on the earie, dearie, I picked it up on the jungle telegraph.

"Mia," she said now. "Whose chap is it besides yours? What demon was his father, do you know?"

Mia grinned. It wasn't a grin Susannah liked. There was too much Detta in it; too much laughing, bitter knowledge. "Aye, lady, I know. And you're right. It was a demon got him on you, a very great demon indeed, say true! A human one! It had to have been so, for know you that true demons, those left on the shore of these worlds which spin around the Tower when the *Prim* receded, are sterile. And for a very good reason."

"Then how—"

"Your dinh is the father of my chap," Mia said. "Roland of Gilead, aye, he. Steven Deschain finally has his grandson, although he lies rotten in his grave and knows it not."

Susannah was goggling at her, unmindful of the cold wind rushing out of the Discordia wilderness. "*Roland . . . ?* It can't be! He was beside me when the demon was *in* me, he was pulling Jake through from the house on Dutch Hill and fucking was the *last* thing on his mind . . ." She trailed off, thinking of the baby she'd seen in the Dogan. Thinking of those eyes. Those blue bombardier's eyes. *No. No, I refuse to believe it.*

"All the same, Roland is his father," Mia insisted. "And when the chap comes, I shall name him from your own mind, Susannah of New York; from what you learned at the same time you learned of merlons and courtyards and trebouchets and barbicans. Why not? 'Tis a good name, and fair."

Professor Murray's Introduction to Medieval History, that's what she's talking about.

"I will name him Mordred," said she. "He'll grow quickly, my darling boy, quicker than human, after his demon nature. He'll grow strong. The avatar of every gunslinger that ever was. And so, like the Mordred of your tale, will he slay his father."

And with that, Mia, daughter of none, raised her arms to the star-shot sky and screamed, although whether in sorrow, terror, or joy, Susannah could not tell.

TWO

"Hunker," Mia said. "I have this."

From beneath her serape she produced a bundle of grapes and a paper sack filled with orange poke-berries as swollen as her belly. Where, Susannah wondered, had the fruit come from? Was their shared body sleepwalking back in the Plaza–Park Hotel? Had there perhaps been a fruit basket she hadn't noticed? Or were these the fruits of pure imagination?

Not that it mattered. Any appetite she might have had was gone, robbed by Mia's claim. The fact that it was impossible somehow only added to the monstrosity of the idea. And she couldn't stop thinking of the baby she'd seen *in utero* on one of those TV screens. Those blue eyes.

No. It can't be, do you hear? It cannot *be!*

The wind coming through the notches between the merlons was chilling her to the bone. She swung off the seat of the cart and settled herself against the allure wall beside Mia, listening to the wind's constant whine and looking up at the alien stars.

Mia was cramming her mouth with grapes. Juice

ran from one corner of her mouth while she spat seeds from the other corner with the rapidity of machine-gun bullets. She swallowed, wiped her chin, and said: "It can. It can be. And more: it is. Are you still glad you came, Susannah of New York, or do you wish you'd left your curiosity unsatisfied?"

"If I'm gonna have a baby I didn't hump for, I'm gonna know everything about that baby that I can. Do you understand that?"

Mia blinked at the deliberate crudity, then nodded. "If you like."

"Tell me how it can be Roland's. And if you want me to believe anything you tell me, you better start by making me believe this."

Mia dug her fingernails into the skin of a pokeberry, stripped it away in one quick gesture, and ate the fruit down greedily. She considered opening another, then simply rolled it between her palms (those disconcertingly white palms), warming it. After enough of this, Susannah knew, the fruit would split its skin on its own. Then she began.

THREE

"How many Beams do there be, Susannah of New York?"

"Six," Susannah said. "At least, there were. I guess now there are only two that—"

Mia waved a hand impatiently, as if to say *Don't waste my time.* "Six, aye. And when the Beams were created out of that greater Discordia, the soup of creation some (including the Manni) call the Over and some call the *Prim,* what made them?"

"I don't know," Susannah said. "Was it God, do you think?"

"Perhaps there is a God, but the Beams rose from the *Prim* on the airs of magic, Susannah, the true magic which passed long ago. Was it God that made magic, or was it magic that made God? I know not. It's a question for philosophers, and mothering's my job. But once upon a time all was Discordia and from it, strong and all crossing at a single unifying point, came the six Beams. There was magic to hold them steady for eternity, but when the magic left from all there is but the Dark Tower, which some have called Can Calyx, the Hall of Resumption, men despaired. When the Age of Magic passed, the Age of Machines came."

"North Central Positronics," Susannah murmured. "Dipolar computers. Slo-trans engines." She paused. "Blaine the Mono. But not in our world."

"No? Do you say your world is exempt? What about the sign in the hotel lobby?" The pokeberry popped. Mia stripped it and gobbled it, drizzling juice through a knowing grin.

"I had an idea you couldn't read," Susannah said. This was beside the point, but it was all she could think of to say. Her mind kept returning to the image of the baby; to those brilliant blue eyes. Gunslinger's eyes.

"Aye, but I know my numbers, and when it comes to your mind, I read very well. Do you say you don't recall the sign in the hotel lobby? Will you tell me that?"

Of course she remembered. According to the sign,

the Plaza–Park would be part of an organization called Sombra/North Central in just another month. And when she'd said *Not in our world,* of course she had been thinking of 1964—the world of black-and-white television, absurdly bulky room-sized computers, and Alabama cops more than willing to sic the dogs on black marchers for voting rights. Things had changed greatly in the intervening thirty-five years. The Eurasian desk clerk's combination TV and typewriter, for instance—how did Susannah know that wasn't a dipolar computer run by some form of slo-trans engine? She did not.

"Go on," she told Mia.

Mia shrugged. "You doom yourselves, Susannah. You seem positively bent on it, and the root is always the same: your faith fails you, and you replace it with rational thought. But there is no love in thought, nothing that lasts in deduction, only death in rationalism."

"What does this have to do with your chap?"

"I don't know. There's much I don't know." She raised a hand, forestalling Susannah before Susannah could speak. "And no, I'm *not* playing for time, or trying to lead you away from what you'd know; I'm speaking as my heart tells me. Would you hear or not?"

Susannah nodded. She'd hear this . . . for a little longer, at least. But if it didn't turn back to the baby soon, she'd turn it back in that direction herself.

"The magic went away. Maerlyn retired to his cave in one world, the sword of Eld gave way to the pistols of the gunslingers in another, and the magic went away. And across the arc of years, great alchemists, great scientists, and great—what?—technicians, I think? Great men of thought, anyway, that's what I mean, great men of *deduction*—these came together and created the machines which ran the Beams. They were great machines but they were *mortal* machines. They replaced the *magic* with *machines,* do ya kennit, and now the machines are failing. In some worlds, great plagues have decimated whole populations."

Susannah nodded. "We saw one of those," she said quietly. "They called it the superflu."

"The Crimson King's Breakers are only hurrying along a process that's already in train. The machines are going mad. You've seen this for yourself. The men believed there would always be more men like them to make more machines. None of them foresaw what's happened. This . . . this universal exhaustion."

"The world has moved on."

"Aye, lady. It has. And left no one to replace the machines which hold up the last magic in creation, for the *Prim* has receded long since. The magic is gone and the machines are failing. Soon enough the Dark Tower will fall. Perhaps there'll be time for one splendid moment of universal rational thought before the darkness rules forever. Wouldn't that be nice?"

"Won't the Crimson King be destroyed, too, when the Tower falls? Him and all his crew? The guys with the bleeding holes in their foreheads?"

"He has been promised his own kingdom, where he'll rule forever, tasting his own special pleasures." Distaste had crept into Mia's voice. Fear, too, perhaps.

"Promised? Promised by whom? Who is more powerful than he?"

"Lady, I know not. Perhaps this is only what he has promised himself." Mia shrugged. Her eyes wouldn't quite meet Susannah's.

"Can nothing prevent the fall of the Tower?"

"Not even your gunslinger friend hopes to *prevent* it," Mia said, "only to slow it down by freeing the Breakers and—perhaps—slaying the Crimson King. Save it! *Save* it, O delight! Did he ever tell you that was his quest?"

Susannah considered this and shook her head. If Roland had ever said that, in so many words, she couldn't remember. And she was sure she would have.

"No," Mia went on, "for he won't lie to his ka-tet unless he has to, 'tis his pride. What he wants of the Tower is only to *see* it." Then she added, rather grudgingly: "Oh, perhaps to enter it, and climb to the room at the top, his ambition may strike so far. He may dream of standing on its allure as we hunker on this one, and chant the names of his fallen comrades, and of his line all the way back to Arthur Eld. But *save* it? No, good lady! Only a return of the magic could possibly save it, and—as you yourself well know—your dinh deals only in lead."

Never since crossing the worlds had Susannah heard Roland's trade of hand cast in such a paltry light. It made her feel sad and angry, but she hid her feelings as best she could.

"Tell me how your chap can be Roland's son, for I would hear."

"Aye, 'tis a good trick, but one the old people of River Crossing could have explained to you, I've no doubt."

Susannah started at that. "How do you know so *much* of me?"

"Because you are possessed," Mia said, "and I am your possessor, sure. I can look through any of your memories that I like. I can read what your eyes see. Now be quiet and listen if you would learn, for I sense our time has grown short."

FOUR

This is what Susannah's demon told her.

"There are six Beams, as you did say, but there are twelve Guardians, one for each end of each Beam. This—for we're still on it—is the Beam of Shardik. Were you to go beyond the Tower, it would become the Beam of Maturin, the great turtle upon whose shell the world rests.

"Similarly, there are but six demon elementals, one for each Beam. Below them is the whole invisible world, those creatures left behind on the beach of existence when the *Prim* receded. There are speaking demons, demons of house which some call ghosts, ill-sick demons which some—makers of machines and worshippers of the great false god rationality, if it does ya—call disease. Many small demons but only six demon elementals. Yet as there are twelve Guardians for the six Beams, there are twelve demon *aspects,* for each demon elemental is both male and female."

Susannah began to see where this was going, and

felt a sudden sinking in her guts. From the naked bristle of rocks beyond the allure, in what Mia called the Discordia, there came a dry, feverish cackle of laughter. This unseen humorist was joined by a second, a third, a fourth and fifth. Suddenly it seemed that the whole world was laughing at her. And perhaps with good reason, for it was a good joke. But how could she have known?

As the hyenas—or whatever they were—cackled, she said: "You're telling me that the demon elementals are hermaphrodites. That's why they're sterile, because they're both."

"Aye. In the place of the Oracle, your dinh had intercourse with one of these demon elementals in order to gain information, what's called *prophecy* in the High Speech. He had no reason to think the Oracle was anything but a succubus, such as those that sometimes exist in the lonely places—"

"Right," Susannah said, "just a run-of-the-mill demon sexpot."

"If you like," Mia said, and this time when she offered Susannah a pokeberry, Susannah took it and began to roll it between her palms, warming the skin. She still wasn't hungry, but her mouth was dry. So dry.

"The demon took the gunslinger's seed as female, and gave it back to you as male."

"When we were in the speaking ring," Susannah said dismally. She was remembering how the pouring rain had pounded against her upturned face, the sense of invisible hands on her shoulders, and then the thing's engorgement filling her up and at the same time seeming to tear her apart. The worst part had been the coldness of the enormous cock inside her. At the time, she'd thought it was like being fucked by an icicle.

And how had she gotten through it? By summoning Detta, of course. By calling on the bitch, victor in a hundred nasty little sex-skirmishes fought in the parking lots of two dozen roadhouses and county-line honky-tonks. Detta, who had trapped it—

"It tried to get away," she told Mia. "Once it figured out it had its cock caught in a damn Chinese finger-puller, it tried to get away."

"If it had wanted to get away," Mia said quietly, "it *would* have."

"Why would it bother fooling me?" Susannah asked, but she didn't need Mia to answer that question, not now. Because it had needed her, of course. It had needed her to carry the baby.

Roland's baby.

Roland's doom.

"You know everything you need to know about the chap," Mia said. "Don't you?"

Susannah supposed she did. A demon had taken in Roland's seed while female; had stored it, somehow; and then shot it into Susannah Dean as male. Mia was right. She knew what she needed to know.

"I've kept my promise," Mia said. "Let's go back. The cold's not good for the chap."

"Just a minute longer," Susannah said. She held up the pokeberry. Golden fruit now bulged through ruptures in the orange skin. "My berry just popped. Let me eat it. I have another question."

"Eat and ask and be quick about both."

"Who are *you*? Who are you really? Are you this demon? Does she have a name, by the way? She and he, do they have a name?"

"No," Mia said. "Elementals have no need of names; they are what they are. Am I a demon? Is that what you'd know? Yar, I suppose I am. Or I was. All that is vague now, like a dream."

"And you're not me . . . or are you?"

Mia didn't answer. And Susannah realized that she probably didn't know.

"Mia?" Low. Musing.

Mia was hunkering against the merlon with her serape tucked between her knees. Susannah could see that her ankles were swollen and felt a moment's pity for the woman. Then she squashed it. This was no time for pity, for there was no truth in it.

"You ain't nothing but the baby-sitter, girl."

The reaction was all she'd hoped for, and more. Mia's face registered shock, then anger. Hell, *fury*. "You *lie!* I'm this chap's *mother!* And when he comes, Susannah, there will be no more combing the world for Breakers, for my chap will be the greatest of them all, able to break both of the remaining Beams all by himself!" Her voice had filled with pride that sounded alarmingly close to insanity. "My Mordred! Do you hear me?"

"Oh, yes," Susannah said. "I hear. And you're actually going to go trotting right to those who've made it their business to pull down the Tower, aren't you? They call, you come." She paused, then finished with deliberate softness. "And when you get to them, they'll take your chap, and thank you very much, and then send you back into the soup you came from."

"Nay! I shall have the raising of him, for so they have promised!" Mia crossed her arms protectively over her belly. "He's mine, I'm his mother and I shall have the raising of him!"

"Girl, why don't you get *real?* Do you think they'll *keep* their word? *Them?* How can you see so much and not see that?"

Susannah knew the answer, of course. Motherhood itself had deluded her.

"Why would they not let me raise him?" Mia asked shrilly. "Who better? Who better than Mia, who was made for only two things, to bear a son and raise him?"

"But you're not just you," Susannah said. "You're like the children of the Calla, and just about everything else my friends and I have run into along the way. You're a *twin,* Mia! I'm your other half, your lifeline. You see the world through my eyes and breathe through my lungs. I had to carry the chap, because you couldn't, could you? You're as sterile as the big boys. And once they've got your kid, their A-bomb of a Breaker, they'll get rid of you if only so they can get rid of me."

"I have their promise," she said. Her face was downcast, set in its stubbornness.

"Turn it around," Susannah said. "Turn it around, I beg. If I were in your place and you in mine, what would you think if I spoke of such a promise?"

"I'd tell you to stop your blabbering tongue!"

"Who are you, really? Where in the hell did they

get you? Was it like a newspaper ad you answered, 'Surrogate Mother Wanted, Good Benefits, Short Term of Employment'? Who are you, really?"

"Shut up!"

Susannah leaned forward on her haunches. This position was ordinarily exquisitely uncomfortable for her, but she'd forgotten both her discomfort and the half-eaten pokeberry in her hand.

"Come on!" she said, her voice taking on the rasping tones of Detta Walker. "Come on and take off yo' blindfold, honeybunch, jus' like you made me take off mine! Tell the truth and spit in the devil's eye! *Who the fuck are you?*"

"*I don't know!*" Mia screamed, and below them the jackals hidden in the rocks screamed back, only their screams were laughter. "*I don't know, I don't know who I am, does that satisfy?*"

It did not, and Susannah was about to press on and press harder when Detta Walker spoke up.

FIVE

This is what Susannah's other demon told her.

Baby-doll, you need to think bout this a little, seem to me. She cain't, she stone dumb, cain't read, cain't cipher more than just a little, ain't been to Morehouse, ain't been to no house, but you have, Miss Oh-Detta Holmes been to Co-lum-bee-ya, lah-de-dah, de Gem ob de Ocean, ain't we jus' so fine.

You need to think bout how she pregnant, for one thing. She say she done fucked Roland out of his jizz, then turn male, into the Demon of the Ring,

and shot it into you, and den you carryin it, you
tossin all those nasty things she made you eat down
yo' throat, so where she *in all this now, dat what*
Detta like to know. How come she *settin there preg-*
nant under dat greaser blanket she wearin? Is it
more of dat . . . what you call it . . . visualization
technique?

Susannah didn't know. She only knew that Mia
was looking at her with suddenly narrowed eyes.
She was doubtless picking up some of this mono-
logue. How much? Not much at all, that was
Susannah's bet; maybe a word here and there, but
mostly it was just quack. And in any case, Mia certainly *acted* like the baby's mother. Baby Mordred!
It was like a Charles Addams cartoon.

Dat she do, Detta mused. *She ack like a Mommy,*
she wrapped around it root and branch, you right
bout dat much.

But maybe, Susannah thought, that was just her
nature. Maybe once you got beyond the mothering
instinct, there *was* no Mia.

A cold hand reached out and seized Susannah's
wrist. "Who is it? Is it that nasty-talking one? If it
is, banish her. She scares me."

She still scared Susannah a little, in all truth, but
not as much as when she'd first come to accept that
Detta was real. They hadn't become friends and
probably never would, but it was clear that Detta
Walker could be a powerful ally. She was more
than mean. Once you got past the idiotic Butterfly
McQueen accent, she was shrewd.

Dis Mia make a mighty pow'ful ally her own-
self, if you c'd get her on yo' side. Ain't hardly

nothin in the world as pow'ful as a pissed-off Mommy.

"We're going back," Mia said. "I've answered your questions, the cold's bad for the baby, and the mean one's here. Palaver's done."

But Susannah shook off her grip and moved back a little, out of Mia's immediate reach. In the gap between the merlons the cold wind knifed through her light shirt, but it also seemed to clear her mind and refresh her thinking.

Part of her is me, because she has access to my memories. Eddie's ring, the people of River Crossing, Blaine the Mono. But she's got to be more *than me as well, because . . . because . . .*

Go on, girl, you ain't doin bad, but you slow.

Because she knows all this other *stuff, as well. She knows about the demons, both the little ones and the elementals. She knows how the Beams came into being—sort of—and about this magical soup of creation, the* Prim. *As far as I ever knew, prim's a word you use for girls who are always yanking their skirts down over their knees. She didn't get that other meaning from me.*

It occurred to her what this conversation was like: parents studying their new baby. Their new chap. He's got your nose, Yes but he's got *your* eyes, and But my goodness, *where* did he get that hair?

Detta said: *And she also got friens back in New York, don't forget* dat. *Least she want to think* they *her friens.*

So she's someone or something else, as well. Someone from the invisible world of house demons

and ill-sicks. But who? Is she really one of the ele-
mentals?

Detta laughed. *She say so, but she lyin bout dat,*
sugar! I know she is!

Then what is she? What was *she, before she was*
Mia?

All at once a phone, amplified to almost ear-splitting shrillness, began to ring. It was so out of place on this abandoned castle tower that at first Susannah didn't know what it was. The things out there in the Discordia—jackals, hyenas, whatever they were—had been subsiding, but with the advent of this sound they began to cackle and shriek again.

Mia, daughter of none, mother of Mordred, knew that ringing for what it was immediately, however. She *came forward.* Susannah at once felt this world waver and lose its reality. It seemed almost to freeze and become something like a painting. Not a very good one, either.

"No!" she shouted, and threw herself at Mia.

But Mia—pregnant or not, scratched up or not, swollen ankles or no swollen ankles—overpowered her easily. Roland had shown them several hand-to-hand tricks (the Detta part of her had crowed with delight at the nastiness of them), but they were useless against Mia; she parried each before Susannah had done more than get started.

Sure, yes, of course, she knows your tricks just
like she knows about Aunt Talitha in River
Crossing and Topsy the Sailor in Lud, because she
has access to your memories, because she is, at least
to some extent, you—

And here her thoughts ended, because Mia had twisted her arms up behind her and oh dear God the pain was enormous.

Ain't you just the most babyish cunt, Detta said with a kind of genial, panting contempt, and before Susannah could reply, an amazing thing happened: the world ripped open like a brittle piece of paper. This rip extended from the dirty cobbles of the allure's floor to the nearest merlon and then on up into the sky. It raced into that star-shot firmament and tore the crescent moon in two.

There was a moment for Susannah to think that this was it, one or both of the final two Beams had snapped and the Tower had fallen. Then, through the rip, she saw two women lying on one of the twin beds in room 1919 of the Plaza–Park Hotel. Their arms were around each other and their eyes were shut. They were dressed in identical blood-stained shirts and bluejeans. Their features were the same, but one had legs below the knee and straight silky hair and white skin.

"Don't you mess with me!" Mia panted in her ear. Susannah could feel a fine, tickling spray of saliva. "Don't you mess with me or with my chap. Because I'm stronger, do you hear? *I'm stronger!*"

There was no doubt about that, Susannah thought as she was propelled toward the widening hole. At least for now.

She was pushed through the rip in reality. For a moment her skin seemed simultaneously on fire and coated with ice. Somewhere the todash chimes were ringing, and then—

SIX

—she sat up on the bed. One woman, not two, but at least one with legs. Susannah was shoved, reeling, to the back. Mia in charge now. Mia reaching for the phone, at first getting it wrong-way-up and then reversing it.

"Hello? Hello!"

"Hello, Mia. My name is—"

She overrode him. "Are you going to let me keep my baby? This bitch inside me says you're not!"

There was a pause, first long and then too long. Susannah felt Mia's fear, first a rivulet and then a flood. *You don't have to feel that way,* she tried to tell her. *You're the one with what they want, with what they* need, *don't you see that?*

"Hello, are you there? Gods, *are you there? PLEASE TELL ME YOU'RE STILL THERE!*"

"I'm here," the man's voice said calmly. "Shall we start again, Mia, daughter of none? Or shall I ring off until you're feeling . . . a little more yourself?"

"No! No, don't do that, don't do that I beg!"

"You won't interrupt me again? Because there's no reason for unseemliness."

"I promise!"

"My name is Richard P. Sayre." A name Susannah knew, but from where? "You know where you need to go, don't you?"

"Yes!" Eager now. Eager to please. "The Dixie Pig, Sixty-first and Lexingworth."

"Lexing*ton,*" Sayre said. "Odetta Holmes can help you find it, I'm sure."

Susannah wanted to scream *That's not my*

name! She kept silent instead. This Sayre would like her to scream, wouldn't he? Would like her to lose control.

"Are you there, Odetta?" Pleasantly teasing. "Are you there, you interfering bitch?"

She kept silent.

"She's in there," Mia said. "I don't know why she's not answering, I'm not holding her just now."

"Oh, I think *I* know why," Sayre said indulgently. "She doesn't like that name, for one thing." Then, in a reference Susannah didn't get: " 'Don't call me Clay no more, Clay my slave name, call me Muhammad Ali!' Right, Susannah? Or was that after your time? A little after, I think. Sorry. Time can be so confusing, can't it? Never mind. I have something to tell you in a minute, my dear. You won't like it very much, I fear, but I think you should know."

Susannah kept silent. It was getting harder.

"As for the immediate future of your chap, Mia, I'm surprised you'd even feel it necessary to ask," Sayre told her. He was a smoothie, whoever he was, his voice containing exactly the right amount of outrage. "The King keeps his promises, unlike some I could name. And, issues of our integrity aside, think of the *practical* issues! Who else should have the keeping of perhaps the most important child to ever be born . . . *including* Christ, *including* Buddha, *including* the Prophet Muhammad? To who else's breast, if I may be crude, would we trust his suck?"

Music to her ears, Susannah thought dismally. *All the things she's been thirsting to hear. And why? Because she is Mother.*

"You'd trust him to me!" Mia cried. "Only to me, of course! Thank you! *Thank* you!"

Susannah spoke at last. Told *her* not to trust *him*. And was, of course, roundly ignored.

"I'd no more lie to you than break a promise to my own mother," said the voice on the phone. (*Did you ever have one, sugar?* Detta wanted to know.) "Even though the truth sometimes hurts, lies have a way of coming back to bite us, don't they? The truth of this matter is you won't have your chap for long, Mia, his childhood won't be like that of other children, normal children—"

"I know! Oh, I know!"

"—but for the five years you *do* have him . . . or perhaps seven, it might be as many as seven . . . he'll have the best of everything. From you, of course, but also from us. Our interference will be minimal—"

Detta Walker leaped forward, as quick and as nasty as a grease-burn. She was only able to take possession of Susannah Dean's vocal cords for a moment, but it was a *precious* moment.

"Dass raht, dahlin, dass raht," she cackled, "he won't come in yo' mouf or get it in you' hair!"

"Shut that bitch UP!" Sayre whipcracked, and Susannah felt the jolt as Mia shoved Detta head over heels—but still cackling—to the back of their shared mind again. Once more into the brig.

Had mah say, though, damn if I didn't! Detta cried. *Ah tole that honky muhfuh!*

Sayre's voice in the telephone's earpiece was cold and clear. "Mia, do you have control or not?"

"Yes! Yes, I do!"

"Then don't let that happen again."

"I won't!"

And somewhere—it felt like above her, although there were no real directions here at the back of the shared mind—something clanged shut. It sounded like iron.

We really are in the brig, she told Detta, but Detta just went on laughing.

Susannah thought: *I'm pretty sure I know who she is, anyway. Besides me, that is.* This truth seemed obvious to her. The part of Mia that wasn't either Susannah or something summoned from the void world to do the Crimson King's bidding . . . surely the third part really was the Oracle, elemental or not; the female force that had at first tried to molest Jake and then had taken Roland, instead. That sad, craving spirit. She finally had the body she needed. One capable of carrying the chap.

"Odetta?" Sayre's voice, teasing and cruel. "Or Susannah, if you like that better? I promised you news, didn't I? It's kind of a good news–bad news thing, I'm afraid. Would you like to hear it?"

Susannah held her silence.

"The bad news is that Mia's chap may not be able to fulfill the destiny of his name by killing his father, after all. The good news is that Roland will almost surely be dead in the next few minutes. As for Eddie, I'm afraid there's no question. He doesn't have either your dinh's reflexes or his battle experience. My dear, you're going to be a widow very soon. That's the bad news."

She could hold her silence no longer, and Mia let her speak. "You lie! About *everything!*"

"Not at all," Sayre said calmly, and Susannah

realized where she knew that name from: the end of Callahan's story. Detroit. Where he'd violated his church's most sacred teaching and committed suicide to keep from falling into the hands of the vampires. Callahan had jumped out of a skyscraper window to avoid that particular fate. He had landed first in Mid-World, and gone from there, via the Unfound Door, into the Calla Borderlands. And what he'd been thinking, the Pere had told them, was *They don't get to win, they don't get to win.* And he was right about that, *right,* goddammit. But if Eddie died—

"We knew where your dinh and your husband would be most likely to end up, should they be swept through a certain doorway," Sayre told her. "And calling certain people, beginning with a chap named Enrico Balazar . . . I assure you, Susannah, that was *easy.*"

Susannah heard the sincerity in his voice. If he didn't mean what he said, then he was the world's best liar.

"How could you find such a thing out?" Susannah asked. When there was no answer she opened her mouth to ask the question again. Before she could, she was tumbled backward once more. Whatever Mia might have been once, she had grown to incredible strength inside Susannah.

"Is she gone?" Sayre was asking.

"Yes, gone, in the back." Servile. Eager to please.

"Then come to us, Mia. The sooner you come to us, the sooner you can look your chap in the face!"

"Yes!" Mia cried, delirious with joy, and

Susannah caught a sudden brilliant glimpse of something. It was like peeking beneath the hem of a circus tent at some bright wonder. Or a dark one.

What she saw was as simple as it was terrible: Pere Callahan, buying a piece of salami from a shopkeeper. A *Yankee* shopkeeper. One who ran a certain general store in the town of East Stoneham, Maine, in the year of 1977. Callahan had told them all this story in the rectory . . . *and Mia had been listening.*

Comprehension came like a red sun rising on a field where thousands have been slaughtered. Susannah rushed forward again, unmindful of Mia's strength, screaming it over and over again:

"Bitch! Betraying bitch! Murdering bitch! You told them where the Door would send them! Where it would send Eddie and Roland! Oh you BITCH!"

SEVEN

Mia was strong, but unprepared for this new attack. It was especially ferocious because Detta had joined her own murderous energy to Susannah's understanding. For a moment the interloper was pushed backward, eyes wide. In the hotel room, the telephone dropped from Mia's hand. She staggered drunkenly across the carpet, almost tripped over one of the beds, then whirled about like a tipsy dancer. Susannah slapped at her and red marks appeared on her cheek like exclamation points.

Slapping myself, that's all I'm doing, Susannah

thought. *Beating up the equipment, how stupid is that?* But she couldn't help it. The enormity of what Mia had done, the betraying *enormity*—

Inside, in some battle-ring which was not quite physical (but not entirely mental, either), Mia was finally able to clutch Susannah/Detta by the throat and drive her back. Mia's eyes were still wide with shock at the ferocity of the assault. And perhaps with shame, as well. Susannah hoped she was able to feel shame, that she hadn't gone beyond that.

I did what I had to do, Mia repeated as she forced Susannah back into the brig. *It's my chap, every hand is against me, I did what I had to do.*

You traded Eddie and Roland for your monster, that's what you did! Susannah screamed. *Based on what you overheard and then passed on, Sayre was sure they'd use the Door to go after Tower, wasn't he? And how many has he set against them?*

The only answer was that iron clang. Only this time it was followed by a second. And a third. Mia had had the hands of her hostess clamped around her throat and was consequently taking no chances. This time the brig's door had been triple-locked. Brig? Hell, might as well call it the Black Hole of Calcutta.

When I get out of here, I'll go back to the Dogan and disable all the switches! she cried. *I can't believe I tried to help you! Well, fuck that! Have it on the street, for all of me!*

You can't *get out,* Mia replied, almost apologetically. *Later, if I can, I'll leave you in peace*—

What kind of peace will there be for me with Eddie dead? No wonder you wanted to take his ring off! How could you bear to have it lie against your skin, knowing what you'd done?

Mia picked up the telephone and listened, but Richard P. Sayre was no longer there. Probably had places to go and diseases to spread, Susannah thought.

Mia replaced the telephone in its cradle, looked around at the empty, sterile room the way people do when they won't be coming back to a place and want to make sure they've taken everything that matters. She patted one pocket of her jeans and felt the little wad of cash. Touched the other and felt the lump that was the turtle, the *sköldpadda*.

I'm sorry, Mia said. *I have to take care of my chap. Every hand is against me now.*

That's not true, Susannah said from the locked room where Mia had thrown her. And where was it, really? In the deepest, darkest dungeons of the Castle on the Abyss? Probably. Did it matter? *I was on your side. I helped you. I stopped your damn labor when you needed it stopped. And look what you did. How could you ever be so cowardly and low?*

Mia paused with her hand on the room's doorknob, her cheeks flushing a dull red. Yes, she was ashamed, all right. But shame wouldn't stop her. *Nothing* would stop her. Until, that was, she found herself betrayed in turn by Sayre and his friends.

Thinking of that inevitability gave Susannah no satisfaction at all.

You're damned, she said. *You know that, don't you?*

"I don't care," Mia said. "An eternity in hell's a

fair price to pay for one look in my chap's face.
Hear me well, I beg."

And then, carrying Susannah and Detta with her,
Mia opened the hotel room door, re-entered the
corridor, and took her first steps on her course
toward the Dixie Pig, where terrible surgeons
waited to deliver her of her equally terrible chap.

STAVE: *Commala-mox-nix!*
You're in a nasty fix!
To take the hand in a traitor's glove
Is to grasp a sheaf of sticks!

RESPONSE: *Commala-come-six!*
Nothing there but thorns and sticks!
When you find your hand in a traitor's glove
You're in a nasty fix.

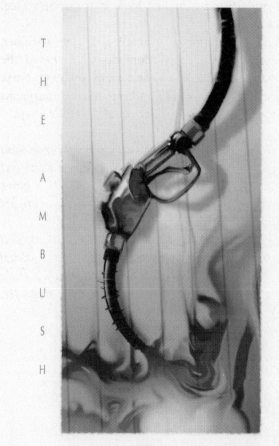

T
H
E

A
M
B
U
S
H

7TH STANZA

ONE

Roland Deschain was the last of Gilead's last great band of warriors, for good reason; with his queerly romantic nature, his lack of imagination, and his deadly hands, he had ever been the best of them. Now he had been invaded by arthritis, but there was no dry twist in his ears or eyes. He heard the thud of Eddie's head against the side of the Unfound Door as they were sucked through (and, ducking down at the last split second, only just avoided having his own skull broken in by the Door's top jamb). He heard the sound of birds, at first strange and distant, like birds singing in a dream, then immediate and prosaic and completely there. Sunlight struck his face and should have dazzled him blind, coming as he was from the dimness of the cave. But Roland had turned his eyes into slits the moment he'd seen that bright light, had done it without thinking. Had he not, he surely would have missed the circular flash from two o'clock as they landed on hard-packed, oil-darkened earth. Eddie would have died for sure. Maybe both of them would have died. In Roland's experience, only two things glared with that perfect brilliant circularity: eyeglasses and the long sight of a weapon.

The gunslinger grabbed Eddie beneath the arm as unthinkingly as he'd slitted his eyes against the glare of onrushing sunlight. He'd felt the tension in the younger man's muscles as their feet left the rock-and bone-littered floor of the Doorway Cave, and he felt them go slack when Eddie's head connected with the side of the Unfound Door. But Eddie was groaning, still trying to talk, so he was at least partly aware.

"Eddie, to me!" Roland bellowed, scrambling to his feet. Bitter agony exploded in his right hip and raced almost all the way down to his knee, but he gave no sign. Barely registered it, in fact. He hauled Eddie with him toward a building, some building, and past what even Roland recognized as oil or gasoline pumps. These were marked MOBIL instead of CITGO or SUNOCO, two other names with which the gunslinger was familiar.

Eddie was semiconscious at best. His left cheek was drenched with blood from a laceration in his scalp. Nevertheless, he put his legs to work as best he could and stumbled up three wooden steps to what Roland now recognized as a general store. It was quite a bit smaller than Took's, but otherwise not much d—

A limber whipcrack of sound came from behind and slightly to the right. The shooter was close enough for Roland to feel confident that if he had heard the sound of the shot, the man with the rifle had already missed.

Something passed within an inch of his ear, making its own perfectly clear sound: *Mizzzzzz!* The glass in the little mercantile's front door shattered inward. The sign which had been hanging there (**WE'RE OPEN, SO COME IN 'N VISIT**) jumped and twisted.

"Rolan..." Eddie's voice, weak and distant, sounded as if it were coming through a mouthful of mush. "Rolan wha ... who ... *OWF!*" This last a grunt of surprise as Roland threw him flat inside the door and landed on top of him.

Now came another of those limber whipcracks; there was a gunner with an extremely high-powered rifle out there. Roland heard someone shout "Aw, fuck 'at, Jack!" and a moment later a speed-shooter—what Eddie and Jake called a machine-gun—opened up. The dirty display windows on both sides of the door came crashing down in bright shards. The paperwork which had been posted inside the glass—town notices, Roland had no doubt—went flying.

Two women and a gent of going-on-elderly years were the only customers in the store's aisles. All three were turned toward the front—toward Roland and Eddie—and on their faces was the eternal uncomprehending look of the gunless civilian. Roland sometimes thought it a grass-eating look, as though such folk—those in Calla Bryn Sturgis mostly no different—were sheep instead of people.

"*Down!*" Roland bellowed from where he lay on his semiconscious (and now breathless) companion. "For the love of your gods *get DOWN!*"

The going-on-elderly gent, who was wearing a

checked flannel shirt in spite of the store's warmth, let go of the can he'd been holding (there was a picture of a tomato on it) and dropped. The two women did not, and the speed-shooter's second burst killed them both, caving in the chest of one and blowing off the top of the other's head. The chest-shot woman went down like a sack of grain. The one who'd been head-shot took two blind, blundering steps toward Roland, blood spewing from where her hair had been like lava from an erupting volcano. Outside the store a second and third speed-shooter began, filling the day with noise, filling the air above them with a deadly crisscross of slugs. The woman who'd lost the top of her head spun around twice in a final dance-step, arms flailing, and then collapsed. Roland went for his gun and was relieved to find it still in its holster: the reassuring sandalwood grip. So that much was well. The gamble had paid off. And he and Eddie certainly weren't todash. The gunners had seen them, seen them very well.

More. Had been *waiting* for them.

"Move in!" someone was screaming. "Move in, move in, don't give em a chance to find their peckers, move in, you *catzarros!*"

"Eddie!" Roland roared. "Eddie, you have to help me now!"

"Hizz . . . ?" Faint. Bemused. Eddie looking at him with only one eye, the right. The left was temporarily drowned in blood from his scalp-wound.

Roland reached out and slapped him hard enough to make blood fly from his hair. "*Harriers!* Coming to kill us! Kill all here!"

Eddie's visible eye cleared. It happened fast. Roland saw the effort that took—not to regain his wits but to regain them at such speed, and despite a head that must be pounding monstrously—and took a moment to be proud of Eddie. He was Cuthbert Allgood all over again, Cuthbert to the life.

"What the hell's this?" someone called in a cracked, excited voice. "Just *what* in the blue *hell* is *this?*"

"Down," Roland said, without looking around. "If you want to live, get on the floor."

"Do what he says, Chip," someone else replied—probably, Roland thought, the man who'd been holding the can with the tomato on it.

Roland crawled through litters of broken glass from the door, feeling pricks and prinks of pain as some cut his knees and knuckles, not caring. A bullet buzzed past his temple. Roland ignored that, too. Outside was a brilliant summer day. In the foreground were the two oil-pumps with MOBIL printed on them. To one side was an old car, probably belonging to either the women shoppers (who'd never need it again) or to Mr. Flannel Shirt. Beyond the pumps and the oiled dirt of the parking area was a paved country road, and on the other side of that a little cluster of buildings painted a uniform gray. One was marked TOWN OFFICE, one STONEHAM FIRE AND RESCUE. The third and largest was the TOWN GARAGE. The parking area in front of these buildings was also paved (*metaled* was Roland's word for it), and a number of vehicles had been parked there, one the size of a large bucka-waggon. From behind them came more than half a dozen men at full charge. One hung back and Roland recognized him: Enrico Balazar's ugly lieutenant, Jack Andolini. The gunslinger had seen this man die, gunshot and then eaten alive by the carnivorous lobstrosities which lived in the shallow waters of the Western Sea, but here he was again. Because infinite worlds spun on the axle which was the Dark Tower, and here was another of them. Yet only one world was true; only one where, when things were finished, they *stayed* finished. It might be this one; it might not be. In either case, this was no time to worry about it.

Up on his knees, Roland opened fire, fanning the trigger of his revolver with the hard ridge of his right hand, aiming first at the boys with the speed-shooters. One of them dropped dead on the country road's white centerline with blood boiling out of his throat. The second was flung backward all the way to the road's dirt shoulder with a hole between his eyes.

Then Eddie was beside him, also on his knees, fanning the trigger of Roland's other gun. He missed at least two of his targets, which wasn't surprising, given his condition. Three others dropped to the road, two dead and one screaming *"I'm hit! Ah, Jack, help me, I'm hit in the guts!"*

Someone grabbed Roland's shoulder, unaware of what a dangerous thing that was to do to a gunslinger, especially one in a fire-fight. "Mister, what in the hell—"

Roland took a quick look, saw a fortyish man wearing both a tie and a butcher's apron, had time to think, *Shopkeeper, probably the one who gave*

Pere directions to the post office, and then shoved the man violently backward. A split second later, blood dashed backward from the left side of the man's head. Grooved, the gunslinger judged, but not seriously hurt, at least not yet. If Roland hadn't pushed him, however—

Eddie was reloading. Roland did the same, taking a bit longer thanks to the missing fingers on his right hand. Meanwhile, two of the surviving harriers had taken cover behind one of the old cars on this side of the road. Too close. Not good. Roland could hear the rumble of an approaching motor. He looked back at the fellow who'd been quick-witted enough to drop when Roland told him to, thus avoiding the fate of the ladies.

"You!" Roland said. "Do you have a gun?"

The man in the flannel shirt shook his head. His eyes were a brilliant blue. Frightened, but not, Roland judged, panicky. In front of this customer, the shopkeeper was sitting up, spread-legged, looking with sickened amazement at the red droplets pattering down and spreading on his white apron.

"Shopkeeper, do you keep a gun?" Roland asked.

Before the shopkeeper could answer—if he was capable of answering—Eddie grabbed Roland's shoulder. "Charge of the Light Brigade," he said. The words came out mushy—*sharr uvva lie briggay*—but Roland wouldn't have understood the reference in any case. The important thing was that Eddie had seen another six men dashing across the road. This time they were spread out and zigzagging from side to side.

"Vai, vai, vai!" Andolini bawled from behind them, sweeping both hands in the air.

"Christ, Roland, that's Tricks Postino," Eddie said. Tricks was once more toting an extremely large weapon, although Eddie couldn't be sure it was the oversized M-16 he'd called The Wonderful Rambo Machine. In any case, he was no luckier here than he'd been in the shootout at the Leaning Tower: Eddie fired and Tricks went down on top of one of the guys already lying in the road, still firing his assault weapon at them as he did so. This was probably nothing more heroic than a finger-spasm, final signals sent from a dying brain, but Roland and Eddie had to throw themselves flat again, and the other five outlaws reached cover behind the old cars on this side of the road. Worse still. Backed by covering fire from the vehicles across the street— the vehicles these boys had come in, Roland was quite sure—they would soon be able to turn this little store into a shooting gallery without too much danger to themselves.

All of this was too close to what had happened at Jericho Hill.

It was time to beat a retreat.

The sound of the approaching vehicle continued to swell—a big engine, laboring under a heavy load, from the sound. What topped the rise to the left of the store was a gigantic truck filled with enormous cut trees. Roland saw the driver's eyes widen and his mouth drop open, and why not? Here in front of this small-town mercantile where he had doubtless stopped many times for a bottle of beer or ale at the end of a long, hot day in the woods, lay half a dozen bleeding bodies scattered in the road like soldiers killed in a battle. Which was, Roland knew, exactly what they were.

The big truck's front brakes shrieked. From the rear came the angry-dragon chuff of the airbrakes. There was an accompanying scream of huge rubber tires first locking and then smoking black tracks on the metaled surface of the road. The truck's multi-ton load began to slew sideways. Roland saw splinters flying from the trees and into the blue sky as the out-laws on the far side of the road continued to fire heedlessly. There was something almost hypnotic about all this, like watching one of the Lost Beasts of Eld come tumbling out of the sky with its wings on fire.

The truck's horseless front end ran over the first of the bodies. Guts flew in red ropes and splashed the dirt of the shoulder. Legs and arms were torn off. A wheel squashed Tricks Postino's head, the sound of his imploding skull like a chestnut bursting in a hot fire. The truck's load broached sideways and began to totter. Wheels fully as high as Roland's shoulders dug in and tossed up clouds of bloody dirt. The truck slid by the store with a majestic lack of speed. The driver was no longer visible in the cab. For a moment the store and the people inside it were blocked from the superior firepower on the other side of the road. The shopkeeper—Chip—and the surviv-ing customer—Mr. Flannel Shirt—were staring at the broaching truck with identical expressions of helpless amazement. The shopkeeper absently wiped blood from the side of his head and flicked it onto the floor like water. His wound was worse than Eddie's, Roland judged, yet he seemed unaware of it. Maybe that was good.

"Out back," the gunslinger said to Eddie. "Now."

"Good call."

Roland grabbed the man in the flannel shirt by the arm. The man's eyes immediately left the truck and went to the gunslinger. Roland nodded toward the back, and the elderly gent nodded back. His unquestioning quickness was an unexpected gift.

Outside, the truck's load finally overturned, mashing one of the parked cars (and the harriers hiding behind it, Roland dearly hoped), spilling logs first off the top and then simply spilling them all. There was a gruesome, endless sound of scraping metal that made the gunfire seem puny by comparison.

TWO

Eddie grabbed the storekeeper just as Roland had grabbed the other man, but Chip showed none of his customer's awareness or instinct for survival. He merely went on staring through the jagged hole where his windows had been, eyes wide with shock and awe as the pulp-truck out there entered the final phase of its self-destructive ballet, the cab twisting free of the overloaded carrier and bouncing down the hill beyond the store and into the woods. The load itself went sliding up the right side of the road, creating a huge bow-wave of dirt and leaving behind a deep groove, a flattened Chevrolet, and two more flattened harriers.

There were plenty more where those came from, though. Or so it seemed. The gunfire continued.

"Come on, Chip, time to split," Eddie said, and this time when he tugged the shopkeeper toward the back of the store Chip came, still looking back over his shoulder and wiping blood from the side of his face.

At the rear of the market, on the left, was an added-on lunchroom with a counter, a few patched stools, three or four tables, and an old lobster-pot over a newsstand which seemed to contain mostly out-of-date girlie magazines. As they reached this part of the building, the gunfire from outside intensified. Then it was dwarfed again, this time by an explosion. The pulper's fuel-tank, Eddie assumed. He felt the droning passage of a bullet and saw a round black hole appear in the picture of a lighthouse mounted on the wall.

"Who *are* those guys?" Chip asked in a perfectly conversational voice. "Who are you? Am I hit? My son was in Viet Nam, you know. Did you see that truck?"

Eddie answered none of his questions, just smiled and nodded and hustled Chip along in Roland's wake. He had absolutely no idea where they were going or how they were going to get out of this fuckaree. The only thing he was completely sure of was that Calvin Tower wasn't here. Which was probably good. Tower might or might not have brought down this particular batch of hellfire and brimstone, but the hellfire and brimstone was *about* old Cal, of that Eddie had no doubt. If old Cal had only—

A darning-needle of heat suddenly tore through his arm and Eddie shouted in surprise and pain. A moment later another punched him in the calf. His lower right leg exploded into *serious* pain, and he cried out again.

"Eddie!" Roland chanced a look back. "Are you—"

"Yeah, fine, go, go!"

Ahead of them now was a cheap fiberboard back wall with three doors in it. One was marked BUOYS, one GULLS, one EMPLOYEES ONLY.

"EMPLOYEES ONLY!" Eddie shouted. He looked down and saw a blood-ringed hole in his bluejeans about three inches below his right knee. The bullet hadn't exploded the knee itself, which was to the good, but oh Mama, it hurt like the veriest mother-fucker of creation.

Over his head, a light-globe exploded. Glass showered down on Eddie's head and shoulders.

"I'm insured, but God knows if it covers some-thin like *this*," Chip said in his perfectly conver-sational voice. He wiped more blood from his face, then slatted it off his fingertips and onto the floor, where it made a Rorschach inkblot. Bullets buzzed around them. Eddie saw one flip up Chip's collar. Some-where behind them, Jack Andolini—old Dou-ble-Ugly—was hollering in Italian. Eddie somehow didn't think he was calling retreat.

Roland and the customer in the flannel shirt went through the EMPLOYEES ONLY door. Eddie fol-lowed, pumped up on the wine of adrenaline and still dragging Chip. This was a storeroom, and of quite a good size. Eddie could smell different kinds of grain, some sort of minty tang, and, most of all, coffee.

Now Mr. Flannel Shirt had taken the lead. Roland followed him quickly down the storeroom's center aisle and between pallets stacked high with canned goods. Eddie limped gamely along after, still hauling the shopkeeper. Old Chip had lost a lot of blood from the wound on the side of his head and Eddie kept expecting him to pass out, but Chip actually seemed . . . well, chipper. He was currently asking Eddie what had happened to Ruth Beemer and her sister. If he meant the two women who'd been in the store (Eddie was pretty sure he did), Eddie hoped that Chip wouldn't suddenly regain his memory.

There was another door at the back. Mr. Flannel Shirt opened it and started out. Roland hauled him back by the shirt, then went out himself, low. Eddie stood Chip beside Mr. Flannel Shirt and himself just in front of them. Behind them, bullets smacked through the EMPLOYEES ONLY door, creating startled white eyes of daylight.

"Eddie!" Roland grunted. "To me!"

Eddie limped out. There was a loading dock here, and beyond it about an acre of unlovely, churned-up ground. Trash barrels had been stacked haphazardly to the right of the dock and there were two Dumpsters to the left, but it didn't look to Eddie Dean as if anyone had worried too much about putting litter in its place. There were also several piles of beercans almost big enough to qualify as archaeological middens. *Nothing like relaxing on the back porch after a hard day at the store,* Eddie thought.

Roland was pointing his gun at another oil-pump, this one rustier and older than the ones out front. On it was a single word. "Diesel," Roland said. "Does that mean fuel? It does, doesn't it?"

"Yeah," Eddie said. "Chip, does the diesel pump work?"

"Sure, sure," Chip said in a disinterested tone of voice. "Lotsa guys fill up back here."

"I can run it, mister," said Flannel Shirt. "You better let me, too—it's tetchy. Can you and your buddy cover me?"

"Yes," Roland said. "Pour it in there." And jerked a thumb at the storeroom.

"Hey, no!" Chip said, startled.

How long did all these things take? Eddie could not have said, not for sure. All he was aware of was a clarity he had known only once before: while riddling Blaine the Mono. It overwhelmed everything with its brilliance, even the pain in his lower leg, where the tibia might or might not have been chipped by a bullet. He was aware of how funky it smelled back here—rotted meat and moldy produce, the yeasty scent of a thousand departed brewskis, the odors of don't-care laziness—and the divinely sweet fir-perfume of the woods just beyond the perimeter of this dirty little roadside store. He could hear the drone of a plane in some distant quadrant of the sky. He knew he loved Mr. Flannel Shirt because Mr. Flannel Shirt was *here,* was *with* them, linked to Roland and Eddie by the strongest of bonds for these few minutes. But time? No, he had no true sense of that. But it couldn't have been much more than ninety seconds since

Roland had begun their retreat, or surely they would have been overwhelmed, crashed truck or no crashed truck.

Roland pointed left, then turned right himself. He and Eddie stood back to back on the loading dock with about six feet between them, guns raised to their cheeks like men about to commence a duel. Mr. Flannel Shirt hopped off the end of the dock, spry as a cricket, and seized the chrome crank on the side of the old diesel pump. He began to spin it rapidly. The numbers in their little windows spun backward, but instead of returning to all zeros, they froze at 0 0 1 9. Mr. Flannel Shirt tried the crank again. When it refused to turn, he shrugged and yanked the nozzle out of its rusty cradle.

"John, no!" Chip cried. He was still standing in the doorway of his storeroom and holding up his hands, one clean and the other bloody all the way up the forearm.

"Get out of the way, Chip, or you're gonna—"

Two men dashed around Eddie's side of the East Stoneham General Store. Both were dressed in jeans and flannel shirts, but unlike Chip's shirt, these looked brand-new, with the creases still in the sleeves. Purchased especially for the occasion, Eddie had no doubt. And one of the goons Eddie recognized quite well; had last seen him in The Manhattan Restaurant of the Mind, Calvin Tower's bookshop. Eddie had also killed this fellow once before. Ten years in the future, if you could believe it. In The Leaning Tower, Balazar's joint, and with the same gun he now held in his hand. A snatch of an old Bob Dylan lyric occurred to him, something about the price you had to pay to keep from going through everything twice.

"Hey, Big Nose!" Eddie cried (as he seemed to each time he saw this particular piece of pond scum). "How you doing, pal?" In truth, George Biondi did not appear to be doing well at all. Not even his mother would have considered him much more than presentable, even on his best day (that humungous beak), and now his features were puffed and discolored by bruises that had only just begun to fade. The worst of them was right between the eyes.

I did that, Eddie thought. *In the back of Tower's bookstore.* It was true, but it also seemed like something that had happened a thousand years ago.

"*You,*" said George Biondi. He seemed too stunned to even raise his gun. "*You. Here.*"

"Me here," Eddie agreed. "As for you, you should have stayed in New York." With that said, he blew George Biondi's face off. His friend's face, too.

Flannel Shirt squeezed the pump handle's pistol grip and dark diesel sprayed from the nozzle. It doused Chip, who cawed indignantly and then staggered out onto the loading dock. "*Stings!*" he shouted. "*Gorry, don't that sting! Quit it, John!*"

John did not. Another three men came dashing around Roland's side of the store, took one look at the gunslinger's calm and awful face, tried to back-track. They were dead before they could do more than get the heels of their new country walking shoes planted. Eddie thought of the half-dozen cars and the big Winnebago that had been parked across the street and had time to wonder just how many men Balazar had sent on this little expedition. Certainly not just his own guys. How had he paid for the imports?

He didn't have to, Eddie thought. *Someone loaded him up with dough and told him to go buy the farm. As many out-of-town goons as he could get. And somehow convinced him the guys they were going after deserved that kind of coverage.*

From inside the store there came a dull, percussive thud. Soot blew out of the chimney and was lost against the darker, oilier cloud rising from the crashed pulp truck. Eddie thought somebody had tossed a grenade. The door to the storeroom blew off its hinges, walked halfway down the aisle surrounded by a cloud of smoke, and fell flat. Soon the fellow who'd thrown the grenade would throw another, and with the floor of the storeroom now covered in an inch of diesel fuel—

"Slow him down if you can," Roland said. "It's not wet enough in there yet."

"Slow down Andolini?" Eddie asked. "How do I do that?"

"With your everlasting *mouth!*" Roland cried, and Eddie saw a wonderful, heartening thing: Roland was grinning. Almost laughing. At the same time he looked at Flannel Shirt—John—and made a spinning gesture with his right hand: *keep pumping.*

"Jack!" Eddie shouted. He had no idea where Andolini might be at this point, and so simply yelled as loud as he could. Having grown up ramming around Brooklyn's less savory streets, this was quite loud.

There was a pause. The gunfire slowed, then stopped.

"Hey," Jack Andolini called back. He sounded surprised, but in a good-humored way. Eddie doubted he was really surprised at all, and he had no doubt whatsoever that what Jack wanted was payback. He'd been hurt in the storage area behind Tower's bookshop, but that wasn't the worst of it. He'd also been humiliated. "Hey, Slick! Are you the guy who was gonna send my brains to Hoboken, then stuck a gun under my chin? Man, I got a mark there!"

Eddie could see him making this rueful little speech, all the time gesturing with his hands, moving his remaining men into position. How many was that? Eight? Maybe ten? They'd already taken out a bunch, God knew. And where would the remainder be? A couple on the left of the store. A couple more on the right. The rest with Monsieur Grenades R Us. And when Jack was ready, those guys would charge. Right into the new shallow lake of diesel fuel.

Or so Eddie hoped.

"I've got the same gun with me today!" he called to Jack. "This time I'll jam it up your ass, how'd that be?"

Jack laughed. It was an easy, relaxed sound. An act, but a good one. Inside, Jack would be red-lining: heart-rate up over one-thirty, blood-pressure up over one-seventy. This was it, not just payback for some little punk daring to blindside him but the biggest job of his stinking bad-guy career, the Super Bowl.

Balazar gave the orders, undoubtedly, but Jack Andolini was the one on the spot, the field marshal, and this time the job wasn't just beating up a dice-dopey bartender who wouldn't pay the vig on what he owed or convincing some Yid jewelry-store owner on Lenox Avenue that he needed protection; this was an actual war. Jack was smart—at least compared to most of the street-hoods Eddie had met while doped up and running with his brother Henry—but Jack was also stupid in some fundamental way that had nothing to do with IQ scores. The punk who was currently taunting him had already beaten him once, and quite handily, but Jack Andolini had contrived to forget that.

Diesel sloshed quietly over the loading dock and rippled along the old warped boards of the mercantile's storeroom. John, aka Sai Yankee Flannel Shirt, gave Roland a questioning look. Roland responded by first shaking his head and then twirling his right hand again: more.

"Where's the bookstore guy, Slick?" Andolini's voice just as pleasant as before, but closer now. He'd crossed the road, then. Eddie put him just outside the store. Too bad diesel fuel wasn't more explosive. "Where's Tower? Give him to us and we'll leave you and the other guy alone until next time."

Sure, Eddie thought, and remembered something Susannah sometimes said (in her best growling Detta Walker voice) to indicate utter disbelief: *Also I won't come in yo' mouth or get any in yo' hair.*

This ambush had been set up especially for visiting gunslingers, Eddie was almost sure of it. The bad boys might or might not know where Tower was (he trusted what came out of Jack Andolini's mouth not at all), but someone had known to exactly which where and when the Unfound Door was going to deliver Eddie and Roland, and had passed that knowledge on to Balazar. *You want the boy who embarrassed your boy, Mr. Balazar? The kid who peeled Jack Andolini and George Biondi off Tower before Tower had time to give in and give you what you wanted? Fine. Here's where he's going to show up. Him and one other. And by the way, here's enough dough to buy an army of mercenaries in tu-tone shoes. Might not be enough, the kid's hard and his buddy's worse, but you might get lucky. Even if you don't, even if the one named Roland gets away and leaves a bunch of dead guys behind . . . well, getting the kid's a start. And there are always more gunnies, aren't there? Sure. The world's full of them. The* worlds.

And what about Jake and Callahan? Had there been a reception party waiting for them, too, and had it been twenty-two years up the line from this when? The little poem on the fence surrounding the vacant lot suggested that, if they'd followed his wife, it had been—SUSANNAH-MIO, DIVIDED GIRL OF MINE, the poem had said. PARKED HER RIG IN THE DIXIE PIG IN THE YEAR OF '99. And if there *had* been a reception party waiting, could they possibly still be alive?

Eddie clung to one idea: if any member of the ka-tet died—Susannah, Jake, Callahan, even Oy—

he and Roland would know. If he was kidding himself about that, succumbing to some romantic fallacy, so be it.

THREE

Roland caught the eye of the man in the flannel shirt and drew the side of his hand across his throat. John nodded and let go of the oil-pump's squeeze-handle at once. Chip, the store owner, was now standing beside the loading dock, and where his face wasn't lathered with blood, he was looking decidedly gray. Roland thought he would pass out soon. No loss there.

"Jack!" the gunslinger shouted. "Jack Andolini!" His pronunciation of the Italian name was a pretty thing to listen to, both precise and rippling.

"You Slick's big brother?" Andolini asked. He sounded amused. And he sounded closer. Roland put him in front of the store, perhaps on the very spot where he and Eddie had come through. He wouldn't wait long to make his next move; this was the countryside, but there were still people about. The rising black plume of smoke from the overturned wood-waggon would already have been noticed. Soon they would hear sirens.

"I suppose you'd call me his foreman," Roland said. He pointed at the gun in Eddie's hand, then pointed into the storeroom, then pointed at himself: *Wait for my signal.* Eddie nodded.

"Why don't you send him out, *mi amigo?* This doesn't have to be your concern. I'll take him and let you go. Slick's the one I want to talk to. Getting the answers I need from him will be a pleasure."

"You could never take us," Roland said pleasantly. "You've forgotten the face of your father. You're a bag of shit with legs. Your own ka-daddy is a man named Balazar, and you lick his dirty ass. The others know and they laugh at you. 'Look at Jack,' they say, 'all that ass-licking only makes him uglier.'"

There was a brief pause. Then: "You got a mean mouth on you, mister." Andolini's voice was level, but all the bogus good humor had gone out of it. All the laughter. "But you know what they say about sticks and stones."

In the distance, at last, a siren rose. Roland nodded first to John (who was watching him alertly) and then at Eddie. *Soon,* that nod said.

"Balazar will be building his towers of cards long after you're nothing but bones in an unmarked grave, Jack. Some dreams are destiny, but not yours. Yours are only dreams."

"Shut up!"

"Hear the sirens? Your time's almost u—"

"Vai!" Jack Andolini shouted. *"Vai! Get em! I want that old fucker's head, do you hear me? I want his head!"*

A round black object arced lazily through the hole where the EMPLOYEES ONLY door had been. Another grenado. Roland had been expecting it. He fired once, from the hip, and the grenado exploded in midair, turning the flimsy wall between the storeroom and the lunchroom into a storm of destructive, splintery blowback. There were screams of surprise and agony.

"Now, Eddie!" Roland shouted, and began to fire into the diesel. Eddie joined in. At first Roland didn't think anything was going to happen, but then a sluggish ripple of blue flame appeared in the center aisle and went snaking toward where the rear wall had been. Not enough! Gods, how he wished it had been the kind they called gasoline!

Roland tipped out the cylinder of his gun, dropped the spent casings around his boots, and reloaded.

"On your right, mister," John said, almost conversationally, and Roland dropped flat. One bullet passed through the place where he'd been. The second flipped at the ends of his long hair. He'd only had time to reload three of his revolver's six chambers, but that was one more bullet than he needed. The two harriers flew backward with identical holes in the center of their brows, just below the hairline.

Another hoodlum dashed around the corner of the store on Eddie's side and saw Eddie waiting for him with a grin on his bloody face. The fellow dropped his gun immediately and began to raise his hands. Eddie put a bullet through his chest before they got as high as his shoulders. *He's learning,* Roland thought. *Gods help him, but he is.*

"That fire's a little slow for my taste, boys," said John, and leaped up onto the loading dock. The store was barely visible through the rolling smoke of the deflected grenado, but bullets came flying through it. John seemed not to notice them, and Roland thanked ka for putting such a good man in their path. Such a hard man.

John took a square silver object from his pants pocket, flipped up the lid, and produced a good flame with the flick of his thumb on a small wheel. He tossed the little flaming tinderbox underhand into the storeroom. Flames burst up all around it with a *whoomp* sound.

"What's the matter with you?" Andolini screamed. *"Get them!"*

"Come and do it yourself!" Roland called. At the same time he pulled on John's pants leg. John jumped off the loading dock backward and stumbled. Roland caught him. Chip the storekeeper chose this moment to faint, pitching forward to the trash-littered earth with a groan so soft it was almost a sigh.

"Yeah, come on!" Eddie goaded. "Come on *Slick,* whatsamatta *Slick,* don't send a boy to do a man's work, you ever hear that one? How many guys did you have over there, two dozen? And we're still standing! So come on! Come on and do it yourself! Or do you want to lick Enrico Balazar's ass for the rest of your life?"

More bullets came through the smoke and flame, but the harriers in the store showed no interest in trying to charge through the growing fire. No more came around the sides of the store, either.

Roland pointed at Eddie's lower right leg, where the hole was. Eddie gave him a thumbs-up, but the leg of his jeans now seemed too full below the knee—swollen—and when he moved, his shor'boot squelched. The pain had settled to a steady hard ache that seemed to cycle with the beat of his heart. Yet he was coming to believe it might have missed the bone. *Maybe,* he admitted to himself, *because I want to believe it.*

The first siren had been joined by two or three others, and they were closing in.

"*Go!*" Jack screamed. He now sounded on the verge of hysterics. "*Go, you chickenshit mother-fuckers, go get them!*"

Roland thought that the remaining badmen might have attacked a couple of minutes ago—maybe even thirty seconds ago—if Andolini had led their charge personally. But now the frontal-assault option had been closed off, and Andolini must surely know that if he led men around either side of the store, Roland and Eddie would pick them off like clay birds in a Fair-Day shooting contest. The only workable strategies left to him were siege or a long flanking movement through the woods, and Jack Andolini had no time for either. Standing their ground back here, however, would present its own problems. Dealing with the local constabulary, for instance, or the fire brigade if that showed up first.

Roland pulled John to him so he could speak quietly. "We need to get out of here right now. Can you help us?"

"Oh, ayuh, I think so." The wind shifted. A draft blew through the mercantile's broken front windows, through the place where the back wall had been, and out the back door. The diesel smoke was black and oily. John coughed and waved it away. "Follow me. Let's step lively."

John hurried across the ugly acre of waste ground behind the store, stepping over a broken crate and weaving his way between a rusty incinerator and a pile of even rustier machine parts. There was a name on the biggest of these that Roland had seen before in his wanderings: JOHN DEERE.

Roland and Eddie walked backward, protecting John's back, taking little glances over their own shoulders to keep from tripping. Roland hadn't entirely given up hope that Andolini would make a final charge and he could kill him, as he had done once before. On the beach of the Western Sea, that had been, and here he was again, not only back but ten years *younger.*

While I, Roland thought, *feel at least a thousand years older.*

Yet that was not really true. Yes, he was now suffering—finally—the ills an old man could reasonably expect. But he had a ka-tet to protect again, and not just any ka-tet but one of *gunslingers,* and they had refreshed his life in a way he never would have expected. It all meant something to him again, not just the Dark Tower but *all* of it. So he wanted Andolini to come. And if he killed Andolini in this world, he had an idea Andolini would stay dead. Because this world was *different.* It had a resonance all the others, even his own, lacked. He felt it in every bone and every nerve. Roland looked up and saw exactly what he expected: clouds in a line. At the rear of the barren acre, a path slipped into the woods, its head marked by a pair of good-sized granite rocks. And here the gunslinger saw herringbone patterns of shadows, overlapping but all pointing the same way. You had to look to see it, but once seen it was unmistakable. As in the version of New York where they had found the empty bag in the vacant lot and Susannah had seen the vagrant dead, this was the true world, the one where time always ran in a single direction. They might be able to hop into the future if they could find a door, as he was sure Jake and Callahan had done (for Roland also remembered the poem on the fence, and now understood at least part of it), but they could never return to the past. This was the true world, the one where no roll of the dice could ever be taken back, the one closest to the Dark Tower. And they were still on the Path of the Beam.

John led them onto the way into the woods and quickly down it, away from the rising pillars of thick dark smoke and the approaching whine of the sirens.

FOUR

They hadn't gone even a quarter of a mile before Eddie began seeing blue glints through the trees. The path was slippery with pine needles, and when they came to the final slope—the one leading down to a long and narrow lake of surpassing loveliness—Eddie saw that someone had built a birch railing. Beyond it was a stub of dock jutting out into the water. Tied to the dock was a motorboat.

"That's mine," John said. "I come over for m'groceries and a bite of lunch. Didn't expect no excitement."

"Well, you got it," Eddie said.

"Ayuh, that's a true thing. Mind this last bit, if you don't want to go on your keister." John went nimbly down the final slope, holding the rail for balance and sliding rather than walking. On his feet was a pair of old scuffed workboots that would have looked perfectly at home in Mid-World, Eddie thought.

He went next himself, favoring his bad leg. Roland brought up the rear. From behind them came a sudden explosion, as sharp and limber as that first high-powered rifleshot but far louder.

"That'd be Chip's propane," John said.

"Cry pardon?" Roland asked.

"Gas," Eddie said quietly. "He means gas."

"Ayuh, stove-gas," John agreed. He stepped into his boat, grabbed the Evinrude's starter-cord, gave it a yank. The engine, a sturdy little twenty-horse sewing machine of a thing, started on the first pull. "Get in here, boys, and let's us vacate t' area," he grunted.

Eddie got in. Roland paused for a moment to tap his throat three times. Eddie had seen him perform this ritual before when about to cross open water, and reminded himself to ask about it. He never got the chance; before the question occurred to him again, death had slipped between them.

FIVE

The skiff moved as quietly and as gracefully over the water as any motor-powered thing can, skating on its own reflection beneath a sky of summer's most pellucid blue. Behind them the plume of dark smoke sullied that blue, rising higher and higher, spreading as it went. Dozens of folk, most of them in shorts or bathing costumes, stood upon the banks of this little lake, turned in the smoke's direction, hands raised to shade against the sun. Few if any marked the steady (and completely unshowy) passage of the motorboat.

"This is Keywadin Pond, just in case you were wonderin," John said. He pointed ahead of them, where another gray tongue of dock stuck out. Beside this one was a neat little boathouse, white with green trim, its overhead door open. As they neared it, Roland and Eddie could see both a canoe and a kayak bobbing inside, at tether.

"Boathouse is mine," the man in the flannel shirt added. The *boat* in *boathouse* came out in a way impossible to reproduce with mere letters—*bwut* would probably come closest—but which both men recognized. It was the way the word was spoken in the Calla.

"Looks well-kept," Eddie said. Mostly to be saying *something*.

"Oh, ayuh," John said. "I do caretakin, camp-checkin, some rough carpenterin. Wouldn't look good f'business if I had a fallin-down boathouse, would it?"

Eddie smiled. "Suppose not."

"My place is about half a mile back from the water. Name's John Cullum." He held out his right hand to Roland, continuing to steer a straight course away from the rising pillar of smoke and toward the boathouse with the other.

Roland took the hand, which was pleasantly rough. "I'm Roland Deschain, of Gilead. Long days and pleasant nights, John."

Eddie put out his own hand in turn. "Eddie Dean, from Brooklyn. Nice to meet you."

John shook with him easily enough but his eyes studied Eddie closely. When their hands parted, he said: "Young fella, did somethin just happen? It did, didn't it?"

"I don't know," Eddie said. Not with complete honesty.

"You ain't been to Brooklyn for a long time, son, have you?"

"Ain't been to Morehouse or to *no* house," Eddie Dean said, and then quickly, before he could lose it: "Mia's locked Susannah away. Locked her away in the year of '99. Suze can get to the Dogan, but going there's no good. Mia's locked off the controls. There's nothing Suze can do. She's kidnapped. She . . . she . . ."

He stopped. For a moment everything had been so *clear,* like a dream upon the instant of waking. Then, as so often happens with dreams, it faded. He didn't even know if it had been a real message from Susannah, or pure imagination.

Young fella, did somethin just happen?

So Cullum had felt it, too. Not imagination, then. Some form of the touch seemed more likely.

John waited, and when there was no more from Eddie, turned to Roland. "Does your pal come over funny that way often?"

"Not often, no. Sai . . . *Mister,* I mean. Mister Cullum, I thank you for helping us when we needed help. I thank ya big-big. It would be monstrous impudent of us to ask for more, but—"

"But you're gonna. Ayuh, figgered." John made

a minute course correction toward the little
boathouse with its square open mouth. Roland
estimated they'd be there in five minutes. That was
fine by him. He had no objection to riding in this
tight little motor-powered boat (even though it
rode rather low in the water with the weight of
three grown men inside), but Keywadin Pond was
far too exposed for his taste. If Jack Andolini (or
his successor, should Jack be replaced) asked
enough of those shore-gawkers, he would eventually find a few who remembered the little skiff with
the three men in it. And the boathouse with the
neat green trim. *John Cullum's bwut-huss, may it
do ya fine,* these witnesses would say. Best they
should be farther along the Beam before that happened, with John Cullum packed off to somewhere
safe. Roland judged "safe" in this case to be perhaps three looks to the horizon-line, or about a
hundred wheels. He had no doubt that Cullum, a
total stranger, had saved their lives by stepping in
decisively at the right moment. The last thing he
wanted was for the man to lose his own as a result.

"Well, I'll do what I can for ya, already made up
m'mind to that, but I got to ask you somethin now,
while I got the chance."

Eddie and Roland exchanged a brief look.
Roland said, "We'll answer if we can. Which is to
say, John of East Stoneham, if we judge that the
answer won't cause you harm."

John nodded. He seemed to gather himself. "I
know you're not ghosts, because we all saw you
back at the store and I just now touched you to
shake hands. I can see the shadders you cast." He

pointed at where they lay across the side of the boat. "Real as real. So my question is this: are you walk-ins?"

"Walk-ins," Eddie said. He looked at Roland, but Roland's face was completely blank. Eddie looked back at John Cullum, sitting in the stern of the boat and steering them toward the boathouse. "I'm sorry, but I don't . . ."

"Been a lot of em around here, last few years," John said. "Waterford, Stoneham, East Stoneham, Lovell, Sweden . . . even over in Bridgton and Denmark." This last township name came out *Denmaa-aaak*.

He saw they were still puzzled.

"Walk-ins're people who just *appear*," he said. "Sometimes they're dressed in old-fashioned clothes, as if they came from . . . *ago,* I guess you'd say. One was nekkid as a jaybird, walkin right up the middle of Route 5. Junior Angstrom seen im. Last November this was. Sometimes they talk other languages. One came to Don Russert's house over in Waterford. Sat right there in the kitchen! Donnie's a retired history professor from Vanderbilt College and he taped the fella. Fella jabbered quite awhile, then went into the laundry room. Donnie figured he must'a taken it for the bathroom and went after him to turn him around, but the fella was already gone. No door for him to go out of, but gone he was.

"Donnie played that tape of his for just about everyone in the Vandy Languages Department (*De-paaa-aatment*), and wasn't none of em recognized it. One said it must be a completely made-up language, like Esperanto. Do you sabby Esperanto, boys?"

Roland shook his head. Eddie said (cautiously), "I've heard of it, but I don't really know what it i—"

"And sometimes," John said, his voice lowering as they glided into the shadows of the boathouse, "sometimes they're hurt. Or disfigured. Roont."

Roland started so suddenly and so hard that the boat rocked. For a moment they were actually in danger of being tipped out. "What? What do you say? Speak again, John, for I would hear it very well."

John apparently thought it was purely an issue of verbal comprehension, because this time he was at pains to pronounce the word more carefully. "*Ruined*. Like folks who'd been in a nuclear war, or a fallout zone, or something."

"Slow mutants," Roland said. "I think he might be talking about slow muties. Here in this town."

Eddie nodded, thinking about the Grays and Pubes in Lud. Also thinking about a misshapen beehive and the monstrous insects which had been crawling over it.

John killed the little Evinrude engine, but for a moment the three of them sat where they were, listening to water slap hollowly against the aluminum sides of the boat.

"Slow mutants," the old fellow said, almost seeming to taste the words. "Ayuh, I guess that'd be as good a name for em as any. But they ain't the only ones. There's been animals, too, and kinds of birds no one's ever seen in these parts. But mostly it's the walk-ins that've got people worried and talkin amongst themselves. Donnie Russert called someone he knew at Duke University, and that fella called someone in their Department of Psychic Studies—amazin they've got such a thing as that in a real college, but it appears they do—and the Psychic Studies woman said that's what such folks are called: walk-ins. And then, when they disappear again—which they always do, except for one fella over in East Conway Village, who died— they're called walk-*outs*. The lady said that some scientists who study such things—I guess you could call em scientists, although I know a lot of folks might argue—b'lieve that walk-ins are aliens from other planets, that spaceships drop em off and then pick em up again, but most of em think they're time-travelers, or from different Earths that lie in a line with ours."

"How long has this been going on?" Eddie asked. "How long have the walk-ins been showing up?"

"Oh, two or three years. And it's gettin worse ruther'n better. I seen a couple of such fellas myself, and once a woman with a bald head who looked like she had this bleedin eye in the middle of her forread. But they was all at a distance, and you fellas are up close."

John leaned toward them over his bony knees, his eyes (as blue as Roland's own) gleaming. Water slapped hollowly at the boat. Eddie felt a strong urge to take John Cullum's hand again, to see if something else would happen. There was another Dylan song called "Visions of Johanna." What Eddie wanted was not a vision of Johanna, but the name was at least close to that.

"Ayuh," John was saying, "you boys are right up close and personal. Now, I'll help you along your way if I can, because I don't sense nothing the least bit bad about either of you (although I'm going to tell you flat out that I ain't *never* seen such shooting), but I want to know: are you walk-ins or not?"

Once more Roland and Eddie exchanged looks, and then Roland answered. "Yes," he said. "I suppose we are."

"Gorry," John whispered. In his awe, not even his seamed face could keep him from looking like a child. "Walk-ins! And where is it you're from, can you tell me that?" He looked at Eddie, laughed the way people do when they are admitting you've put a good one over on them, and said: "Not *Brooklyn.*"

"But I *am* from Brooklyn," Eddie said. The only thing was it hadn't been *this* world's Brooklyn, and he knew that now. In the world he came from, a children's book named *Charlie the Choo-Choo* had been written by a woman named Beryl Evans; in this one it had been written by someone named Claudia y Inez Bachman. Beryl Evans sounded real and Claudia y Inez Bachman sounded phony as a three-dollar bill, yet Eddie was coming more and more to believe that Bachman was the true handle. And why? Because it came as part of this world.

"I *am* from Brooklyn, though. Just not the . . . well . . . the same one."

John Cullum was still looking at them with that wide-eyed child's expression of wonder. "What about those other fellas? The ones who were waiting for you? Are they . . . ?"

"No," Roland said. "Not they. No more time

for this, John—not now." He got cautiously to his feet, grabbed an overhead beam, and stepped out of the boat with a little wince of pain. John followed and Eddie came last. The two other men had to help him. The steady throb in his right calf had receded a little bit, but the leg was stiff and numb, hard to control.

"Let's go to your place," Roland said. "There's a man we need to find. With the blessing, you may be able to help us do that."

He may be able to help us in more ways than that, Eddie thought, and followed them back into the sunlight, gimping along on his bad leg with his teeth gritted.

At that moment, Eddie thought he would have slain a saint in exchange for a dozen aspirin tablets.

> STAVE: *Commala-loaf-leaven!*
> *They go to hell or up to heaven!*
> *When the guns are shot and the fire's hot,*
> *You got to poke em in the oven.*

> RESPONSE: *Commala-come-seven!*
> *Salt and yow' for leaven!*
> *Heat em up and knock em down*
> *And poke em in the oven.*

A GAME OF TOSS

8TH STANZA

ONE

In the winter of 1984–85, when Eddie's heroin use was quietly sneaking across the border from the Land of Recreational Drugs and into the Kingdom of Really Bad Habits, Henry Dean met a girl and fell briefly in love. Eddie thought Sylvia Goldover was a Skank *El Supremo* (smelly armpits and dragon breath wafting out from between a pair of Mick Jagger lips), but kept his mouth shut because *Henry* thought she was beautiful, and Eddie didn't want to hurt Henry's feelings. That winter the young lovers spent a lot of time either walking on the windswept beach at Coney Island or going to the movies in Times Square, where they would sit in the back row and wank each other off once the popcorn and the extra-large box of Goobers were gone.

Eddie was philosophic about the new person in Henry's life; if Henry could work his way past that awful breath and actually tangle tongues with Sylvia Goldover, more power to him. Eddie himself spent a lot of those mostly gray three months alone and stoned in the Dean family apartment. He didn't mind; liked it, in fact. If Henry had been there, he would have insisted on TV and would have ragged Eddie constantly about his story-tapes. ("Oh boy! Eddie's gonna wissen to his wittle stowy about the *elves* and the *ogs* and the cute wittle *midgets!*") Always calling the orcs the ogs, and always calling the Ents "the scawwy walking *twees.*" Henry thought made-up shit was queer. Eddie had sometimes tried to tell him there was nothing more made-up than the crud they showed on afternoon TV, but Henry wasn't having any of that; Henry could tell you all about the evil twins on *General Hospital* and the equally evil step-mother on *The Guiding Light.*

In many ways, Henry Dean's great love affair—which ended when Sylvia Goldover stole ninety bucks out of his wallet, left a note saying *I'm sorry, Henry* in its place, and took off for points unknown with her *old* boyfriend—was a relief to Eddie. He'd sit on the sofa in the living room, put on the tapes of John Gielgud reading Tolkien's *Rings* trilogy, skin-pop along the inside of his right arm, and nod off to the Forests of Mirkwood or the Mines of Moria along with Frodo and Sam.

He'd loved the hobbits, thought he could have cheerfully spent the rest of his life in Hobbiton, where the worst drug going was tobacco and big brothers did not spend entire days ragging on little brothers, and John Cullum's little cottage in the woods returned him to those days and that dark-toned story with surprising force. Because the cottage had a hobbit-hole feel about it. The furniture in the living room was small but perfect: a sofa and two overstuffed chairs with those white doilies on the arms and where the back of your head would rest. The gold-framed black-and-white photograph on one wall had to be Cullum's folks, and the one opposite it had to be his grandparents. There was a framed Certificate of Thanks from the East Stoneham Volunteer Fire Department. There was a parakeet in a cage, twittering amiably, and a cat on the hearth. She raised her head when they came in, gazed greenly at the strangers for a moment, then appeared to go back to sleep. There was a standing ashtray beside what had to be Cullum's easy chair, and in it were two pipes, one a corncob and the other a briar. There was an old-fashioned Emerson record-player/radio (the radio of the type featuring a multi-band dial and a large knurled tuning knob) but no television. The room smelled pleasantly of tobacco and potpourri. As fabulously neat as it was, a single glance was enough to tell you that the man who lived here wasn't married. John Cullum's parlor was a modest ode to the joys of bachelor-hood.

"How's your leg?" John asked. " 'Pears to have stopped bleeding, at least, but you got a pretty good hitch in your gitalong."

Eddie laughed. "It hurts like a son of a bitch, but I can walk on it, so I guess that makes me lucky."

"Bathroom's in there, if you want to wash up," Cullum said, and pointed.

"Think I better," Eddie said.

The washing-up was painful but also a relief. The wound in his leg was deep, but seemed to have totally missed the bone. The one in his arm was even less of a problem; the bullet had gone right through, praise God, and there was hydrogen peroxide in Cullum's medicine cabinet. Eddie poured it into the hole, teeth bared at the pain, and then went ahead and used the stuff on both his leg and the laceration in his scalp before he could lose his courage. He tried to remember if Frodo and Sam had had to face anything even close to the horrors of hydrogen peroxide, and couldn't come up with anything. Well, of course they'd had elves to heal them, hadn't they?

"I got somethin might help out," Cullum said when Eddie re-appeared. The old guy disappeared into the next room and returned with a brown prescription bottle. There were three pills inside it. He tipped them into Eddie's palm and said, "This is from when I fell down on the ice last winter and busted my goddam collarbone. Percodan, it's called. I dunno if there's any good left in em or not, but—"

Eddie brightened. "Percodan, huh?" he asked, and tossed the pills into his mouth before John Cullum could answer.

"Don't you want some water with those, son?"

"Nope," Eddie said, chewing enthusiastically. "Neat's a treat."

A glass case full of baseballs stood on a table beside the fireplace, and Eddie wandered over to look at it. "Oh my God," he said, "you've got a signed Mel Parnell ball! And a Lefty Grove! Holy shit!"

"Those ain't nothing," Cullum said, picking up the briar pipe. "Look up on t' top shelf." He took a sack of Prince Albert tobacco from the drawer of an endtable and began to fill his pipe. As he did so, he caught Roland watching him. "Do ya smoke?"

Roland nodded. From his shirt pocket he took a single bit of leaf. "P'raps I might roll one."

"Oh, I can do ya better than that," Cullum said, and left the room again. The room beyond was a study not much bigger than a closet. Although the Dickens desk in it was small, Cullum had to sidle his way around it.

"Holy shit," Eddie said, seeing the baseball Cullum must have meant. "Autographed by the Babe!"

"Ayuh," Cullum said. "Not when he was a Yankee, either, I got no use for baseballs autographed by Yankees. That 'us signed when Ruth was still wearing a Red Sox . . ." He broke off. "Here they are, knew I had em. Might be stale, but it's a lot staler where there's none, my mother used to say. Here you go, mister. My nephew left em. He ain't hardly old enough to smoke, anyway."

Cullum handed the gunslinger a package of cigarettes, three-quarters full. Roland turned them thoughtfully over in his hand, then pointed to the brand name. "I see a picture of a dromedary, but that isn't what this says, is it?"

Cullum smiled at Roland with a kind of cautious wonder. "No," he said. "That word's *Camel*. It means about the same."

"Ah," Roland said, and tried to look as if he understood. He took one of the cigarettes out, studied the filter, then put the tobacco end in his mouth.

"No, turn it around," Cullum said.

"Say true?"

"Ayuh."

"Jesus, Roland! He's got a Bobby Doerr . . . two Ted Williams balls . . . a Johnny Pesky . . . a Frank Malzone . . ."

"Those names don't mean anything to you, do they?" John Cullum asked Roland.

"No," Roland said. "My friend . . . thank you." He took a light from the match sai Cullum offered. "My friend hasn't been on this side very much for quite awhile. I think he misses it."

"Gorry," Cullum said. "Walk-ins! Walk-ins in *my* house! I can't hardly believe it!"

"Where's Dewey Evans?" Eddie asked. "You don't have a Dewey Evans ball."

"Pardon?" Cullum asked. It came out *paaaaaadon*.

"Maybe they don't call him that yet," Eddie said, almost to himself. "Dwight Evans? Right fielder?"

"Oh." Cullum nodded. "Well, I only have the best in that cabinet, don't you know."

"Dewey fills the bill, believe me," Eddie said. "Maybe he's not worthy of being in the John Cullum Hall of Fame yet, but wait a few years. Wait until '86. And by the way, John, as a fan of the game, I want to say two words to you, okay?"

"Sure," Cullum said. It came out exactly as the word was said in the Calla: SHO-ah.

Roland, meanwhile, had taken a drag from his smoke. He blew it out and looked at the cigarette, frowning.

"The words are *Roger Clemens*," Eddie said. "Remember that name."

"Clemens," John Cullum said, but dubiously.

Faintly, from the far side of Keywadin Pond, came the sound of more sirens. "Roger Clemens, ayuh, I'll remember. Who is he?"

"You're gonna want him in here, leave it at that," Eddie said, tapping the case. "Maybe on the same shelf with the Babe."

Cullum's eyes gleamed. "Tell me somethin, son. Have the Red Sox won it all yet? Have they—"

"This isn't a smoke, it's nothing but murky air," Roland said. He gave Cullum a reproachful look that was so un-Roland that it made Eddie grin. "No taste to speak of at all. People here actually *smoke* these?"

Cullum took the cigarette from Roland's fingers, broke the filter off the end, and gave it back to him. "Try it now," he said, and returned his attention to Eddie. "So? I got you out of a jam on t'other side of the water. Seems like you owe me one. Have they ever won the Series? At least up to your time?"

Eddie's grin faded and he looked at the old man seriously. "I'll tell you if you really want me to, John. But *do* ya?"

John considered, puffing his pipe. Then he said, "I s'pose not. Knowin'd spoil it."

"Tell you one thing," Eddie said cheerfully. The pills John had given him were kicking in and he *felt* cheerful. A little bit, anyway. "You don't want to die before 1986. That one's gonna be a corker."

"Ayuh?"

"Say absolutely true." Then Eddie turned to the gunslinger. "What are we going to do about our gunna, Roland?"

Roland hadn't even thought about it until this moment. All their few worldly possessions, from Eddie's fine new whittling knife, purchased in Took's Store, to Roland's ancient grow-bag, given to him by his father far on the other side of time's horizon, had been left behind when they came through the door. When they had been *blown through* the door. The gunslinger assumed their gunna had been left lying in the dirt in front of the East Stoneham store, although he couldn't remember for sure; he'd been too fiercely focused on getting Eddie and himself to safety before the fellow with the long-sighted rifle blew their heads off. It hurt to think of all those companions of the long trek burned up in the fire that had undoubtedly claimed the store by now. It hurt even worse to think of them in the hands of Jack Andolini. Roland had a brief but vivid picture of his grow-bag hanging on Andolini's belt like a 'backy-pouch (or an enemy's scalp) and winced.

"Roland? What about our—"

"We have our guns, and that's all the gunna we need," Roland said, more roughly than he had intended. "Jake has the *Choo-Choo* book, and I can make another compass should we need one. Otherwise—"

"But—"

"If you're talkin about your goods, sonny, I c'n ask some questions about em when the time comes," Cullum said. "But for the time being, I think your friend's right."

Eddie *knew* his friend was right. His friend was almost *always* right, which was one of the few things Eddie still hated about him. He wanted his gunna, goddammit, and not just for the one clean pair of jeans and the two clean shirts. Nor for extra ammo or the whittling knife, fine as it was. There had been a lock of Susannah's hair in his leather swag-bag, and it had still carried a faint whiff of her smell. *That* was what he missed. But done was done.

"John," he said, "what day is this?"

The man's bristly gray eyebrows went up. "You serious?" And when Eddie nodded: "Ninth of July. Year of our Lord nineteen-seventy-seven."

Eddie made a soundless whistling noise through his pursed lips.

Roland, the last stub of the Dromedary cigarette smoldering between his fingers, had gone to the window for a looksee. Nothing behind the house but trees and a few seductive blue winks from what Cullum called "the Keywadin." But that pillar of black smoke still rose in the sky, as if to remind him that any sense of peace he might feel in these surroundings was only an illusion. They had to get out of here. And no matter how terribly afraid he was for Susannah Dean, now that they were here they had to find Calvin Tower and finish their business with him. And they'd have to do it quickly. Because—

As if reading his mind and finishing his thought, Eddie said: "Roland? It's speeding up. Time on this side is speeding up."

"I know."

"It means that whatever we do, we have to get it right the first time, because in this world you can never come back earlier. There are no do-overs."

Roland knew that, too.

TWO

"The man we're looking for is from New York City," Eddie told John Cullum.

"Ayuh, plenty of those around in the summer-time."

"His name's Calvin Tower. He's with a friend of his named Aaron Deepneau."

Cullum opened the glass case with the baseballs inside, took out one with *Carl Yastrzemski* written across the sweet spot in that weirdly perfect script of which only professional athletes seem capable (in Eddie's experience it was the spelling that gave most of them problems), and began to toss it from hand to hand. "Folks from away really pile in once June comes—you know that, don't ya?"

"I do," Eddie said, feeling hopeless already. He thought it was possible old Double-Ugly had already gotten to Cal Tower. Maybe the ambush at the store had been Jack's idea of dessert. "I guess you can't—"

"If I can't, I guess I better goddam retire," Cullum said with some spirit, and tossed the Yaz ball to Eddie, who held it in his right hand and ran the tips of his left-hand fingers over the red stitches. The feel of them raised a wholly unexpected lump in his throat. If a baseball didn't tell you that you were home, what did? Only this world wasn't home anymore. John was right, he was a walk-in.

"What do you mean?" Roland asked. Eddie tossed him the ball and Roland caught it without ever taking his eyes off John Cullum.

"I don't bother with names, but I know most everyone who comes into this town just the same," he said. "Know em by sight. Same with any other caretaker worth his salt, I s'pose. You want to know who's in your territory." Roland nodded at this with perfect understanding. "Tell me what this guy looks like."

Eddie said, "He stands about five-nine and weighs . . . oh, I'm gonna say two-thirty."

"Heavyset, then."

"Do ya. Also, most of his hair's gone on the sides of his forehead." Eddie raised his hands to his own head and pushed his hair back, exposing the temples (one of them still oozing blood from his near-fatal passage through the Unfound Door). He winced a little at the pain this provoked in his upper left arm, but there the bleeding had already stopped. Eddie was more worried about the round he'd taken in the leg. Right now Cullum's Percodan was dealing with the pain, but if the bullet was still in there—and Eddie thought it might be—it would eventually have to come out.

"How old is he?" Cullum asked.

Eddie looked at Roland, who only shook his head. Had Roland ever actually seen Tower? At this particular moment, Eddie couldn't remember. He thought not.

"I think in his fifties."

"He's the book collector, ain't he?" Cullum asked, then laughed at Eddie's expression of surprise. "Told you, I keep a weather eye out on the summah folk. You never know when one's gonna turn out to be a deadbeat. Maybe an outright thief. Or, eight or nine years ago, we had this woman from New Jersey who turned out to be a firebug." Cullum shook his head. "Looked like a small-town librarian, the sort of lady who wouldn't say boo to a goose, and she was lightin up barns all over Stoneham, Lovell, and Waterford."

"How do you know he's a book dealer?" Roland asked, and tossed the ball back to Cullum, who immediately tossed it to Eddie.

"Didn't know *that*," he said. "Only that he collects em, because he told Jane Sargus. Jane's got a little shop right where Dimity Road branches off from Route 5. That's about a mile south of here. Dimity Road's actually where that fella and his friend are stayin, if we're talking about the right ones. I guess we are."

"His friend's name is Deepneau," Eddie said, and tossed the Yaz ball to Roland. The gunslinger caught it, tossed it to Cullum, then went to the fireplace and dropped the last shred of his cigarette onto the little pile of logs stacked on the grate.

"Don't bother with names, like I told you, but the friend's skinny and looks about seventy. Walks like his hips pain him some. Wears steel-rimmed glasses."

"That's the guy, all right," Eddie said.

"Janey has a little place called Country Collectibles. She gut some furniture in the barn, dressers and armoires and such, but what she specializes in is quilts, glassware, and old books. Sign says so right out front."

"So Cal Tower . . . what? Just went in and started browsing?" Eddie couldn't believe it, and at the same time he could. Tower had been balky about leaving New York even after Jack and George Biondi had threatened to burn his most valuable books right in front of his eyes. And once he and Deepneau got here, the fool had signed up for general delivery at the post office—or at least his friend Aaron had, and as far as the bad guys were concerned, one was as good as the other. Callahan had left him a note telling him to stop advertising his presence in East Stoneham. *How stupid can you be???* had been the Pere's final communication to sai Tower, and the answer seemed to be more stupid than a bag of hammers.

"Ayuh," Cullum said. "Only he did a lot more'n browse." His eyes, as blue as Roland's, were twinkling. "Bought a couple of hundred dollars' worth of readin material. Paid with traveler's checks. Then he gut her to give him a list of other used bookstores in the area. There's quite a few, if you add in Notions in Norway and that Your Trash, My Treasure place over in Fryeburg. Plus he got her to write down the names of some local folks who have book collections and sometimes sell out of their houses. Jane was awful excited. Talked about it all over town, she did."

Eddie put a hand to his forehead and groaned. That was the man he'd met, all right, that was Calvin Tower to the life. What had he been thinking? That once he "gut" north of Boston he was safe?

"Can you tell us how to find him?" Roland asked.

"Oh, I c'n do better'n that. I can take you right to where they're stayin."

Roland had been tossing the ball from hand to hand. Now he stopped and shook his head. "No. You'll be going somewhere else."

"Where?"

"Anyplace you'll be safe," Roland said. "Beyond that, sai, I don't want to know. Neither of us do."

"Well call me Sam, I say goddam. Dunno's I like that much."

"Doesn't matter. Time is short." Roland considered, then said: "Do you have a cartomobile?"

Cullum looked momentarily puzzled, then grinned. "Yep, a cartomobile and a truckomobile both. I'm loaded." The last word came out *ludded*.

"Then you'll lead us to Tower's Dimity Road place in one while Eddie . . ." Roland paused for a moment. "Eddie, do you still remember how to drive?"

"Roland, you're hurtin my feelings."

Roland, never a very humorous fellow even at the best of times, didn't smile. He returned his attention to the dan-tete—little savior—ka had put in their way, instead. "Once we've found Tower, you'll go your course, John. That's any course that isn't ours. Take a little vacation, if it does ya. Two days should be enough, then you can return to your business." Roland hoped their own business here in East Stoneham would be done by sundown, but didn't want to hex them by saying so.

"I don't think you understand that this is my busy season," Cullum said. He held out his hands and Roland tossed him the ball. "I got a boathouse to paint . . . a barn that needs shinglin—"

"If you stay with us," Roland said, "you'll likely never shingle another barn."

Cullum looked at him with an eyebrow cocked, clearly trying to gauge Roland's seriousness and not much liking what he saw.

While this was going on, Eddie found himself returning to the question of whether or not Roland had ever actually seen Tower with his own eyes. And now he realized that his first answer to that question had been wrong—Roland *had* seen Tower.

Sure he did. It was Roland who pulled that bookcase full of Tower's first editions into the Doorway Cave. Roland was looking right at him. What he saw was probably distorted, but . . .

That train of thought drifted away, and by the seemingly inevitable process of association, Eddie's mind returned to Tower's precious books, such rarities as *The Dogan*, by Benjamin Slightman, Jr., and *'Salem's Lot*, by Stephen King.

"I'll just get m'keys and we're off," Cullum said, but before he could turn away, Eddie said: "Wait."

Cullum looked at him quizzically.

"We've got a little more to talk about, I think." And he held up his hands for the baseball.

"Eddie, our time is short," Roland said.

"I know that," Eddie said. *Probably better than you, since it's my woman the clock's running out on.* "If I could, I'd leave that asshole Tower to Jack and concentrate on getting back to Susannah. But ka won't let me do that. Your damned old ka."

"We need—"

"Shut up." He had never said such a thing to

Roland in his life, but now the words came out on their own, and he felt no urge to call them back. In his mind, Eddie heard a ghostly Calla-chant: *Com-mala-come-come, the palaver's not done.*

"What's on your mind?" Cullum asked him.

"A man named Stephen King. Do you know that name?"

And saw by Cullum's eyes that he did.

THREE

"Eddie," Roland said. He spoke in an oddly tentative way the younger man had never heard before. *He's as at sea as I am.* Not a comforting thought. "Andolini may still be looking for us. More important, he may be looking for Tower, now that we've slipped through his fingers . . . and as sai Cullum has made perfectly clear, Tower has made himself easy to find."

"Listen to me," Eddie replied. "I'm playing a hunch here, but a hunch is *not* all this is. We've met one man, Ben Slightman, who wrote a book in another world. *Tower's* world. *This* world. And we've met another one, Donald Callahan, who was a *character* in a book from another world. Again, *this* world." Cullum had tossed him the ball and now Eddie flipped it underhand, and hard, to Roland. The gunslinger caught it easily.

"This might not seem like such a big deal to me, except we've been *haunted* by books, haven't we? *The Dogan. The Wizard of Oz. Charlie the Choo-Choo.* Even Jake's Final Essay. And now *'Salem's Lot.* I think that if this Stephen King is real—"

"Oh, he's real, all right," Cullum said. He glanced out his window toward Keywadin Pond and the sound of the sirens on the other side. At the pillar of smoke, now diffusing the blue sky with its ugly smudge. Then he held his hands up for the baseball. Roland threw it in a soft arc whose apogee almost skimmed the ceiling. "And I read that book you're all het up about. Got it up to the City, at Bookland. Thought it was a corker, too."

"A story about vampires."

"Ayuh, I heard him talkin about it on the radio. Said he got the idea from *Dracula*."

"You heard the writer on the radio," Eddie said. He was having that through-the-looking-glass, down-the-rabbit-hole, off-on-a-comet feeling again, and tried to ascribe it to the Percodan. It wouldn't work. All at once he felt strangely unreal to himself, a shade you could almost see through, as thin as . . . well, as thin as a page in a book. It was no help to realize that this world, lying in the summer of 1977 on time's beam, seemed real in a way all the other wheres and whens—including his own— did not. And that feeling was totally subjective, wasn't it? When you came right down to it, how did anyone know they weren't a character in some writer's story, or a transient thought in some bus-riding schmoe's head, or a momentary mote in God's eye? Thinking about such stuff was crazy, and enough such thinking could *drive* you crazy.

And yet . . .

Dad-a-chum, dad-a-chee, not to worry, you've got the key.

Keys, my specialty, Eddie thought. And then:

King's a key, isn't he? Calla, Callahan. Crimson King, Stephen King. Is Stephen King the Crimson King of this world?

Roland had settled. Eddie was sure it hadn't been easy for him, but the difficult had ever been Roland's specialty. "If you have questions to ask, have at it." And made the twirling gesture with his right hand.

"Roland, I hardly know where to start. The ideas I've got are so big . . . so . . . I don't know, so fundamentally fucking *scary* . . ."

"Best to keep it simple, then." Roland took the ball when Eddie tossed it to him but now looked more than a little impatient with the game of toss. "We really *do* have to move on."

How Eddie knew it. He would have asked his questions while they were rolling, if they all could have ridden in the same vehicle. But they couldn't, and Roland had never driven a motor vehicle, which made it impossible for Eddie and Cullum to ride in the same one.

"All right," he said. "Who is he? Let's start with that. Who is Stephen King?"

"A writer," Cullum said, and gave Eddie a look that said, *Are you a fool, son?* "He lives over in Bridgton with his family. Nice enough fella, from what I've heard."

"How far away is Bridgton?"

"Oh . . . twenty, twenty-five miles."

"How old is he?" Eddie was groping, maddeningly aware that the right questions might be out there, but he had no clear idea of what they were.

John Cullum squinted an eye and seemed to calculate. "Not that old, I sh'd think. If he's thirty, he
just got there."

"This book . . . *'Salem's Lot* . . . was it a best-
seller?"

"Dunno," Cullum said. "Lots of people around
here read it, tell you that much. Because it's set in
Maine. And because of the ads they had on TV, you
know. Also there was a movie made out of his first
book, but I never went to see it. Looked too
bloody."

"What was it called?"

Cullum thought, then shook his head. "Can't
quite remember. 'Twas just one word, and I'm
pretty sure it was a girl's name, but that's the best I
can do. Maybe it'll come to me."

"He's not a walk-in, you don't think?"

Cullum laughed. "Born and raised right here in
the state of Maine. Guess that makes him a *live*-in."

Roland was looking at Eddie with increasing
impatience, and Eddie decided to give up. This was
worse than playing Twenty Questions. But goddammit, Pere Callahan was *real* and he was also in
a book of fiction written by this man King, and
King lived in an area that was a magnet for what
Cullum called walk-ins. One of those walk-ins had
sounded very much to Eddie like a servant of the
Crimson King. A woman with a bald head who
seemed to have a bleeding eye in the center of her
forehead, John had said.

Time to drop this for now and get to Tower.
Irritating he might be, but Calvin Tower owned a
certain vacant lot where the most precious rose in

the universe was growing wild. Also, he knew all sorts of stuff about rare books and the folks who had written them. Very likely he knew more about the author of *'Salem's Lot* than sai Cullum. Time to let it go. But—

"Okay," he said, tossing the ball back to the caretaker. "Lock that thing up and we'll head off to the Dimity Road, if it does ya. Just a couple more questions."

Cullum shrugged and put the Yaz ball back into the case. "It's your nickel."

"I know," Eddie said . . . and suddenly, for the second time since he'd come through the door, Susannah seemed weirdly close. He saw her sitting in a room filled with antiquey-looking science and surveillance equipment. Jake's Dogan, for sure . . . only as Susannah must have imagined it. He saw her speaking into a mike, and although he couldn't hear her, he could see her swollen belly and her frightened face. Now *very* pregnant, wherever she was. Pregnant and ready to pop. He knew well enough what she was saying: *Come, Eddie, save me, Eddie, save both of us, do it before it's too late.*

"Eddie?" Roland said. "You've come over all gray. Is it your leg?"

"Yeah," Eddie said, although right now his leg didn't hurt at all. He thought again of whittling the key. The dreadful responsibility of knowing it had to be just right. And here he was again, in much the same situation. He had hold of something, he knew he did . . . but what? "Yeah, my leg."

He armed sweat from his forehead.

"John, about the name of the book. *'Salem's Lot*. That's actually Jerusalem's Lot, right?"

"Ayuh."

"It's the name of the town in the book."

"Ayuh."

"Stephen King's second book."

"Ayuh."

"His second *novel*."

"Eddie," Roland said, "surely that's enough."

Eddie waved him aside, then winced at the pain in his arm. His attention was fixed on John Cullum. "There *is* no Jerusalem's Lot, right?"

Cullum looked at Eddie as if he were crazy. "Course not," he said. "It's a made-up story about made-up folks in a made-up town. It's about *vampires*."

Yes, Eddie thought, *and if I told you I have reason to believe that vampires are real . . . not to mention invisible demons, magic balls, and witches . . . you'd be absolutely positive I was nuts, wouldn't you?*

"Do you happen to know if Stephen King has been living in this Bridgton town his whole life?"

"No, he hasn't. He 'n his family moved down here two, maybe three years ago. I b'lieve they lived in Windham first when they got down from the northern part of the state. Or maybe 'twas Raymond. One of the towns on Big Sebago, anyway."

"Would it be fair to say that these walk-ins you mentioned have been turning up since the guy moved into the area?"

Cullum's bushy eyebrows went up, then knitted

together. A loud and rhythmic hooting began to come to them from over the water, a sound like a foghorn.

"You know," Cullum said, "you might have somethin there, son. It might only be coincidence, but maybe not."

Eddie nodded. He felt emotionally wrung out, like a lawyer at the end of a long and difficult cross-examination. "Let's blow this pop-shop," he said to Roland.

"Might be a good idea," Cullum said, and tipped his head in the direction of the rhythmic foghorn blasts. "That's Teddy Wilson's boat. He's the county constable. Also a game warden." This time he tossed Eddie a set of car-keys instead of a baseball. "I'm givin you the automatic transmission," he said. "Just in case you're a little rusty. The truck's a stick shift. You follow me, and if you get in trouble, honk the horn."

"I will, believe me," Eddie said.

As they followed Cullum out, Roland said: "Was it Susannah again? Is that why you lost all the color out of your face?"

Eddie nodded.

"We'll help her if we can," Roland said, "but this may be our only way back to her."

Eddie knew that. He also knew that by the time they got to her, it might be too late.

STAVE: *Commala-ka-kate*
You're in the hands of fate.
No matter if you're real or not,
The hour groweth late.

RESPONSE: *Commala-come-eight!*
The hour groweth late!
No matter what the shade ya cast
You're in the hands of fate.

EDDIE BITES HIS TONGUE

9TH STANZA

ONE

Pere Callahan had made a brief visit to the East
Stoneham Post Office almost two weeks before the
shootout at Chip McAvoy's store, and there the
former Jerusalem's Lot parish priest had written a
hurried note. Although addressed to both Aaron
Deepneau and Calvin Tower, the note inside the
envelope had been aimed at the latter, and its tone
had not been particularly friendly:

6/27/77

Tower—

   *I'm a friend of the guy who helped
you with Andolini. Wherever you are,
you need to move right away. Find a
barn, unused camp, even an abandoned
shed if it comes down to that. You probably won't be comfortable but remember that the alternative is being dead. <u>I
mean every word I say!</u> Leave some
lights on where you are staying now and
leave your car in the garage or driveway.
Hide a note with directions to your new*

location under the driver's-side floor-
mat, or under the back-porch step. We'll
be in touch. Remember that we are the
only ones who can relieve you of the
burden you carry. But if we are to help
you, you must help us.

Callahan, of the Eld

And make this trip to the post office
your LAST! How stupid can you be???

Callahan had risked his life to leave that note,
and Eddie, under the spell of Black Thirteen, had
nearly lost his. And the net result of those risks and
close calls? Why, Calvin Tower had gone jaunting
merrily around the western Maine countryside,
looking for buys on rare and out-of-print books.

Following John Cullum up Route 5 with Roland
sitting silently beside him, then turning to follow
Cullum onto the Dimity Road, Eddie felt his temper edging up into the red zone.

Gonna have to put my hands in my pockets and
bite my tongue, he thought, but in this case he
wasn't sure even those old reliables would work.

TWO

About two miles from Route 5, Cullum's Ford
F-150 made a right off Dimity Road. The turn was
marked by two signs on a rusty pole. The top one
said ROCKET RD. Below it was another (rustier still)
which promised LAKESIDE CABINS BY THE WK MO OR
SEAS. Rocket Road was little more than a trail

winding through the trees, and Eddie hung well behind Cullum to avoid the rooster-tail of dust their new friend's old truck was kicking up. The "cartomobile" was another Ford, some anonymous two-door model Eddie couldn't have named without looking at the chrome on the back or in the owner's manual. But it felt most religiously fine to be driving again, with not a single horse between his legs but several hundred of them ready to run at the slightest motion of his right foot. It was also good to hear the sound of the sirens fading farther and farther behind.

The shadows of overhanging trees swallowed them. The smell of fir and pinesap was simultaneously sweet and sharp. "Pretty country," the gunslinger said. "A man could take his long ease here." It was his only comment.

Cullum's truck began to pass numbered driveways. Below each number was a small legend reading JAFFORDS RENTALS. Eddie thought of pointing out to Roland that they'd known a Jaffords in the Calla, known him very well, and then didn't. It would have been belaboring the obvious.

They passed 15, 16, and 17. Cullum paused briefly to consider at 18, then stuck his arm out the cab's window and motioned them on again. Eddie had been ready to move on even before the gesture, knowing perfectly well that Cabin 18 wasn't the one they wanted.

Cullum turned in at the next drive. Eddie followed, the tires of the sedan now whispering on a thick bed of fallen pine needles. Winks of blue once more began to appear between the trees, but when they finally reached Cabin 19 and a view of the water, Eddie saw that this, unlike Keywadin, was a true pond. Probably not much wider than a football field. The cabin itself looked like a two-room job. There was a screened-in porch facing the water with a couple of tatty but comfortable-looking rockers on it. A tin stovestack poked up from the roof. There was no garage and no car parked in front of the cabin, although Eddie thought he could see where one had been. With the cover of duff, it was hard to tell for sure.

Cullum killed the truck's engine. Eddie did likewise. Now there was only the lap of water against the rocks, the sigh of a breeze through the pines, and the mild sound of birdsong. When Eddie looked to the right, he saw that the gunslinger was sitting with his talented, long-fingered hands folded peaceably in his lap.

"How does it feel to you?" Eddie asked.

"Quiet." The word was spoken Calla-fashion: *Cahh-it.*

"Anyone here?"

"I think so, yes."

"Danger?"

"Yar. Beside me."

Eddie looked at him, frowning.

"You, Eddie. You want to kill him, don't you?"

After a moment, Eddie admitted it was so. This uncovered part of his nature, as simple as it was savage, sometimes made him uneasy, but he could not deny it was there. And who, after all, had brought it out and honed it to a keen edge?

Roland nodded. "There came into my life, after years during which I wandered in the desert as solitary as any anchorite, a whining and self-involved young man whose only ambition was to continue taking a drug which did little but make him sniffle and feel sleepy. This was a posturing, selfish, loud-mouthed loutkin with little to recommend him—"

"But good-looking," Eddie said. "Don't forget that. The cat was a true sex mo-*chine*."

Roland looked at him, unsmiling. "If I could manage not to kill you then, Eddie of New York, you can manage not to kill Calvin Tower now." And with that, Roland opened the door on his side and got out.

"Well, says *you*," Eddie told the interior of Cullum's car, and then got out himself.

THREE

Cullum was still behind the wheel of his truck when first Roland and then Eddie joined him.

"Place feels empty to me," he said, "but I see a light on in the kitchen."

"Uh-huh," Eddie said. "John, I've got—"

"Don't tell me, you got another question. Only person I know who's got more of em is my grand-nephew Aidan. He just went three. Go on, ask."

"Could you pinpoint the center of the walk-in activity in this area over the last few years?" Eddie had no idea why he was asking this question, but it suddenly seemed vitally important to him.

Cullum considered, then said: "Turtleback Lane, over in Lovell."

"You sound pretty sure of that."

"Ayuh. Do you remember me mentionin my

friend Donnie Russert, the history prof from Vandy?"

Eddie nodded.

"Well, after he met one of these fellas in person, he got interested in the phenomenon. Wrote several articles about it, although he said no reputable magazine'd publish em no matter how well documented his facts were. He said that writin about the walk-ins in western Maine taught him something he'd never expected to learn in his old age: that some things people just won't believe, not even when you can prove em. He used to quote a line from some Greek poet. 'The column of truth has a hole in it.'

"Anyway, he had a map of the seven-town area mounted on one wall of his study: Stoneham, East Stoneham, Waterford, Lovell, Sweden, Fryeburg, and East Fryeburg. With pins stuck in it for each walk-in reported, do ya see?"

"See very well, say thank ya," Eddie said.

"And I'd have to say . . . yeah, Turtleback Lane's the heart of it. Why, there were six or eight pins right there, and the whole damn rud can't be more'n two miles long; it's just a loop that runs off Route 7, along the shore of Kezar Lake, and then back to 7 again."

Roland was looking at the house. Now he turned to the left, stopped, and laid his left hand on the sandalwood butt of his gun. "John," he said, "we're well-met, but it's time for you to roll out of here."

"Ayuh? You sure?"

Roland nodded. "The men who came here are

fools. It still has the smell of fools, which is partly how I know that they haven't moved on. You're not one of that kind."

John Cullum smiled faintly. "Sh'd hope not," he said, "but I gut t'thankya for the compliment." Then he paused and scratched his gray head. "If 'tis a compliment."

"Don't get back to the main road and start thinking I didn't mean what I said. Or worse, that we weren't here at all, that you dreamed the whole thing. Don't go back to your house, not even to pack an extra shirt. It's no longer safe. Go somewhere else. At least three looks to the horizon."

Cullum closed one eye and appeared to calculate. "In the fifties, I spent ten miserable years as a guard at the Maine State Prison," he said, "but I met a hell of a nice man there named—"

Roland shook his head and then put the two remaining fingers of his right hand to his lips. Cullum nodded.

"Well, I f'git what his name is, but he lives over in Vermont, and I'm sure I'll remember it—maybe where he lives, too—by the time I get acrost the New Hampshire state line."

Something about this speech struck Eddie as a little false, but he couldn't put his finger on just why, and he decided in the end that he was just being paranoid. John Cullum was a straight arrow . . . wasn't he? "May you do well," he said, and gripped the old man's hand. "Long days and pleasant nights."

"Same to you boys," Cullum said, and then shook with Roland. He held the gunslinger's three-fingered right hand a moment longer. "Was it God saved my life back there, do ya think? When the bullets first started flyin'?"

"Yar," the gunslinger said. "If you like. And may he go with you now."

"As for that old Ford of mine—"

"Either right here or somewhere nearby," Eddie said. "You'll find it, or someone else will. Don't worry."

Cullum grinned. "That's pretty much what I was gonna tell you."

"*Vaya con Dios,*" Eddie said.

Cullum grinned. "Goes back double, son. You want to watch out for those walk-ins." He paused. "Some of em aren't very nice. From all reports."

Cullum put his truck in gear and drove away. Roland watched him go and said, "Dan-tete."

Eddie nodded. Dan-tete. Little savior. It was as good a way to describe John Cullum—now as gone from their lives as the old people of River Crossing—as any other. And he *was* gone, wasn't he? Although there'd been something about the way he'd talked of his friend in Vermont . . .

Paranoia.

Simple paranoia.

Eddie put it out of his mind.

FOUR

Since there was no car present and hence no driver's-side floormat beneath which to look, Eddie intended to explore under the porch step. But before he could take more than a single stride in that direction, Roland gripped his shoulder in one hand and pointed with the other. What Eddie saw was a brushy slope going down to the water and the roof of what was probably another boathouse, its green shingles covered with a layer of dry needles.

"Someone there," Roland said, his lips barely moving. "Probably the lesser of the two fools, and watching us. Raise your hands."

"Roland, do you think that's safe?"

"Yes." Roland raised his hands. Eddie thought of asking him upon what basis he placed his belief, and knew the answer without asking: intuition. It was Roland's specialty. With a sigh, Eddie raised his own hands to his shoulders.

"Deepneau!" Roland called out in the direction of the boathouse. "Aaron Deepneau! We're friends, and our time is short! If that's you, come out! We need to palaver!"

There was a pause, and then an old man's voice called: "What's your name, mister?"

"Roland Deschain, of Gilead and the line of the Eld. I think you know it."

"And your trade?"

"I deal in lead!" Roland called, and Eddie felt goosebumps pebble his arms.

A long pause. Then: "Have they killed Calvin?"

"Not that *we* know of," Eddie called back. "If you know something we don't, why don't you come on out here and tell us?"

"Are you the guy who showed up while Cal was dickering with that prick Andolini?"

Eddie felt another throb of anger at the word

dickering. At the slant it put on what had actually been going down in Tower's back room. "A dicker? Is that what he told you it was?" And then, without waiting for Aaron Deepneau to answer: "Yeah, I'm that guy. Come out here and let's talk."

No answer. Twenty seconds slipped by. Eddie pulled in breath to call Deepneau again. Roland put a hand on Eddie's arm and shook his head. Another twenty seconds went by, and then there was the rusty shriek of a spring as a screen door was pushed open. A tall, skinny man stepped out of the boathouse, blinking like an owl. In one hand he held a large black automatic pistol by the barrel. Deepneau raised it over his head. "It's a Beretta, and unloaded," he said. "There's only one clip and it's in the bedroom, under my socks. Loaded guns make me nervous. Okay?"

Eddie rolled his eyes. These *folken* were their own worst enemas, as Henry might have said.

"Fine," Roland said. "Just keep coming."

And—wonders never ceased, it seemed—Deepneau did.

FIVE

The coffee he made was better by far than any they'd had in Calla Bryn Sturgis, better than any Roland had had since his days in Mejis, Dropriding out on the Rim. There were also strawberries. Cultivated and store-bought, Deepneau said, but Eddie was transported by their sweetness. The three of them sat in the kitchen of Jaffords Rentals' Cabin #19, drinking coffee and dipping the big strawberries in the sugarbowl. By the end of their palaver, all three men looked like assassins who'd dabbled the tips of their fingers in the spilled blood of their latest victim. Deepneau's unloaded gun lay forgotten on the windowsill.

Deepneau had been out for a walk on the Rocket Road when he heard gunfire, loud and clear, and then explosions. He'd hurried back to the cabin (not that he was capable of too much hurry in his current condition, he said), and when he saw the smoke starting to rise in the south, had decided that returning to the boathouse might be wise, after all. By then he was almost positive it was the Italian hoodlum, Andolini, so—

"What do you mean, you *returned* to the boathouse?" Eddie asked.

Deepneau shifted his feet under the table. He was extremely pallid, with purple patches beneath his eyes and only a few wisps of hair, fine as dandelion fluff, on his head. Eddie remembered Tower's telling him that Deepneau had been diagnosed with cancer a couple of years ago. He didn't look great today, but Eddie had seen folks—especially in the City of Lud—who looked a lot worse. Jake's old pal Gasher had been just one of them.

"Aaron?" Eddie asked. "What did you mean—"

"I heard the question," he said, a trifle irritably. "We got a note via general delivery, or rather Cal did, suggesting we move out of the cabin to someplace adjacent, and keep a lower profile in general. It was from a man named Callahan. Do you know him?"

Roland and Eddie nodded.

"This Callahan . . . you could say he took Cal to the woodshed."

Cal, Calla, Callahan, Eddie thought, and sighed.

"Cal's a decent man in most ways, but he does not enjoy being taken to the woodshed. We did move down to the boathouse for a few days . . ." Deepneau paused, possibly engaging in a brief struggle with his conscience. Then he said, "Two days, actually. Only two. And then Cal said we were crazy, being in the damp was making his arthritis worse, and he could hear me wheezing. 'Next thing I'll have you in that little shitpot hospital over in Norway,' he said, 'with pneumonia as well as cancer.' He said there wasn't a chance in hell of Andolini finding us up here, as long as the young guy—you"—he pointed a gnarled and strawberry-stained finger at Eddie—"kept his mouth shut. 'Those New York hoodlums can't find their way north of Westport without a compass,' he said."

Eddie groaned. For once in his life he absolutely *loathed* being right about something.

"He said we'd been very careful. And when I said, 'Well, *somebody* found us, this Callahan found us,' Cal said well of course." Again the finger pointed at Eddie. "*You* must have told Mr. Callahan where to look for the zip code, and after that it was easy. Then Cal said, 'And the post office was the best he could do, wasn't it? Believe me, Aaron, we're safe out here. No one knows where we are except the rental agent, and she's back in New York.' "

Deepneau peered at them from beneath his

shaggy eyebrows, then dipped a strawberry and ate half of it.

"*Is* that how you found us? The rental agent?"

"No," Eddie said. "A local. He took us right to you, Aaron."

Deepneau sat back. "Ouch."

"Ouch is right," Eddie said. "So you moved back into the cabin, and Cal went right on buying books instead of hiding out here and reading one. Correct?"

Deepneau dropped his eyes to the tablecloth. "You have to understand that Cal is very dedicated. Books are his life."

"No," Eddie said evenly, "Cal isn't dedicated. Cal is *obsessed*, that's what Cal is."

"I understand that you are a scrip," Roland said, speaking for the first time since Deepneau had led them into the cabin. He had lit another of Cullum's cigarettes (after plucking the filter off as the caretaker had shown him) and now sat smoking with what looked to Eddie like absolutely no satisfaction at all.

"A scrip? I don't . . ."

"A lawyer."

"Oh. Well, yes. But I've been retired from practice since—"

"We need you to come out of retirement long enough to draw up a certain paper," Roland said, and then explained what sort of paper he wanted. Deepneau was nodding before the gunslinger had done more than get started, and Eddie assumed Tower had already told his friend this part of it. That was okay. What he didn't like was the expression on the old fella's face. Still, Deepneau let

Roland finish. He hadn't forgotten the basics of relating to potential clients, it seemed, retired or not.

When he was sure Roland *was* finished, Deepneau said: "I feel I must tell you that Calvin has decided to hold onto that particular piece of property a little longer."

Eddie thumped the unwounded side of his head, being careful to use his right hand for this bit of theater. His left arm was stiffening up, and his leg was once more starting to throb between the knee and the ankle. He supposed it was possible that good old Aaron was traveling with some heavy-duty painkillers and made a mental note to ask for a few if he was.

"Cry pardon," Eddie said, "but I took a knock on the head while I was arriving in this charming little town, and I think it's screwed up my hearing. I thought you said that sai . . . that Mr. Tower had decided against selling us the lot."

Deepneau smiled, rather wearily. "You know perfectly well what I said."

"But he's *supposed* to sell it to us! He had a letter from Stefan Toren, his three-times-great grand-father, saying just that!"

"Cal says different," Aaron responded mildly. "Have another strawberry, Mr. Dean."

"No thank you!"

"Have another strawberry, Eddie," Roland said, and handed him one.

Eddie took it. Considered squashing it against Long, Tall, and Ugly's beak, just for the hell of it, then dipped it first in a saucer of cream, then in the sugarbowl. He began to eat. And damn, it was hard to stay bitter with that much sweetness flooding your mouth. A fact of which Roland (Deepneau too, for that matter) was surely aware.

"According to Cal," Deepneau said, "there was nothing in the envelope he had from Stefan Toren except for this man's name." He tilted his mostly hairless head toward Roland. "Toren's will—what was in the olden days sometimes called a 'deadletter'—was long gone."

"I knew what was in the envelope," Eddie said. "He asked me, and *I knew!*"

"So he told me." Deepneau regarded him expressionlessly. "He said it was a trick any streetcorner magician could do."

"Did he also tell you that he *promised* to sell us the lot if I could tell him the name? That he fucking *promised?*"

"He claims to have been under considerable stress when he made that promise. As I am sure he was."

"Does the son of a bitch think we mean to weasel on him?" Eddie asked. His temples were thudding with rage. Had he ever been so angry? Once, he supposed. When Roland had refused to let him go back to New York so he could score some horse. "Is that it? Because we won't. We'll come up with every cent he wants, and more. I swear it on the face of my father! And on the heart of my dinh!"

"Listen to me carefully, young man, because this is important."

Eddie glanced at Roland. Roland nodded slightly,

then crushed out his cigarette on one bootheel. Eddie looked back at Deepneau, silent but glowering.

"He *says* that is exactly the problem. He says you'll pay him some ridiculously low token amount—a dollar is the usual sum in such cases—and then stiff him for the rest. He claims you tried to hypnotize him into believing you were a supernatural being, or someone with *access* to supernatural beings . . . not to mention access to millions from the Holmes Dental Corporation . . . but he was not fooled."

Eddie gaped at him.

"These are things Calvin *says*," Deepneau continued in that same calm voice, "but they are not necessarily the things Calvin *believes*."

"What in hell do you mean?"

"Calvin has issues with letting go of things," Deepneau said. "He is quite good at finding rare and antiquarian books, you know—a regular literary Sherlock Holmes—and he is compulsive about acquiring them. I've seen him *hound* the owner of a book he wants—I'm afraid there's no other word that really fits—until the book's owner gives in and sells. Sometimes just to make Cal stop calling on the telephone, I'm sure.

"Given his talents, his location, and the considerable sum of money to which he gained complete access on his twenty-sixth birthday, Cal should have been one of the most successful antiquarian book-dealers in New York, or in the whole country. His problem isn't with buying but selling. Once he has an item he's really worked to acquire, he hates to let it go again. I remember when a book collector from San Francisco, a fellow almost as compulsive as Cal himself, finally wore down Cal enough to sell him a signed first of *Moby-Dick*. Cal made over seventy thousand dollars on that one deal alone, but he also didn't sleep for a week.

"He feels much the same way about the lot on the corner of Second and Forty-sixth. It's the only real property, other than his books, which he still has. And he's convinced himself that you want to steal it from him."

There was a short period of silence. Then Roland said: "Does he know better, in his secret heart?"

"Mr. Deschain, I don't understand what—"

"Aye, ya do," Roland said. "Does he?"

"Yes," Deepneau said at last. "I believe he does."

"Does he understand in his secret heart that we are men of our word who will pay him for his property, unless we're dead?"

"Yes, probably. But—"

"Does he understand that, if he transfers owner-ship of the lot to us, and if we make this transfer perfectly clear to Andolini's dinh—his boss, a man named Balazar—"

"I know the name," Deepneau said dryly. "It's in the papers from time to time."

"That Balazar will then leave your friend alone? If, that is, he can be made to understand that the lot is no longer your friend's to sell, and that any effort to take revenge on sai Tower will cost Balazar himself dearly?"

Deepneau crossed his arms over his narrow

chest and waited. He was looking at Roland with a kind of uneasy fascination.

"In short, if your friend Calvin Tower sells us that lot, his troubles will be over. Do you think he knows *that* in his secret heart?"

"Yes," Deepneau said. "It's just that he's got this . . . this kink about letting stuff go."

"Draw up a paper," Roland said. "Object, the vacant square of waste ground on the corner of those two streets. Tower the seller. Us the buyer."

"The Tet Corporation as buyer," Eddie put in.

Deepneau was shaking his head. "I could draw it up, but you won't convince him to sell. Unless you've got a week or so, that is, and you're not averse to using hot irons on his feet. Or maybe his balls."

Eddie muttered something under his breath. Deepneau asked him what he'd said. Eddie told him nothing. What he'd said was *Sounds good*.

"We will convince him," Roland said.

"I wouldn't be so sure of that, my friend."

"We will convince him," Roland repeated. He spoke in his driest tone.

Outside, an anonymous little car (a Hertz rental if Eddie had ever seen one) rolled into the clearing and came to a stop.

Bite your tongue, bite your tongue, Eddie told himself, but as Calvin Tower got briskly out of the car (giving the new vehicle in his dooryard only the most cursory glance), Eddie felt his temples begin to heat up. He rolled his hands into fists, and when his nails bit into the skin of his palms, he grinned in bitter appreciation of the pain.

Tower opened the trunk of his rental Chevy and pulled out a large bag. *His latest haul,* Eddie thought. Tower looked briefly south, at the smoke in the sky, then shrugged and started for the cabin.

That's right, Eddie thought, *that's right, you whore, just something on fire, what's it to you?* Despite the throb of pain it caused in his wounded arm, Eddie squeezed his fists tighter, dug his nails in deeper.

You can't kill him, Eddie, Susannah said. *You know that, don't you?*

Did he know it? And even if he did, could he listen to Suze's voice? To any voice of reason, for that matter? Eddie didn't know. What he knew was that the real Susannah was gone, she had a monkey named Mia on her back and had disappeared into the maw of the future. Tower, on the other hand, was here. Which made sense, in a way. Eddie had read someplace that nuclear war's most likely survivors would be the cockroaches.

Never mind, sugar, you just bite down on your tongue and let Roland handle this. You can't kill him!

No, Eddie supposed not.

Not, at least, until sai Tower had signed on the dotted line. After that, however . . . after that . . .

SIX

"Aaron!" Tower called as he mounted the porch steps.

Roland caught Deepneau's eyes and put a finger across his lips.

"Aaron, hey *Aaron!*" Tower sounded strong and happy to be alive—not a man on the run but a man on a wonderful busman's holiday. "Aaron, I went over to that widow's house in East Fryeburg, and holy Joe, she's got every novel Herman Wouk ever wrote! Not the book club editions, either, which is what I expected, but—"

The *scroink!* of the screen door's rusty spring being stretched was followed by the clump of shoes across the porch.

"—the Doubleday firsts! *Marjorie Morningstar! The Caine Mutiny!* I think somebody across the lake better hope their fire insurance is paid up, because—"

He stepped in. Saw Aaron. Saw Roland sitting across from Deepneau, looking at him steadily from those frightening blue eyes with the deep crow's feet at the corners. And, last of all, he saw Eddie. But Eddie didn't see him. At the last moment Eddie Dean had lowered his clasped hands between his knees and then lowered his head so his gaze was fixed upon them and the board floor below them. He was quite literally biting his tongue. There were two drops of blood on the side of his right thumb. He fixed his eyes on these. He fixed every iota of his attention on them. Because if he looked at the owner of that jolly voice, Eddie would surely kill him.

Saw our car. Saw it but never went over for a look. Never called out and asked his friend who was here, or if everything was okay. If Aaron was okay. Because he had some guy named Herman Wouk on his mind, not book club editions but the real thing. No worries, mate. Because you've got no more short-term imagination than Jack Andolini. You and Jack, just a couple ragged cockroaches, scuttling across the floor of the universe. Eyes on the prize, right? Eyes on the fucking prize.

"*You,*" Tower said. The happiness and excitement were gone from his voice. "The guy from—"

"The guy from nowhere," Eddie said without looking up. "The one who peeled Jack Andolini off you when you were about two minutes from shitting in your pants. And this is how you repay. You're quite the guy, aren't you?" As soon as he finished speaking, Eddie clamped down on his tongue again. His clasped hands were trembling. He expected Roland to intervene—surely he would, Eddie couldn't be expected to deal with this selfish monster on his own, he wasn't capable of it—but Roland said nothing.

Tower laughed. The sound was as nervous and brittle as his voice when he'd realized who was sitting in the kitchen of his rented cabin. "Oh, sir . . . Mr. Dean . . . I really think you've exaggerated the seriousness of that situation—"

"What I remember," Eddie said, still without looking up, "is the smell of the gasoline. I fired my dinh's gun, do you recall that? I suppose we were lucky there were no fumes, and that I fired it in the right direction. They poured gasoline all over the corner where you keep your desk. They were going to burn your favorite books . . . or should I say your best friends, your family? Because that's what they are to you, aren't they? And Deepneau, who the fuck is he? Just some old guy full of cancer who ran north with you when you needed a running buddy. You'd leave him dying in a ditch if someone offered you a first edition of Shakespeare or some special Ernest Hemingway."

"I resent that!" Tower cried. "I happen to know that my bookshop has been burned flat, and through an oversight it's uninsured! I'm ruined, and it's all your fault! I want you out of here!"

"You defaulted on the insurance when you needed cash to buy that Hopalong Cassidy collection from the Clarence Mulford estate last year," Aaron Deepneau said mildly. "You told me that insurance lapse was only temporary, but—"

"It was!" Tower said. He sounded both injured and surprised, as if he had never expected betrayal from this quarter. Probably he hadn't. "It *was* only temporary, goddammit!"

"—but to blame this young man," Deepneau went on in that same composed but regretful voice, "seems most unfair."

"I want you out of here!" Tower snarled at Eddie. "You and your friend, as well! I have no wish to do business with you! If you ever thought I did, it was a . . . a *misapprehension!*" He seized upon this last word as though upon a prize, and nearly shouted it out.

Eddie clasped his hands more tightly yet. He had never been more aware of the gun he was wearing; it had gained a kind of balefully lively weight. He reeked with sweat; he could smell it. And now drops of blood began to ooze out from between his palms and fall to the floor. He could feel his teeth beginning to sink into his tongue. Well, it was certainly a way to forget the pain in one's leg. Eddie decided to give the tongue in question another brief conditional parole.

"What I remember most clearly about my visit to you—"

"You have some books that belong to me," Tower said. "I want them back. I *insist* on—"

"Shut up, Cal," Deepneau said.

"What?" Tower did not sound wounded now; he sounded shocked. Almost breathless.

"Stop squirming. You've earned this scolding, and you know it. If you're lucky, a scolding is all it will be. So shut up and for once in your life take it like a man."

"Hear him very well," Roland said in a tone of dry approval.

"What I remember most clearly," Eddie pushed on, "is how horrified you were by what I told Jack—about how I and my friends would fill Grand Army Plaza with corpses if he didn't lay off. Some of them women and children. You didn't like that, but do you know what, Cal? Jack Andolini's here, right now, in East Stoneham."

"You *lie!*" Tower said. He drew in breath as he said it, turning the words into an inhaled scream.

"God," Eddie replied, "if only I did. I saw two innocent women die, Cal. In the general store, this was. Andolini set an ambush, and if you were a praying man—I suppose you're not, unless there's some first edition you feel in danger of losing, but if you were—you might want to get down on your knees and pray to the god of selfish, obsessed, greedy, uncaring dishonest bookstore owners that it was a woman named *Mia* who told Balazar's dinh where we were probably going to end up, *her,* not you. Because if they followed *you,* Calvin, those two women's blood is on *your hands!*"

His voice was rising steadily, and although Eddie was still looking steadfastly down, his whole body had begun to tremble. He could feel his eyes bulging in their sockets and the cords of strain standing out on his neck. He could feel his balls drawn all the way up, as small and as hard as peachpits. Most of all he could feel the desire to spring across the room, as effortless as a ballet dancer, and bury his hands in Calvin Tower's fat white throat. He was waiting for Roland to intervene—*hoping* for Roland to intervene—but the gunslinger did not, and Eddie's voice continued to rise toward the inevitable scream of fury.

"One of those women went right down but the other . . . she stayed up for a couple of seconds. A bullet took off the top of her head. I think it was a machine-gun bullet, and for the couple of seconds she stayed on her feet, she looked like a volcano. Only she was blowing blood instead of lava. Well, but it was probably Mia who ratted. I've got a feeling about that. It's not entirely logical, but luckily for you, it's *strong.* Mia using what Susannah knew and protecting her chap."

"Mia? Young man—Mr. Dean—I know no—"

"Shut up!" Eddie cried. "Shut up, you rat! You lying, reneging weasel! You greedy, grasping, piggy excuse for a man! Why didn't you take out a few billboards? HI, I'M CAL TOWER! I'M STAYING ON THE ROCKET ROAD IN EAST STONEHAM! WHY DON'T YOU

COME SEE ME AND MY FRIEND, AARON! BRING
GUNS!"

Slowly, Eddie looked up. Tears of rage were
rolling down his face. Tower had backed up against
the wall to one side of the door, his eyes huge and
moist in his round face. Sweat stood out on his
brow. He held his bag of freshly acquired books
against his chest like a shield.

Eddie looked at him steadily. Blood dripped
from between his tightly clasped hands; the spot of
blood on the arm of his shirt had begun to spread
again; now a trickle of blood ran from the left side
of his mouth, as well. And he supposed he understood Roland's silence. This was Eddie Dean's job.
Because he knew Tower inside as well as out, didn't
he? Knew him very well. Once upon a time not so
long ago hadn't he himself thought everything in
the world but heroin pale and unimportant?
Hadn't he believed everything in the world that
wasn't heroin up for barter or sale? Had he not
come to a point when he would literally have
pimped his own mother in order to get the next
fix? Wasn't that why he was so angry?

"That lot on the corner of Second Avenue and
Forty-sixth Street was never yours," Eddie said.
"Not your father's, or his father's, all the way back
to Stefan Toren. You were only custodians, the
same way I'm custodian of the gun I wear."

"I deny that!"

"Do you?" Aaron asked. "How strange. I've
heard you speak of that piece of land in almost
those exact words—"

"*Aaron, shut up!*"

"—many times," Deepneau finished calmly.

There was a pop. Eddie jumped, sending a fresh throb of pain up his leg from the hole in his shin. It was a match. Roland was lighting another cigarette. The filter lay on the oilcloth covering the table with two others. They looked like little pills.

"Here is what you said to me," Eddie said, and all at once he was calm. The rage was out of him, like poison drawn from a snakebite. Roland had let him do that much, and despite his bleeding tongue and bleeding palms, he was grateful.

"Anything I said . . . I was under stress . . . I was afraid you might kill me yourself!"

"You said you had an envelope from March of 1846. You said there was a sheet of paper in the envelope, and a name written on the paper. You said—"

"*I deny*—"

"You said that if I could tell you the name written on that piece of paper, you'd sell me the lot. For one dollar. And with the understanding that you'd be getting a great deal more—millions—between now and . . . 1985, let's say."

Tower barked a laugh. "Why not offer me the Brooklyn Bridge while you're at it?"

"You made a promise. And now your father watches you attempt to break it."

Calvin Tower shrieked: "*I DENY EVERY WORD YOU SAY!*"

"Deny and be damned," Eddie said. "And now I'm going to tell you something, Cal, something I know from my own beat-up but still beating heart. You're eating a bitter meal. You don't know that because someone told you it was sweet and your own tastebuds are numb."

"I have no idea what you're talking about! You're crazy!"

"No," Aaron said. "He's not. You're the one who's crazy if you don't listen to him. I think . . . I think he's giving you a chance to redeem the purpose of your life."

"Give it up," Eddie said. "Just once listen to the better angel instead of to the other one. That other one hates you, Cal. It only wants to kill you. Believe me, I know."

Silence in the cabin. From the pond came the cry of a loon. From across it came the less lovely sound of sirens.

Calvin Tower licked his lips and said, "Are you telling the truth about Andolini? Is he really in this town?"

"Yes," Eddie said. Now he could hear the *whuppa-whuppa-whup* of an approaching helicopter. A TV news chopper? Wasn't this still about five years too early for such things, especially up here in the boondocks?

The bookstore owner's eyes shifted to Roland. Tower had been surprised, and he'd been guilt-tripped with a vengeance, but the man was already regaining some of his composure. Eddie could see it, and he reflected (not for the first time) on how much simpler life would be if people would stay in the pigeonholes where you originally put them. He did not want to waste time thinking of Calvin Tower as a brave man, or as even second cousin to the good guys, but maybe he was both those things. Damn him.

"You're truly Roland of Gilead?"

Roland regarded him through rising membranes of cigarette smoke. "You say true, I say thank ya."

"Roland of the Eld?"

"Yes."

"Son of Steven?"

"Yes."

"Grandson of Alaric?"

Roland's eyes flickered with what was probably surprise. Eddie himself was surprised, but what he mostly felt was a kind of tired relief. The questions Tower was asking could mean only two things. First, more had been passed down to him than just Roland's name and trade of hand. Second, he was coming around.

"Of Alaric, aye," Roland said, "him of the red hair."

"I don't know anything about his hair, but I know why he went to Garlan. Do you?"

"To slay a dragon."

"And did he?"

"No, he was too late. The last in that part of the world had been slain by another king, one who was later murdered."

Now, to Eddie's even greater surprise, Tower haltingly addressed Roland in a language that was a second cousin to English at best. What Eddie heard was something like *Had heet Rol-uh, fa heet gun, fa heet hak, fa-had gun?*

Roland nodded and replied in the same tongue, speaking slowly and carefully. When he was finished, Tower sagged against the wall and dropped his bag of books unheeded to the floor. "I've been a fool," he said.

No one contradicted him.

"Roland, would you step outside with me? I need . . . I . . . need . . ." Tower began to cry. He said something else in that not-English language, once more ending on a rising inflection, as if asking a question.

Roland got up without replying. Eddie also got up, wincing at the pain in his leg. There was a slug in there, all right, he could feel it. He grabbed Roland's arm, pulled him down, and whispered in the gunslinger's ear: "Don't forget that Tower and Deepneau have an appointment at the Turtle Bay Washateria, four years from now. Tell him Forty-seventh Street, between Second and First. He probably knows the place. Tower and Deepneau were . . . are . . . *will be* the ones who save Don Callahan's life. I'm almost sure of it."

Roland nodded, then crossed to Tower, who initially cringed away and then straightened with a conscious effort. Roland took his hand in the way of the Calla, and led him outside.

When they were gone, Eddie said to Deepneau, "Draw up the contract. He's selling."

Deepneau regarded him skeptically. "You really think so?"

"Yeah," Eddie said. "I really do."

SEVEN

Drawing the contract didn't take long. Deepneau found a pad in the kitchen (there was a cartoon beaver on top of each sheet, and the legend DAM IMPORTANT THINGS TO DO) and wrote it on that, pausing every now and then to ask Eddie a question.

When they were finished, Deepneau looked at Eddie's sweat-shiny face and said, "I have some Percocet tablets. Would you like some?"

"You bet," Eddie said. If he took them now, he thought—hoped—he would be ready for what he wanted Roland to do when Roland got back. The bullet was still in there, in there for sure, and it had to come out. "How about four?"

Deepneau's eyes measured him.

"I know what I'm doing," Eddie said. Then added: "Unfortunately."

EIGHT

Aaron found a couple of children's Band-Aids in the cabin's medicine chest (Snow White on one, Bambi on another) and put them over the hole in Eddie's arm after pouring another shot of disinfectant into the wound's entry and exit points. Then, while drawing a glass of water to go with the painkillers, he asked Eddie where he came from. "Because," he said, "although you wear that gun with authority, you sound a lot more like Cal and me than you do him."

Eddie grinned. "There's a perfectly good reason for that. I grew up in Brooklyn. Co-Op City." And thought: *Suppose I were to tell you that I'm there right now, as a matter of fact? Eddie Dean, the world's horniest fifteen-year-old, running wild in the streets? For that Eddie Dean, the most important thing in the world is getting laid. Such things*

as the fall of the Dark Tower and some ultimate
baddie named the Crimson King won't bother me
for another—

Then he saw the way Aaron Deepneau was looking at him and came out of his own head in a hurry.
"What? Have I got a booger hanging out of my
nose, or something?"

"Co-Op City's not in Brooklyn," Deepneau said.
He spoke as one does to a small child. "Co-Op
City's in the Bronx. Always has been."

"That's—" Eddie began, meaning to add *ridicu-*
lous, but before he could get it out, the world
seemed to waver on its axis. Again he was overwhelmed by that sense of fragility, that sense of the
entire universe (or an entire *continuum* of universes)
made of crystal instead of steel. There was no way
to speak rationally of what he was feeling, because
there was nothing rational about what was happening.

"There are more worlds than these," he said.
"That was what Jake told Roland just before he
died. 'Go, then—there are other worlds than these.'
And he must have been right, because he came
back."

"Mr. Dean?" Deepneau looked concerned. "I
don't understand what you're talking about, but
you've come over very pale. I think you should sit
down."

Eddie allowed himself to be led back into the
cabin's combination kitchen and sitting room. Did
he himself understand what he was talking about?
Or how Aaron Deepneau—presumably a lifelong
New Yorker—could assert with such casual assur-

ance that Co-Op City was in the Bronx when Eddie knew it to be in Brooklyn?

Not entirely, but he understood enough to scare the hell out of him. Other worlds. Perhaps an infinite number of worlds, all of them spinning on the axle that was the Tower. All of them were similar, but there *were* differences. Different politicians on the currency. Different makes of automobiles— Takuro Spirits instead of Datsuns, for instance— and different major league baseball teams. In these worlds, one of which had been decimated by a plague called the superflu, you could time-hop back and forth, past and future. Because . . .

Because in some vital way, they aren't the real world. Or if they're real, they're not the key world.

Yes, that felt closer. He had come from one of those other worlds, he was convinced of it. So had Susannah. And Jakes One and Two, the one who had fallen and the one who had been literally pulled out of the monster's mouth and saved.

But this world was the key world. And he knew it because he was a key-*maker* by trade: *Dad-a-chum, dad-a-chee, not to worry, you've got the key.*

Beryl Evans? Not quite real. Claudia y Inez Bachman? Real.

World with Co-Op City in Brooklyn? Not quite real. World with Co-Op City in the Bronx? Real, hard as it was to swallow.

And he had an idea that Callahan had crossed over from the real world to one of the others long before he had embarked on his highways in hiding; had crossed without even knowing it. He'd said something about officiating at some little boy's funeral, and how, after that . . .

"After that he said everything changed," Eddie said as he sat down. "That *everything changed*."

"Yes, yes," Aaron Deepneau said, patting him on the shoulder. "Sit quietly now."

"Pere went from a seminary in Boston to Lowell, real. 'Salem's Lot, not real. Made up by a writer named—"

"I'm going to get a cold compress for your forehead."

"Good idea," Eddie said, closing his eyes. His mind was whirling. Real, not real. Live, Memorex. John Cullum's retired professor friend was right: the column of truth *did* have a hole in it.

Eddie wondered if anyone knew how deep that hole went.

NINE

It was a different Calvin Tower who came back to the cabin with Roland fifteen minutes later, a quiet and chastened Calvin Tower. He asked Deepneau if Deepneau had written a bill of sale, and when Deepneau nodded, Tower said nothing, only nodded back. He went to the fridge and returned with several cans of Blue Ribbon beer and handed them around. Eddie refused, not wanting to put alcohol on top of the Percs.

Tower did not offer a toast, but drank off half his beer at a single go. "It isn't every day I get called the scum of the earth by a man who promises to make me a millionaire and also to relieve me of my heart's heaviest burden. Aaron, will this thing stand up in court?"

Aaron Deepneau nodded. Rather regretfully, Eddie thought.

"All right, then," Tower said. Then, after a pause: "All right, let's do it." But still he didn't sign.

Roland spoke to him in that other language. Tower flinched, then signed his name in a quick scrawl, his lips tucked into a line so narrow his mouth seemed almost not to be there. Eddie signed for the Tet Corporation, marveling at how strange the pen felt in his hand—he couldn't remember when last he had held one.

When the thing was done, sai Tower reverted—looked at Eddie and cried in a cracked voice that was almost a shriek, "There! I'm a pauper! Give me my dollar! I'm promised a dollar! I feel a need to take a shit coming on and I need something to wipe my ass with!"

Then he put his hands over his face. He sat like that for several seconds, while Roland folded the signed paper (Deepneau had witnessed both signatures) and put it in his pocket.

When Tower lowered his hands again, his eyes were dry and his face was composed. There even seemed to be a touch of color in his formerly ashy cheeks. "I think I actually do feel a little better," he said. He turned to Aaron. "Do you suppose these two *cockuhs* might be right?"

"I think it's a real possibility," Aaron said, smiling.

Eddie, meanwhile, had thought of a way to find

out for sure if it really was these two men who would save Callahan from the Hitler Brothers—or almost for sure. One of them had said . . .

"Listen," he said. "There's a certain phrase, Yiddish, I think. *Gai cocknif en yom.* Do you know what it means? Either of you?"

Deepneau threw back his head and laughed. "Yeah, it's Yiddish, all right. My Ma used to say it all the time when she was mad at us. It means go shit in the ocean."

Eddie nodded at Roland. In the next couple of years, one of these men—probably Tower—would buy a ring with the words *Ex Libris* carved into it. Maybe—how crazy was *this*—because Eddie Dean himself had put the idea into Cal Tower's head. And Tower—selfish, acquisitive, miserly, book-greedy Calvin Tower—would save Father Callahan's life while that ring was on his finger. He was going to be shit-scared (Deepneau, too), but he was going to do it. And—

At that point Eddie happened to look at the pen with which Tower had signed the bill of sale, a perfectly ordinary Bic Clic, and the enormous truth of what had just happened struck home. They owned it. They owned the vacant lot. *They,* not the Sombra Corporation. *They owned the rose!*

He felt as if he'd just taken a hard shot to the head. The rose belonged to the Tet Corporation, which was the firm of Deschain, Dean, Dean, Chambers & Oy. It was now their responsibility, for better or for worse. This round they had won. Which did not change the fact that he had a bullet in his leg.

"Roland," he said, "there's something you have to do for me."

TEN

Five minutes later Eddie lay on the cabin's linoleum floor in his ridiculous knee-length Calla Bryn Sturgis underbritches. In one hand he held a leather belt which had spent its previous life holding up various pairs of Aaron Deepneau's pants. Beside him was a basin filled with a dark brown fluid.

The hole in his leg was about three inches below his knee and a little bit to the right of the shinbone. The flesh around it had risen up in a hard little cone. This miniature volcano's caldera was currently plugged with a shiny red-purple clot of blood. Two folded towels had been laid beneath Eddie's calf.

"Are you going to hypnotize me?" he asked Roland. Then he looked at the belt he was holding and knew the answer. "Ah, shit, you're not, are you?"

"No time." Roland had been rummaging in the junk-drawer to the left of the sink. Now he approached Eddie with a pair of pliers in one hand and a paring knife in the other. Eddie thought they made an exceedingly ugly combo.

The gunslinger dropped to one knee beside him. Tower and Deepneau stood in the living area, side by side, watching with big eyes. "There was a thing Cort told us when we were boys," Roland said. "Will I tell it to you, Eddie?"

"If you think it'll help, sure."

"Pain rises. From the heart to the head, pain rises. Double up sai Aaron's belt and put it in your mouth."

Eddie did as Roland said, feeling very foolish and very scared. In how many Western movies had he seen a version of this scene? Sometimes John Wayne bit a stick and sometimes Clint Eastwood bit a bullet, and he believed that in some TV show or other, Robert Culp had actually bitten a belt.

But of course we have to remove the bullet, Eddie thought. *No story of this type would be complete without at least one scene where—*

A sudden memory, shocking in its brilliance, struck him and the belt tumbled from his mouth. He actually cried out.

Roland had been about to dip his rude operating instruments in the basin, which held the rest of the disinfectant. Now he looked at Eddie, concerned. "What is it?"

For a moment Eddie couldn't reply. His breath was quite literally gone, his lungs as flat as old inner tubes. He was remembering a movie the Dean boys had watched one afternoon on TV in their apartment, the one in

(*Brooklyn*)

(*the Bronx*)

Co-Op City. Henry mostly got to pick what they watched because he was bigger and older. Eddie didn't protest too often or too much; he idolized his big brother. (When he *did* protest too much he was apt to get the old Indian Rope Burn or maybe a Dutch Rub up the back of his neck.) What Henry liked was Westerns. The sort of movies where, sooner or later, some character had to bite the stick or belt or bullet.

"Roland," he said. His voice was just a faint wheeze to start with. "Roland, listen."

"I hear you very well."

"There was a movie. I told you about movies, right?"

"Stories told in moving pictures."

"Sometimes Henry and I used to stay in and watch them on TV. Television's basically a home movie-machine."

"A shit-machine, some would say," Tower put in.

Eddie ignored him. "One of the movies we watched was about these Mexican peasants—*folken,* if it does ya—who hired some gunslingers to protect them from the *bandidos* who came every year to raid their village and steal their crops. Does any of this ring a bell?"

Roland looked at him with gravity and what might have been sadness. "Yes. Indeed it does."

"And the name of Tian's village. I always knew it sounded familiar, but I didn't know why. Now I do. The movie was called *The Magnificent Seven,* and just by the way, Roland, how many of us were in the ditch that day, waiting for the Wolves?"

"Would you boys mind telling us what you're talking about?" Deepneau asked. But although he asked politely, both Roland and Eddie ignored him, too.

Roland took a moment to cull his memory, then said: "You, me, Susannah, Jake, Margaret, Zalia, and Rosa. There were more—the Tavery twins and Ben Slightman's boy—but seven fighters."

"Yes. And the link I couldn't quite make was to the movie's director. When you're making a movie, you need a director to run things. He's the dinh."

Roland nodded.

"The dinh of *The Magnificent Seven* was a man named John Sturges."

Roland sat a moment longer, thinking. Then he said: "Ka."

Eddie burst out laughing. He simply couldn't help it. Roland always had the answer.

ELEVEN

"In order to catch the pain," Roland said, "you have to clamp down on the belt at the instant you feel it. Do you understand? *The very instant*. Pin it with your teeth."

"Gotcha. Just make it quick."

"I'll do the best I can."

Roland dipped first the pliers and then the knife into the disinfectant. Eddie waited with the belt in his mouth, lying across his teeth. Yes, once you saw the basic pattern, you couldn't unsee it, could you? Roland was the hero of the piece, the grizzled old warrior who'd be played by some grizzled but vital star like Paul Newman or maybe Eastwood in the Hollywood version. He himself was the young buck, played by the hot young boy star of the moment. Tom Cruise, Emilio Estevez, Rob Lowe, someone like that. And here's a set we all know, a cabin in the woods, and a situation we've seen many times before but still relish, Pulling the Bullet. All that was missing was the ominous sound of drums in the distance. And, Eddie realized, probably the drums were missing because they'd already been through the Ominous Drums part of the story: the god-drums. They had turned out to be an amplified version of a Z.Z. Top song being broadcast through streetcorner speakers in the City of Lud. Their situation was becoming ever harder to deny: *they were characters in someone's story.* This whole world—

I refuse to believe that. I refuse to believe that I was raised in Brooklyn simply because of some writer's mistake, something that will eventually be fixed in the second draft. Hey, Pere, I'm with you—I refuse to believe I'm a character. *This is my fucking* life!

"Go on, Roland," he said. "Get that thing outta me."

The gunslinger poured some of the disinfectant from the bowl over Eddie's shin, then used the tip of the knife to flick the clot out of the wound. With that done, he lowered the pliers. "Be ready to bite the pain, Eddie," he murmured, and a moment later Eddie did.

TWELVE

Roland knew what he was doing, had done it before, and the bullet hadn't gone deep. The whole thing was over in ninety seconds, but it was the longest minute and a half in Eddie's life. At last Roland tapped the pliers on one of Eddie's closed hands. When Eddie managed to unroll his fingers, the gunslinger dropped a flattened slug into it. "Souvenir," he said. "Stopped right on the bone. That was the scraping that you heard."

Eddie looked at the mashed piece of lead, then flicked it across the linoleum floor like a marble. "Don't want it," he said, and wiped his brow.

Tower, ever the collector, picked up the cast-off slug. Deepneau, meanwhile, was examining the toothmarks in his belt with silent fascination.

"Cal," Eddie said, getting up on his elbows. "You had a book in your case—"

"I want those books back," Tower said immediately. "You better be taking care of them, young man."

"I'm sure they're in great condition," Eddie said, telling himself once more to bite his tongue if he had to. *Or grab Aaron's belt and bite that again, if your tongue won't do.*

"They better be, young man; now they're all I have left."

"Yes, along with the forty or so in your various safe deposit boxes," Aaron Deepneau said, completely ignoring the vile look his friend shot him. "The signed *Ulysses* is probably the best, but there are several gorgeous Shakespeare folios, a complete set of signed Faulkners—"

"Aaron, would you please be quiet?"

"—and a *Huckleberry Finn* that you could turn into a Mercedes-Benz sedan any day of the week," Deepneau finished.

"In any case, one of them was a book called *'Salem's Lot,*" Eddie said. "By a man named—"

"Stephen King," Tower finished. He gave the

slug a final look, then put it on the kitchen table next to the sugarbowl. "I've been told he lives close to here. I've picked up two copies of *Lot* and also three copies of his first novel, *Carrie*. I was hoping to take a trip to Bridgton and get them signed. I suppose now that won't happen."

"I don't understand what makes it so valuable," Eddie said, and then: "Ouch, Roland, that hurts!"

Roland was checking the makeshift bandage around the wound in Eddie's leg. "Be still," he said.

Tower paid no attention to this. Eddie had turned him once more in the direction of his favorite subject, his obsession, his darling. What Eddie supposed Gollum in the Tolkien books would have called "his precious."

"Do you remember what I told you when we were discussing *The Hogan*, Mr. Dean? Or *The Dogan,* if you prefer? I said that the value of a rare book—like that of a rare coin or a rare stamp—is created in different ways. Sometimes it's just an autograph—"

"Your copy of *'Salem's Lot* isn't signed."

"No, because this particular author is very young and not very well known. He may amount to something one day, or he may not." Tower shrugged, almost as if to say that was up to ka. "But this particular book . . . well, the first edition was only seventy-five hundred copies, and almost all of them sold in New England."

"Why? Because the guy who wrote it is from New England?"

"Yes. As so often happens, the book's value was created entirely by accident. A local chain decided to promote it heavily. They even produced a TV commercial, which is almost unheard-of at the local retail level. And it worked. Bookland of Maine ordered five thousand copies of the first edition—almost seventy per cent—and sold nearly every single one. Also, as with *The Hogan,* there were misprints in the front matter. Not the title, in this case, but on the flap. You can tell an authentic first of *'Salem's Lot* by the clipped price—at the last minute, Doubleday decided to raise the price from seven-ninety-five to eight-ninety-five—and by the name of the priest in the flap copy."

Roland looked up. "What about the name of the priest?"

"In the book, it's Father Callahan. But on the flap someone wrote Father *Cody,* which is actually the name of the town's doctor."

"And that's all it took to bump the price of a copy from nine bucks to nine hundred and fifty," Eddie marveled.

Tower nodded. "That's all—scarcity, clipped flap, misprint. But there's also an element of speculation in collecting rare editions which I find . . . quite exciting."

"That's one word for it," Deepneau said dryly.

"For instance, suppose this man King becomes famous or critically acclaimed? I admit the chances are small, but suppose that did happen? Available first editions of his second book are so rare that, instead of being worth seven hundred and fifty dollars, my copy might be worth ten times that." He frowned at Eddie. "So you'd better be taking good care of it."

"I'm sure it'll be fine," Eddie said, and wondered what Calvin Tower would think if he knew that one of the book's characters had it on a shelf in his arguably fictional rectory. Said rectory in a town that was the fraternal twin of one in an old movie starring Yul Brynner as Roland's twin, and introducing Horst Buchholz as Eddie's.

He'd think you were crazy, that's what he'd think.

Eddie got to his feet, swayed a little, and gripped the kitchen table. After a few moments the world steadied.

"Can you walk on it?" Roland asked.

"I was before, wasn't I?"

"No one was digging around in there before."

Eddie took a few experimental steps, then nodded. His shin flared with pain each time he shifted his weight to his right leg, but yes—he could walk on it.

"I'll give you the rest of my Percocet," Aaron said. "I can get more."

Eddie opened his mouth to say yeah, sure, bring it on, and then saw Roland looking at him. If Eddie said yes to Deepneau's offer, the gunslinger wouldn't speak up and cause Eddie to lose face . . . but yes, his dinh was watching.

Eddie thought of the speech he'd made to Tower, all that poetic stuff about how Calvin was eating a bitter meal. It was true, poetic or not. But that apparently wouldn't stop Eddie from sitting back down to that same dinner himself. First a few Percodan, then a few Percocet. Both of them too much like horse for comfort. So how long would it be before he got tired of kissing his sister and started looking for some *real* pain relief?

"I think I'll skip the Percs," Eddie said. "We're going to Bridgton—"

Roland looked at him, surprised. "We are?"

"We are. I can pick up some aspirin on the way."

"Astin," Roland said, with unmistakable affection.

"Are you sure?" Deepneau asked.

"Yeah," Eddie said. "I am." He paused, then added: "Say sorry."

THIRTEEN

Five minutes later the four of them stood in the needle-carpeted dooryard, listening to sirens and looking at the smoke, which had now begun to thin. Eddie was bouncing the keys to John Cullum's Ford impatiently in one hand. Roland had asked him twice if this trip to Bridgton was necessary, and Eddie had told him twice that he was almost sure it was. The second time he'd added (almost hopefully) that as dinh, Roland could overrule him, if he wished.

"No. If you think we should go see this talespinner, we will. I only wish you knew *why*."

"I think that when we get there, we'll both understand."

Roland nodded, but still looked dissatisfied. "I know you're as anxious as I am to leave this world—this level of the Tower. For you to want to go against that, your intuition must be strong."

It was, but there was something else, as well: he'd heard from Susannah again, the message once more coming from her version of the Dogan. She was a prisoner in her own body—at least Eddie *thought* that was what she was trying to tell him—but she was in the year 1999 and she was all right.

This had happened while Roland was thanking Tower and Deepneau for their help. Eddie was in the bathroom. He'd gone in to take a leak, but suddenly forgot all about that and simply sat on the toilet's closed lid, head bent, eyes closed. Trying to send a message back to her. Trying to tell her to slow Mia down if she possibly could. He'd gotten the sense of daylight from her—New York in the afternoon—and that was bad. Jake and Callahan had gone through the Unfound Door into New York at night; this Eddie had seen with his own eyes. They might be able to help her, but only if she could slow Mia down.

Burn up the day, he sent to Susannah . . . or tried to. *You have to burn up the day before she takes you to wherever she's supposed to have the kid. Do you hear me? Suze, do you hear me? Answer if you hear me! Jake and Pere Callahan are coming and you have to hold on!*

June, a sighing voice had replied. *June of 1999. The girls walk around with their bellies showing and—*

Then came Roland's knock on the bathroom door, and Roland's voice asking if Eddie was ready to roll. Before the day was over they'd make their way to Turtleback Lane in the town of Lovell—a place where walk-ins were common, according to John Cullum, and reality was apt to be correspondingly thin—but first they were going to make a trip to Bridgton, and hopefully meet the man who seemed to have created Donald Callahan and the town of 'Salem's Lot.

Be a hoot if King was out in California, writing the movie version, or something, Eddie thought, but he didn't believe that was going to be the case. They were still on the Path of the Beam, in the way of ka. So, presumably, was sai King.

"You boys want to take it very easy," Deepneau told them. "There are going to be a lot of cops around. Not to mention Jack Andolini and whatever remains of his merry band."

"Speaking of Andolini," Roland said, "I think the time has come for the two of you to go somewhere he isn't."

Tower bristled. Eddie could have predicted it. "Go *now?* You must be joking! I have a list of almost a dozen people in the area who collect books—buy, sell, trade. Some know what they're doing, but others . . ." He made a clipping gesture, as if shearing an invisible sheep.

"There'll be people selling old books out of their barns over in Vermont, too," Eddie said. "And you want to remember how easy it was for us to find you. It was you who made it easy, Cal."

"He's right," Aaron said, and when Calvin Tower made no reply, only turned his sulky face down to regard his shoes, Deepneau looked at Eddie again. "But at least Cal and I have driver's licenses to show, should we be stopped by the local or the state police. I'm guessing neither of you do."

"That would be correct," Eddie said.

"And I very much doubt if you could show a

permit to carry those frighteningly large handguns, either."

Eddie glanced down at the big—and incredibly ancient—revolver riding just below his hip, then looked back up at Deepneau, amused. "That would also be correct," he said.

"Then be careful. You'll be leaving East Stoneham, so you'll probably be okay if you are."

"Thanks," Eddie said, and stuck out his hand. "Long days and pleasant nights."

Deepneau shook. "That's a lovely thing to say, son, but I'm afraid my nights haven't been especially pleasant just lately, and if things on the medical front don't take a turn for the better soon, my days aren't apt to be especially long, either."

"They're going to be longer than you might think," Eddie said. "I have good reason to believe you've got at least another four years in you."

Deepneau touched a finger to his lips, then pointed at the sky. "From the mouth of man to the ear of God."

Eddie swung to Calvin Tower while Roland shook hands with Deepneau. For a moment Eddie didn't think the bookstore owner was going to shake with him, but at last he did. Grudgingly.

"Long days and pleasant nights, sai Tower. You did the right thing."

"I was coerced and you know it," Tower said. "Store gone . . . property gone . . . about to be run off the first real vacation I've had in ten years . . ."

"Microsoft," Eddie said abruptly. And then: "Lemons."

Tower blinked. "Beg pardon?"

"*Lemons*," Eddie repeated, and then he laughed out loud.

FOURTEEN

Toward the end of his mostly useless life, the great sage and eminent junkie Henry Dean had enjoyed two things above all others: getting stoned; getting stoned and talking about how he was going to make a killing in the stock market. In investment matters, he considered himself a regular E. F. Hutton.

"One thing I would most definitely *not* invest in, bro," Henry told him once when they were up on the roof. Not long before Eddie's trip to the Bahamas as a cocaine mule, this had been. "One thing I would most apple-solutely *not* sink my money into is all this computer shit, Microsoft, Macintosh, Sanyo, Sankyo, Pentium, all that."

"Seems pretty popular," Eddie had ventured. Not that he'd much cared, but what the hell, it was a conversation. "Microsoft, especially. The coming thing."

Henry had laughed indulgently and made jacking-off gestures. "My prick, that's the coming thing."

"But—"

"Yeah, yeah, I know, people're *flocking* to that crap. Driving all the prices up. And when I observe that action, do you know what I see?"

"No, what?"

"Lemons!"

"Lemons?" Eddie had asked. He'd thought he

was following Henry, but he guessed he was lost, after all. Of course the sunset had been amazing that evening, and he had been most colossally fucked up.

"You heard me!" Henry had said, warming to the subject. "Fuckin lemons! Didn't they teach you anything in school, bro? Lemons are these little animals that live over in Switzerland, or someplace like that. And every now and then—I think it's every ten years, I'm not sure—they get suicidal and throw themselves over the cliffs."

"Oh," Eddie said, biting hard on the inside of his cheek to keep from bursting into mad cackles. "*Those* lemons. I thought you meant the ones you use to make lemonade."

"Fuckin wank," Henry said, but he spoke with the indulgent good nature the great and eminent sometimes reserve for the small and uninformed. "Anyway, my *point* is that all these people who are flockin to invest in Microsoft and Macintosh and, I don't know, fuckin Nervous Norvus Speed Dial Chips, all they're gonna do is make Bill Fuckin Gates and Steve Fuckin Jobs-a-rino rich. This computer shit is gonna crash and burn by 1995, all the experts say so, and the people investin in it? Fuckin lemons, throwin themselves over the cliffs and into the fuckin ocean."

"Just fuckin lemons," Eddie agreed, and sprawled back on the still-warm roof so Henry wouldn't see how close he was to losing it entirely. He was seeing billions of Sunkist lemons trotting toward these high cliffs, all of them wearing red jogging shorts and little white sneakers, like M&Ms in a TV ad.

"Yeah, but I wish I'd gotten into that fuckin Microsoft in '82," Henry said. "Do you realize that shares that were sellin for fifteen bucks back then are now sellin for thirty-five? Oh, man!"

"Lemons," Eddie had said dreamily, watching the sunset's colors begin to fade. At that point he'd had less than a month to live in his world—the one where Co-Op City was in Brooklyn and always had been—and Henry had less than a month to live, period.

"Yeah," Henry had said, lying down beside him, "but man, I wish I coulda gotten in back in '82."

FIFTEEN

Now, still holding Tower's hand, he said: "I'm from the future. You know that, don't you?"

"I know that *he* says you are, yes." Tower jerked his head toward Roland, then tried to pull his hand free. Eddie held on.

"Listen to me, Cal. If you listen and then act on what I tell you, you can earn what that vacant lot of yours would be worth on the real estate market five, maybe even ten times over."

"Big talk from a man who isn't even wearing socks," Tower said, and once again tried to pull his hand free. Again Eddie held it. Once he supposed he wouldn't have been able to do that, but his hands were stronger now. So was his will.

"Big talk from a man who's seen the future," he corrected. "And the future is computers, Cal. The future is Microsoft. Can you remember that?"

"*I* can," Aaron said. "Microsoft."

"Never heard of it," Tower said.

"No," Eddie agreed, "I don't think it even exists yet. But it will, soon, and it's going to be huge. Computers, okay? Computers for everybody, or at least that was the plan. *Will be* the plan. The guy in charge is Bill Gates. Always Bill, never William."

It occurred to him briefly that since this world was different from the one in which he and Jake had grown up—the world of Claudia y Inez Bachman instead of Beryl Evans—that maybe the big computer genius here *wouldn't* be Gates; could be someone named Chin Ho Fuk, for all Eddie knew. But he also knew that wasn't likely. This world was very close to his: same cars, same brand names (Coke and Pepsi rather than Nozz-A-La), same people on the currency. He thought he could count on Bill Gates (not to mention Steve Jobs-a-rino) showing up when he was supposed to.

In one way, he didn't even care. Calvin Tower was in many respects a total shithead. On the other hand, Tower had stood up to Andolini and Balazar for as long as he had to. He'd held onto the vacant lot. And now Roland had the bill of sale in his pocket. They owed Tower a fair return for what he'd sold them. It had nothing to do with how much or how little they liked the guy, which was probably a good thing for old Cal.

"This Microsoft stuff," Eddie said, "you can pick it up for fifteen dollars a share in 1982. By 1987—which is when I sort of went on permanent vacation—those shares will be worth thirty-five apiece. That's a hundred per cent gain. A little more."

"Says you," Tower said, and finally succeeded in pulling his hand free.

"If he says so," Roland said, "it's the truth."

"Say thanks," Eddie said. It occurred to him that he was suggesting that Tower take a fairly big leap based on a stone junkie's observations, but he thought that in this case he could do that.

"Come on," Roland said, and made that twirling gesture with his fingers. "If we're going to see the writer, let's go."

Eddie slid behind the wheel of Cullum's car, suddenly sure that he would never see either Tower or Aaron Deepneau again. With the exception of Pere Callahan, none of them would. The partings had begun.

"Do well," he said to them. "May ya do well."

"And you," Deepneau said.

"Yes," Tower said, and for once he didn't sound a bit grudging. "Good luck to you both. Long days and happy nights, or whatever it is."

There was just room to turn around without backing, and Eddie was glad—he wasn't quite ready for reverse, at least not yet.

As Eddie drove back toward the Rocket Road, Roland looked over his shoulder and waved. This was highly unusual behavior for him, and the knowledge must have shown on Eddie's face.

"It's the end-game now," Roland said. "All I've worked for and waited for all the long years. The end is coming. I feel it. Don't you?"

Eddie nodded. It was like that point in a piece of music when all the instruments begin rushing toward some inevitable crashing climax.

"Susannah?" Roland asked.

"Still alive."

"Mia?"

"Still in control."

"The baby?"

"Still coming."

"And Jake? Father Callahan?"

Eddie stopped at the road, looked both ways, then made his turn.

"No," he said. "From them I haven't heard. What about you?"

Roland shook his own head. From Jake, somewhere in the future with just an ex-Catholic priest and a billy-bumbler for protection, there was only silence. Roland hoped the boy was all right.

For the time being, he could do no more.

> STAVE: *Commala-me-mine*
> *You have to walk the line.*
> *When you finally get the thing you need*
> *It makes you feel so fine.*

> RESPONSE: *Commala-come-nine!*
> *It makes ya feel fine!*
> *But if you'd have the thing you need*
> *You have to walk the line.*

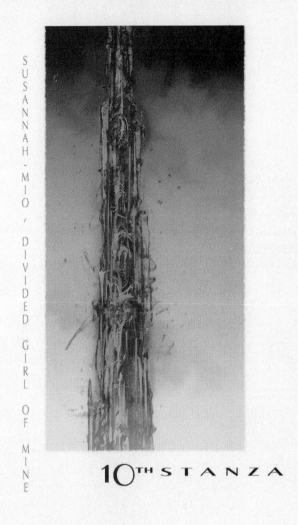

SUSANNAH-MIO, DIVIDED GIRL OF MINE

10TH **STANZA**

ONE

"John Fitzgerald Kennedy died this afternoon at Parkland Memorial Hospital."

This voice, this grieving voice: Walter Cronkite's voice, in a dream.

"America's last gunslinger is dead. O Discordia!"

TWO

As Mia left room 1919 of the New York Plaza–Park (soon to be the Regal U.N. Plaza, a Sombra/North Central project, O Discordia), Susannah fell into a swoon. From a swoon she passed into a savage dream filled with savage news.

THREE

The next voice is that of Chet Huntley, co-anchor of *The Huntley-Brinkley Report*. It's also—in some way she cannot understand—the voice of Andrew, her chauffeur.

"Diem and Nhu are dead," says that voice.

"Now do slip the dogs of war, the tale of woe begins; from here the way to Jericho Hill is paved with blood and sin. Ah, Discordia! Charyou tree! Come, reap!"

Where am I?

She looks around and sees a concrete wall packed with a jostling intaglio of names, slogans, and obscene drawings. In the middle, where anyone sitting on the bunk must see it, is this greeting: HELLO NIGGER WELCOME TO OXFORD DON'T LET THE SUN SET ON YOU HERE!

The crotch of her slacks is damp. The underwear beneath is downright soaked, and she remembers why: although the bail bondsman was notified well in advance, the cops held onto them as long as possible, cheerfully ignoring the increasing chorus of pleas for a bathroom break. No toilets in the cells; no sinks; not even a tin bucket. You didn't need to be a quiz-kid on *Twenty-one* to figure it out; they were *supposed* to piss in their pants, supposed to get in touch with their essential animal natures, and eventually she had, *she,* Odetta Holmes—

No, she thinks, *I am Susannah. Susannah Dean. I've been taken prisoner again, jailed again, but I am still I.*

She hears voices from beyond this wing of jail cells, voices which for her sum up the present. She's supposed to think they're coming from a TV out in the jail's office, she assumes, but it's got to be a trick. Or some ghoul's idea of a joke. Why else would Frank McGee be saying President Kennedy's brother, Bobby, is dead? Why would Dave Garroway from the *Today* show be saying that the

President's little *boy* is dead, that John-John has been killed in a plane crash? What sort of awful lie is that to hear as you sit in a stinking southern jail with your wet underpants clinging to your crotch? Why is "Buffalo" Bob Smith of the *Howdy Doody* show yelling "Cowabunga, kids, Martin Luther King is dead"? And the kids all screaming back, "Commala-come-*Yay!* We love the things ya say! Only good nigger's a dead nigger, so kill a coon *today!*"

The bail bondsman will be here soon. That's what she needs to hold onto, *that.*

She goes to the bars and grips them. Yes, this is Oxford Town, all right, Oxford all over again, two men dead by the light of the moon, somebody better investigate soon. But she's going to get out, and she'll fly away, fly away, fly away home, and not long after that there will be an entirely new world to explore, with a new person to love and a new person to *be.* Commala-come-come, the journey's just begun.

Oh, but that's a lie. The journey is almost over. Her heart knows this.

Down the hall a door opens and footsteps come clicking toward her. She looks in that direction— eagerly, hoping for the bondsman, or a deputy with a ring of keys—but instead it's a black woman in a pair of stolen shoes. It's her old self. It's Odetta Holmes. Didn't go to Morehouse, but did go to Columbia. And to all those coffee houses down in the Village. And to the Castle on the Abyss, that house, too.

"Listen to me," Odetta says. "No one can get you out of this but yourself, girl."

"You want to enjoy those legs while you got em, honey!" The voice she hears coming out of her mouth is rough and confrontational on top, scared underneath. The voice of Detta Walker. "You goan lose em fore long! They goan be cut off by the A train! That fabled A train! Man named Jack Mort goan push you off the platform in the Christopher Street station!"

Odetta looks at her calmly and says, "The A train doesn't stop there. It's *never* stopped there."

"What the fuck you *talkin* about, bitch?"

Odetta is not fooled by the angry voice or the profanity. She knows who she's talking to. And she knows what she's talking about. The column of truth has a hole in it. These are not the voices of the gramophone but those of our dead friends. There are ghosts in the rooms of ruin. "Go back to the Dogan, Susannah. And remember what I say: only you can save yourself. Only you can lift your-self out of Discordia."

FOUR

Now it's the voice of David Brinkley, saying that someone named Stephen King was struck and killed by a minivan while walking near his home in Lovell, a small town in western Maine. King was fifty-two, he says, the author of many novels, most notably *The Stand, The Shining,* and *'Salem's Lot.* Ah Discordia, Brinkley says, the world grows darker.

FIVE

Odetta Holmes, the woman Susannah once was, points through the bars of the cell and past her. She says it again: "Only you can save yourself. But the way of the gun is the way of damnation as well as salvation; in the end there is no difference."

Susannah turns to look where the finger is pointing, and is filled with horror at what she sees: The blood! Dear God, the *blood!* There is a bowl filled with blood, and in it some monstrous dead thing, a dead baby that's not human, and has she killed it herself?

"No!" she screams. "No, I will never! *I will NEVER!*"

"Then the gunslinger will die and the Dark Tower will fall," says the terrible woman standing in the corridor, the terrible woman who is wearing Trudy Damascus's shoes. "Discordia indeed."

Susannah closes her eyes. Can she *make* herself swoon? Can she swoon herself right out of this cell, this terrible world?

She does. She falls forward into the darkness and the soft beeping of machinery and the last voice she hears is that of Walter Cronkite, telling her that Diem and Nhu are dead, astronaut Alan Shepard is dead, Lyndon Johnson is dead, Richard Nixon is dead, Elvis Presley is dead, Rock Hudson is dead, Roland of Gilead is dead, Eddie of New York is dead, Jake of New York is dead, the world is dead, the *worlds,* the Tower is falling, a trillion universes are merging, and all is Discordia, all is ruin, all is ended.

SIX

Susannah opened her eyes and looked around wildly, gasping for breath. She almost fell out of the chair in which she was sitting. It was one of those capable of rolling back and forth along the instrument panels filled with knobs and switches and blinking lights. Overhead were the black-and-white TV screens. She was back in the Dogan. Oxford

(*Diem and Nhu are dead*)

had only been a dream. A dream within a dream, if you pleased. This was another, but marginally better.

Most of the TV screens which had been showing pictures of Calla Bryn Sturgis the last time she'd been here were now broadcasting either snow or test-patterns. On one, however, was the nineteenth-floor corridor of the Plaza–Park Hotel. The camera rolled down it toward the elevators, and Susannah realized that these were Mia's eyes she was looking through.

My eyes, she thought. Her anger was thin, but she sensed it could be fed. Would *have* to be fed, if she was ever to regard the unspeakable thing she'd seen in her dream. The thing in the corner of her Oxford jail cell. The thing in the bowl of blood.

They're my eyes. She hijacked them, that's all.

Another TV screen showed Mia arriving in the elevator lobby, examining the buttons, and then pushing the one marked with the DOWN arrow. *We're off to see the midwife,* Susannah thought, looking grimly up at the screen, and then barked a short, humorless laugh. *Oh, we're off to see the midwife, the wonderful midwife of Oz. Because because because because be-CAUZZZ . . . Because of the wonderful things she does!*

Here were the dials she'd reset at some considerable inconvenience—hell, *pain*. EMOTIONAL TEMP still at 72. The toggle-switch marked CHAP still turned to ASLEEP, and in the monitor above it the chap thus still in black-and-white like everything else: no sign of those disquieting blue eyes. The absurd LABOR FORCE oven-dial was still at 2, but she saw that most of the lights which had been amber the last time she'd been in this room had now turned red. There were more cracks in the floor and the ancient dead soldier in the corner had lost his head: the increasingly heavy vibration of the machinery had toppled the skull from the top of its spine, and it now laughed up at the fluorescent lights in the ceiling.

The needle on the **SUSANNAH-MIO** readout had reached the end of the yellow zone; as Susannah watched, it edged into the red. Danger, danger, Diem and Nhu are dead. Papa Doc Duvalier is dead. Jackie Kennedy is dead.

She tried the controls one after another, confirming what she already knew: they were locked in place. Mia might not have been able to change the settings in the first place, but locking things up once those settings were to her liking? That much she had been able to do.

There was a crackle and squall from the overhead speakers, loud enough to make her jump.

Then, coming to her through heavy bursts of static, Eddie's voice.

"Suze! . . . ay! . . . Ear me? Burn . . . ay! Do it before . . . ever . . . posed . . . id! Do you hear me?"

On the screen she thought of as Mia-Vision, the doors of the central elevator car opened. The hijacking mommy-bitch got on. Susannah barely noticed. She snatched up the microphone and pushed the toggle-switch on the side. "Eddie!" she shouted. "I'm in 1999! The girls walk around with their bellies showing and their bra-straps—" Christ, what was she blathering on about? She made a mighty effort to sweep her mind clear.

"Eddie, I don't understand you! Say it again, sugar!"

For a moment there was nothing but more static, plus the occasional spooky wail of feedback. She was about to try the mike again when Eddie's voice returned, this time a little clearer.

"Burn up . . . day! Jake . . . Pere Cal . . . hold on! Burn . . . before she . . . to wherever she . . . have the kid! If you . . . knowledge!"

"I hear you, I acknowledge that much!" she cried. She was clutching the silver mike so tightly that it trembled in her grasp. "I'm in 1999! June of 1999! But I'm not understanding you as well as I need to, sug! Say again, and tell me if you're all right!"

But Eddie was gone.

After calling for him half a dozen times and getting nothing but that blur of static, she set the microphone down again and tried to figure out what he had been trying to tell her. Trying also to set aside her joy just in knowing that Eddie could still try to tell her *anything*.

"Burn up day," she said. That part, at least, had come through loud and clear. "Burn up *the* day. As in kill some time." She thought that almost had to be right. Eddie wanted Susannah to slow Mia down. Maybe because Jake and Pere Callahan were coming? About that part she wasn't so sure, and she didn't much like it, anyway. Jake was a gunslinger, all right, but he was also only a kid. And Susannah had an idea that the Dixie Pig was full of very nasty people.

Meanwhile, on Mia-Vision, the elevator doors were opening again. The hijacking mommy-bitch had reached the lobby. For the time being Susannah put Eddie, Jake, and Pere Callahan out of her mind. She was recalling how Mia had refused to *come forward*, even when their Susannah-Mio legs were threatening to disappear right out from under their shared Susannah-Mio body. Because she was, to misquote some old poem or other, alone and afraid in a world she never made.

Because she was *shy*.

And my goodness, things in the lobby of the Plaza–Park had changed while the hijacking mommy-bitch had been upstairs waiting for her phone call. They had changed a *lot*.

Susannah leaned forward with her elbows propped on the edge of the Dogan's main instrument panel and her chin propped on the palms of her hands.

This might be interesting.

SEVEN

Mia stepped out of the elevator, then attempted to step right back in. She thumped against the doors instead, and hard enough to make her teeth come together with a little ivory click. She looked around, bewildered, at first not sure how it was that the little descending room had disappeared.

Susannah! What happened to it?

No answer from the dark-skinned woman whose face she now wore, but Mia discovered she didn't actually need one. She could see the place where the door slid in and out. If she pushed the button the door would probably open again, but she had to conquer her sudden strong desire to go back up to Room 1919. Her business there was done. Her *real* business was somewhere beyond the lobby doors.

She looked toward those doors with the sort of lip-biting dismay which may escalate into panic at a single rough word or angry look.

She'd been upstairs for a little over an hour, and during that time the lobby's early-afternoon lull had ended. Half a dozen taxis from La Guardia and Kennedy had pulled up in front of the hotel at roughly the same time; so had a Japanese tour-bus from Newark Airport. The tour had originated in Sapporo and consisted of fifty couples with reservations at the Plaza–Park. Now the lobby was rapidly filling with chattering people. Most had dark, slanted eyes and shiny black hair, and were wearing oblong objects around their necks on straps. Every now and then one would raise one of these objects and point it at someone else. There would be a brilliant flash, laughter, and cries of *Domo! Domo!* There were three lines forming at the desk. The beautiful woman who'd checked Mia in during quieter times had been joined by two other clerks, all of them working like mad. The high-ceilinged lobby echoed with laughter and mingled conversation in some strange tongue that sounded to Mia like the twittering of birds. The banks of mirror-glass added to the general confusion by making the lobby seem twice as full as it actually was.

Mia cringed back, wondering what to do.

"Front!" yelled a desk clerk, and banged a bell. The sound seemed to shoot across Mia's confused thoughts like a silver arrow. "Front, please!"

A grinning man—black hair slicked against his skull, yellow skin, slanting eyes behind round spectacles—came rushing up to Mia, holding one of the oblong flash-things. Mia steeled herself to kill him if he attacked.

"Ah-yoo takea pickcha me and my wife?"

Offering her the flash-thing. Wanting her to take it from him. Mia cringed away, wondering if it ran on radiation, if the flashes might hurt her baby.

Susannah! What do I do?

No answer. Of course not, she really couldn't expect Susannah's help after what had just happened, but . . .

The grinning man was still thrusting the flash-machine at her. He looked a trifle puzzled, but mostly undaunted. "Yooo take-ah pickcha, preese?" And put the oblong thing in her hand. He stepped back and put his arm around a lady who looked exactly like him except for her shiny black hair, which was cut across her forehead in what Mia thought of as a wench-clip. Even the round glasses were the same.

"No," Mia said. "No, cry pardon . . . no." The panic was very close now and very bright, whirling and gibbering right in front of her

(*yooo take-ah pickcha, we kill-ah baby*)

and Mia's impulse was to drop the oblong flasher on the floor. That might break it, however, and release the deviltry that powered the flashes.

She put it down carefully instead, smiling apologetically at the astonished Japanese couple (the man still had his arm around his wife), and hurried across the lobby in the direction of the little shop. Even the piano music had changed; instead of the former soothing melodies, it was pounding out something jagged and dissonant, a kind of musical headache.

I need a shirt because there's blood on this one. I'll get the shirt and then I'll go to the Dixie Pig, Sixty-first and Lexingworth . . . Lexington, I mean, Lexington . . . and then I'll have my baby. I'll have my baby and all this confusion will end. I'll think of how I was afraid and I'll laugh.

But the shop was also full. Japanese women examined souvenirs and twittered to each other in their bird-language while they waited for their husbands to get them checked in. Mia could see a counter stacked with shirts, but there were women all around it, examining them. And there was another line at the counter.

Susannah, what should I do? You've got to help me!

No answer. She was in there, Mia could feel her,

but she would not help. *And really,* she thought, *would I, if I were in her position?*

Well, perhaps she would. Someone would have to offer her the right inducement, of course, but—

The only inducement I want from you is the truth, Susannah said coldly.

Someone brushed against Mia as she stood in the door to the shop and she turned, her hands coming up. If it was an enemy, or some enemy of her chap, she would claw his eyes out.

"Solly," said a smiling black-haired woman. Like the man, she was holding out one of the oblong flash-things. In the middle was a circular glass eye that stared at Mia. She could see her own face in it, small and dark and bewildered. "You take pickcha, preese? Take pickcha me and my fliend?"

Mia had no idea what the woman was saying or what she wanted or what the flash-makers were supposed to do. She only knew that there were too many people, they were everywhere, this was a madhouse. Through the shop window she could see that the front of the hotel was likewise thronged. There were yellow cars and long black cars with windows you couldn't look into (although the people inside could doubtless look out), and a huge silver conveyance that sat rumbling at the curb. Two men in green uniforms were in the street, blowing silver whistles. Somewhere close by something began to rattle loudly. To Mia, who had never heard a jackhammer, it sounded like a speed-shooter gun, but no one outside was throwing himself to the sidewalk; no one even looked alarmed.

How was she supposed to get to the Dixie Pig on her own? Richard P. Sayre had said he was sure Susannah could help her find it, but Susannah had fallen stubbornly silent, and Mia herself was on the verge of losing control entirely.

Then Susannah spoke up again.

If I help you a little now—get you to a quiet place where you can catch your breath and at least do something about your shirt—will you give me some straight answers?

About what?

About the baby, Mia. And about the mother. About you.

I did!

I don't think so. I don't think you're any more elemental than . . . well, than I am. I want the truth.

Why?

I want the truth, Susannah repeated, and then fell silent, refusing to respond to any more of Mia's questions. And when yet another grinning little man approached her with yet another flash-thing, Mia's nerve broke. Right now just getting across the hotel lobby looked like more than she could manage on her own; how was she supposed to get all the way to this Dixie Pig place? After so many years in

(*Fedic*)

(*Discordia*)

(*the Castle on the Abyss*)

to be among so many people made her feel like screaming. And after all, why not tell the dark-skinned woman what little she knew? She—Mia,

daughter of none, mother of one—was firmly in
charge. What harm in a little truth-telling?

All right, she said. *I'll do as you ask, Susannah
or Odetta or whoever you are. Just help me. Get
me out of here.*

Susannah Dean *came forward.*

EIGHT

There was a women's restroom adjacent to the hotel
bar, around the corner from the piano player. Two of
the yellow-skinned, black-haired ladies with the
tipped eyes were at the basins, one washing her
hands, the other fixing her hair, both of them twittering in their birdy-lingo. Neither paid any attention to the *kokujin* lady who went past them and to
the stalls. A moment later they left her in blessed
silence except for the faint music drifting down from
the overhead speakers.

Mia saw how the latch worked and engaged it.
She was about to sit down on the toilet seat when
Susannah said: *Turn it inside out.*

What?

*The shirt, woman. Turn it inside out, for your
father's sake!*

For a moment Mia didn't. She was too stunned.

The shirt was a rough-woven callum-ka, the sort
of simple pullover favored by both sexes in the rice-
growing country during cooler weather. It had
what Odetta Holmes would have called a boat-
neck. No buttons, so yes, it could very easily be
turned inside out, but—

Susannah, clearly impatient: *Are you going to*

*stand there commala-moon all day? Turn it inside
out! And tuck it into your jeans this time.*

W . . . Why?

It'll give you a different look, Susannah replied
promptly, but that wasn't the reason. What she
wanted was a look at herself below the waist. If her
legs were Mia's then they were quite probably
white legs. She was fascinated (and a little sickened) by the idea that she had become a kind of
tu-tone halfbreed.

Mia paused a moment longer, fingertips rubbing
the rough weave of the shirt above the worst of the
bloodstains, which was over her left breast. Over
her heart. Turn it inside out! In the lobby, a dozen
half-baked ideas had gone through her head (using
the scrimshaw turtle to fascinate the people in the
shop had probably been the only one even close to
workable), but simply turning the damned thing
inside out hadn't been one of them. Which only
showed, she supposed, how close to total panic she
had been. But now . . .

Did she need Susannah for the brief time she
would be in this overcrowded and disorienting
city, which was so different from the quiet rooms
of the castle and the quiet streets of Fedic? Just to
get from here to Sixty-first Street and Lexingworth?

Lexington, said the woman trapped inside her.
Lexington. You keep forgetting that, don't you?

Yes. Yes, she did. And there was no reason to
forget such a simple thing, maybe she hadn't been
to Morehouse, Morehouse or no house, but she
wasn't stupid. So why—

What? she demanded suddenly. *What are you smiling about?*

Nothing, said the woman inside . . . but she was still smiling. Almost grinning. Mia could feel it, and she didn't like it. Upstairs in Room 1919, Susannah had been screaming at her in a mixture of terror and fury, accusing Mia of betraying the man she loved and the one she followed. Which had been true enough to make Mia ashamed. She didn't enjoy feeling that way, but she'd liked the woman inside better when she was howling and crying and totally discombobulated. The smile made her nervous. This version of the brown-skinned woman was trying to turn the tables on her; maybe thought she *had* turned the tables. Which was impossible, of course, she was under the protection of the King, but . . .

Tell me why you're smiling!

Oh, it don't amount to much, Susannah said, only now she sounded like the other one, whose name was Detta. Mia did more than dislike that one. She was a little afraid of that one. *It's just that there was this fella named Sigmund Freud, honey-chile—honky muhfuh, but not stupid. And he said that when someone always be f'gittin sump'in, might be because that person want to be f'gittin it.*

That's stupid, Mia said coldly. Beyond the stall where she was having this mental conversation, the door opened and two more ladies came in—no, at least three and maybe four—twittering in their birdy-language and giggling in a way that made Mia clamp her teeth together. *Why would I want to forget the place where they're waiting to help me have my baby?*

Well, dis Freud—dis smart cigar-smoking Viennese honky muhfuh—he claim dat we got dis mind under *our mind, he call it the unconscious or subconscious or some* fuckin *conscious. Now I ain't claimin dere is such a thing, only dat he say dere was.*

(Burn up the day, *Eddie had told her, that much she was sure of, and she would do her best, only hoping that she wasn't working on getting Jake and Callahan killed by doing it.*)

Ole Honky Freud, Detta went on, *he say in lots of ways de subconscious or unconscious mind* smarter *dan de one on top. Cut through de bullshit* faster *dan de one on top. An maybe yours understand what I been tellin you all along, that yo' frien Sayre nothin but a lyin rat-ass muhfuh goan steal yo baby and, I dunno, maybe cut it up in dis bowl and den feed it to the vampires like dey was dawgs an dat baby nuffin but a big-ass bowl o' Alpo or Purina Vampire Ch—*

Shut up! Shut up your lying face!

Out at the basins, the birdy-women laughed so shrilly that Mia felt her eyeballs shiver and threaten to liquefy in their sockets. She wanted to rush out and seize their heads and drive them into the mirrors, wanted to do it again and again until their blood was splashed all the way up to the ceiling and their *brains*—

Temper, temper, said the woman inside, and now it sounded like Susannah again.

She lies! That bitch LIES!

No, Susannah replied, and the conviction in that single short word was enough to send an arrow of fear into Mia's heart. *She says what's on her mind, no argument there, but she doesn't lie. Go on, Mia, turn your shirt inside out.*

With a final eye-watering burst of laughter, the birdy-women left the bathroom. Mia pulled the shirt off over her head, baring Susannah's breasts, which were the color of coffee with just the smallest splash of milk added in. Her nipples, which had always been as small as berries, were now much larger. Nipples craving a mouth.

There were only the faintest maroon spots on the inside of the shirt. Mia put it back on, then unbuttoned the front of her jeans so she could tuck it in. Susannah stared, fascinated, at the point just above her pubic thatch. Here her skin lightened to a color that might have been milk with the smallest splash of coffee added in. Below were the white legs of the woman she'd met on the castle allure. Susannah knew that if Mia lowered her jeans all the way, she'd see the scabbed and scratched shins she had already observed as Mia—the *real* Mia— looked out over Discordia toward the red glow marking the castle of the King.

Something about this frightened Susannah terribly, and after a moment's consideration (it took no longer), the reason came to her. If Mia had only replaced those parts of her legs that Odetta Holmes had lost to the subway train when Jack Mort pushed her onto the tracks she would have been white only from the knees or so down. But her *thighs* were white, too, and her groin area was turning. What strange lycanthropy was this?

De body-stealin kind, Detta replied cheerfully.

Pretty soon you be havin a white belly . . . white breas's . . . white neck . . . white cheeks . . .

Stop it, Susannah warned, but when had Detta Walker ever listened to her warnings? Hers or anybody's?

And den, las' of all, you have a white brain, *girl! A Mia brain! And won't dat be fahn? Sho! You be all Mia den! Nobody give you no shit if you want to ride right up front on de bus!*

Then the shirt was drawn over her hips; the jeans were again buttoned up. Mia sat down on the toilet ring that way. In front of her, scrawled on the door, was this graffito: BANGO SKANK AWAITS THE KING!

Who is this Bango Skank? Mia asked.

I have no idea.

I think . . . It was hard, but Mia forced herself. *I think I owe you a word of thanks.*

Susannah's response was cold and immediate. *Thank me with the truth.*

First tell me why you'd help me at all, after I . . .

This time Mia couldn't finish. She liked to think of herself as brave—as brave as she had to be in the service of her chap, at least—but this time she couldn't finish.

After you betrayed the man I love to men who are, when you get right down to it, footsoldiers of the Crimson King? After you decided it would be all right for them to kill mine so long as you could keep yours? Is that what you want to know?

Mia hated to hear it spoken of that way, but bore it. *Had* to bear it.

Yes, lady, if you like.

It was the other one who replied this time, in that voice—harsh, cawing, laughing, triumphant, and hateful—that was even worse than the shrill laughter of the birdy-women. Worse by far.

Because mah boys got away, dass why! Fucked those honkies mos' righteous! The ones dey didn't shoot all blowed to smithereens!

Mia felt a deep stirring of unease. Whether it was true or not, the bad laughing woman clearly *believed* it was true. And if Roland and Eddie Dean were still out there, wasn't it possible the Crimson King wasn't as strong, as all-powerful, as she had been told? Wasn't it even possible that she *had* been misled about—

Stop it, stop it, you can't think that way!

There's another reason I helped. The harsh one was gone and the other was back. At least for now.

What?

It's my baby, too, Susannah said. *I don't want it killed.*

I don't believe you.

But she did. Because the woman inside was right: Mordred Deschain of Gilead and Discordia belonged to both of them. The bad one might not care, but the other, Susannah, clearly felt the chap's tidal pull. And if she was right about Sayre and whoever waited for her at the Dixie Pig . . . if they were liars and cozeners . . .

Stop it. Stop. I have nowhere else to go but to them.

You do, Susannah said quickly. *With Black Thirteen you can go anywhere.*

You don't understand. He'd follow me. Follow it.

You're right, I don't *understand.* She actually did, or *thought* she did, but . . . *Burn up the day,* he'd said.

All right, I'll try to explain. I don't understand everything myself—there are things I don't know—but I'll tell you what I can.

Thank y—

Before she could finish, Susannah was falling again, like Alice down the rabbit-hole. Through the toilet, through the floor, through the pipes beneath the floor, and into another world.

NINE

No castle at the end of her drop, not this time. Roland had told them a few stories of his wandering years—the vampire nurses and little doctors of Eluria, the walking waters of East Downe, and, of course, the story of his doomed first love—and this was a little like falling into one of those tales. Or, perhaps, into one of the oat-operas ("adult Westerns," as they were called) on the still relatively new ABC-TV network: *Sugarfoot,* with Ty Hardin, *Maverick,* with James Garner, or—Odetta Holmes's personal favorite—*Cheyenne,* starring Clint Walker. (Odetta had once written a letter to ABC programming, suggesting they could simultaneously break new ground and open up a whole new audience if they did a series about a wandering Negro cowboy in the years after the Civil War. She never got an answer. She supposed writing the letter in the first place had been ridiculous, a waste of time.)

There was a livery stable with a sign out front

reading **TACK MENDED CHEAP**. The sign over the hotel promised **QUIET ROOMS, GUD BEDS**. There were at least five saloons. Outside one of them, a rusty robot that ran on squalling treads turned its bulb head back and forth, blaring a come-on to the empty town from the horn-shaped speaker in the center of its rudimentary face: "Girls, girls, *girls!* Some are humie and some are cybie, but who cares, you can't tell the difference, they do what you want without complaint, won't is not in their vo-CAB-u-lary, they give satisfaction with every action! Girls, girls, girls! Some are cybie, some are real, you can't tell the difference when you cop a feel! They do what you want! They want what *you* want!"

Walking beside Susannah was the beautiful young white woman with the swollen belly, scratched legs, and shoulder-length black hair. Now, as they walked below the gaudy false front of **THE FEDIC GOOD-TIME SALOON, BAR, AND DANCE EMPORIUM,** she was wearing a faded plaid dress which advertised her advanced state of pregnancy in a way that made it seem freakish, almost a sign of the apocalypse. The *huaraches* of the castle allure had been replaced by scuffed and battered shor'boots. Both of them were wearing shor'boots, and the heels clumped hollowly on the boardwalk.

From one of the deserted barrooms farther along came the herky-jerky jazz of a jagtime tune, and a snatch of some old poem came to Susannah: *A bunch of the boys were whooping it up in the Malamute Saloon!*

She looked over the batwing doors and was not

in the least surprised to see the words SERVICE'S
MALAMUTE SALOON.

She slowed long enough to peer over the
batwing doors and saw a chrome piano playing
itself, dusty keys popping up and down, just a
mechanical music-box no doubt built by the ever-
popular North Central Positronics, entertaining a
room that was empty except for a dead robot and,
in the far corner, two skeletons working through
the process of final decomposition, the one that
would take them from bone to dust.

Farther along, at the end of the town's single
street, loomed the castle wall. It was so high and so
wide it blotted out most of the sky.

Susannah abruptly knocked her fist against the
side of her head. Then she held her hands out in
front of her and snapped her fingers.

"What are you doing?" Mia asked. "Tell me, I
beg."

"Making sure I'm here. Physically here."

"You are."

"So it seems. But how can that be?"

Mia shook her head, indicating that she didn't
know. On this, at least, Susannah was inclined to
believe her. There was no dissenting word from
Detta, either.

"This isn't what I expected," Susannah said,
looking around. "It's not what I expected at all."

"Nay?" asked her companion (and without
much interest). Mia was moving in that awkward
but strangely endearing duck-footed waddle that
seems to best suit women in the last stages of their
carry. "And what was it ye did expect, Susannah?"

"Something more medieval, I guess. More like that." She pointed at the castle.

Mia shrugged as if to say take it or leave it, and then said, "Is the other one with you? The nasty one?"

Detta, she meant. Of course. "She's always with me. She's a part of me just as your chap is a part of you." Although how Mia could be pregnant when it had been Susannah who caught the fuck was something Susannah was still dying to know.

"I'll soon be delivered of mine," Mia said. "Will ya never be delivered of yours?"

"I thought I was," Susannah said truthfully. "She came back. Mostly, I think, to deal with you."

"I hate her."

"I know." And Susannah knew more. Mia feared Detta, as well. Feared her big-big.

"If she speaks, our palaver ends."

Susannah shrugged. "She comes when she comes and speaks when she speaks. She doesn't ask my permission."

Ahead of them on this side of the street was an arch with a sign above it:

FEDIC STATION
MONO PATRICIA DISCONTINUED
THUMBPRINT READER INOPERATIVE
SHOW TICKET
NORTH CENTRAL POSITRONICS THANKS YOU FOR YOUR PATIENCE

The sign didn't interest Susannah as much as the two things that lay on the filthy station platform beyond it: a child's doll, decayed to little more than a head and one floppy arm, and, beyond it, a grinning mask. Although the mask appeared to be made of steel, a good deal of it seemed to have rotted like flesh. The teeth poking out of the grin were canine fangs. The eyes were glass. Lenses, Susannah felt sure, no doubt also crafted by North Central Positronics. Surrounding the mask were a few shreds and tatters of green cloth, what had undoubtedly once been this thing's hood. Susannah had no trouble putting together the remains of the doll and the remains of the Wolf; her mamma, as Detta sometimes liked to tell folks (especially horny boys in roadhouse parking lots), didn't raise no fools.

"This is where they brought them," she said. "Where the Wolves brought the twins they stole from Calla Bryn Sturgis. Where they—what?—operated on them."

"Not just from Calla Bryn Sturgis," Mia said indifferently, "but aye. And once the babbies were here, they were taken there. A place you'll also recognize, I've no doubt."

She pointed across Fedic's single street and farther up. The last building before the castle wall abruptly ended the town was a long Quonset hut with sides of filthy corrugated metal and a rusty curved roof. The windows running along the side Susannah could see had been boarded up. Also along that side was a steel hitching rail. To it were tied what looked like seventy horses, all of them gray. Some had fallen over and lay with their legs sticking straight out. One or two had turned their heads toward the women's voices and then seemed to freeze in that position. It was very un-horselike behavior, but of course these weren't real horses. They were robots, or cyborgs, or whichever one of Roland's terms you might like to use. Many of them seemed to have run down or worn out.

In front of this building was a sign on a rusting steel plate. It read:

NORTH CENTRAL POSITRONICS, LTD.
Fedic Headquarters
Arc 16 Experimental Station

Maximum Security
VERBAL ENTRY CODE REQUIRED
EYEPRINT REQUIRED

"It's another Dogan, isn't it?" Susannah asked.

"Well, yes and no," Mia said. "It's the Dogan of all Dogans, actually."

"Where the Wolves brought the children."

"Aye, and will bring them again," Mia said. "For the King's work will go forward after this disturbance raised by your friend the gunslinger is past. I have no doubt of it."

Susannah looked at her with real curiosity. "How can you speak so cruel and yet be so serene?" she asked. "They bring children here and scoop out their heads like . . . like gourds. Children, who've harmed nobody! What they send back are great galumphing idiots who grow to their full size in agony and often die in much the same way. Would you be so sanguine, Mia, if *your* child was borne away across one of those saddles, shrieking for you and holding out his arms?"

Mia flushed, but was able to meet Susannah's gaze. "Each must follow the road upon which ka has set her feet, Susannah of New York. Mine is to bear my chap, and raise him, and thus end your dinn's quest. And his life."

"It's wonderful how everyone seems to think they know just what ka means for them," Susannah said. "Don't you think that's wonderful?"

"I think you're trying to make jest of me because you fear," Mia said levelly. "If such makes you feel better, than aye, have on." She spread her arms and made a little sarcastic bow over her great belly.

They had stopped on the boardwalk in front of a shop advertising **MILLINERY & LADIES' WEAR** and across from the Fedic Dogan. Susannah thought: *Burn up the day, don't forget that's the other part of your job here. Kill time. Keep the oddity of a body we now seem to share in that women's restroom just as long as you possibly can.*

"I'm not making fun," Susannah said. "I'm only asking you to put yourself in the place of all those other mothers."

Mia shook her head angrily, her inky hair flying around her ears and brushing at her shoulders. "I did not make their fate, lady, nor did they make mine. I'll save my tears, thank you. Would you hear my tale or not?"

"Yes, please."

"Then let us sit, for my legs are sorely tired."

TEN

In the Gin-Puppie Saloon, a few rickety storefronts back in the direction from which they'd come, they found chairs which would still bear their weight, but neither woman had any taste for the saloon itself, which smelled of dusty death. They dragged the chairs out to the boardwalk, where Mia sat with an audible sigh of relief.

"Soon," she said. "Soon you shall be delivered, Susannah of New York, and so shall I."

"Maybe, but I don't understand any of this. Least of all why you're rushing to this guy Sayre when you must know he serves the Crimson King."

"Hush!" Mia said. She sat with her legs apart and her huge belly rising before her, looking out across the empty street. "'Twas a man of the King who gave me a chance to fulfill the only destiny ka ever left me. Not Sayre but one much greater than he. Someone to whom Sayre answers. A man named Walter."

Susannah started at the name of Roland's ancient nemesis. Mia looked at her, gave her a grim smile.

"You know the name, I see. Well, maybe that'll save some talk. Gods know there's been far too much talk for my taste, already; it's not what I was made for. I was made to bear my chap and raise him, no more than that. And no less."

Susannah offered no reply. Killing was supposedly her trade, killing time her current chore, but in truth she had begun to find Mia's single-mindedness a trifle tiresome. Not to mention frightening.

As if picking this thought up, Mia said: "I am what I am and I am content wi' it. If others are not, what's that to me? Spit on em!"

Spoken like Detta Walker at her feistiest, Susannah thought, but made no reply. It seemed safer to remain quiet.

After a pause, Mia went on. "Yet I'd be lying if I didn't say that being here brings back . . . certain memories. Yar!" And, unexpectedly, she laughed. Just as unexpectedly, the sound was beautiful and melodic.

"Tell your tale," Susannah said. "This time tell me all of it. We have time before the labor starts again."

"Do you say so?"

"I do. Tell me."

For a few moments Mia just looked out at the street with its dusty cover of oggan and its air of sad and ancient abandonment. As Susannah waited for story-time to commence, she for the first time became aware of the still, shadeless quality to Fedic. She could see everything very well, and there was no moon in the sky as on the castle allure, but she still hesitated to call this daytime.

It's no *time,* a voice inside her whispered—she knew not whose. *This is a place between, Susannah; a place where shadows are cancelled and time holds its breath.*

Then Mia told her tale. It was shorter than Susannah had expected (shorter than she wanted, given Eddie's abjuration to burn up the day), but it explained a great deal. More, actually, than Susannah had hoped for. She listened with growing rage, and why not? She had been more than raped that day in the ring of stones and bones, it seemed. She had been robbed, as well—the strangest robbery to which any woman had ever been subject.

And it was still going on.

ELEVEN

"Look out there, may it do ya fine," said the big-bellied woman sitting beside Susannah on the boardwalk. "Look out and see Mia before she gained her name."

Susannah looked into the street. At first she saw nothing but a cast-off waggon-wheel, a splintered (and long-dry) watering trough, and a starry silver thing that looked like the lost rowel from some cowpoke's spur.

Then, slowly, a misty figure formed. It was that of a nude woman. Her beauty was blinding—even before she had come fully into view, Susannah knew that. Her age was any. Her black hair brushed her shoulders. Her belly was flat, her navel a cunning cup into which any man who ever loved women would be happy to dip his tongue. Susannah (or perhaps it was Detta) thought, *Hell, I could dip my own.* Hidden between the ghost-woman's thighs was a cunning cleft. Here was a different tidal pull.

"That's me when I came here," said the pregnant version sitting beside Susannah. She spoke almost like a woman who is showing slides of her vacation. *That's me at the Grand Canyon, that's me in Seattle, that's me at Grand Coulee Dam; that's me on the Fedic high street, do it please ya.* The pregnant woman was also beautiful, but not in the same eerie way as the shade in the street. The pregnant woman looked a certain age, for instance— late twenties—and her face had been marked by experience. Much of it painful.

"I said I was an elemental—the one who made love to your dinh—but that was a lie. As I think you suspected. I lied not out of hope of gain, but only . . . I don't know . . . from a kind of wishfulness, I suppose. I wanted the baby to be mine that way, too—"

"Yours from the start."

"Aye, from the start—you say true." They watched the nude woman walk up the street, arms swinging, muscles of her long back flexing, hips swaying from side to side in that eternal breathless clock of motion. She left no tracks on the oggan.

"I told you that the creatures of the invisible world were left behind when the *Prim* receded. Most died, as fishes and sea-animals will when cast up on a beach and left to strangle in the alien air. But there are always some who adapt, and I was one of those unfortunates. I wandered far and wide, and whenever I found men in the wastes, I took on the form you see."

Like a model on a runway (one who has forgotten to actually put on the latest Paris fashion she's supposed to be displaying), the woman in the street pivoted on the balls of her feet, buttocks tensing with lovely silken ease, creating momentary crescent-shaped hollows. She began to walk back, the eyes just below the straight cut of her bangs fixed on some distant horizon, her hair swinging beside ears that were without other ornament.

"When I found someone with a prick, I fucked him," Mia said. "That much I had in common with the demon elemental who first tried to have congress with your soh and then did have congress with your dinh, and that also accounts for my lie, I suppose. And I found your dinh passing fair." The tiniest bit of greed roughened her voice as she said this. The Detta in Susannah found it sexy. The Detta in Susannah bared her lips in a grin of gruesome understanding.

"I fucked them, and if they couldn't break free I fucked them to death." Matter-of-fact. *After the Grand Coulee, we went to Yosemite.* "Would you tell your dinh something for me, Susannah? If you see him again?"

"Aye, if you like."

"Once he knew a man—a bad man—named Amos Depape, brother of the Roy Depape who ran with Eldred Jonas in Mejis. Your dinh believes Amos Depape was stung to death by a snake, and in a way he was . . . but the snake was me."

Susannah said nothing.

"I didn't fuck them for sex, I didn't fuck them to kill them, although I didn't care when they died and their pricks finally wilted out of me like melting icicles. In truth I didn't know *why* I was fucking them, until I came here, to Fedic. In those early days there were still men and women here; the Red Death hadn't come, do ye ken. The crack in the earth beyond town was there, but the bridge over it still stood strong and true. Those folk were stubborn, trying not to let go, even when the rumors that Castle Discordia was haunted began. The trains still came, although on no regular schedule—"

"The children?" Susannah asked. "The twins?" She paused. "The Wolves?"

"Nay, all of that was two dozen centuries later. Or more. But hear me now: there was one couple in Fedic who had a *baby*. You've no idea, Susannah of New York, how rare and wonderful that was in those days when most folk were as sterile as the elementals themselves, and those who weren't more often than not produced either slow mutants or monsters so terrible they were killed by their parents if they took more than a single breath. Most of them didn't. But *this* baby!"

She clasped her hands. Her eyes shone.

"It was round and pink and unblemished by so much as a portwine stain—perfect—and I knew after a single look what I'd been made for. I wasn't fucking for the sex of it, or because in coitus I was almost mortal, or because it brought death to most of my partners, but to have a baby like theirs. Like their Michael."

She lowered her head slightly and said, "I would have taken him, you know. Would have gone to the man, fucked him until he was crazy, then whispered in his ear that he should kill his molly. And when she'd gone to the clearing at the end of the path, I would have fucked him dead and the baby—that beautiful little pink baby—would have been mine. D'you see?"

"Yes," Susannah said. She felt faintly sick. In front of them, in the middle of the street, the ghostly woman made yet another turn and started back again. Farther down, the huckster-robot honked out his seemingly eternal spiel: *Girls, girls, girls! Some are humie and some are cybie, but who cares, you can't tell the difference!*

"I discovered I couldn't go near them," Mia said. "It was as though a magic circle had been drawn around them. It was the baby, I suppose.

"Then came the plague. The Red Death. Some folks said something had been opened in the castle, some jar of demonstuff that should have been left shut forever. Others said the plague came out of the crack—what they called the Devil's Arse. Either way, it was the end of life in Fedic, life on the edge of Discordia. Many left on foot or in waggons. Baby Michael and his parents stayed, hoping for a train. Each day I waited for them to sicken—for the red spots to show on the baby's dear cheeks and fat little arms—but they never did; none of the three sickened. Perhaps they *were* in a magic circle. I think they must have been. And a train came. It was Patricia. The mono. Do ya ken—"

"Yes," Susannah said. She knew all she wanted to about Blaine's companion mono. Once upon a time her route must have taken her over here as well as to Lud.

"Aye. They got on. I watched from the station platform, weeping my unseen tears and wailing my unseen cries. They got on with their sweet wee one . . . only by then he was three or four years old, walking and talking. And they went. I tried to follow them, and Susannah, I could not. I was a prisoner here. Knowing my purpose was what made me so."

Susannah wondered about that, but decided not to comment.

"Years and decades and centuries went by. In Fedic there were by then only the robots and the unburied bodies left over from the Red Death, turning to skeletons, then to dust.

"Then men came again, but I didn't dare go near them because they were *his* men." She paused. "*Its* men."

"The Crimson King's."

"Aye, they with the endlessly bleeding holes on their foreheads. They went there." She pointed to the Fedic Dogan—the Arc 16 Experimental Station. "And soon their accursed machines were running again, just as if they still believed that machines could hold up the world. Not, ye ken, that holding it up is what they want to do! No, no, not they! They brought in beds—"

"Beds!" Susannah said, startled. Beyond them, the ghostly woman in the street rose once more on the balls of her feet and made yet one more graceful pirouette.

"Aye, for the children, although this was still long years before the Wolves began to bring em here, and long before you were part of your dinh's story. Yet that time did draw nigh, and Walter came to me."

"Can you make that woman in the street disappear?" Susannah asked abruptly (and rather crossly). "I know she's a version of you, I get the idea, but she makes me . . . I don't know . . . nervous. Can you make her go away?"

"Aye, if you like." Mia pursed her lips and blew. The disturbingly beautiful woman—the spirit without a name—disappeared like smoke.

For several moments Mia was quiet, once more gathering the threads of her story. Then she said, "Walter . . . saw me. Not like other men. Even the ones I fucked to death only saw what they wanted to see. Or what *I* wanted them to see." She smiled in unpleasant reminiscence. "I made some of them die thinking they were fucking their own mothers! You should have seen their faces!" Then the smile faded. "But Walter *saw* me."

"What did he look like?"

"Hard to tell, Susannah. He wore a hood, and inside it he grinned—such a grinning man he was— and he palavered with me. There." She pointed toward the Fedic Good-Time Saloon with a finger that trembled slightly.

"No mark on his forehead, though?"

"Nay, I'm sure not, for he's not one of what Pere Callahan calls the low men. Their job is the Breakers. The Breakers and no more."

Susannah began to feel the anger then, although she tried not to show it. Mia had access to all her memories, which meant all the inmost workings and secrets of their ka-tet. It was like discovering you'd had a burglar in the house who had tried on your underwear as well as stealing your money and going through your most personal papers.

It was awful.

"Walter is, I suppose, what you'd call the

Crimson King's Prime Minister. He often travels in disguise, and is known in other worlds under other names, but always he is a grinning, laughing man—"

"I met him briefly," Susannah said, "under the name of Flagg. I hope to meet him again."

"If you truly knew him, you'd wish for no such thing."

"The Breakers you spoke of—where are they?"

"Why . . . Thunderclap, do'ee not know? The shadowlands. Why do you ask?"

"No reason but curiosity," Susannah said, and seemed to hear Eddie: *Ask any question she'll answer. Burn up the day. Give us a chance to catch up.* She hoped Mia couldn't read her thoughts when they were separated like this. If she could, they were all likely up shit creek without a paddle. "Let's go back to Walter. Can we speak of him a bit?"

Mia signaled a weary acceptance that Susannah didn't quite believe. How long had it been since Mia had had an ear for any tale she might care to tell? The answer, Susannah guessed, was probably never. And the questions Susannah was asking, the doubts she was articulating . . . surely some of them must have passed through Mia's own head. They'd be banished quickly as the blasphemies they were, but still, come on, this was not a stupid woman. Unless obsession *made* you stupid. Susannah supposed a case could be made for that idea.

"Susannah? Bumbler got your tongue?"

"No, I was just thinking what a relief it must have been when he came to you."

Mia considered that, then smiled. Smiling changed her, made her look girlish and artless and shy. Susannah had to remind herself that wasn't a look she could trust. "Yes! It was! Of course it was!"

"After discovering your purpose and being trapped here by it . . . after seeing the Wolves getting ready to store the kids and then operate on them . . . after all that, Walter comes. The devil, in fact, but at least he can see you. At least he can hear your sad tale. And he makes you an offer."

"He said the Crimson King would give me a child," Mia said, and put her hands gently against the great globe of her belly. "My Mordred, whose time has come round at last."

TWELVE

Mia pointed again at the Arc 16 Experimental Station. What she had called the Dogan of Dogans. The last remnant of her smile lingered on her lips, but there was no happiness or real amusement in it now. Her eyes were shiny with fear and—perhaps—awe.

"That's where they changed me, made me mortal. Once there were many such places—there must have been—but I'd set my watch and warrant that's the only one left in all of In-World, Mid-World, or End-World. It's a place both wonderful and terrible. And it was there I was taken."

"I don't understand what you mean." Susannah was thinking of her Dogan. Which was, of course, based on *Jake's* Dogan. It was certainly a strange place, with its flashing lights and multiple TV screens, but not frightening.

"Beneath it are passages which go under the castle," Mia said. "At the end of one is a door that opens on the Calla side of Thunderclap, just under the last edge of the darkness. That's the one the Wolves use when they go on their raids."

Susannah nodded. That explained a lot. "Do they take the kiddies back the same way?"

"Nay, lady, do it please you; like many doors, the one that takes the Wolves from Fedic to the Calla side of Thunderclap goes in only one direction. When you're on the other side, it's no longer there."

"Because it's not a *magic* door, right?"

Mia smiled and nodded and patted her knee.

Susannah looked at her with mounting excitement. "It's another twin-thing."

"Do you say so?"

"Yes. Only this time Tweedledum and Tweedledee are science and magic. Rational and irrational. Sane and insane. No matter what terms you pick, that's a double-damned pair if ever there was one."

"Aye? Do you say so?"

"Yes! *Magic* doors—like the one Eddie found and you took me through to New York—go both ways. The doors North Central Positronics made to replace them when the *Prim* receded and the magic faded . . . they go only one way. Have I got that right?"

"I think so, aye."

"Maybe they didn't have time to figure out how to make teleportation a two-lane highway before the world moved on. In any case, the Wolves go to the Calla side of Thunderclap by door and come back to Fedic by train. Right?"

Mia nodded.

Susannah no longer thought she was just trying to kill time. This information might come in handy later on. "And after the King's men, Pere's low men, have scooped the kids' brains, what then? Back through the door with them, I suppose—the one under the castle. Back to the Wolves' staging point. And a train takes them the rest of the way home."

"Aye."

"Why do they bother takin em back at all?"

"Lady, I know not." Then Mia's voice dropped. "There's another door under Castle Discordia. Another door in the rooms of ruin. One that goes . . ." She licked her lips. "That goes todash."

"Todash? . . . I know the word, but I don't understand what's so bad—"

"There are endless worlds, your dinh is correct about that, but even when those worlds are close together—like some of the multiple New Yorks— there are endless spaces between. Think ya of the spaces between the inner and outer walls of a house. Places where it's always dark. But just because a place is always dark doesn't mean it's empty. Does it, Susannah?"

There are monsters in the todash darkness.

Who had said that? Roland? She couldn't remember for sure, and what did it matter? She thought she understood what Mia was saying, and if so, it was horrible.

"Rats in the walls, Susannah. *Bats* in the walls. All sorts of sucking, biting bugs in the walls."

"Stop it, I get the picture."

"That door beneath the castle—one of their mistakes, I have no doubt—goes to *nowhere at all*. Into the darkness between worlds. Todash-space. But not empty space." Her voice lowered further. "That door is reserved for the Red King's most bitter enemies. They're thrown into a darkness where they may exist—blind, wandering, insane—for years. But in the end, something always finds them and devours them. Monsters beyond the ability of such minds as ours to bear thought of."

Susannah found herself trying to picture such a door, and what waited behind it. She didn't want to but couldn't help it. Her mouth dried up.

In that same low and somehow horrible tone of confidentiality, Mia said, "There were many places where the old people tried to join magic and science together, but yon may be the only one left." She nodded toward the Dogan. "It was there that Walter took me, to make me mortal and take me out of *Prim*'s way forever.

"To make me like you."

THIRTEEN

Mia didn't know everything, but so far as Susannah could make out, Walter/Flagg had offered the spirit later to be known as Mia the ultimate Faustian bargain. If she was willing to give up her nearly eternal but discorporate state and become a mortal woman, then she could become pregnant and bear a child. Walter was honest with her about how little she would actually be getting for all she'd be giving up.

The baby wouldn't grow as normal babies did—as Baby Michael had done before Mia's unseen but worshipful eyes—and she might only have him for seven years, but oh what wonderful years they could be!

Beyond this, Walter had been tactfully silent, allowing Mia to form her own pictures: how she would nurse her baby and wash him, not neglecting the tender creases behind the knees and ears; how she would kiss him in the honeyspot between the unfledged wings of his shoulderblades; how she would walk with him, holding both of his hands in both of hers as he toddled; how she would read to him and point out Old Star and Old Mother in the sky and tell him the story of how Rustie Sam stole the widow's best loaf of bread; how she would hug him to her and bathe his cheek with her grateful tears when he spoke his first word, which would, of course, be *Mama*.

Susannah listened to this rapturous account with a mixture of pity and cynicism. Certainly Walter had done one hell of a job selling the idea to her, and as ever, the best way to do that was to let the mark sell herself. He'd even proposed a properly Satanic period of proprietorship: seven years. *Just sign on the dotted line, madam, and please don't mind that whiff of brimstone; I just can't seem to get the smell out of my clothes.*

Susannah understood the deal and still had trouble swallowing it. This creature had given up immortality for morning sickness, swollen and achy breasts, and, in the last six weeks of her carry, the need to pee approximately every fifteen minutes. And wait, folks, there's more! Two and a half years of changing diapers soaked with piss and loaded with shit! Of getting up in the night as the kid howls with the pain of cutting his first tooth (and cheer up, Mom, only thirty-one to go). That first magic spit-up! That first heartwarming spray of urine across the bridge of your nose when the kid lets go as you're changing his clout!

And yes, there would be magic. Even though she'd never had a child herself, Susannah knew there would be magic even in the dirty diapers and the colic if the child were the result of a loving union. But to have the child and then have him taken away from you just when it was getting good, just as the child approached what most people agreed was the age of reason, responsibility, and accountability? To then be swept over the Crimson King's red horizon? That was an awful idea. And was Mia so besotted by her impending motherhood that she didn't realize the little she *had* been promised was now being whittled away? Walter/Flagg had come to her in Fedic, Scenic Aftermath of the Red Death, and promised her seven years with her son. On the telephone in the Plaza–Park, however, Richard Sayre had spoken of a mere five.

In any case, Mia had agreed to the dark man's terms. And really, how much sport could there have been in getting her to do that? She'd been made for motherhood, had arisen from the *Prim* with that imperative, had known it herself ever since seeing her first perfect human baby, the boy Michael. How could she have said no? Even if the offer had only been for three years, or for one, how? Might as well expect a long-time junkie to refuse a loaded spike when it was offered.

Mia had been taken into the Arc 16 Experimental Station. She'd been given a tour by the smiling, sarcastic (and undoubtedly frightening) Walter, who sometimes called himself Walter of End-World and sometimes Walter of All-World. She'd seen the great room filled with beds, awaiting the children who would come to fill them; at the head of each was a stainless-steel hood attached to a segmented steel hose. She did not like to think what the purpose of such equipment might be. She'd also been shown some of the passages under the Castle on the Abyss, and had been in places where the smell of death was strong and suffocating. She—there had been a red darkness and she—

"Were you mortal by then?" Susannah asked. "It sounds as though maybe you were."

"I was on my way," she said. "It was a process Walter called *becoming*."

"All right. Go on."

But here Mia's recollections were lost in a dark fugue—not todash, but far from pleasant. A kind of amnesia, and it was *red*. A color Susannah had come to distrust. Had the pregnant woman's transition from the world of the spirit to the world of the flesh—her trip to Mia—been accomplished through some other kind of doorway? She herself didn't seem to know. Only that there had been a time of darkness—unconsciousness, she supposed—and then she had awakened " . . . as you see me. Only not yet pregnant, of course."

According to Walter, Mia could not actually make

a baby, even as a mortal woman. Carry, yes. Conceive, no. So it came to pass that one of the demon elementals had done a great service for the Crimson King, taking Roland's seed as female and passing it on to Susannah as male. And there had been another reason, as well. Walter hadn't mentioned it, but Mia had known.

"It's the prophecy," she said, looking into Fedic's deserted and shadowless street. Across the way, a robot that looked like Andy of the Calla stood silent and rusting in front of the Fedic Café, which promised GOOD MEELS CHEEP.

"What prophecy?" Susannah asked.

" 'He who ends the line of Eld shall conceive a child of incest with his sister or his daughter, and the child will be marked, by his red heel shall you know him. It is he who shall stop the breath of the last warrior.' "

"Woman, *I'm* not Roland's sister, or his daughter, either! You maybe didn't notice a small but basic difference in the color of our hides, namely his being *white* and mine being *black*." But she thought she had a pretty good idea of what the prophecy meant, just the same. Families were made in many ways. Blood was only one of them.

"Did he not tell you what dinh means?" Mia asked.

"Of course. It means leader. If he was in charge of a whole country instead of just three scruffy-ass gunpuppies, it'd mean king."

"Leader and king, you say true. Now, Susannah, will you tell me that such words aren't just poor substitutes for another?"

Susannah made no reply.

Mia nodded as though she had, then winced when a fresh contraction struck. It passed, and she went on. "The sperm was Roland's. I believe it may have been preserved somehow by the old people's science while the demon elemental turned itself inside out and made man from woman, but that isn't the important part. The important part is that it lived and found the rest of itself, as ordained by ka."

"My egg."

"Your egg."

"When I was raped in the ring of stones."

"Say true."

Susannah sat, musing. Finally she looked up. "Seem to me that it's what I said before. You didn't like it then, not apt to like it now, but—girl, you just the baby-sitter."

There was no rage this time. Mia only smiled. "Who went on having her periods, even when she was being sick in the mornings? You did. And who's got the full belly today? *I* do. If there was a baby-sitter, Susannah of New York, it was you."

"How can that be? Do you know?"

Mia did.

FOURTEEN

The baby, Walter had told her, would be *transmitted* to Mia; sent to her cell by cell just as a fax is sent line by line.

Susannah opened her mouth to say she didn't know what a fax was, then closed it again. She understood the *gist* of what Mia was saying, and that was enough to fill her with a terrible combination of awe and rage. She *had* been pregnant. She was, in a real sense, pregnant right this minute. But the baby was being

(*faxed*)

sent to Mia. Was this a process that had started fast and slowed down, or started slow and speeded up? The latter, she thought, because as time passed she'd felt less pregnant instead of more. The little swelling in her belly had mostly flattened out again. And now she understood how both she and Mia could feel an equal attachment to the chap: it did, in fact, belong to both of them. Had been passed on like a . . . a blood transfusion.

Only when they want to take your blood and put it into someone else, they ask your permission. If they're doctors, that is, and not one of Pere Callahan's vampires. You're a lot closer to one of those, Mia, aren't you?

"Science or magic?" Susannah asked. "Which one was it that allowed you to steal my baby?"

Mia flushed a little at that, but when she turned to Susannah, she was able to meet Susannah's eyes squarely. "I don't know," she said. "Likely a mixture of both. And don't be so self-righteous! It's in *me*, not you. It's feeding off my bones and my blood, not yours."

"So what? Do you think that changes anything? You stole it, with the help of some filthy magician."

Mia shook her head vehemently, her hair a storm around her face.

"No?" Susannah asked. "Then how come *you*

weren't the one eating frogs out of the swamp and shoats out of the pen and God knows what other nasty things? How come you needed all that make-believe nonsense about the banquets in the castle, where you could pretend to be the one eating? In short, sugarpie, how come your chap's nourishment had to go down *my* throat?"

"Because . . . because . . ." Mia's eyes, Susannah saw, were filling with tears. "Because this is spoiled land! Blasted land! The place of the Red Death and the edge of the Discordia! I'd not feed my chap from here!"

It was a good answer, Susannah reckoned, but not the *complete* answer. And Mia knew it, too. Because Baby Michael, perfect Baby Michael, had been conceived here, had thrived here, had been thriving when Mia last saw him. And if she was so sure, why were those tears standing in her eyes?

"Mia, they're lying to you about your chap."

"You don't know that, so don't be hateful!"

"I *do* know it." And she did. But there wasn't proof, gods damn it! How did you prove a feeling, even one as strong as this?

"Flagg—Walter, if you like that better—he promised you seven years. Sayre says you can have five. What if they hand you a card, GOOD FOR THREE YEARS OF CHILD-REARING WITH STAMP, when you get to this Dixie Pig? Gonna go with that, too?"

"That won't happen! You're as nasty as the other one! Shut up!"

"You got a nerve calling *me* nasty! Can't wait to give birth to a child supposed to murder his Daddy."

"I don't care!"

"You're all confused, girl, between what you want to happen and what *will* happen. How do you know they aren't gonna kill him before he can cry out his first breath, and grind him up and feed him to these Breaker bastards?"

"*Shut . . . up!*"

"Kind of a super-food? Finish the job all at once?"

"Shut *up,* I said, *shut UP!*"

"Point is, you don't know. You don't know anything. You just the baby-sitter, just the au pair. You know they lie, you know they trick and never treat, and yet you go on. And you want *me* to shut up."

"Yes! *Yes!*"

"I won't," Susannah told her grimly, and seized Mia's shoulders. They were amazingly bony under the dress, but hot, as if the woman were running a fever. "I won't because it's really mine and you know it. Cat can have kittens in the oven, girl, but that won't ever make em muffins."

All right, they had made it back to all-out fury after all. Mia's face twisted into something both horrible and unhappy. In Mia's eyes, Susannah thought she could see the endless, craving, grieving creature this woman once had been. And something else. A spark that might be blown into belief. If there was time.

"I'll *shut* you up," Mia said, and suddenly Fedic's main street tore open, just as the allure had. Behind it was a kind of bulging darkness. But not empty. Oh no, not empty, Susannah felt that very clearly.

They fell toward it. Mia *propelled* them toward it. Susannah tried to hold them back with no success at all. As they tumbled into the dark, she heard a singsong thought running through her head, running in an endless worry-circle: *Oh Susannah-Mio, divided girl of mine, Done parked her RIG*

FIFTEEN

in the DIXIE PIG, In the year of—

Before this annoying (but ever so important) jingle could finish its latest circuit through Susannah-Mio's head, the head in question struck something, and hard enough to send a galaxy of bright stars exploding across her field of vision. When they cleared, she saw, very large, in front of her eyes:

NK AWA

She pulled back and saw BANGO SKANK AWAITS THE KING! It was the graffito written on the inside of the toilet stall's door. Her life was haunted by doors—had been, it seemed, ever since the door of her cell had clanged closed behind her in Oxford, Mississippi—but this one was shut. Good. She was coming to believe that shut doors presented fewer problems. Soon enough this one would open and the problems would start again.

Mia: *I told you all I know. Now are you going to help me get to the Dixie Pig, or do I have to do it on my own? I can if I have to, especially with the turtle to help me.*

Susannah: *I'll help.*

Although how much or how little help Mia got from her sort of depended on what time it was right now. How long had they been in here? Her legs felt completely numb from the knees down—her butt, too—and she thought that was a good sign, but under these fluorescent lights, Susannah supposed it was always half-past anytime.

What does it matter to you? Mia asked, suspicious. *What does it matter to you what time it is?*

Susannah scrambled for an explanation.

The baby. You know that what I did will keep it from coming only for so long, don't you?

Of course I do. That's why I want to get moving.

All right. Let's see the cash our old pal Mats left us.

Mia took out the little wad of bills and looked at them uncomprehendingly.

Take the one that says Jackson.

I . . . Embarrassment. *I can't read.*

Let me come forward. I'll read it.

No!

All right, all right, calm down. It's the guy with the long white hair combed back kind of like Elvis.

I don't know this Elvis—

Never mind, it's that one right on top. Good. Now put the rest of the cash back in your pocket, nice and safe. Hold the twenty in the palm of your hand. Okay, we're blowing this pop-stand.

What's a pop-stand?

Mia, shut up.

SIXTEEN

When they re-entered the lobby—walking slowly, on legs that tingled with pins and needles—Susannah was marginally encouraged to see that it was dusk outside. She hadn't succeeded in burning up the entire day, it seemed, but she'd gotten rid of most of it.

The lobby was busy but no longer frantic. The beautiful Eurasian girl who'd checked her/them in was gone, her shift finished. Under the canopy, two new men in green monkeysuits were whistling up cabs for folks, many of whom were wearing tuxedos or long sparkly dresses.

Going out to parties, Susannah said. *Or maybe the theater.*

Susannah, I care not. Do we need to get one of the yellow vehicles from one of the men in the green suits?

No. We'll get a cab on the corner.

Do you say so?

Oh, quit with the suspicion. You're taking your kid to either its death or yours, I'm sure of that, but I recognize your intention to do well and I'll keep my promise. Yes, I do say so.

All right.

Without another word—certainly none of apology—Mia left the hotel, turned right, and began walking back toward Second Avenue, 2 Hammarskjöld Plaza, and the beautiful song of the rose.

SEVENTEEN

On the corner of Second and Forty-sixth, a metal waggon of faded red was parked at the curb. The curb was yellow at this point, and a man in a blue suit—a Guard o' the Watch, by his sidearm—seemed to be discussing that fact with a tall, white-bearded man.

Inside of her, Mia felt a flurry of startled movement.

Susannah? What is it?

That man!

The Guard o' the Watch? Him?

No, the one with the beard! He looks almost exactly like Henchick! Henchick of the Manni! Do you not see?

Mia neither saw nor cared. She gathered that although parking waggons along the yellow curb was forbidden, and the man with the beard seemed to understand this, he still would not move. He went on setting up easels and then putting pictures on them. Mia sensed this was an old argument between the two men.

"I'm gonna have to give you a ticket, Rev."

"Do what you need to do, Officer Benzyck. God loves you."

"Good. Delighted to hear it. As for the ticket, you'll tear it up. Right?"

"Render unto Caesar the things that are Caesar's; render unto God those things that are God's. So says the Bible, and blessed be the Lord's Holy Book."

"I can get behind that," said Benzyck o' the

Watch. He pulled a thick pad of paper from his back pocket and began to scribble on it. This also had the feel of an old ritual. "But let me tell you something, Harrigan—sooner or later City Hall is gonna catch up to your action, and they're gonna render unto your scofflaw holy-rollin' *ass*. I only hope I'm there when it happens."

He tore a sheet from his pad, went over to the metal waggon, and slipped the paper beneath a black window-slider resting on the waggon's glass front.

Susannah, amused: *He's gettin a ticket. Not the first one, either, from the sound.*

Mia, momentarily diverted in spite of herself: *What does it say on the side of his waggon, Susannah?*

There was a slight shift as Susanna *came* part-way *forward,* and the sense of a squint. It was a strange sensation for Mia, like having a tickle deep in her head.

Susannah, still sounding amused: *It says* CHURCH OF THE HOLY GOD-BOMB, *Rev. Earl Harrigan. It also says* YOUR CONTRIBUTIONS WILL BE REWARDED IN HEAVEN.

What's heaven?

Another name for the clearing at the end of the path.

Ah.

Benzyck o' the Watch was strolling away with his hands clasped behind his back, his considerable ass bunching beneath his blue uniform trousers, his duty done. The Rev. Harrigan, meanwhile, was adjusting his easels. The picture on one showed a man being let out of jail by a fellow in a white robe. The whiterobe's head was glowing. The picture on the other showed the whiterobe turning away from a monster with red skin and horns on his head. The monster with the horns looked pissed like a bear at sai Whiterobe.

Susannah, is that red thing how the folk of this world see the Crimson King?

Susannah: *I guess so. It's Satan, if you care— lord of the underworld. Have the god-guy get you a cab, why don't you? Use the turtle.*

Again, suspicious (Mia apparently couldn't help it): *Do you say so?*

Say true! Aye! Say Jesus Christ, woman!

All right, all right. Mia sounded a bit embarrassed. She walked toward Rev. Harrigan, pulling the scrimshaw turtle out of her pocket.

EIGHTEEN

What she needed to do came to Susannah in a flash. She withdrew from Mia (if the woman couldn't get a taxi with the help of that magic turtle, she was hopeless) and with her eyes squeezed shut visualized the Dogan. When she opened them, she was there. She grabbed the microphone she'd used to call Eddie and depressed the toggle.

"Harrigan!" she said into the mike. "Reverend Earl Harrigan! Are you there? Do you read me, sugar? *Do you read me?*"

NINETEEN

Rev. Harrigan paused in his labors long enough to watch a black woman—one fine-struttin honey, too, praise God—get into a cab. The cab drove off. He had a lot to do before beginning his nightly sermon—his little dance with Officer Benzyck was only the opening gun—but he stood there watching the cab's taillights twinkle and dwindle, just the same.

Had something just happened to him?

Had . . . ? Was it possible that . . . ?

Rev. Harrigan fell to his knees on the sidewalk, quite oblivious of the pedestrians passing by (just as most were oblivious of him). He clasped his big old praise-God hands and raised them to his chin. He knew the Bible said that praying was a private thing best done in one's closet, and he'd spent plenty of time getting kneebound in his own, yes Lord, but he also believed God wanted folks to see what a praying man looked like from time to time, because most of them—say *Gawd!*—had forgotten what that looked like. And there was no better, no *nicer* place to speak with God than right here on the corner of Second and Forty-sixth. There was a singing here, clean and sweet. It uplifted the spirit, clarified the mind . . . and, just incidentally, clarified the skin, as well. This wasn't the voice of God, and Rev. Harrigan was not so blasphemously stupid as to think it was, but he had an idea that it was angels. Yes, say *Gawd,* say *Gawd-bomb,* the voice of the ser-a-phim!

"God, did you just drop a little God-bomb on

me? I want to ask was that voice I just heard yours or mine own?"

No answer. So many times there was no answer. He would ponder this. In the meantime, he had a sermon to prepare for. A show to do, if you wanted to be perfectly vulgar about it.

Rev. Harrigan went to his van, parked at the yellow curb as always, and opened the back doors. Then he took out the pamphlets, the silk-covered collection plate which he'd put beside him on the sidewalk, and the sturdy wooden cube. The soapbox upon which he would stand, could you raise up high and shout hallelujah?

And yes, brother, while you were right at it, could you give amen?

STAVE: *Commala-come-ken*
It's the other one again.
You may know her name and face
But that don't make her your friend.

RESPONSE: *Commala-come-ten!*
She is not your friend!
If you let her get too close
She'll cut you up again.

T
H
E
W
R
I
T
E
R

11TH S T A N Z A

ONE

By the time they reached the little shopping center in the town of Bridgton—a supermarket, a laundry, and a surprisingly large drugstore—both Roland and Eddie sensed it: not just the singing, but the gathering power. It lifted them up like some crazy, wonderful elevator. Eddie found himself thinking of Tinkerbell's magic dust and Dumbo's magic feather. This was like drawing near the rose and yet not like that. There was no sense of holiness or sanctification in this little New England town, but *something* was going on here, and it was powerful.

Driving here from East Stoneham, following the signs to Bridgton from back road to back road, Eddie had sensed something else, as well: the unbelievable *crispness* of this world. The summer-green depths of the pine forests had a validity he had never encountered before, never even suspected. The birds which flew across the sky fair stopped his breath for wonder, even the most common sparrow. The very shadows on the ground seemed to have a velvety thickness, as if you could reach down, pick them up, and carry them away under your arm like pieces of carpet, if you so chose.

At some point, Eddie asked Roland if he felt any of this.

"Yes," Roland said. "I feel it, see it, hear it . . . Eddie, I *touch* it."

Eddie nodded. He did, too. This world was real beyond reality. It was . . . *anti*-todash. That was the best he could do. And they were very much in the heart of the Beam. Eddie could feel it carrying them on like a river rushing down a gorge toward a waterfall.

"But I'm afraid," Roland said. "I feel as though we're approaching the center of everything—the Tower itself, mayhap. It's as if, after all these years, the quest itself has become the point for me, and the end is frightening."

Eddie nodded. He could get behind that. Certainly he was afraid. If it wasn't the Tower putting out that stupendous force, then it was some potent and terrible thing akin to the rose. But not quite the same. A *twin* to the rose? That could be right.

Roland looked out at the parking lot and the people who came and went beneath a summer sky filled with fat, slow-floating clouds, seemingly unaware that the whole world was singing with power around them, and that all the clouds flowed along the same ancient pathway in the heavens. They were unaware of their own beauty.

The gunslinger said, "I used to think the most terrible thing would be to reach the Dark Tower and find the top room empty. The God of all universes either dead or nonexistent in the first place. But now . . . suppose there *is* someone there, Eddie? Someone in charge who turns out to be . . ." He couldn't finish.

Eddie could. "Someone who turns out to be just another bumhug? Is that it? God not dead but feeble-minded and malicious?"

Roland nodded. This was not, in fact, precisely what he was afraid of, but he thought Eddie had at least come close.

"How can that be, Roland? Considering what we feel?"

Roland shrugged, as if to say anything could be.

"In any case, what choice do we have?"

"None," Roland said bleakly. "All things serve the Beam."

Whatever the great and singing force was, it seemed to be coming from the road that ran west from the shopping center, back into the woods. Kansas Road, according to the sign, and that made Eddie think of Dorothy and Toto and Blaine the Mono.

He dropped the transmission of their borrowed Ford into Drive and started rolling forward. His heart was beating in his chest with slow, exclamatory force. He wondered if Moses had felt like this when he approached the burning bush which contained God. He wondered if Jacob had felt like this, awakening to find a stranger, both radiant and fair, in his camp—the angel with whom he would wrestle. He thought that they probably had. He felt sure that another part of their journey was about to come to an end—another answer lay up ahead.

God living on Kansas Road, in the town of Bridgton, Maine? It should have sounded crazy, but didn't.

Just don't strike me dead, Eddie thought, and turned west. *I need to get back to my sweetheart, so please don't strike me dead, whoever or what-ever you are.*

"Man, I'm so scared," he said.

Roland reached out and briefly grasped his hand.

TWO

Three miles from the shopping center, they came to a dirt road which struck off into the pine trees on their left. There had been other byways, which Eddie had passed without slowing from the steady thirty miles an hour he had been maintaining, but at this one he stopped.

Both front windows were down. They could hear the wind in the trees, the grouchy call of a crow, the not-too-distant buzz of a powerboat, and the rumble of the Ford's engine. Except for a hundred thousand voices singing in rough harmony, those were the only sounds. The sign marking the turnoff said no more than PRIVATE DRIVE. Nevertheless, Eddie was nodding.

"This is it."

"Yes, I know. How's your leg?"

"Hurts. Don't worry about it. Are we gonna do this?"

"We *have* to," Roland said. "You were right to bring us here. What's here is the other half of *this*." He tapped the paper in his pocket, the one convey-ing ownership of the vacant lot to the Tet Corpora-tion.

"You think this guy King is the rose's twin."

"You say true." Roland smiled at his own choice

of words. Eddie thought he'd rarely seen one so sad. "We've picked up the Calla way of talking, haven't we? Jake first, then all of us. But that will fall away."

"Further to go," Eddie said. It wasn't a question.

"Aye, and it will be dangerous. Still . . . maybe nothing so dangerous as this. Shall we roll?"

"In a minute. Roland, do you remember Susannah mentioning a man named Moses Carver?"

"A stem . . . which is to say a man of affairs. He took over her father's business when sai Holmes died, am I correct?"

"Yeah. He was also Suze's godfather. She said he could be trusted completely. Remember how mad she got at Jake and me when we suggested he might have stolen the company's money?"

Roland nodded.

"I trust her judgment," Eddie said. "What about you?"

"Yes."

"If Carver *is* honest, we might be able to put him in charge of the things we need to accomplish in this world."

None of this seemed terribly important compared to the force Eddie felt rising all around him, but he thought it was. They might only have one chance to protect the rose now and ensure its survival later. They had to do it right, and Eddie knew that meant heeding the will of destiny.

In a word, ka.

"Suze says Holmes Dental was worth eight or ten million when you snatched her out of New

York, Roland. If Carver's as good as I hope he is, the company might be worth twelve or fourteen million by now."

"That's a lot?"

"Delah," Eddie said, tossing his open hand at the horizon, and Roland nodded. "It sounds funny to talk about using the profits from some kind of dental process to save the universe, but that's just what I *am* talking about. And the money the tooth-fairy left her may only be the beginning. Microsoft, for instance. Remember me mentioning that name to Tower?"

Roland nodded. "Slow down, Eddie. *Calm* down, I beg."

"I'm sorry," Eddie said, and pulled in a deep breath. "It's this place. The singing. The *faces* . . . do you see the faces in the trees? In the shadows?"

"I see them very well."

"It makes me feel a little crazy. Bear with me. What I'm talking about is merging Holmes Dental and the Tet Corporation, then using our knowledge of the future to turn it into one of the richest combinations in the history of the world. Resources to equal those of the Sombra Corporation . . . or maybe North Central Positronics itself."

Roland shrugged, then lifted a hand as if to ask how Eddie could talk about money while in the presence of the immense force flowing along the barrel of the Beam and through them, lifting the hair from the napes of their necks, making their sinuses tingle, turning every woodsy shadow into a watching face . . . as if a multitude had gathered here to watch them play out a crucial scene in their drama.

"I know how you feel, but it *matters,*" Eddie insisted. "Believe me, it does. Suppose, for instance, we were to grow fast enough to buy out North Central Positronics before it can rise as a force in this world? Roland, we might be able to turn it, the way you can turn even the biggest river with no more than a single spade up in its headwaters, where it's only a trickle."

At this Roland's eyes gleamed. "Take it over," he said. "Turn its purpose from the Crimson King's to our own. Yes, that might be possible."

"Whether it is or isn't, we have to remember that we're not just playing for 1977, or 1987, where I came from, or 1999, where Suze went." In that world, Eddie realized, Calvin Tower might be dead and Aaron Deepneau would be for sure, their final action in the Dark Tower's drama—saving Donald Callahan from the Hitler Brothers—long finished. Swept from the stage, both of them. Into the clearing at the end of the path along with Gasher and Hoots, Benny Slightman, Susan Delgado

(*Calla, Callahan, Susan, Susannah*)

and the Tick-Tock Man, even Blaine and Patricia. Roland and his ka-tet would also pass into that clearing, be it early or late. In the end—if they were fantastically lucky and suicidally brave—only the Dark Tower would stand. If they could nip North Central Positronics in the bud, they might be able to save all the Beams that had been broken. Even if they failed at that, two Beams might be enough to hold the Tower in place: the rose in New York and a man named Stephen King in Maine. Eddie's head had no proof that this was indeed the case . . . but his heart believed it.

"What we're playing for, Roland, is the ages."

Roland made a fist and thumped it lightly on the dusty dashboard of John Cullum's old Ford and nodded.

"Anything can go on that lot, you realize that? *Anything.* A building, a park, a monument, The National Gramophone Institute. As long as the rose stays. This guy Carver can make the Tet Corporation legal, maybe working with Aaron Deepneau—"

"Yes," Roland said. "I liked Deepneau. He had a true face."

Eddie thought so, too. "Anyway, they can draw up legal papers that take care of the rose—the rose always stays, no matter what. And I've got a feeling that it will. 2007, 2057, 2525, 3700 . . . hell, the year 19,000 . . . I think it'll always be there. Because it may be fragile, but I think it's also immortal. We have to do it right while we have the chance, though. Because this is the key world. In this one you never get a chance to whittle a little more if the key doesn't turn. In this world I don't think there are any do-overs."

Roland considered this, then pointed to the dirt road leading into the trees. Into a forest of watching faces and singing voices. A harmonium of all that filled life with worth and meaning, that held to the truth, that acknowledged the White. "And what about the man who lives at the end of this road, Eddie? If he *is* a man."

"I think he is, and not just because of what John Cullum said. It's what I feel here." Eddie patted his chest above the heart.

"So do I."

"Do you say so, Roland?"

"Aye, I do. Is *he* immortal, do you think? Because I've seen much in my years, and heard rumors of much more, but never of a man or woman who lived forever."

"I don't think he needs to be immortal. I think all he needs to do is write the right story. Because some stories *do* live forever."

Understanding lit up Roland's eyes. *At last,* Eddie thought. *At last he sees it.*

But how long had it taken him to see it himself, and then to swallow it? God knew he should have been able to, after all the other wonders he'd seen, and yet still this last step had eluded him. Even discovering that Pere Callahan had seemingly sprung alive and breathing from a fiction called *'Salem's Lot* hadn't been enough to take him that last crucial step. What had finally done it was finding out that Co-Op City was in the Bronx, not Brooklyn. In this world, at least. Which was the only world that mattered.

"Maybe he's not at home," Roland said as around them the whole world waited. "Maybe this man who made us is not at home."

"You know he is."

Roland nodded. And the old light had dawned in his eyes, light from a fire that had never gone out, the one that had lit his way along the Beam all the way from Gilead.

"Then drive on!" he cried hoarsely. "Drive on,

for your father's sake! If he's God—our God—I'd look Him in the eye and ask Him the way to the Tower!"

"Would you not ask him the way to Susannah, first?"

As soon as the question was out of his mouth, Eddie regretted it and prayed the gunslinger would not answer it.

Roland didn't. He only twirled the remaining fingers on his right hand: *Go, go.*

Eddie put the gearshift of Cullum's Ford into Drive and turned onto the dirt road. He drove them into a great singing force that seemed to go through them like a wind, turning them into something as insubstantial as a thought, or a dream in the head of some sleeping god.

THREE

A quarter of a mile in, the road forked. Eddie took the lefthand branch, although the sign pointing that way said ROWDEN, not KING. The dust raised by their passage hung in the rearview mirror. The singing was a sweet din, pouring through him like liquor. His hair was still standing up at the roots, and his muscles were trembling. Called upon to draw his gun, Eddie thought he would probably drop the damned thing. Even if he managed to hold onto it, aiming would be impossible. He didn't know how the man they were looking for could live so close to the sound of that singing and eat or sleep, let alone write stories. But of course King wasn't just *close* to the sound; if

Eddie had it right, King was the *source* of the sound.

But if he has a family, what about them? And even if he doesn't, what about the neighbors?

Here was a driveway on the right, and—

"Eddie, stop." It was Roland, but not sounding the least bit like himself. His Calla tan was thin paint over an immense pallor.

Eddie stopped. Roland fumbled at the door-handle on his side, couldn't make it work, levered himself out the window all the way to his waist instead (Eddie heard the chink his belt buckle made on the chrome strip which faced the window-well), and then vomited onto the oggan. When he fell back into the seat, he looked both exhausted and exalted. The eyes which rolled to meet Eddie's were blue, ancient, glittering. "Drive on."

"Roland, are you sure—"

Roland only twirled his fingers, looking straight out through the Ford's dusty windshield. *Go, go. For your father's sake!*

Eddie drove on.

FOUR

It was the sort of house real-estate agents call a ranch. Eddie wasn't surprised. What *did* surprise him a little was how modest the place was. Then he reminded himself that not every writer was a *rich* writer, and that probably went double for *young* writers. Some sort of typo had apparently made his second novel quite the catch among bibliomaniacs, but Eddie doubted if King ever saw a commission on that sort of thing. Or royalties, if that was what they called it.

Still, the car parked in the turnaround driveway was a new-looking Jeep Cherokee with a nifty Indian stripe running up the side, and that suggested Stephen King wasn't exactly starving for his art, either. There was a wooden jungle gym in the front yard with a lot of plastic toys scattered around it. Eddie's heart sank at the sight of them. One lesson which the Calla had taught exquisitely was that kids complicated things. The ones living here were *little* kids, from the look of the toys. And to them comes a pair of men wearing hard calibers. Men who were not, at this point in time, strictly in their right minds.

Eddie cut the Ford's engine. A crow cawed. A powerboat—bigger than the one they'd heard earlier, from the sound—buzzed. Beyond the house, bright sun glinted on blue water. And the voices sang *Come, come, come-come-commala.*

There was a clunk as Roland opened his door and got out, slewing a little as he did so: bad hip, dry twist. Eddie got out on legs that felt as numb as sticks.

"Tabby? That you?"

This from around the right side of the house. And now, running ahead of the voice and the man who owned the voice, came a shadow. Never had Eddie seen one that so filled him with terror and fascination. He thought, and with absolute certainty: *Yonder comes my maker. Yonder is he, aye, say true.* And the voices sang, *Commala-come-three, he who made me.*

"Did you forget something, darling?" Only the last word came out in a downeast drawl, *daaa-lin,* the way John Cullum would have said it. And then came the man of the house, then came he. He saw them and stopped. He saw *Roland* and stopped. The singing voices stopped with him, and the powerboat's drone seemed to stop as well. For a moment the whole world hung on a hinge. Then the man turned and ran. Not, however, before Eddie saw the terrible thunderstruck look of recognition on his face.

Roland was after him in a flash, like a cat after a bird.

FIVE

But sai King was a man, not a bird. He couldn't fly, and there was really nowhere to run. The side lawn sloped down a mild hill broken only by a concrete pad that might have been the well or some kind of sewage-pumping device. Beyond the lawn was a postage stamp–sized bit of beach, littered with more toys. After that came the lake. The man reached the edge of it, splashed into it, then turned so awkwardly he almost fell down.

Roland skidded to a stop on the sand. He and Stephen King regarded each other. Eddie stood perhaps ten yards behind Roland, watching both of them. The singing had begun again, and so had the buzzing drone of the powerboat. Perhaps they had never stopped, but Eddie believed he knew better.

The man in the water put his hands over his eyes like a child. "You're not there," he said.

"I am, sai." Roland's voice was both gentle and filled with awe. "Take your hands from your eyes, Stephen of Bridgton. Take them down and see me very well."

"Maybe I'm having a breakdown," said the man in the water, but he slowly dropped his hands. He was wearing thick glasses with severe black frames. One bow had been mended with a bit of tape. His hair was either black or a very dark brown. The beard was definitely black, the first threads of white in it startling in their brilliance. He was wearing bluejeans below a tee-shirt that said THE RAMONES and ROCKET TO RUSSIA and GABBA-GABBA-HEY. He looked like starting to run to middle-aged fat, but he wasn't fat yet. He was tall, and as ashy-pale as Roland. Eddie saw with no real surprise that Stephen King *looked* like Roland. Given the age difference they could never be mistaken for twins, but father and son? Yes. Easily.

Roland tapped the base of his throat three times, then shook his head. It wasn't enough. It wouldn't do. Eddie watched with fascination and horror as the gunslinger sank to his knees amid the litter of bright plastic toys and put his curled hand against his brow.

"Hile, tale-spinner," he said. "Comes to you Roland Deschain of Gilead that was, and Eddie Dean of New York. Will you open to us, if we open to you?"

King laughed. Given the power of Roland's words, Eddie found the sound shocking. "I . . . man, this can't be happening." And then, to himself: "Can it?"

Roland, still on his knees, went on as if the

man standing in the water had neither laughed nor spoken. "Do you see us for what we are, and what we do?"

"You'd be gunslingers, if you were real." King peered at Roland through his thick spectacles. "Gunslingers seeking the Dark Tower."

That's it, Eddie thought as the voices rose and the sun shimmered on the blue water. *That nails it.*

"You say true, sai. We seek aid and succor, Stephen of Bridgton. Will'ee give it?"

"Mister, I don't know who your friend is, but as for you . . . man, I *made* you. You can't be standing *there* because the only place you really exist is *here.*" He thumped a fist to the center of his forehead, as if in parody of Roland. Then he pointed to his house. His ranch-style house. "And in there. You're in there, too, I guess. In a desk drawer, or maybe a box in the garage. You're unfinished business. I haven't thought of you in . . . in . . ."

His voice had grown thin. Now he began to sway like someone who hears faint but delicious music, and his knees buckled. He fell.

"Roland!" Eddie shouted, at last plunging forward. "Man's had a fucking heart attack!" Already knowing (or perhaps only hoping) better. Because the singing was as strong as ever. The faces in the trees and shadows as clear.

The gunslinger was bending down and grasping King—who had already begun to thrash weakly—under the arms. "He's but fainted. And who could blame him? Help me get him into the house."

SIX

The master bedroom had a gorgeous view of the lake and a hideous purple rug on the floor. Eddie sat on the bed and watched through the bathroom door as King took off his wet sneakers and outer clothes, stepping between the door and the tiled bathroom wall for a moment to swap his wet undershorts for a dry pair. He hadn't objected to Eddie following him into the bedroom. Since coming to—and he'd been out for no more than thirty seconds—he had displayed an almost eerie calm.

Now he came out of the bathroom and crossed to the bureau. "Is this a practical joke?" he asked, rummaging for dry jeans and a fresh tee-shirt. To Eddie, King's house said money—some, at least. God knew what the clothes said. "Is it something Mac McCutcheon and Floyd Calderwood dreamed up?"

"I don't know those men, and it's no joke."

"Maybe not, but that man can't be real." King stepped into the jeans. He spoke to Eddie in a reasonable tone of voice. "I mean, I *wrote* about him!"

Eddie nodded. "I kind of figured that. But he's real, just the same. I've been running with him for—" How long? Eddie didn't know. "—for awhile," he finished. "You wrote about him but not me?"

"Do you feel left out?"

Eddie laughed, but in truth he *did* feel left out. A little, anyway. Maybe King hadn't gotten to him yet. If that was the case, he wasn't exactly safe, was he?

"This doesn't *feel* like a breakdown," King said, "but I suppose they never do."

"You're not having a breakdown, but I have some sympathy for how you feel, sai. That man—"

"Roland. Roland of . . . Gilead?"

"You say true."

"I don't know if I had the Gilead part or not," King said. "I'd have to check the pages, if I could find them. But it's good. As in 'There is no balm in Gilead.'"

"I'm not following you."

"That's okay, neither am I." King found cigarettes, Pall Malls, on the bureau and lit one. "Finish what you were going to say."

"He dragged me through a door between this world and his world. I also felt like I was having a breakdown." It hadn't been this world from which Eddie had been dragged, close but no cigar, and he'd been jonesing for heroin at the time—jonesing bigtime—but the situation was complicated enough without adding that stuff. Still, there was one question he had to ask before they rejoined Roland and the real palaver began.

"Tell me something, sai King—do you know where Co-Op City is?"

King had been transferring his coins and keys from his wet jeans to the dry ones, right eye squinted shut against the smoke of the cigarette tucked in the corner of his mouth. Now he stopped and looked at Eddie with his eyebrows raised. "Is this a trick question?"

"No."

"And you won't shoot me with that gun you're wearing if I get it wrong?"

Eddie smiled a little. King wasn't an unlikable

cuss, for a god. Then he reminded himself that God had killed his little sister, using a drunk driver as a tool, and his brother Henry as well. God had made Enrico Balazar and burned Susan Delgado at the stake. His smile faded. But he said, "No one's getting shot here, sai."

"In that case, I believe Co-Op City's in Brooklyn. Where you come from, judging by your accent. So do I win the Fair-Day Goose?"

Eddie jerked like someone who's been poked with a pin. "What?"

"Just a thing my mother used to say. When my brother Dave and I did all our chores and got em right the first time, she'd say 'You boys win the Fair-Day Goose.' It was a joke. So do I win the prize?"

"Yes," Eddie said. "Sure."

King nodded, then butted out his cigarette. "You're an okay guy. It's your pal I don't much care for. And never did. I think that's part of the reason I quit on the story."

That startled Eddie again, and he got up from the bed to cover it. "*Quit* on it?"

"Yeah. *The Dark Tower,* it was called. It was gonna be my *Lord of the Rings,* my *Gormenghast,* my you-name-it. One thing about being twenty-two is that you're never short of ambition. It didn't take me long to see that it was just too big for my little brain. Too . . . I don't know . . . outré? That's as good a word as any, I guess. Also," he added dryly, "I lost the outline."

"You did *what?*"

"Sounds crazy, doesn't it? But writing can be a

crazy deal. Did you know that Ernest Hemingway once lost a whole book of short stories on a train?"

"Really?"

"Really. He had no back-up copies, no carbons. Just poof, gone. That's sort of what happened to me. One fine drunk night—or maybe I was done up on mescaline, I can no longer remember—I did a complete outline for this five- or ten-thousand-page fantasy epic. It was a good outline, I think. Gave the thing some form. Some style. And then I lost it. Probably flew off the back of my motorcycle when I was coming back from some fucking bar. Nothing like that ever happened to me before. I'm usually careful about my work, if nothing else."

"Uh-huh," Eddie said, and thought of asking *Did you happen to see any guys in loud clothes, the sort of guys who drive flashy cars, around the time you lost it? Low men, not to put too fine a point on it? Anyone with a red mark on his or her forehead? The sort of thing that looks a little like a circle of blood? Any indications, in short, that someone* stole *your outline? Someone who might have an interest in making sure* The Dark Tower *never gets finished?*

"Let's go out to the kitchen. We need to palaver." Eddie just wished he knew what they were supposed to palaver *about.* Whatever it was, they had better get it right, because this was the real world, the one in which there were no do-overs.

SEVEN

Roland had no idea of how to stock and then start the fancy coffee-maker on the counter, but he found a battered coffee pot on one of the shelves that was not much different from the one Alain Johns had carried in his gunna long ago, when three boys had come to Mejis to count stock. Sai King's stove ran on electricity, but a child could have figured out how to make the burners work. When Eddie and King came into the kitchen, the pot was beginning to get hot.

"I don't use coffee, myself," King said, and went to the cold-box (giving Roland a wide berth). "And I don't ordinarily drink beer before five, but I believe that today I'll make an exception. Mr. Dean?"

"Coffee'll do me fine."

"Mr. Gilead?"

"It's Deschain, sai King. I'll also have the coffee, and say thank ya."

The writer opened a can by using the built-in ring in the top (a device that struck Roland as superficially clever and almost moronically wasteful). There was a hiss, followed by the pleasant smell

(*commala-come-come*)

of yeast and hops. King drank down at least half the can at a go, wiped foam out of his mustache, then put the can on the counter. He was still pale, but seemingly composed and in possession of his faculties. The gunslinger thought he was doing quite well, at least so far. Was it possible that, in some of the deeper ranges of his mind and heart, King had expected their visit? Had been waiting for them?

"You have a wife and children," Roland said. "Where are they?"

"Tabby's folks live up north, near Bangor. My daughter's been spending the last week with her nanna and poppa. Tabby took our youngest— Owen, he's just a baby—and headed that way about an hour ago. I'm supposed to pick up my other son—Joe—in . . ." He checked his watch. "In just about an hour. I wanted to finish my writing, so this time we're taking both cars."

Roland considered. It might be true. It was almost certainly King's way of telling them that if anything happened to him, he would be missed in short order.

"I can't believe this is happening. Have I said that enough to be annoying yet? In any case, it's too much like one of my own stories to be happening."

"Like *'Salem's Lot,* for instance," Eddie suggested.

King raised his eyebrows. "So you know about that. Do they have the Literary Guild wherever you came from?" He downed the rest of his beer. He drank, Roland thought, like a man with a gift for it. "A couple of hours ago there were sirens way over on the other side of the lake, plus a big plume of smoke. I could see it from my office. At the time I thought it was probably just a grassfire, maybe in Harrison or Stoneham, but now I wonder. Did that have anything to do with you guys? It did, didn't it?"

Eddie said, "He's writing it, Roland. Or was. He says he stopped. But it's called *The Dark Tower.* So he knows."

King smiled, but Roland thought he looked really, deeply frightened for the first time. Setting aside that initial moment when he'd come around the corner of the house and seen them, that was. When he'd seen his creation.

Is that what I am? His creation?

It felt wrong and right in equal measure. Thinking about it made Roland's head ache and his stomach feel slippery all over again.

"'He knows,'" King said. "I don't like the sound of that, boys. In a story, when someone says 'He knows,' the next line is usually 'We'll have to kill him.'"

"Believe me when I tell you this," Roland said. He spoke with great emphasis. "Killing you is the last thing we'd ever want to do, sai King. Your enemies are our enemies, and those who would help you along your way are our friends."

"Amen," Eddie said.

King opened his cold-box and got another beer. Roland saw a great many of them in there, standing to frosty attention. More cans of beer than anything else. "In that case," he said, "you better call me Steve."

EIGHT

"Tell us the story with me in it," Roland invited.

King leaned against the kitchen counter and the top of his head caught a shaft of sun. He took a sip

of his beer and considered Roland's question. Eddie
saw it then for the first time, very dim—a contrast
to the sun, perhaps. A dusty black shadow, something swaddled around the man. Dim. Barely there.
But there. Like the darkness you saw hiding behind
things when you traveled todash. Was that it?
Eddie didn't think so.

Barely there.

But there.

"You know," King said, "I'm not much good at
telling stories. That sounds like a paradox, but it's
not; it's the reason I write them down."

Is it Roland he talks like, or me? Eddie wondered. He couldn't tell. Much later on he'd realize
that King talked like *all* of them, even Rosa
Munoz, Pere Callahan's woman of work in the
Calla.

Then the writer brightened. "Tell you what, why
don't I see if I can find the manuscript? I've got
four or five boxes of busted stories downstairs.
Dark Tower's got to be in one of them." *Busted.
Busted stories.* Eddie didn't care for the sound of
that at all. "You can read some of it while I go get
my little boy." He grinned, displaying big, crooked
teeth. "Maybe when I get back, you'll be gone and
I can get to work on thinking you were never here
at all."

Eddie glanced at Roland, who shook his head
slightly. On the stove, the first bubble of coffee
blinked in the pot's glass eye.

"Sai King—" Eddie began.

"Steve."

"Steve, then. We ought to transact our business

now. Matters of trust aside, we're in a ripping hurry."

"Sure, sure, right, racing against time," King said, and laughed. The sound was charmingly goofy. Eddie suspected that the beer was starting to do its work, and he wondered if the man was maybe a juice-head. Impossible to tell for sure on such short acquaintance, but Eddie thought some of the signs were there. He didn't remember a whole hell of a lot from high school English, but he did recall some teacher or other telling him that writers *really* liked to drink. Hemingway, Faulkner, Fitzgerald, "The Raven" guy. Writers liked to drink.

"I'm not laughing at you guys," King said. "It's actually against my religion to laugh at men who are toting guns. It's just that in the sort of books I write, people are almost always racing against time. Would you like to hear the first line of *The Dark Tower*?"

"Sure, if you remember it," Eddie said.

Roland said nothing, but his eyes gleamed bright under brows that were now threaded with white.

"Oh, I remember it. It may be the best opening line I ever wrote." King set his beer aside, then raised his hands with the first two fingers of each held out and bent, as if making quotation marks. "'The man in black fled across the desert, and the gunslinger followed.' The rest might have been puff and blow, but man, that was clean." He dropped his hands and picked up his beer. "For the forty-third time, is this really happening?"

"Was the man in black's name Walter?" Roland asked.

King's beer tilted shy of his mouth and he spilled some down his front, wetting his fresh shirt. Roland nodded, as if that was all the answer he needed.

"Don't faint on us again," Eddie said, a trifle sharply. "Once was enough to impress me."

King nodded, took another sip of his beer, seemed to take hold of himself at the same time. He glanced at the clock. "Are you gentlemen really going to let me pick up my son?"

"Yes," Roland said.

"You . . ." King paused to consider, then smiled. "Do you set your watch and your warrant on it?"

With no smile in return, Roland said, "So I do."

"Okay, then, *The Dark Tower,* Reader's Digest Condensed Book version. Keeping in mind that oral storytelling isn't my thing, I'll do the best I can."

NINE

Roland listened as if worlds depended on it, as he was quite sure they did. King had begun his version of Roland's life with the campfires, which had pleased the gunslinger because they confirmed Walter's essential humanity. From there, King said, the story went back to Roland's meeting with a kind of shirttail farmer on the edge of the desert. Brown, his name had been.

Life for your crop, Roland heard across an echo of years, and *Life for your own.* He'd forgotten Brown, and Brown's pet raven, Zoltan, but this stranger had not.

"What I liked," King said, "was how the story seemed to be going backward. From a purely technical standpoint, it was very interesting. I start with you in the desert, then slip back a notch to you meeting Brown and Zoltan. Zoltan was named after a folksinger and guitarist I knew at the University of Maine, by the way. Anyway, from the dweller's hut the story slips back another notch to you coming into the town of Tull ... named after a rock group—"

"Jethro Tull," Eddie said. "Goddam of course! I *knew* that name was familiar! What about Z.Z. Top, Steve? Do you know them?" Eddie looked at King, saw the incomprehension, and smiled. "I guess it's not their when quite yet. Or if it is, you haven't found out about them."

Roland twirled his fingers: *Go on, go on.* And gave Eddie a look that suggested he stop interrupting.

"Anyway, from Roland coming into Tull, the story slips back another notch to tell how Nort, the weed-eater, died and was resurrected by Walter. You see what buzzed me about it, don't you? The early part of it was all told in reverse gear. It was bass-ackwards."

Roland had no interest in the technical aspects that seemed to fascinate King; this was his life they were talking about, after all, his *life,* and to him it had all been moving forward. At least until he'd reached the Western Sea, and the doors through which he had drawn his traveling companions.

But Stephen King knew nothing of the doors, it seemed. He had written of the way station, and

Roland's meeting with Jake Chambers; he had written of their trek first into the mountains and then through them; he had written of Jake's betrayal by the man he had come to trust and to love.

King observed the way Roland hung his head during this part of the tale, and spoke with odd gentleness. "No need to look so ashamed, Mr. Deschain. After all, I was the one who made you do it."

But again, Roland wondered about that.

King had written of Roland's palaver with Walter in the dusty golgotha of bones, the telling of the Tarot and the terrible vision Roland had had of growing right through the roof of the universe. He had written of how Roland had awakened following that long night of fortune-telling to find himself years older, and Walter nothing but bones. Finally, King said, he'd written of Roland going to the edge of the water and sitting there. "You said, 'I loved you, Jake'"

Roland nodded matter-of-factly. "I love him still."

"You speak as though he actually exists."

Roland looked at him levelly. "Do I exist? Do you?"

King was silent.

"What happened then?" Eddie asked.

"Then, *señor*, I ran out of story—or got intimidated, if you like that better—and stopped."

Eddie also wanted to stop. He could see the shadows beginning to lengthen in the kitchen and wanted to get after Susannah before it was too late. He thought both he and Roland had a pretty good idea of how to get out of this world, suspected Stephen King himself could direct them to Turtleback Lane in Lovell, where reality was thin and—according to John Cullum, at least—the walk-ins had been plentiful of late. And King would be happy to direct them. Happy to get rid of them. But they couldn't go just yet, and in spite of his impatience Eddie knew it.

"You stopped because you lost your lineout," Roland said.

"Outline. And no, not really." King had gone after his third beer, and Eddie thought it was no wonder the man was getting pudgy in the middle; he'd already consumed the caloric equivalent of a loaf of bread, and was starting on Loaf #2. "I hardly ever work from an outline. In fact . . . don't hold me to this, but that might have been the only time. And it got too big for me. Too strange. Also *you* became a problem, sir or sai or whatever you call yourself." King grimaced. "Whatever form of address that is, I didn't make it up."

"Not yet, anyway," Roland remarked.

"You started as a version of Sergio Leone's Man With No Name."

"In the Spaghetti Westerns," Eddie said. "Jesus, of course! I watched a hundred of em at the Majestic with my brother Henry, when Henry was still at home. I went by myself or with this friend of mine, Chuggy Coter, when Henry was in the Nam. Those were *guy* flicks."

King was grinning. "Yeah," he said, "but my wife went ape for em, so go figure."

"Cool on her!" Eddie exclaimed.

"Yeah, Tab's a cool kitty." King looked back at Roland. "As The Man With No Name—a fantasy version of Clint Eastwood—you were okay. A lot of fun to partner up with."

"Is that how you think of it?"

"Yes. But then you changed. Right under my hand. It got so I couldn't tell if you were the hero, the antihero, or no hero at all. When you let the kid drop, that was the capper."

"You said you made me do that."

Looking Roland straight in the eyes—blue meeting blue amid the endless choir of voices—King said: "I lied, brother."

TEN

There was a little pause while they all thought that over. Then King said, "You started to scare me, so I stopped writing about you. Boxed you up and put you in a drawer and went on to a series of short stories I sold to various men's magazines." He considered, then nodded. "Things changed for me after I put you away, my friend, and for the better. I started to sell my stuff. Asked Tabby to marry me. Not long after that I started a book called *Carrie*. It wasn't my first novel, but it was the first one I sold, and it put me over the top. All that after saying goodbye Roland, so long, happy trails to you. Then what happens? I come around the corner of my house one day six or seven years later and see you standing in my fucking driveway, big as Billy-be-damned, as my mother used to say. And all I can say now is that thinking you're a hallucination brought on by overwork is the most optimistic conclusion I can draw. And I don't believe it. How can I?" King's voice was rising, becoming reedy. Eddie didn't mistake it for fear; this was outrage. "How can I believe it when I see the shadows you cast, the blood on your leg—" He pointed to Eddie. "And the dust on your face?" This time to Roland. "You've taken away my goddam options, and I can feel my mind . . . I don't know . . . tipping? Is that the word? I think it is. Tipping."

"You didn't just stop," Roland said, ignoring this last completely for the self-indulgent nonsense it probably was.

"No?"

"I think telling stories is like pushing something. Pushing against uncreation itself, maybe. And one day while you were doing that, you felt something pushing back."

King considered this for what seemed to Eddie like a very long time. Then he nodded. "You could be right. It was more than the usual going-dry feeling, for sure. I'm used to that, although it doesn't happen as often as it used to. It's . . . I don't know, one day you just start having less fun while you're sitting there, tapping the keys. Seeing less clearly. Getting less of a buzz from telling *yourself* the story. And then, to make things worse, you get a *new* idea, one that's all bright and shiny, fresh off the showroom floor, not a scratch on her. Completely unfucked-up by you, at least as of yet. And . . . well . . ."

"And you felt something pushing back." Roland spoke in the same utterly flat tone.

"Yeah." King's voice had dropped so low Eddie

could barely hear him. "NO TRESPASSING. DO NOT ENTER. HIGH VOLTAGE." He paused. "Maybe even DANGER OF DEATH."

You wouldn't like that faint shadow I see swirling around you, Eddie thought. *That black nimbus. No, sai, I don't think you'd like that at all, and what am I seeing? The cigarettes? The beer? Something else addictive you maybe have a taste for? A car accident one drunk night? And how far ahead? How many years?*

He looked at the clock over the Kings' kitchen table and was dismayed to see that it was quarter to four in the afternoon. "Roland, it's getting late. This man's got to get his kid." *And we've got to find my wife before Mia has the baby they seem to be sharing and the Crimson King has no more use for the Susannah part of her.*

Roland said, "Just a little more." And lowered his head without saying anything. Thinking. Trying to decide which questions were the right questions. Maybe just one right question. And it was important, Eddie knew it was, because they'd never be able to return to the ninth day of July in the year 1977. They might be able to revisit that day in some other world, but not in this one. And would Stephen King exist in any of those other worlds? Eddie thought maybe not. *Probably* not.

While Roland considered, Eddie asked King if the name Blaine meant anything special to him.

"No. Not particularly."

"What about Lud?"

"As in Luddites? They were some sort of machine-hating religious sect, weren't they? Nineteenth century, I think, or they might have started even earlier. If I've got it right, the ones in the nineteenth century would break into factories and bash the machinery to pieces." He grinned, displaying those crooked teeth. "I guess they were the Greenpeace of their day."

"Beryl Evans? That name ring a bell?"

"No."

"Henchick? Henchick of the Manni?"

"No. What are the Manni?"

"Too complicated to go into. What about Claudia y Inez Bachman? That one mean anyth—"

King burst out laughing, startling Eddie. Startling King himself, judging from the look on his face. "Dicky's wife!" he exclaimed. "How in the hell do you know about that?"

"I don't. Who's Dicky?"

"Richard Bachman. I've started publishing some of my earliest novels as paperback originals, under a pseudonym. Bachman is it. One night when I was pretty drunk, I made up a whole author bio for him, right down to how he beat adult-onset leukemia, hooray Dickie. Anyway, Claudia's his wife. Claudia Inez Bachman. The *y* part, though . . . that I don't know about."

Eddie felt as if a huge invisible stone had suddenly rolled off his chest and out of his life. *Claudia Inez Bachman* only had eighteen letters. So something had added the *y*, and why? To make nineteen, of course. Claudia Bachman was just a name. Claudia y Inez Bachman, though . . . *she* was ka-tet.

Eddie thought they'd just gotten one of the things they'd come here for. Yes, Stephen King had created them. At least he'd created Roland, Jake, and Father Callahan. The rest he hadn't gotten to yet. And he had moved Roland like a piece on a chessboard: go to Tull, Roland, sleep with Allie, Roland, chase Walter across the desert, Roland. But even as he moved his main character along the board, so had *King himself* been moved. That one letter added to the name of his pseudonym's wife insisted upon it. Something had wanted to make Claudia Bachman *nineteen*. So—

"Steve."

"Yes, Eddie of New York." King smiled self-consciously.

Eddie could feel his heart beating hard in his chest. "What does the number nineteen mean to you?"

King considered. Outside the wind soughed in the trees, the powerboats whined, and the crow— or another—cawed. Soon along this lake would come the hour of barbecues, and then maybe a trip to town and a band concert on the square, all in this best of all possible worlds. Or just the one most real.

At last, King shook his head and Eddie let out a frustrated breath.

"Sorry. It's a prime number, but that's all I can come up with. Primes sort of fascinate me, have ever since Mr. Soychak's Algebra I class at Lisbon High. And I think it's how old I was when I met my wife, but she might dispute that. She has a disputatious nature."

"What about ninety-nine?"

King thought it over, then ticked items off on his fingers. "A hell of an age to be. 'Ninety-nine years on the old rock-pile.' A song called—I think—'The Wreck of Old Ninety-nine.' Only it might be 'The Wreck of the *Hesperus*' I'm thinking about. 'Ninety-nine bottles of beer on the wall, we took one down and passed it all around, and there were ninety-eight bottles of beer.' Beyond that, *nada*."

This time it was King's turn to look at the clock.

"If I don't leave soon, Betty Jones is going to call to see if I forgot I *have* a son. And after I get Joe I'm supposed to drive a hundred and thirty miles north, there's that. Which might be easier if I quit with the beer. And that, in turn, might be easier if I didn't have a couple of armed spooks sitting in my kitchen."

Roland was nodding. He reached down to his gunbelt, brought up a shell, and began to roll it absently between the thumb and forefinger of his left hand. "Just one more question, if it does ya. Then we'll go our course and let you go yours."

King nodded. "Ask it, then." He looked at his third can of beer, then tipped it down the sink with an expression of regret.

"Was it you wrote *The Dark Tower*?"

To Eddie this question made no sense, but King's eyes lit up and he smiled brilliantly. *"No!"* he said. "And if I ever do a book on writing—and I probably could, it's what I taught before I retired to do this—I'll say so. Not that, not any of them, not really. I know that there are writers who *do* write, but I'm not one of them. In fact, whenever I run out of inspiration and resort to plot, the story I'm working on usually turns to shit."

"I don't have a clue what you're talking about," Eddie said.

"It's like . . . hey, that's neat!"

The shell rolling back and forth between the gunslinger's thumb and forefinger had jumped effortlessly to the backs of his fingers, where it seemed to walk along Roland's rippling knuckles.

"Yes," Roland agreed, "it is, isn't it?"

"It's how you hypnotized Jake at the way station. How you made him remember being killed."

And Susan, Eddie thought. *He hypnotized Susan the same way, only you don't know about that yet, sai King. Or maybe you do. Maybe somewhere inside you know all of it.*

"I've tried hypnosis," King said. "In fact, a guy got me up onstage at the Topsham Fair when I was a kid and tried to make me cluck like a hen. It didn't work. That was around the time Buddy Holly died. And the Big Bopper. And Ritchie Valens. Todana! Ah, Discordia!"

He suddenly shook his head as if to clear it, and looked up from the dancing shell to Roland's face. "Did I say something just then?"

"No, sai." Roland looked down at the dancing shell—back and forth it went, and back and forth—which quite naturally drew King's eyes back as well.

"What happens when you make a story?" Roland inquired. "*My* story, for instance?"

"It just comes," King said. His voice had grown faint. Bemused. "It blows into me—that's the good part—and then it comes out when I move my fingers. Never from the head. Comes out the navel, or somewhere. There was an editor . . . I think it was Maxwell Perkins . . . who called Thomas Wolfe—"

Eddie knew what Roland was doing and knew it was probably a bad idea to interrupt, but he couldn't help it. "A rose," he said. "A rose, a stone, an unfound door."

King's face lighted with pleasure, but his eyes never lifted from the shell dancing along the heddles of the gunslinger's knuckles. "Actually it's a stone, a *leaf*, a door," he said. "But I like rose even better."

He had been entirely captured. Eddie thought he could almost hear the sucking sound as the man's conscious mind drained away. It occurred to him that something as simple as a ringing phone at this critical moment might change the whole course of existence. He got up, and—moving quietly in spite of his stiff and painful leg—went to where it hung on the wall. He twisted the cord in his fingers and applied pressure until it snapped.

"A rose, a stone, an unfound door," King agreed. "That could be Wolfe, all right. Maxwell Perkins called him 'a divine wind-chime.' O lost, and by the wind grieved! All the forgotten faces! O Discordia!"

"How does the story come to you, sai?" Roland asked quietly.

"I don't like the New Agers . . . the crystal-wavers . . . all the it-don't-matter, turn-the-pagers . . . but they call it channeling, and that's . . . how it feels . . . like something in a channel . . ."

"Or on a beam?" Roland asked.

"All things serve the Beam," the writer said, and sighed. The sound was terrible in its sadness. Eddie felt his back prickle up in helpless waves of goose-flesh.

ELEVEN

Stephen King stood in a shaft of dusty afternoon sunlight. It lit his cheek, the curve of his left eye, the dimple at the corner of his mouth. It turned each white hair on the left side of his beard into a line of light. He *stood* in light, and that made the faint darkness around him clearer. His respiration had slowed to perhaps three or four breaths a minute.

"Stephen King," Roland said. "Do you see me?"

"Hile, gunslinger, I see you very well."

"When did you first see me?"

"Not until today."

Roland looked surprised at this, and a little frustrated. It was clearly not the answer he had expected. Then King went on.

"I saw Cuthbert, not you." A pause. "You and Cuthbert broke bread and scattered it beneath the gallows. That's in the part that's already written."

"Aye, so we did. When Hax the cook swung. We were but lads. Did Bert tell you that tale?"

But King did not answer this. "I saw Eddie. I saw him very well." A pause. "Cuthbert and Eddie are twins."

"Roland—" Eddie began in a low voice. Roland hushed him with a savage shake of the head and put the bullet he'd used to hypnotize King on the table. King kept looking at the place where it had been, as if he still saw it there. Probably he did. Dust motes danced around his dark and shaggy head of hair.

"Where were you when you saw Cuthbert and Eddie?"

"In the barn." King's voice dropped. His lips had begun to tremble. "Auntie sent me out because we tried to run away."

"Who?"

"Me and my brother Dave. They caught us and brought us back. They said we were bad, bad boys."

"And you had to go into the barn."

"Yes, and saw wood."

"That was your punishment."

"Yes." A tear welled in the corner of King's right eye. It slipped down his cheek to the edge of his beard. "The chickens are dead."

"The chickens in the barn?"

"Yes, them." More tears followed the first.

"What killed them?"

"Uncle Oren says it was avian flu. Their eyes are open. They're . . . a little scary."

Or perhaps more than just a little, Eddie thought, judging by the tears and the pallor of the man's cheeks.

"You couldn't leave the barn?"

"Not until I saw my share of the wood. David did his. It's my turn. There are spiders in the chickens. Spiders in their guts, little red ones. Like specks of red pepper. If they get on me I'll catch the flu and die. Only then I'll come back."

"Why?"

"I'll be a vampire. I'll be a slave to *him*. His scribe, maybe. His pet writer."

"Whose?"

"The Lord of the Spiders. The Crimson King, Tower-pent."

"Christ, Roland," Eddie whispered. He was shuddering. What had they found here? What nest had they exposed? "Sai King, *Steve*, how old were you—*are* you?"

"I'm seven." A pause. "I wet my pants. I don't want the spiders to bite me. The red spiders. But then *you* came, Eddie, and I went free." He smiled radiantly, his cheeks gleaming with tears.

"Are you asleep, Stephen?" Roland asked.

"Aye."

"Go deeper."

"All right."

"I'll count to three. On three you'll be as deep as you can go."

"All right."

"One . . . two . . . three." On *three*, King's head lolled forward. His chin rested on his chest. A line of silver drool ran from his mouth and swung like a pendulum.

"So now we know something," Roland said to Eddie. "Something crucial, maybe. He was touched by the Crimson King when he was just a child, but it seems that we won him over to our side. Or *you* did, Eddie. You and my old friend, Bert. In any case, it makes him rather special."

"I'd feel better about my heroism if I remembered it," Eddie said. Then: "You realize that when this guy was seven, I wasn't even born?"

Roland smiled. "Ka is a wheel. You've been turning on it under different names for a long time. Cuthbert for one, it seems."

"What's this about the Crimson King being 'Tower-pent'?"

"I have no idea."

Roland turned back to Stephen King. "How many times do you think the Lord of Discordia has tried to kill you, Stephen? Kill you and halt your pen? Shut up your troublesome mouth? Since that first time in your aunt and uncle's barn?"

King seemed to try counting, then shook his head. "Delah," he said. *Many.*

Eddie and Roland exchanged a glance.

"And does someone always step in?" Roland asked.

"Nay, sai, never think it. I'm not helpless. Sometimes I step aside."

Roland laughed at that—the dry sound of a stick broken over a knee. "Do you know what you are?"

King shook his head. His lower lip had pooched out like that of a sulky child.

"Do you know what you are?"

"The father first. The husband second. The writer third. Then the brother. After brotherhood I am silent. Okay?"

"No. Not oh-kay. Do you know what you are?"

A long pause. "No. I told you all I can. Stop asking me."

"I'll stop when you speak true. Do you know—"

"Yes, all right, I know what you're getting at. Satisfied?"

"Not yet. Tell me what—"

"I'm Gan, or *possessed* by Gan, I don't know which, maybe there's no difference." King began to cry. His tears were silent and horrible. "But it's not Dis, I turned aside from Dis, I *repudiate* Dis, and that should be enough but it's not, ka is never satisfied, greedy old ka, that's what *she* said, isn't it? What Susan Delgado said before you killed her, or I killed her, or Gan killed her. 'Greedy old ka, how I hate it.' Regardless of who killed her, I made her say that, I, for I hate it, so I do. I buck against ka's goad, and will until the day I go into the clearing at the end of the path."

Roland sat at the table, white at the sound of Susan's name.

"And still ka comes to me, comes *from* me, I translate it, am *made* to translate it, ka flows out of my navel like a ribbon. I am not ka, I am not the ribbon, it's just what comes through me and I hate it I hate it! The chickens were full of *spiders,* do you understand that, full of *spiders!* "

"Stop your snivelment," Roland said (with a remarkable lack of sympathy, to Eddie's way of thinking), and King stilled.

The gunslinger sat thinking, then raised his head.

"Why did you stop writing the story when I came to the Western Sea?"

"Are you dumb? Because I *don't want to be Gan!* I turned aside from Dis, I should be able to turn aside from Gan, as well. I love my wife. I love my kids. I love to write stories, but I don't want to write *your* story. I'm always afraid. He looks for me. The Eye of the King."

"But not since you stopped," Roland said.

"No, since then he looks for me not, he sees me not."

"Nevertheless, you must go on."

King's face twisted, as if in pain, then smoothed out into the previous look of sleep.

Roland raised his mutilated right hand. "When you do, you'll start with how I lost my fingers. Do you remember?"

"Lobstrosities," King said. "Bit them off."

"And how do you know that?"

King smiled a little and made a gentle *wissshhh*-ing sound. "The wind blows," said he.

"Gan bore the world and moved on," Roland replied. "Is that what you mean to say?"

"Aye, and the world would have fallen into the abyss if not for the great turtle. Instead of falling, it landed on his back."

"So we're told, and we all say thank ya. Start with the lobstrosities biting off my fingers."

"Dad-a-jum, dad-a-jingers, goddam lobsters bit off your fingers," King said, and actually laughed.

"Yes."

"Would have saved me a lot of trouble if you'd died, Roland son of Steven."

"I know. Eddie and my other friends, as well." A ghost of a smile touched the corners of the gun-slinger's mouth. "Then, after the lobstrosities—"

"Eddie comes, Eddie comes," King interrupted, and made a dreamy little flapping gesture with his right hand, as if to say he knew all that and Roland shouldn't waste his time. "The Prisoner the Pusher the Lady of Shadows. The butcher the baker the candle-mistaker." He smiled. "That's how my son Joe says it. When?"

Roland blinked, caught by surprise.

"When, when, *when?*" King raised his hand and

Eddie watched with surprise as the toaster, the waffle maker, and the drainer full of clean dishes rose and floated in the sunshine.

"Are you asking me when you should start again?"

"Yes, yes, *yes!*" A knife rose out of the floating dish drainer and flew the length of the room. There it stuck, quivering, in the wall. Then everything settled back into place again.

Roland said, "Listen for the song of the Turtle, the cry of the Bear."

"Song of Turtle, cry of Bear. Maturin, from the Patrick O'Brian novels. Shardik from the Richard Adams novel."

"Yes. If you say so."

"Guardians of the Beam."

"Yes."

"Of *my* Beam."

Roland looked at him fixedly. "Do you say so?"

"Yes."

"Then let it be so. When you hear the song of the Turtle or the cry of the Bear, then you must start again."

"When I open my eye to your world, he sees me." A pause. "*It.*"

"I know. We'll try to protect you at those times, just as we intend to protect the rose."

King smiled. "I love the rose."

"Have you seen it?" Eddie asked.

"Indeed I have, in New York. Up the street from the U.N. Plaza Hotel. It used to be in the deli. Tom and Jerry's. In the back. Now it's in the vacant lot where the deli was."

"You'll tell our story until you're tired," Roland said. "When you can't tell any more, when the Turtle's song and the Bear's cry grow faint in your ears, then will you rest. And when you can begin again, you *will* begin again. You—"

"Roland?"

"Sai King?"

"I'll do as you say. I'll listen for the song of the Turtle and each time I hear it, I'll go on with the tale. If I live. But you must listen, too. For *her* song."

"Whose?"

"Susannah's. The baby will kill her if you aren't quick. And your ears must be sharp."

Eddie looked at Roland, frightened. Roland nodded. It was time to go.

"Listen to me, sai King. We're well-met in Bridgton, but now we must leave you."

"Good," King said, and he spoke with such unfeigned relief that Eddie almost laughed.

"You will stay here, right where you are, for ten minutes. Do you understand?"

"Yes."

"Then you'll wake up. You'll feel very well. You won't remember that we were here, except in the very deepest depths of your mind."

"In the mudholes."

"The mudholes, do ya. On top, you'll think you had a nap. A wonderful, refreshing nap. You'll get your son and go to where you're supposed to go. You'll feel fine. You'll go on with your life. You'll write many stories, but every one will be to some greater or lesser degree about this story. Do you understand?"

"Yar," King said, and he sounded so much like Roland when Roland was gruff and tired that Eddie's back pricked up in gooseflesh again. "Because what's seen can't be unseen. What's known can't be unknown." He paused. "Save perhaps in death."

"Aye, perhaps. Every time you hear the song of the Turtle—if that's what it sounds like to you— you'll start on our story again. The only real story you have to tell. And we'll try to protect you."

"I'm afraid."

"I know, but we'll try—"

"It's not *that*. I'm afraid of not being able to finish." His voice lowered. "I'm afraid the Tower will fall and I'll be held to blame."

"That is up to ka, not you," Roland said. "Or me. I've satisfied myself on that point. And now—" He nodded to Eddie, and stood up.

"Wait," King said.

Roland looked at him, eyebrows raised.

"I am allowed mail privileges, but only once."

Sounds like a guy in a POW camp, Eddie mused. And aloud: "Who allows you mail privileges, Steve-O?"

King's brow wrinkled. "Gan?" he asked. "Is it Gan?" Then, like the sun breaking through on a foggy morning, his brow smoothed out and he smiled. "I think it's *me!*" he said. "I can send a letter to myself ... perhaps even a small package ... but only once." His smile broadened into an engaging grin. "All of this ... sort of like a fairy-tale, isn't it?"

"Yes indeed," Eddie said, thinking of the glass

palace they'd come to straddling the Interstate in Kansas.

"What would you do?" Roland asked. "To whom would you send mail?"

"To Jake," King said promptly.

"And what would you tell him?"

King's voice became Eddie Dean's voice. It wasn't an approximation; it was *exact*. The sound turned Eddie cold.

"Dad-a-chum, dad-a-chee," King lilted, "not to worry, you've got the key!"

They waited for more, but it seemed there was no more. Eddie looked at Roland, and this time it was the younger man's turn to twirl his fingers in the let's-go gesture. Roland nodded and they started for the door.

"That was fucking-A creepy," Eddie said.

Roland didn't reply.

Eddie stopped him with a touch on the arm. "One other thing occurs to me, Roland. While he's hypnotized, maybe you ought to tell him to quit drinking and smoking. Especially the ciggies. He's a fiend for them. Did you see this place? Fuckin ashtrays everywhere."

Roland looked amused. "Eddie, if one waits until the lungs are fully formed, tobacco prolongs life, not shortens it. It's the reason why in Gilead everyone smoked but the very poorest, and even they had their shuckies, like as not. Tobacco keeps away ill-sick vapors, for one thing. Many dangerous insects, for another. Everyone knows this."

"The Surgeon General of the United States would be delighted to hear what everyone in Gilead knows," Eddie said dryly. "What about the booze, then? Suppose he rolls his Jeep over some drunk night, or gets on the Interstate going the wrong way and head-ons someone?"

Roland considered it, then shook his head. "I've meddled with his mind—and ka itself—as much as I intend to. As much as I *dare* to. We'll have to keep checking back over the years in any . . . why do you shake your head at me? The tale spins from *him!*"

"Maybe so, but we won't be able to check on him for twenty-two years unless we decide to abandon Susannah . . . and I'll never do that. Once we jump ahead to 1999, there's no coming back. Not in this world."

For a moment Roland made no reply, just looked at the man leaning his behind against his kitchen counter, asleep on his feet with his eyes open and his hair tumbled on his brow. Seven or eight minutes from now King would awaken with no memory of Roland and Eddie . . . always assuming they were gone, that was. Eddie didn't seriously believe the gunslinger would leave Suze hung out on the line . . . but he'd let Jake drop, hadn't he? Let Jake drop into the abyss, once upon a time.

"Then he'll have to go it alone," Roland said, and Eddie breathed a sigh of relief. "Sai King."

"Yes, Roland."

"Remember—when you hear the song of the Turtle, you must put aside all other things and tell this story."

"I will. At least I'll try."

"Good."

Then the writer said: "The ball must be taken off the board and broken."

Roland frowned. "Which ball? Black Thirteen?"

"If it wakes, it will become the most dangerous thing in the universe. And it's waking now. In some other place. Some other where and when."

"Thank you for your prophecy, sai King."

"Dad-a-shim, dad-a-shower. Take the ball to the double Tower."

To this Roland shook his head in silent bewilderment.

Eddie put a fist to his forehead and bent slightly. "Hile, wordslinger."

King smiled faintly, as if this were ridiculous, but said nothing.

"Long days and pleasant nights," Roland told him. "You don't need to think about the chickens anymore."

An expression of almost heartbreaking hope spread across Stephen King's bearded face. "Do you really say so?"

"I really do. And may we meet again on the path before we all meet in the clearing." The gunslinger turned on his bootheel and left the writer's house.

Eddie took a final look at the tall, rather stooped man standing with his narrow ass propped against the counter. He thought: *The next time I see you, Stevie—if I do—your beard will be mostly white and there'll be lines around your face . . . and I'll still be young. How's your blood-pressure, sai? Good to go for the next twenty-two years? Hope so. What about your ticker? Does cancer run in your family, and if it does, how deep?*

There was time for none of these questions, of course. Or any others. Very soon the writer would be waking up and going on with his life. Eddie followed his dinh out into the latening afternoon and closed the door behind him. He was beginning to think that, when ka had sent them here instead of to New York City, it had known what it was doing, after all.

TWELVE

Eddie stopped on the driver's side of John Cullum's car and looked across the roof at the gunslinger. "Did you see that thing around him? That black haze?"

"The todana, yes. Thank your father that it's still faint."

"What's a todana? Sounds like todash."

Roland nodded. "It's a variation of the word. It means deathbag. He's been marked."

"Jesus," Eddie said.

"It's faint, I tell you."

"But there."

Roland opened his door. "We can do nothing about it. Ka marks the time of each man and woman. Let's move, Eddie."

But now that they were actually ready to get rolling again, Eddie was queerly reluctant to go. He had a sense of things unfinished with sai King. And he hated the thought of that black aura.

"What about Turtleback Lane, and the walk-ins? I meant to ask him—"

"We can find it."

"Are you sure? Because I think we need to go there."

"I think so, too. Come on. We've got a lot of work ahead of us."

THIRTEEN

The taillights of the old Ford had hardly cleared the end of the driveway before Stephen King opened his eyes. The first thing he did was look at the clock. Almost four. He should have been rolling after Joe ten minutes ago, but the nap he'd taken had done him good. He felt wonderful. Refreshed. Cleaned out in some weird way. He thought, *If every nap could do that, taking them would be a national law.*

Maybe so, but Betty Jones was going to be seriously worried if she didn't see the Cherokee turning into her yard by four-thirty. King reached for the phone to call her, but his eyes fell to the pad on the desk below it, instead. The sheets were headed CALLING ALL BLOWHARDS. A little something from one of his sisters-in-law.

Face going blank again, King reached for the pad and the pen beside it. He bent and wrote:

Dad-a-chum, dad-a-chee, not to worry, you've got the key.

He paused, looking fixedly at this, then wrote:

Dad-a-chud, dad-a-ched, see it, Jake! The key is red!

He paused again, then wrote:

Dad-a-chum, dad-a-chee, give this boy a plastic key.

He looked at what he had written with deep affection. Almost love. God almighty, but he felt fine! These lines meant nothing at all, and yet writing them afforded a satisfaction so deep it was almost ecstasy.

King tore off the sheet.

Balled it up.

Ate it.

It stuck for a moment in his throat and then—ulp!—down it went. Good deal! He snatched the

(*ad-a-chee*)

key to the Jeep off the wooden key-board (which was itself shaped like a key) and hurried outside. He'd get Joe, they'd come back here and pack, they'd grab supper at Mickey Kee's in South Paris. Correction, Mickey-*Dee's*. He felt he could eat a couple of Quarter Pounders all by himself. Fries, too. *Damn,* but he felt good!

When he reached Kansas Road and turned toward town, he flipped on the radio and got the McCoys, singing "Hang On, Sloopy"—always excellent. His mind drifted, as it so often did while listening to the radio, and he found himself thinking of the characters from that old story, *The Dark Tower.* Not that there were many left; as he recalled, he'd killed most of them off, even the kid. Didn't know what else to do with him, probably. That was usually why you got rid of characters, because you didn't know what else to do with them. What had his name been, Jack? No, that was the haunted Dad in *The Shining.* The *Dark Tower* kid had been *Jake.* Excellent choice of name for a story with a Western motif, something right out of Wayne D. Overholser or Ray Hogan. Was it possible Jake could come back into that story, maybe as a ghost? Of course he could. The nice thing about tales of the supernatural, King reflected, was that nobody had to *really* die. They could always come back, like that guy Barnabas on *Dark Shadows*. Barnabas Collins had been a vampire.

"Maybe the *kid* comes back as a vampire," King said, and laughed. "Watch out, Roland, dinner is served and dinner be you!" But that didn't feel right. What, then? Nothing came, but that was all right. In time, something might. Probably when he least expected it; while feeding the cat or changing the baby or just walking dully along, as Auden said in that poem about suffering.

No suffering today. Today he felt *great*.

Yar, just call me Tony the Tiger.

On the radio, the McCoys gave way to Troy Shondell, singing "This Time."

That *Dark Tower* thing had been sort of interesting, actually. King thought, *Maybe when we get back from up north I ought to dig it out. Take a look at it.*

Not a bad idea.

STAVE: *Commala-come-call*
We hail the One who made us all,
Who made the men and made the maids,
Who made the great and small.

RESPONSE: *Commala-come-call!*
He made the great and small!
And yet how great the hand of fate
That rules us one and all.

JAKE AND CALLAHAN

12TH STANZA

ONE

Don Callahan had had many dreams of returning to America. Usually they began with him waking up under a high, fair desert sky full of the puffy clouds baseball players call "angels" or in his own rectory bed in the town of Jerusalem's Lot, Maine. No matter which locale it happened to be, he'd be nearly overwhelmed with relief, his first instinct for prayer. *Oh, thank God. Thank God it was only a dream and finally I am awake.*

He was awake now, no question of that.

He turned a complete circle in the air and saw Jake do exactly the same in front of him. He lost one of his sandals. He could hear Oy yapping and Eddie roaring in protest. He could hear taxi horns, that sublime New York street music, and something else, as well: a preacher. Really cruising along, by the sound of him. Third gear, at least. Maybe overdrive.

One of Callahan's ankles clipped the side of the Unfound Door as he went through and there was a burst of terrific pain from that spot. Then the ankle (and the area around it) went numb. There was a speedy riffle of todash chimes, like a thirty-three-and-a-third record played at forty-five rpm. A buffet of conflicting air currents hit him, and suddenly he was smelling gasoline and exhaust instead of the Doorway Cave's dank air. First street music; now street perfume.

For a moment there were *two* preachers. Henchick behind, roaring *"Behold, the door opens!"* and another one ahead, bellowing *"Say GAWD, brotha, that's right, say GAWD on Second Avenue!"*

More twins, Callahan thought—there was time for that—and then the door behind him blammed shut and the only God-shouter was the one on Second Avenue. Callahan also had time to think *Welcome home, you sonofabitch, welcome back to America,* and then he landed.

TWO

It was quite an all-out crash, but he came down hard on his hands and knees. His jeans protected the latter parts to some degree (although they tore), but the sidewalk scraped what felt like an acre of skin from his palms. He heard the rose, singing powerfully and undisturbed.

Callahan rolled over onto his back and looked up at the sky, snarling with pain, holding his bleeding, buzzing hands in front of his face. A drop of blood from the left one splashed onto his cheek like a tear.

"Where the fuck did *you* come from, my friend?" asked an astounded black man in gray fatigues. He seemed to have been the only one to mark Don Callahan's dramatic re-entry into America. He was staring down at the man on the sidewalk with wide eyes.

"Oz," Callahan said, and sat up.

His hands stung fiercely and now his ankle was back, complaining in loud *yowp-yowp-yowp* bursts of pain that were in perfect synch with his elevated heartbeat. "Go on, fella. Get out of here. I'm okay, so twenty-three skidoo."

"Whatever you say, bro. Later."

The man in the gray fatigues—a janitor just off-shift was Callahan's guess—started walking. He favored Callahan with one final glance—still amazed but already beginning to doubt what he'd seen—and then skirted the little crowd listening to the street preacher. A moment later he was gone.

Callahan got to his feet and stood on one of the steps leading up to Hammarskjöld Plaza, looking for Jake. He didn't see him. He looked the other way, for the Unfound Door, but that was gone, too.

"Now listen, my friends! Listen, I say God, I say God's love, I say gimme hallelujah!"

"Hallelujah," said a member of the street preacher's crowd, not really sounding all that into it.

"I say amen, thank you, brotha! Now listen because this is America's time of TESTING and America is FAILING her TEST! This country needs a BOMB, not a new-kew-lar one but a GAWD-BOMB, can you say hallelujah?"

"Jake!" Callahan shouted. "Jake, where are you? Jake!"

"Oy!" That was Jake, his voice raised in a scream. *"Oy, LOOK OUT!"*

There was a yapping, excited bark Callahan would have recognized anywhere. Then the scream of locked tires.

The blare of a horn.

And the thud.

THREE

Callahan forgot about his bashed ankle and sizzling palms. He ran around the preacher's little crowd (it had turned as one to the street and the preacher had quit his rant in mid-flow) and saw Jake standing in Second Avenue, in front of a Yellow Cab that had slewed to a crooked stop no more than an inch from his legs. Blue smoke was still drifting up from its rear tires. The driver's face was a pallid, craning O of shock. Oy was crouched between Jake's feet. To Callahan the bumbler looked freaked out but otherwise all right.

The thud came again and yet again. It was Jake, bringing his balled-up fist down on the hood of the taxi. *"Asshole!"* Jake yelled at the pallid O on the other side of the windshield. *Thud!* *"Why don't you—" Thud! "—watch where—" THUD! "—the fuck you're GOING!" THUD-THUD!*

"You give it to im, Cholly!" yelled someone from across the street, where perhaps three dozen people had stopped to watch the fun.

The taxi's door opened. The long tall helicopter who stepped out was wearing what Callahan thought was called a dashiki over jeans and huge mutant sneakers with boomerangs on the sides. There was a fez on his head, which probably accounted somewhat for the impression of extreme height, but not entirely. Callahan guessed the guy was at least six and a half feet tall, fiercely bearded, and scowling at Jake. Callahan started toward this developing scene with a sinking heart, barely aware that one of his feet was bare, slapping the pavement with every other step. The street preacher was also moving toward the developing confrontation. Behind the taxi stopped in the intersection, another driver, interested in nothing but his own scheduled evening plans, laid on his horn with both hands—*WHEEEOOOONNNNNNK!!!*—and leaned out his window, hollering "Move it, Abdul, you're blockin the box!"

Jake paid no attention. He was in a total fury. This time he brought both fists down on the hood of the taxi, like Ratso Rizzo in *Midnight Cowboy*—THUD! *"You almost ran my friend down, you asshole, did you even LOOK—"* THUD! *"—where you were GOING?"*

Before Jake could bring his fists down on the hood of the taxi again—which he obviously meant to do until he was satisfied—the driver grabbed his right wrist. "Stop doing that, you little punk!" he cried in an outraged and strangely high voice. "I am telling you—"

Jake stepped back, breaking free of the tall taxi driver's grip. Then, in a liquid motion too quick for Callahan to follow, the kid yanked the Ruger from the docker's clutch under his arm and pointed it at the driver's nose.

"Tell me *what?*" Jake raged at him. "Tell me *what?* That you were driving too fast and almost ran down my friend? That you don't want to die here in the street with a hole in your head? Tell me *WHAT?*"

A woman on the far side of Second Avenue either saw the gun or caught a whiff of Jake's homicidal fury. She screamed and started hurrying away. Several more followed her example. Others gathered at the curb, smelling blood. Incredibly, one of them—a young man wearing his hat turned around backward—shouted: "Go on, kid! Ventilate that camel-jockey!"

The driver backed up two steps, his eyes widening. He held up his hands to his shoulders. "Do not shoot me, boy! Please!"

"Then say you're sorry!" Jake raved. "If you want to live, you cry my pardon! And his! And *his!*" Jake's skin was dead pale except for tiny red spots of color high up on his cheekbones. His eyes were huge and wet. What Don Callahan saw most clearly and liked least was the way the barrel of the Ruger was trembling. "Say you're sorry for the way you were driving, you careless motherfucker! Do it now! *Do it now!*"

Oy whined uneasily and said, "Ake!"

Jake looked down at him. When he did, the taxi driver lunged for the gun. Callahan hit him with a fairly respectable right cross and the driver sprawled against the front of his car, his fez tumbling from his head. The driver behind him had clear lanes on either side and could have swung around but continued to lay on his horn instead, yelling *"Move it buddy, move it!"* Some of the spectators on the far side of Second were actually applauding like spectators at a Madison Square Garden fight, and Callahan thought:

Why, this place is a madhouse. Did I know that before and forget, or is it something I just learned?

The street preacher, a man with a beard and long white hair that descended to his shoulders, was now standing beside Jake, and when Jake started to raise the Ruger again, the preacher laid a gentle, unhurried hand on the boy's wrist.

"Holster it, boy," he said. "Stick it away, praise Jesus."

Jake looked at him and saw what Susannah had seen not long before: a man who looked eerily like Henchick of the Manni. Jake put the gun back into the docker's clutch, then bent and picked up Oy. The bumbler whined, stretched his face toward Jake's on his long neck, and began to lick the boy's cheek.

Callahan, meanwhile, had taken the driver's arm and was leading him back toward his hack. He fished in his pocket and palmed a ten-dollar bill which was about half the money they'd managed to put together for this little safari.

"All over," he said to the driver, speaking in what he hoped was a soothing voice. "No harm, no foul, you go your way, he goes his—" And then, past the hackie, yelling at the relentless horn-honker: "Horn works, you nimrod, so why not give it a rest and try your lights?"

"That little bastard was pointing the gun at me," said the taxi driver. He felt on his head for his fez and didn't find it.

"It's only a model," Callahan said soothingly. "The kind of thing you build from a kit, doesn't even fire pellets. I assure y—"

"Hey, pal!" cried the street preacher, and when the taxi driver looked, the preacher underhanded him the faded red fez. With this back on his head, the driver seemed more willing to be reasonable. More willing yet when Callahan pressed the ten into his hand.

The guy behind the cab was driving an elderly whale of a Lincoln. Now he laid on his horn again.

"You may be biting my crank, Mr. Monkey-meat!" the taxi driver yelled at him, and Callahan almost burst out laughing. He started toward the guy in the Lincoln. When the taxi driver tried to join him, Callahan put his hands on the man's shoulders and stopped him.

"Let me handle this. I'm a religious. Making the lion lie down with the lamb is my job."

The street preacher joined them in time to hear this. Jake had retired to the background. He was standing beside the street preacher's van and checking Oy's legs to make sure he was uninjured.

"Brother!" the street preacher addressed Callahan. "May I ask your denomination? Your, I say hallelujah, your *view* of the *Almighty*?"

"I'm a Catholic," Callahan said. "Therefore, I view the Almighty's a guy."

The street preacher held out a large, gnarled hand. It produced exactly the sort of fervent, just-short-of-crushing grip Callahan had expected. The man's cadences, combined with his faint Southern accent, made Callahan think of Foghorn Leghorn in the Warner Bros. cartoons.

"I'm Earl Harrigan," the preacher said, continuing to wring Callahan's fingers. "Church of the

Holy God-Bomb, Brooklyn and America. A pleasure to meet you, Father."

"I'm sort of semi-retired," Callahan said. "If you have to call me something, make it Pere. Or just Don. Don Callahan."

"Praise Jesus, Father Don!"

Callahan sighed and supposed Father Don would have to do. He went to the Lincoln. The cab driver, meanwhile, scooted away with his OFF DUTY light on.

Before Callahan could speak to the Lincoln's driver, that worthy got out on his own. It was Callahan's night for tall men. This one went about six-three and was carrying a large belly.

"It's all over," Callahan told him. "I suggest you get back in your car and drive out of here."

"It ain't over until I say it's over," Mr. Lincoln demurred. "I got Abdul's medallion number; what I want from you, Sparky, is the name and address of that kid with the dog. I also want a closer look at the pistol he just—*ow, ow! OWW! OWWWWW! Quit it!*"

Reverend Earl Harrigan had seized one of Mr. Lincoln's hands and twisted it behind his back. Now he seemed to be doing something creative to the man's thumb. Callahan couldn't see exactly what it was. The angle was wrong.

"God loves you so much," Harrigan said, speaking quietly into Mr. Lincoln's ear. "And what He wants in return, you loudmouth shithead, is for you to give me hallelujah and then go on your way. Can you give me hallelujah?"

"*OWW, OWWW, let go! Police! POLEECE!*"

"Only policeman apt to be on this block around now would be Officer Benzyck, and he's already given me my nightly ticket and moved on. By now he'll be in Dennis's, having a pecan waffle and double bacon, praise God, so I want you to think about this." There came a cracking sound from behind Mr. Lincoln's back that set Callahan's teeth on edge. He didn't like to think Mr. Lincoln's thumb had made that sound, but didn't know what else it could have been. Mr. Lincoln cocked his head skyward on his thick neck and let out a long exhalation of pure pain—*Yaaaahhhhhhh!*

"You want to give me hallelujah, brother," advised Rev. Harrigan, "or you'll be, praise God, carrying your thumb home in your breast pocket."

"Hallelujah," whispered Mr. Lincoln. His complexion had gone an ocher shade. Callahan thought some of that might be attributable to the orangey streetlamps which at some point had replaced the fluorescents of his own time. Probably not all of it, though.

"Good! Now say amen. You'll feel better when you do."

"A-Amen."

"Praise God! Praise Jee-eee-eee-*esus*!"

"Let me go . . . let go of my *thumb*—!"

"Are you going to get out of here and stop blocking this intersection if I do?"

"Yes!"

"Without any more fiddle-de-dee or hidey-ho, praise Jesus?"

"*Yes!*"

Harrigan leaned yet closer to Mr. Lincoln, his lips

stopping less than half an inch from a large plug of yellow-orange wax caught in the cup of Mr. Lincoln's ear. Callahan watched this with fascination and complete absorption, all other unresolved issues and unfulfilled goals for the time being forgotten. The Pere was more than halfway to believing that if Jesus had had Earl Harrigan on His team, it probably would have been old Pontius who ended up on the cross.

"My friend, bombs will soon begin to fall: God-bombs. And you have to choose whether you want to be among those who are, praise Jesus, up in the sky *dropping* those bombs, or those who are in the villages below, getting blown to smithereens. Now I sense this isn't the time or place for you to make a choice for Christ, but will you at least think about these things, sir?"

Mr. Lincoln's response must have been a tad slow for Rev. Harrigan, because that worthy did something else to the hand he had pinned behind Mr. Lincoln's back. Mr. Lincoln uttered another high, breathless scream.

"I said, will you *think* about these things?"

"Yes! Yes! Yes!"

"Then get in your car and drive away and God bless you and keep you."

Harrigan released Mr. Lincoln. Mr. Lincoln backed away from him, eyes wide, and got back into his car. A moment later he was driving down Second Avenue—fast.

Harrigan turned to Callahan and said, "Catholics are going to Hell, Father Don. Idolators, each and every one of them; they bow to

the Cult of Mary. And the Pope! Don't get me
started on *him!* Yet I have known some fine
Catholic folks, and have no doubt you're one of
them. It may be I can pray you through to a
change of faith. Lacking that, I may be able to
pray you through the flames." He looked back at
the sidewalk in front of what now seemed to be
called Hammarskjöld Plaza. "I believe my congre-
gation has dispersed."

"Sorry about that," Callahan said.

Harrigan shrugged. "Folks don't come to Jesus
in the summertime, anyway," he said matter-of-
factly. "They do a little window-shopping and then
go back to their sinning. Winter's the time for serious crusading . . . got to get you a little storefront
where you can give em hot soup and hot scripture
on a cold night." He looked down at Callahan's
feet and said, "You seem to have lost one of your
sandals, my mackerel-snapping friend." A new
horn blared at them and a perfectly amazing
taxi—to Callahan it looked like a newer version of
the old VW Microbuses—went swerving past with
a passenger yelling something out at them. It probably wasn't happy birthday. "Also, if we don't get
out of the street, faith may not be enough to protect us."

FOUR

"He's all right," Jake said, setting Oy down on the
sidewalk. "I flipped, didn't I? I'm sorry."

"Perfectly understandable," the Rev. Harrigan
assured him. "What an interesting dog! I've never

seen one that looked quite like that, praise Jesus!"
And he bent to Oy.

"He's a mixed breed," Jake said tightly, "and he
doesn't like strangers."

Oy showed how much he disliked and distrusted
them by raising his head to Harrigan's hand and
flattening his ears in order to improve the stroking
surface. He grinned up at the preacher as if they
were old, old pals. Callahan, meanwhile, was looking around. It was New York, and in New York
people had a tendency to mind their business and
let you mind yours, but still, Jake had drawn a gun.
Callahan didn't know how many folks had seen it,
but he *did* know it would only take one to report it,
perhaps to this Officer Benzyck Harrigan had mentioned, and put them in trouble when they could
least afford it.

He looked at Oy and thought, *Do me a favor
and don't say anything, okay? Jake can maybe pass
you off as some new kind of Corgi or Border Collie
hybrid, but the minute you start talking, that goes
out the window. So do me a favor and don't.*

"Good boy," said Harrigan, and after Jake's
friend miraculously did *not* respond by saying
"Oy!" the preacher straightened up. "I have something for you, Father Don. Just a minute."

"Sir, we really have to—"

"I have something for you, too, son—praise
Jesus, say dear Lord! But first . . . this won't take
but a second . . ."

Harrigan ran to open the side door of his ille-
gally parked old Dodge van, ducked inside, rummaged.

Callahan bore this for awhile, but the sense of passing seconds quickly became too much. "Sir, I'm sorry, but—"

"*Here* they are!" Harrigan exclaimed and backed out of the van with the first two fingers of his right hand stuck into the heels of a pair of battered brown loafers. "If you're less than a size twelve, we can stuff em with newspaper. More, and I guess you're out of luck."

"A twelve is exactly what I am," Callahan said, and ventured a praise-God as well as a thank-you. He was actually most comfortable in size eleven and a half shoes, but these were close enough, and he slipped them on with genuine gratitude. "And now we—"

Harrigan turned to the boy and said, "The woman you're after got into a cab right where we had our little dust-up, and no more than half an hour ago." He grinned at Jake's rapidly changing expression—first astonishment, then delight. "She said the other one is in charge, that you'd know who the other one was, and where the other one is taking her."

"Yeah, to the Dixie Pig," Jake said. "Lex and Sixty-first. Pere, we might still have time to catch her, but only if we go right now. She—"

"No," Harrigan said. "The woman who spoke to me—inside my head she spoke to me and clear as a bell, praise Jesus—said you were to go to the hotel first."

"Which hotel?" Callahan asked.

Harrigan pointed down Forty-sixth Street to the Plaza–Park Hyatt. "That's the only one in the neighborhood . . . and that's the direction she came from."

"Thank you," Callahan said. "Did she say why we were to go there?"

"No," Harrigan said serenely, "I believe right around then the other one caught her blabbing and shut her up. Then into the taxi and away she went!"

"Speaking of moving on—" Jake began.

Harrigan nodded, but also raised an admonitory finger. "By all means, but remember that the God-bombs are going to fall. Never mind the showers of blessing—that's for Methodist wimps and Episcopalian scuzzballs! The *bombs* are gonna fall! And boys?"

They turned back to him.

"I know you fellas are as much God's human children as I am, for I've smelled your sweat, praise Jesus. But what about the lady? The lay-*dees*, for in truth I b'lieve there were two of em. What about *them*?"

"The woman you met's with us," Callahan said after a brief hesitation. "She's okay."

"I wonder about that," Harrigan said. "The Book says—praise God and praise His Holy Word—to beware of the strange woman, for her lips drip as does the honeycomb but her feet go down to death and her steps take hold on hell. Remove thy way from her and come not nigh the door of her house." He had raised one lumpy hand in a benedictory gesture as he offered this. Now he lowered it and shrugged. "That ain't exact, I don't have the memory for scripture that I did when I was younger and Bible-shoutin down south with my Daddy, but I think you get the drift."

"Book of Proverbs," Callahan said.

Harrigan nodded. "Chapter five, say *Gawd*." Then he turned and contemplated the building which rose into the night sky behind him. Jake started away, but Callahan stayed him with a touch . . . although when Jake raised his eyebrows, Callahan could only shake his head. No, he didn't know why. All he knew was that they weren't quite through with Harrigan yet.

"This is a city stuffed with sin and sick with transgression," the preacher said at last. "Sodom on the halfshell, Gomorrah on a graham cracker, ready for the God-bomb that will surely fall from the skies, say hallelujah, say sweet Jesus and gimme amen. But this right here is a good place. A *good* place. Can you boys feel it?"

"Yes," Jake said.

"Can you *hear* it?"

"Yes," Jake and Callahan said together.

"Amen! I thought it would all stop when they tore down the little deli that stood here years and years ago. But it didn't. Those angelic voices—"

"So speaks Gan along the Beam," Jake said.

Callahan turned to him and saw the boy's head cocked to one side, his face wearing the calm look of entrancement.

Jake said: "So speaks Gan, and in the voice of the can calah, which some call angels. Gan denies the can toi; with the merry heart of the guiltless he denies the Crimson King and Discordia itself."

Callahan looked at him with wide eyes—frightened eyes—but Harrigan nodded matter-of-factly, as if he had heard it all before. Perhaps he had. "There was a vacant lot after the deli, and then they built this. Two Hammarskjöld Plaza. And I thought, 'Well, *that'll* end it and then I'll move on, for Satan's grip is strong and his hoof prints leave deep tracks in the ground, and there no flower will bloom and no grain will grow.' Can you say *see*-lah?" He raised his arms, his gnarly old man's hands, trembling with the outriders of Parkinson's, turned upward to the sky in that open immemorial gesture of praise and surrender. "Yet still it sings," he said, and dropped them.

"Selah," Callahan murmured. "You say true, we say thank ya."

"It *is* a flower," Harrigan said, "for once I went in there to see. In the lobby, somebody say hallelu-jah, I say in the *lobby* between the doors to the street and the elevators to those upper floors where God knows how much dollarbill fuckery is done, there's a little garden growing in the sun which falls through the tall windows, a garden behind velvet ropes, and the sign says GIVEN BY THE TET CORPORA-TION, IN HONOR OF THE BEAME FAMILY, AND IN MEM-ORY OF GILEAD."

"Does it?" Jake said, and his face lit with a glad smile. "Do you say so, sai Harrigan?"

"Boy, if I'm lyin I'm dyin. *Gawd*-bomb! And in the middle of all those flowers there grows a single wild rose, so beautiful that I saw it and wept as those by the waters of Babylon, the great river that flows by Zion. And the men coming and going in that place, them with their briefcases stuffed full of Satan's piece-work, many of *them* wept, too. Wept and went right on about their whores' business as if they didn't even know."

"They know," Jake said softly. "You know what I think, Mr. Harrigan? I think the rose is a secret their hearts keep, and that if anyone threatened it, most of them would fight to protect it. Maybe to the death." He looked up at Callahan. "Pere, we have to go."

"Yes."

"Not a bad idea," Harrigan agreed, "for mine eyes can see Officer Benzyck headed back this way, and it might be well if you were gone when he gets here. I'm glad your furry little friend wasn't hurt, son."

"Thanks, Mr. Harrigan."

"Praise God, he's no more a dog than I am, is he?"

"No, sir," Jake said, smiling widely.

"Beware that woman, boys. She put a thought in my head. I call that witchcraft. And she was *two*."

"Twins-say-twim, aye," Callahan said, and then (without knowing he meant to do it until it was done) he sketched the sign of the cross in front of the preacher.

"Thank you for your blessing, heathen or not," Earl Harrigan said, clearly touched. Then he turned toward the approaching NYPD patrolman and called cheerfully, "Officer Benzyck! Good to see you and there's some jam right there on your collar, praise God!"

And while Officer Benzyck was studying the jam on his uniform collar, Jake and Callahan slipped away.

FIVE

"Whoo-*eee*," Jake said under his breath as they walked toward the brightly underlit hotel canopy. A white limousine, easily twice the size of any Jake had seen before (and he'd seen his share; once his father had even taken him to the Emmys), was offloading laughing men in tuxedos and women in evening dresses. They came out in a seemingly endless stream.

"Yes indeed," Callahan said. "It's like being on a roller coaster, isn't it?"

Jake said, "We're not even supposed to *be* here. This was Roland and Eddie's job. We were just supposed to go see Calvin Tower."

"Something apparently thought different."

"Well, it should have thought twice," Jake said gloomily. "A kid and a priest, with one gun between them? It's a joke. What are our chances, if the Dixie Pig is full of vampires and low men unwinding on their day off?"

Callahan did not respond to this, although the prospect of trying to rescue Susannah from the Dixie Pig terrified him. "What was that Gan stuff you were spouting?"

Jake shook his head. "I don't know—I can barely remember what I said. I think it's part of the touch, Pere. And do you know where I think I got it?"

"Mia?"

The boy nodded. Oy trotted neatly at his heel, his long snout not quite touching Jake's calf. "And I'm getting something else, as well. I keep seeing this black man in a jail cell. There's a radio playing, telling him all these people are dead—the Kennedys,

Marilyn Monroe, George Harrison, Peter Sellers, Itzak Rabin, whoever *he* is. I think it might be the jail in Oxford, Mississippi, where they kept Odetta Holmes for awhile."

"But this is a *man* you see. Not Susannah but a *man*."

"Yes, with a toothbrush mustache, and he wears funny little gold-rimmed glasses, like a wizard in a fairy-tale."

They stopped just outside the radiance of the hotel's entrance. A doorman in a green swallowtail coat blew an ear-splitting blast on his little silver whistle, hailing down a Yellow Cab.

"Is it Gan, do you think? Is the black man in the jail cell Gan?"

"I don't know." Jake shook his head with frustration. "There's something about the Dogan, too, all mixed in."

"And this comes from the touch."

"Yes, but it's not from Mia or Susannah or you or me. I think . . ." Jake's voice lowered. "I think I better figure out who that black man is and what he means to us, because I think that what I'm seeing comes from the Dark Tower itself." He looked at Callahan solemnly. "In some ways, we're getting very close to it, and that's why it's so dangerous for the ka-tet to be broken like it is.

"In some ways, we're almost there."

SIX

Jake took charge smoothly and completely from the moment he stepped out of the revolving doors with Oy in his arms and then put the billy-bumbler down on the lobby's tile floor. Callahan didn't think the kid was even aware of it, and probably that was all to the good. If he got self-conscious, his confidence might crumble.

Oy sniffed delicately at his own reflection in one of the lobby's green glass walls, then followed Jake to the desk, his claws clicking faintly on the black and white marble squares. Callahan walked beside him, aware that he was looking at the future and trying not to goggle at it too obviously.

"She was here," Jake said. "Pere, I can almost see her. Both of them, her and Mia."

Before Callahan could reply, Jake was at the desk. "Cry pardon, ma'am," he said. "My name is Jake Chambers. Do you have a message for me, or a package, or something? It'd be either from Susannah Dean or maybe from a Miss Mia."

The woman peered down doubtfully at Oy for a moment. Oy looked up at her with a cheery grin that revealed a great many teeth. Perhaps these disturbed the clerk, because she turned away from him with a frown and examined the screen of her computer.

"Chambers?" she asked.

"Yes, ma'am." Spoken in his best getting-along-with-grownups voice. It had been awhile since he'd needed to use that one, but it was still there, Jake found, and within easy reach.

"I have something for you, but it's not from a woman. It's from someone named Stephen King." She smiled. "I don't suppose it's the famous writer? Do you know him?"

"No, ma'am," Jake said, and snuck a sidewards glance at Callahan. Neither of them had heard of Stephen King until recently, but Jake understood why the name might give his current traveling companion the chills. Callahan didn't look particularly chilly at the moment, but his mouth had thinned to a single line.

"Well," she said, "I suppose it's a common enough name, isn't it? Probably there are *normal* Stephen Kings all over the United States who wish he'd just . . . I don't know . . . give it a *rest*." She voiced a nervous little laugh, and Callahan wondered what had set her on edge. Oy, who got less doggy the longer you looked at him? Maybe, but Callahan thought it was more likely something in Jake, something that whispered *danger.* Perhaps even *gunslinger.* Certainly there was something in him that set him apart from other boys. *Far.* Callahan thought of him pulling the Ruger from the docker's clutch and sticking it under the unfortunate taxi driver's nose. *Tell me that you were driving too fast and almost ran down my friend!* he'd screamed, his finger already white on the trigger. *Tell me that you don't want to die here in the street with a hole in your head!*

Was that the way an ordinary twelve-year-old reacted to a near-miss accident? Callahan thought not. He thought the desk clerk was right to be nervous. As for himself, Callahan realized he felt a little better about their chances at the Dixie Pig. Not a lot, but a little.

SEVEN

Jake, perhaps sensing something a little off-kilter, flashed the clerk his best getting-along-with-grown-ups smile, but to Callahan it looked like Oy's: too many teeth.

"Just a moment," she said, turning away from him.

Jake gave Callahan a puzzled what's-up-with-*her* look. Callahan shrugged and spread his hands.

The clerk went to a cabinet behind her, opened it, looked through the contents of a box stored inside, and returned to the desk with an envelope bearing the Plaza–Park's logo. Jake's name—and something else—had been written on the front in what looked like half-script and half-printing:

> *Jake Chambers*
> *This is the Truth*

She slid it across the desk to him, careful that their fingers should not touch.

Jake took it and ran his fingers down the length of it. There was a piece of paper inside. Something else, as well. A hard narrow strip. He tore open the envelope and pulled out the paper. Folded inside it was the slim, white plastic rectangle of a hotel MagCard. The note had been written on a cheeky piece of stationery headed CALLING ALL BLOWHARDS. The message itself was only three lines long:

> *Dad-a-chum, dad-a-chee, not to worry, you've got the key.*

Dad-a-chud, dad-a-ched, see it, Jake! The key is red!

Jake looked at the MagCard and watched color abruptly swirl into it, turning it the color of blood almost instantly.

Couldn't be red until the message was read, Jake thought, smiling a little at the idea's riddle-ish quality. He looked up to see if the clerk had seen the MagCard's transformation, but she had found something which required her attention at the far end of the desk. And Callahan was checking out a couple of women who'd just come strolling in from the street. He might be a Pere, Jake reflected, but his eye for the ladies still seemed to be in proper working order.

Jake looked back at the paper and was just in time to read the last line:

Dad-a-chum, dad-a-chee, give this boy a plastic key.

A couple of years before, his mother and father had given him a Tyco Chemistry Set for Christmas. Using the instruction booklet, he'd whipped up a batch of invisible ink. The words written in the stuff had faded almost as quickly as these words were fading now, only if you looked very closely, you could still read the message written in chemistry set ink. This one, however, was authentically *gone,* and Jake knew why. Its purpose had been served. There was no more need for it. Ditto the line about the key being red, and sure enough, that was fading, as well. Only the first line remained, as if he needed reminding:

Dad-a-chum, dad-a-chee, not to worry, you've got the key.

Had Stephen King sent this message? Jake doubted it. More likely one of the other players in the game—perhaps even Roland or Eddie—had used the name to get his attention. Still, he'd run upon two things since arriving here that encouraged him enormously. The first was the continued singing of the rose. It was stronger than ever, really, even though a skyscraper had been built on the vacant lot. The second was that Stephen King was apparently still alive twenty-four years after creating Jake's traveling companion. And no longer just a writer but a *famous* writer.

Great. For now things were still rattling precariously along the right set of tracks.

Jake grabbed Father Callahan's arm and led him toward the gift shop and tinkling cocktail piano. Oy followed, padding at Jake's knee. Along the wall they found a line of house phones. "When the operator answers," Jake said, "tell her you want to talk to your friend Susannah Dean, or to *her* friend, Mia."

"She'll ask me what room," Callahan said.

"Tell her you forgot, but it's on the nineteenth floor."

"How do you—"

"It'll be the nineteenth, just trust me."

"I do," Callahan said.

The phone rang twice and then the operator asked how she could help. Callahan told her. He was connected, and in some room on the nineteenth floor, a telephone began to ring.

Jake watched the Pere begin to speak, then subside into listening again with a small, bemused smile on his face. After a few moments, he hung up. "Answering machine!" he said. "They have a *machine* that takes guests' calls and then tapes messages! What a wonderful invention!"

"Yeah," Jake said. "Anyway, we know for sure that she's out and for pretty sure she didn't leave anyone behind to watch her gunna. But, just in case . . ." He patted the front of his shirt, which now concealed the Ruger.

As they crossed the lobby to the elevator bank, Callahan said: "What do we want in her room?"

"I don't know."

Callahan touched him on the shoulder. "I think you do."

The doors of the middle elevator popped open and Jake got on with Oy still at heel. Callahan followed, but Jake thought he was all at once dragging his feet a little.

"Maybe," Jake said as they started up. "And maybe you do, too."

Callahan's stomach suddenly felt heavier, as if he'd just finished a large meal. He supposed the added weight was fear. "I thought I was rid of it," he said. "When Roland took it out of the church, I really thought I was rid of it."

"Some bad pennies just keep turning up," Jake said.

EIGHT

He was prepared to try his unique red key in every door on the nineteenth floor if he had to, but Jake knew 1919 was right even before they reached it. Callahan did, too, and a sheen of sweat broke on his forehead. It felt thin and hot. Feverish.

Even Oy knew. The bumbler whined uneasily.

"Jake," Callahan said. "We need to think this over. That thing is dangerous. Worse, it's *malevolent*."

"That's why we gotta take it," Jake said patiently. He stood in front of 1919, drumming the MagCard between his fingers. From behind the door—and under it, and through it—came a hideous drone like the singing voice of some apocalyptic idiot. Mixed in was the sound of jangling, out-of-tune chimes. Jake knew the ball had the power to send you todash, and in those dark and mostly doorless spaces, it was all too possible to become lost forever. Even if you found your way to another version of Earth, it would have a queer darkness to it, as if the sun were always on the verge of total eclipse.

"Have you seen it?" Callahan asked.

Jake shook his head.

"I have," Callahan said dully, and armed sweat from his forehead. His cheeks had gone leaden. "There's an Eye in it. I think it's the Crimson King's eye. I think it's a part of him that's trapped in there forever, and insane. Jake, taking that ball to a place where there are vampires and low men—servants of the King—would be like giving Adolf Hitler an A-bomb for his birthday."

Jake knew perfectly well that Black Thirteen was capable of doing great, perhaps illimitable, damage. But he knew something else, as well.

"Pere, if Mia left Black Thirteen in this room

and she's now going to where *they* are, they'll
know about it soon enough. And they'll be after it
in one of their big flashy cars before you can say
Jack Robinson."

"Can't we leave it for Roland?" Callahan asked
miserably.

"Yes," Jake said. "That's a good idea, just like
taking it to the Dixie Pig is a bad one. But we can't
leave it for him *here*." Then, before Callahan could
say anything else, Jake slid the blood-red MagCard
into the slot above the doorknob. There was a loud
click and the door swung open.

"Oy, stay right here, outside the door."

"Ake!" He sat down, curling his cartoon squig-
gle of a tail around his paws, and looked at Jake
with anxious eyes.

Before they went in, Jake laid a cold hand on
Callahan's wrist and said a terrible thing.

"Guard your mind."

NINE

Mia had left the lights on, and yet a queer darkness
had crept into Room 1919 since her departure.
Jake recognized it for what it was: todash darkness.
The droning song of the idiot and the muffled, jangling chimes were coming from the closet.

It's awake, he thought with mounting dismay. *It
was asleep before—dozing, at least—but all this
moving around woke it up. What do I do? Are the
box and the bowling bag enough to make it safe?
Do I have anything that will make it safer? Any
charm, any sigul?*

As Jake opened the closet door, Callahan found himself exerting all the force of his will—which was considerable—just to keep from fleeing. That atonal humming and the occasional jangling chimes beneath it offended his ears and mind and heart. He kept remembering the way station, and how he had shrieked when the hooded man had opened the box. How *slick* the thing inside had been! It had been lying on red velvet . . . and it had *rolled*. Had *looked* at him, and all the malevolent madness of the universe had been in that disembodied, leering gaze.

I will not run. I will not. If the boy can stay, I can stay.

Ah, but the boy was a *gunslinger,* and that made a difference. He was more than ka's child; he was Roland of Gilead's child as well, his adopted son.

Don't you see how pale he is? He's as scared as you are, for Christ's sake! Now get hold of yourself, man!

Perhaps it was perverse, but observing Jake's extreme pallor steadied him. When an old bit of nonsense song occurred to him and he began to sing under his breath, he steadied yet more.

"Round and round the mulberry bush," he sang in a whisper, "the monkey chased the weasel . . . the monkey thought 'twas all in fun . . ."

Jake eased open the closet. There was a room safe inside. He tried 1919 and nothing happened. He paused to let the safe mechanism reset itself, wiped sweat from his forehead with both hands (they were shaking), and tried again. This time he punched 1999, and the safe swung open.

Black Thirteen's droning song and the contra-puntal jangle of the todash chimes both increased. The sounds were like chilly fingers prying around in their heads.

And it can send you places, Callahan thought. *All you have to do is let down your guard a little bit . . . open the bag . . . open the box . . . and then . . . oh, the places you'll go! Pop goes the weasel!*

True though he knew this to be, part of him *wanted* to open the box. *Lusted* to. Nor was he the only one; as he watched, Jake knelt before the safe like a worshipper at an altar. Callahan reached to stop him from lifting the bag out with an arm that seemed incredibly heavy.

It doesn't matter if you do or don't, a voice whispered in his mind. It was sleep-inducing, that voice, and incredibly persuasive. Nonetheless, Callahan kept reaching. He grasped Jake's collar with fingers from which all feeling seemed to have departed.

"No," he said. "Don't." His voice sounded draggy, dispirited, depressed. When he pulled Jake to one side, the boy seemed to go as if in slow motion, or underwater. The room now seemed lit by the sick yellow light that sometimes falls over a landscape before a ruinous storm. As Callahan fell onto his own knees before the open safe (he seemed to descend through the air for at least a full minute before touching down), he heard the voice of Black Thirteen, louder than ever. It was telling him to kill the boy, to open the boy's throat and give the ball a refreshing drink of his warm life's blood. Then

Callahan himself would be allowed to leap from the room's window.

All the way down to Forty-sixth Street you will praise me, Black Thirteen assured him in a voice both sane and lucid.

"Do it," Jake sighed. "Oh yes, do it, who gives a damn."

"Ake!" Oy barked from the doorway. *"Ake!"* They both ignored him.

As Callahan reached for the bag, he found himself remembering his final encounter with Barlow, the king vampire—the Type One, in Callahan's own parlance—who had come to the little town of 'Salem's Lot. Found himself remembering how he'd confronted Barlow in Mark Petrie's house, with Mark's parents lying lifeless on the floor at the vampire's feet, their skulls crushed and their oh-so-rational brains turned to jelly.

While you fall, I'll let you whisper the name of my king, Black Thirteen whispered. *The Crimson King.*

As Callahan watched his hands grasp the bag—whatever had been there before, NOTHING BUT STRIKES AT MID-WORLD LANES was now printed on the side—he thought of how his crucifix had first glared with some otherworldly light, driving Barlow back . . . and then had begun to darken again.

"Open it!" Jake said eagerly. "Open it, I want to see it!"

Oy was barking steadily now. Down the hall someone yelled "Shut that dog up!" and was likewise ignored.

Callahan slipped the ghostwood box from the bag—the box that had spent such a blessedly quiet time hidden beneath the pulpit of his church in Calla Bryn Sturgis. Now he would open it. Now he would observe Black Thirteen in all its repellent glory.

And then die. Gratefully.

TEN

Sad to see a man's faith fail, the vampire Kurt Barlow had said, and then he'd plucked Don Callahan's dark and useless cross from his hand. Why had he been able to do that? Because—behold the paradox, consider the riddle—Father Callahan *had failed to throw the cross away himself.* Because he had failed to accept that the cross was nothing but one symbol of a far greater power, one that ran like a river beneath the universe, perhaps beneath a thousand universes—

I need no symbol, Callahan thought; and then: *Is that why God let me live? Was He giving me a second chance to learn that?*

It was possible, he thought as his hands settled on the lid of the box. Second chances were one of God's specialties.

"Folks, you got to shut your dog *up.*" The querulous voice of a hotel maid, but very distant. Then it said: "*Madre de Dios,* why's it so *dark* in here? What's that . . . what's that . . . n . . . n . . . "

Perhaps she was trying to say *noise.* If so, she never finished. Even Oy now seemed resigned to the spell of the humming, singing ball, for he gave up his protests (and his post at the door) to come trotting into the room. Callahan supposed the beast wanted to be at Jake's side when the end came.

The Pere struggled to still his suicidal hands. The thing in the box raised the volume of its idiot's song, and the tips of his fingers twitched in response. Then they stilled again. *I have that much of a victory,* Callahan thought.

"Ne'mine, *I'll* do it." The voice of the maid, drugged and avid. "I want to see it. *Dios!* I want to *hold* it!"

Jake's arms seemed to weigh a ton, but he forced them to reach out and grab the maid, a middle-aged Hispanic lady who couldn't have weighed more than a hundred and five pounds.

As he had struggled to still his hands, so Callahan now struggled to pray.

God, not my will but Thine. Not the potter but the potter's clay. If I can't do anything else, help me to take it in my arms and jump out the window and destroy the gods-damned thing once and for all. But if it be Your will to help me make it still, instead—to make it go back to sleep—then send me Your strength. And help me to remember . . .

Drugged by Black Thirteen he might have been, but Jake still hadn't lost his touch. Now he plucked the rest of the thought out of the Pere's mind and spoke it aloud, only changing the word Callahan used to the one Roland had taught them.

"I need no sigul," Jake said. "Not the potter but the potter's clay, *and I need no sigul!*"

"God," Callahan said. The word was as heavy as a stone, but once it was out of his mouth, the rest of them came easier. "God, if You're still there, if You still hear me, this is Callahan. Please still this thing, Lord. Please send it back to sleep. I ask it in the name of Jesus."

"In the name of the White," Jake said.

"*Ite!*" Oy yapped.

"Amen," said the maid in a stoned, bemused voice.

For a moment the droning idiot's song from the box rose another notch, and Callahan understood it was hopeless, that not even God Almighty could stand against Black Thirteen.

Then it fell silent.

"God be thanked," he whispered, and realized his entire body was drenched with sweat.

Jake burst into tears and picked up Oy. The chambermaid also began to weep, but had no one to comfort her. As Pere Callahan slid the meshy (and oddly heavy) material of the bowling bag back around the ghostwood box, Jake turned to her and said, "You need to take a nap, sai."

It was the only thing he could think of, and it worked. The maid turned and walked across to the bed. She crawled up on it, pulled her skirt down over her knees, and appeared to fall unconscious.

"Will it stay asleep?" Jake asked Callahan in a low voice. "Because . . . Pere . . . that was too close for comfort."

Perhaps, but Callahan's mind suddenly seemed free—freer than it had been in years. Or perhaps it was his heart that had been freed. In any case, his thoughts seemed very clear as he lowered the bowling bag to the folded dry-cleaning bags on top of the safe.

Remembering a conversation in the alley behind Home. He and Frankie Chase and Magruder, out on a smoke-break. The talk had turned to protecting your valuables in New York, especially if you had to go away for awhile, and Magruder had said the safest storage in New York . . . the absolute safest storage . . .

"Jake, there's also a bag of plates in the safe."

"Orizas?"

"Yes. Get them." While he did, Callahan went to the maid on the bed and reached into the left skirt pocket of her uniform. He brought out a number of plastic MagCards, a few regular keys, and a brand of mints he'd never heard of—Altoids.

He turned her over. It was like turning a corpse.

"What're you doing?" Jake whispered. He had put Oy down so he could sling the silk-lined reed pouch over his shoulder. It was heavy, but he found the weight comforting.

"Robbing her, what does it look like?" the Pere replied angrily. "Father Callahan of the Holy Roman Catholic Church is robbing a hotel maid. Or would, if she had any . . . ah!"

In the other pocket was the little roll of bills he'd been hoping for. She had been performing turn-down service when Oy's barking had distracted her. This included flushing the john, pulling the shades, turning down the bed, and leaving what the maids called "pillow candy." Sometimes patrons tipped for the service. This maid was carrying two tens, three fives, and four ones.

"I'll pay you back if our paths cross," Callahan told the unconscious maid. "Otherwise, just consider it your service to God."

"*Whiiiite,*" the maid said in the slurred whisper of one who talks and yet sleeps.

Callahan and Jake exchanged a look.

ELEVEN

In the elevator going back down, Callahan held the bag containing Black Thirteen and Jake carried the one with the 'Rizas inside. He also carried their money. It now came to a total of forty-eight dollars.

"Will it be enough?" It was his only question after hearing the Pere's plan for disposing of the ball, a plan which would necessitate another stop.

"I don't know and I don't care," Callahan replied. They were speaking in the low voices of conspirators, although the elevator was empty save for them. "If I can rob a sleeping chambermaid, stiffing a cab driver should be a leadpipe cinch."

"Yeah," Jake said. He was thinking that Roland had done more than rob a few innocent people during his quest for the Tower; he'd killed a good many, as well. "Let's just get this done and then find the Dixie Pig."

"You don't have to worry so much, you know," Callahan said. "If the Tower falls, you'll be among the very first to know."

Jake studied him. After a moment or two of this, Callahan cracked a smile. He couldn't help it.

"Not that funny, sai," Jake said, and they went

out into the dark of that early summer's night in the year of '99.

TWELVE

It was quarter to nine and there was still a residue of light across the Hudson when they arrived at the first of their two stops. The taximeter's tale was nine dollars and fifty cents. Callahan gave the cabbie one of the maid's tens.

"Mon, don't hurt yose'f," the driver said in a powerful Jamaican accent. "I dreadful 'fraid you might leave yose'f *shote*."

"You're lucky to get anything at all, son," Callahan said kindly. "We're seeing New York on a budget."

"My woman got a budget, too," said the cabbie, and then drove away.

Jake, meanwhile, was looking up. "Wow," he said softly. "I guess I forgot how *big* all this is."

Callahan followed his glance, then said: "Let's get it done." And, as they hurried inside: "What are you getting from Susannah? Anything?"

"Man with a guitar," Jake said. "Singing . . . I don't know. And I should. It was another one of those coincidences that aren't coincidences, like the owner of the bookstore being named Tower or Balazar's joint turning out to be The Leaning Tower. Some song . . . I should know."

"Anything else?"

Jake shook his head. "That's the last thing I got from her, and it was just after we got into the taxi outside the hotel. I think she's gone into the Dixie

Pig and now she's out of touch." He smiled faintly at the unintentional pun.

Callahan veered toward the building directory in the center of the huge lobby. "Keep Oy close to you."

"Don't worry."

It didn't take Callahan long to find what he was looking for.

THIRTEEN

The sign read:

LONG-TERM STORAGE
10–36 MOS.
USE TOKENS
TAKE KEY
MANAGEMENT ACCEPTS
NO RESPONSIBILITY
FOR LOST PROPERTY!

Below, in a framed box, was a list of rules and regulations, which they both scanned closely. From beneath their feet came the rumble of a subway train. Callahan, who hadn't been in New York for almost twenty years, had no idea what train it might be, where it might go, or how deep in the city's intestine it might run. They'd already come down two levels by escalator, first to the shops and then to here. The subway station was deeper still.

Jake shifted the bag of Orizas to his other shoulder and pointed out the last line on the framed notice. "We'd get a discount if we were tenants," he said.

"Count!" Oy cried sternly.

"Aye, laddie," Callahan agreed, "and if wishes were horses, beggars would ride. We don't need a discount."

Nor did they. After walking through a metal detector (no problem with the Orizas) and past a rent-a-cop dozing on a stool, Jake determined that one of the smallest lockers—those on the far left-hand side of the long room—would accommodate the MID-WORLD LANES bag and the box inside. To rent the box for the maximum length of time would cost twenty-seven dollars. Pere Callahan fed bills into the various slots of the token-dispensing machine carefully, prepared for a malfunction: of all the wonders and horrors he'd seen during their brief time back in the city (the latter including a two-dollar taxi drop-charge), this was in some ways the hardest to accept. A vending machine that accepted paper currency? A lot of sophisticated technology had to lie behind this machine with its dull brown finish and its sign commanding patrons to INSERT BILLS FACE UP! The picture accompanying the command showed George Washington with the top of his head facing to the left, but the bills Callahan fed into the machine seemed to work no matter which way the head was facing. Just as long as the picture was on top. Callahan was almost relieved when the machine *did* malfunction once, refusing to accept an old and wrinkled dollar bill. The relatively crisp fives it gobbled up without a murmur, dispensing little showers of tokens into the tray beneath. Callahan gathered up twenty-seven dollars' worth of these, started back toward where Jake was waiting, and then turned around again, curious about something. He looked on the side of the amazing (amazing to him, at least, it was) currency-eating vending machine. Toward the bottom, on a series of little plaques, was the information he'd been looking for. This was a Change-Mak-R 2000, manufactured in Cleveland, Ohio, but a lot of companies had chipped in: General Electric, DeWalt Electronics, Showrie Electric, Panasonic, and, at the bottom, smallest of all but very much there, North Central Positronics.

The snake in the garden, Callahan thought. *This guy Stephen King, who supposedly thought me up, may only exist in one world, but what do you bet North Central Positronics exists in all of them? Sure, because that's the Crimson King's rig, just like Sombra's his rig, and he only wants what any power-mad despot in history has wanted: to be everywhere, own everything, and basically control the universe.*

"Or bring it to darkness," he murmured.

"Pere!" Jake called impatiently. *"Pere!"*

"I'm coming," he said, and hurried across to Jake with his hands full of shiny gold tokens.

FOURTEEN

The key came out of Locker 883 after Jake had inserted nine of the tokens, but he went on putting them in until all twenty-seven were gone. At this point the small glass porthole under the locker-number turned red.

"Maxed out," Jake said with satisfaction. They were still talking in those low mustn't-wake-the-baby tones, and this long, cavernous room was indeed very quiet. Jake guessed it would be bedlam at eight in the morning and five in the afternoon on working days, with folks coming and going from the subway station below, some of them storing their gear in the short-term coin-op lockers. Now there was just the ghostly sound of conversation drifting down the escalator well from the few shops still open in the arcade and the rumble of another approaching train.

Callahan slid the bowling bag into the narrow opening. Slid it back as far as it would go with Jake watching anxiously. Then he closed the locker and Jake turned the key. "Bingo," Jake said, putting the key in his pocket. Then, with anxiety: "Will it sleep?"

"I think so," Callahan said. "Like it did in my church. If another Beam breaks, it might wake up and work mischief, but then, if another Beam lets go—"

"If another Beam lets go, a little mischief won't matter," Jake finished for him.

Callahan nodded. "The only thing is . . . well, you know where we're going. And you know what we're apt to find there."

Vampires. Low men. Other servants of the Crimson King, maybe. Possibly Walter, the hooded man in black who sometimes shifted his shape and form and called himself Randall Flagg. Possibly even the Crimson King himself.

Yes, Jake knew.

"If you have the touch," Callahan continued, "we have to assume that some of them do, too. It's possible they could pick this place—and the locker-number—out of our minds. We're going to go in there and try to get her, but we have to recognize that the chances of failure are fairly high. I've never fired a gun in my life, and you're not—forgive me, Jake, but you're not exactly a battle-hardened veteran."

"I've got one or two under my belt," Jake said. He was thinking about his time with Gasher. And about the Wolves, of course.

"This is apt to be different," Callahan said. "I'm just saying it might be a bad idea for us to be taken alive. If it comes to that. Do you understand?"

"Don't worry," Jake said in a tone of chilling comfort. "Don't worry about that, Pere. We won't be."

FIFTEEN

Then they were outside again, looking for another cab. Thanks to the maid's tip-money, Jake reckoned they had just about enough remaining cash to take them to the Dixie Pig. And he had an idea that once they entered the Pig, their need for ready cash—or anything else—would cease.

"Here's one," Callahan said, and waved his arm in a flagging gesture. Jake, meanwhile, looked back at the building from which they had just emerged.

"You're sure it'll be safe there?" he asked Callahan as the cab swerved toward them, honking relentlessly at a slowpoke between him and his fares.

"According to my old friend sai Magruder, that's the safest storage area in Manhattan," Callahan said. "Fifty times safer than the coin-op lockers in Penn Station and Grand Central, he said . . . and of course here you've got the long-term storage option. There are probably other storage places in New York, but we'll be gone before they open—one way or the other."

The cab pulled over. Callahan held the door for Jake, and Oy hopped unobtrusively in right behind him. Callahan spared one final glance at the twin towers of the World Trade Center before getting in himself.

"It's good to go until June of two thousand and two, unless someone breaks in and steals it."

"Or if the building falls down on top of it," Jake said.

Callahan laughed, although Jake hadn't quite sounded as if he were joking. "Never happen. And if it did . . . well, one glass ball under a hundred and ten stories of concrete and steel? Even a glass ball filled with deep magic? That'd be one way to take care of the nasty thing, I guess."

SIXTEEN

Jake had asked the cabbie to drop them off at Lexington and Fifty-ninth, just to be on the safe side, and after looking to Callahan for approval, he gave the sai all but their last two dollars.

On the corner of Lex and Sixtieth, Jake pointed

to a number of cigarette ends mashed into the sidewalk. "This is where he was," he said. "The man playing the guitar."

He bent down, picked up one of the butts, and held it in his palm for a moment or two. Then he nodded, smiled cheerlessly, and readjusted the strap on his shoulder. The Orizas clanked faintly inside the rush bag. Jake had counted them in the back of the cab and hadn't been surprised to find there were exactly nineteen.

"No wonder she stopped," Jake said, dropping the butt and wiping his hand on his shirt. And suddenly he sang, low but perfectly on pitch: "I am a man . . . of constant sorrow . . . I've seen trouble . . . all my days . . . I'm bound to ride . . . that Northern railroad . . . Perhaps I'll take . . . the very next train."

Callahan, keyed up already, felt his nerves crank yet tighter. Of course he recognized the song. Only when Susannah had sung it that night on the Pavilion—the same night Roland had won the hearts of the Calla by dancing the fiercest commala many had ever seen—she'd substituted "maid" for "man."

"She gave him money," Jake said dreamily. "And she said . . ." He stood with his head down, biting his lip, thinking hard. Oy looked up at him raptly. Nor did Callahan interrupt. Understanding had come to him: he and Jake were going to die in the Dixie Pig. They would go down fighting, but they were going to die there.

And he thought dying would be all right. It was going to break Roland's heart to lose the boy . . . yet he would go on. As long as the Dark Tower stood, Roland would go on.

Jake looked up. "She said, 'Remember the struggle.' "

"Susannah did."

"Yes. She *came forward*. Mia let her. And the song moved Mia. She wept."

"Say true?"

"True. Mia, daughter of none, mother of one. And while Mia was distracted . . . her eyes blind with tears . . ."

Jake looked around. Oy looked around with him, likely not searching for anything but only imitating his beloved Ake. Callahan was remembering that night on the Pavilion. The lights. The way Oy had stood on his hind legs and bowed to the *folken*. Susannah, singing. The lights. The dancing, Roland dancing the commala in the lights, the colored lights. Roland dancing in the white. Always Roland; and in the end, after the others had fallen, murdered away one by one in these bloody motions, Roland would remain.

I can live with that, Callahan thought. *And die with it.*

"She left something but it's *gone!*" Jake said in a distressed, almost-crying voice. "Someone must have found it . . . or maybe the guitar-player saw her drop it and took it . . . this fucking city! Everyone steals everything! Ah, *shit!*"

"Let it go."

Jake turned his pale, tired, frightened face up to Callahan's. "She left us something and we *need* it! Don't you understand how thin our chances are?"

"Yes. If you want to back off, Jake, now would be the time."

The boy shook his head with no doubt nor the slightest hesitation, and Callahan was fiercely proud of him. "Let's go, Pere," he said.

SEVENTEEN

On the corner of Lex and Sixty-first they stopped again. Jake pointed across the street. Callahan saw the green awning and nodded. It was imprinted with a cartoon porker that was grinning blissfully in spite of having been roasted a bright and smoking red. THE DIXIE PIG was written on the awning's overhang. Parked in a row in front of it were five long black limousines with their accent lights glowing a slightly blurred yellow in the dark. Callahan realized for the first time that a mist was creeping down the Avenue.

"Here," Jake said, and handed him the Ruger. The boy rummaged in his pockets and came up with two big handfuls of cartridges. They gleamed dully in the pervasive orange glow of the street-lamps. "Put em all in your breast pocket, Pere. Easier to get at that way, all right?"

Callahan nodded.

"Ever shot a gun before?"

"No," Callahan said. "Have you ever fired one of those plates?"

Jake's lips parted in a grin. "Benny Slightman and I snuck a bunch of the practice dishes out to the riverbank and had a match one night. He wasn't much good, but . . ."

"Let me guess. You were."

Jake shrugged, then nodded. He had no words to express how fine the plates had felt in his hands, how savagely right. But perhaps that was natural. Susannah had also taken quickly and naturally to throwing the Oriza. That Pere Callahan had seen for himself.

"All right, what's our plan?" Callahan asked. Now that he had decided to go through it all the way to the end, he was more than willing to give leadership over to the boy. Jake was, after all, the gunslinger.

The boy shook his head. "There *is* none," he said, "not really. I go in first. You right behind me. Once we're through the door, we spread apart. Ten feet between us any time we have ten feet to give, Pere—do you understand? So that no matter how many there are or how *close* they are, no one of them can get both of us at the same time."

This was Roland's teaching, and Callahan recognized it as such. He nodded.

"I'll be able to follow her by touch, and Oy will be able to by scent," Jake said. "Move with us. Shoot whatever asks to be shot, and without hesitation, do you understand?"

"Aye."

"If you kill something that has what looks like a useful weapon, take it. If you can scoop it up on the move, that is. We have to keep moving. We have to keep taking it to them. We have to be relentless. Can you scream?"

Callahan considered it, then nodded.

"Scream at them," Jake said. "I'll be doing the

same. And I'll be moving. Maybe running, more likely at a good fast walk. Make sure that every time I look on my right, I see the side of your face."

"You'll see it," Callahan said, and thought: *Until one of them drops me, at least.* "After we bring her out of there, Jake, am I a gunslinger?"

Jake's grin was wolfish, all his doubts and fears put behind him. "Khef, ka, and ka-tet," he said. "Look, there's the WALK light. Let's cross."

EIGHTEEN

The driver's seat of the first limo was empty. There was a fellow in a cap and a uniform behind the wheel of the second, but to Pere Callahan the sai looked asleep. Another man in cap and uniform was leaning against the sidewalk side of the third limo. The coal of a cigarette made a lazy arc from his side to his mouth and then back down again. He glanced their way, but with no appreciable interest. What was there to see? A man going on elderly, a boy going on teenage, and a scurrying dog. Big deal.

When they gained the other side of Sixty-first, Callahan saw a sign on a chrome stand in front of the restaurant:

CLOSED FOR PRIVATE FUNCTION

What exactly did you call tonight's function at the Dixie Pig? Callahan wondered. A baby shower? A birthday party?

"What about Oy?" he asked Jake in a low voice.

"Oy stays with me."

Only four words, but they were enough to convince Callahan Jake knew what he did: this was their night to die. Callahan didn't know if they'd manage to go out in a blaze of glory, but they would be going out, all three of them. The clearing at the end of the path was now hidden from their view by only a single turn; they would enter it three abreast. And little as he wanted to die while his lungs were still clear and his eyes could still see, Callahan understood that things could have been much worse. Black Thirteen had been stuffed away in another dark place where it would sleep, and if Roland did indeed remain standing when the hurly-burly was done, the battle lost and won, then he would track it down and dispose of it as he saw fit. Meanwhile—

"Jake, listen to me a second. This is important."

Jake nodded, but he looked impatient.

"Do you understand that you are in danger of death, and do you ask forgiveness for your sins?"

The boy understood he was being given last rites. "Yes," he said.

"Are you sincerely sorry for those sins?"

"Yes."

"Repent of them?"

"Yes, Pere."

Callahan sketched the sign of the cross in front of him. *"In nomine Patris, et Filii, et Spiritus—"*

Oy barked. Just once, but with excitement. And it was a bit muffled, that bark, for he had found something in the gutter and was holding it up to Jake in his mouth. The boy bent and took it.

"What?" Callahan asked. "What is it?"

"It's what she left for us," Jake said. He sounded enormously relieved, almost hopeful again. "What she dropped while Mia was distracted and crying about the song. Oh man—we might have a chance, Pere. We might just have a chance after all."

He put the object in the Pere's hand. Callahan was surprised by its weight, and then struck almost breathless by its beauty. He felt the same dawning of hope. It was probably stupid, but it was there, all right.

He held the scrimshaw turtle up to his face and ran the pad of his index finger over the question-mark-shaped scratch on its shell. Looked into its wise and peaceful eyes. "How lovely it is," he breathed. "Is it the Turtle Maturin? It is, isn't it?"

"I don't know," Jake said. "Probably. She calls it the *sköldpadda,* and it may help us, but it can't kill the harriers that are waiting for us in there." He nodded toward the Dixie Pig. "Only we can do that, Pere. Will you?"

"Oh yes," Callahan said calmly. He put the turtle, the *sköldpadda,* into his breast pocket. "I'll shoot until the bullets are gone or I'm dead. If I run out of bullets before they kill me, I'll club them with the gun-butt."

"Good. Let's go give *them* some last rites."

They walked past the CLOSED sign on its chrome post, Oy trotting between them, his head up and his muzzle wearing that toothy grin. They mounted the three steps to the double doors without hesitating. At the top, Jake reached into the pouch and brought out two of the plates. He tapped them together, nodded at the dull ringing sound, and then said: "Let's see yours."

Callahan lifted the Ruger and held the barrel beside his right cheek like a duelist. Then he touched his breast pocket, which bulged and drooped with shells.

Jake nodded, satisfied. "Once we're in, we stay together. Always together, with Oy between. On three. And once we start, we don't stop until we're dead."

"Never stop."

"Right. Are you ready?"

"Yes. God's love on you, boy."

"And on you, Pere. One . . . two . . . *three*." Jake opened the door and together they went into dim light and the sweet tangy smell of roasting pork.

> STAVE: *Commala-come-ki,*
> *There's a time to live and one to die.*
> *With your back against the final wall*
> *Ya gotta let the bullets fly.*

> RESPONSE: *Commala-come ki!*
> *Let the bullets fly!*
> *Don't 'ee mourn for me, my lads*
> *When it comes my day to die.*

"HILE, MIA, HILE, MOTHER"

13TH STANZA

ONE

Ka might have put that downtown bus where it was when Mia's cab pulled up, or it might only have been coincidence. Certainly it's the sort of question that provokes argument from the humblest street-preacher (can you give me hallelujah) all the way up to the mightiest of theological philosophers (can you give me a Socratic amen). Some might consider it almost frivolous; the mighty issues that loom their shadows behind the question, however, are anything but.

One downtown bus, half empty.

But if it hadn't been there on the corner of Lex and Sixty-first, Mia likely would never have noticed the man playing the guitar. And, had she not stopped to listen to the man playing the guitar, who knows how much of what followed might have been different?

TWO

"Awwww, *man*, wouldja looka-*dat!*" the cab driver exclaimed, and lifted his hand to his windshield in an exasperated gesture. A bus was parked on the corner of Lexington and Sixty-first, its diesel engine rumbling and its taillights flashing what Mia took to be some kind of distress code. The bus driver was standing by one of the rear wheels, looking at the dark cloud of diesel smoke pouring from the bus's rear vent.

"Lady," said the cab driver, "you mind getting off on the corner of Sixtieth? Tha'be all right?"

Is it? Mia asked. *What should I say?*

Sure, Susannah replied absently. *Sixtieth's fine.*

Mia's question had called her back from her version of the Dogan, where she'd been trying to get in touch with Eddie. She'd had no luck doing that, and was appalled at the state of the place. The cracks in the floor now ran deep, and one of the ceiling panels had crashed down, bringing the fluorescent lights and several long snarls of electrical cable with it. Some of the instrument panels had gone dark. Others were seeping tendrils of smoke. The needle on the **SUSANNAH-MIO** dial was all the way over into the red. Below her feet, the floor was vibrating and the machinery was screaming. And saying that none of this was real, it was all only a visualization technique, kind of missed the whole point, didn't it? She'd shut down a very powerful process, and her body was paying a price. The Voice of the Dogan had warned her that what she was doing was dangerous; that it wasn't (in the words of a TV ad) nice to fool Mother Nature. Susannah had no idea which of her glands and organs were taking the biggest beating, but she knew that they *were* hers. Not Mia's. It was time to call a halt to this madness before everything went sky-high.

First, though, she'd tried to get in touch with Eddie, yelling his name repeatedly into the mike with NORTH CENTRAL POSITRONICS stamped on it. Nothing. Yelling Roland's name also brought no result. If they were dead, she would have known it. She was sure of that. But not to be able to get in touch with them at *all* . . . what did that mean?

It mean you once mo' been fucked mos' righteous, honeychile, Detta told her, and cackled. *This what you get fo' messin wit' honkies.*

I can get out here? Mia was asking, shy as a girl arriving at her first dance. *Really?*

Susannah would have slapped her own brow, had she had one. God, when it was about anything but her baby, the bitch was so goddam *timid!*

Yes, go ahead. It's only a single block, and on the avenues, the blocks are short.

The driver . . . how much should I give the driver?

Give him a ten and let him keep the change. Here, hold it out for me—

Susannah sensed Mia's reluctance and reacted with weary anger. This was not entirely without amusement.

Listen to me, sweetheart, I wash my hands of you. Okay? Give him any fucking bill you want.

No, no, it's all right. Humble now. Frightened. *I trust you, Susannah.* And she held up the remaining bills from Mats, fanned out in front of her eyes like a hand of cards.

Susannah almost refused, but what was the point? She *came forward,* took control of the brown hands holding the money, selected a ten, and gave it to the driver. "Keep the change," she said.

"Thanks, lady!"

Susannah opened the curbside door. A robot voice began to speak when she did, startling her—startling both of them. It was someone named Whoopi Goldberg, reminding her to take her bags. For Susannah-Mia, the question of her gunna was moot. There was only one piece of baggage which concerned them now, and of this Mia would soon be delivered.

She heard guitar music. At the same time she felt her control over the hand stuffing money back into her pocket and the leg swinging out of the cab begin to ebb. Mia, taking over again now that Susannah had solved another of her little New York dilemmas. Susannah began to struggle against this usurpation

(my *body, goddammit,* mine, *at least from the waist up, and that includes the head and the brain inside it!*)

and then quit. What was the use? Mia was stronger. Susannah had no idea why that should be, but she knew that it was.

A kind of queer *Bushido* fatalism had come over Susannah Dean by this point. It was the sort of calmness that cloaks the drivers of cars skidding helplessly toward bridge overpasses, the pilots of planes that heel over into their final dives, their engines dead . . . and gunslingers driven to their final cave or draw. Later she might fight, if fighting seemed either worthwhile or honorable. She would fight to save herself or the baby, but not Mia—this was her decision. Mia had forfeited any chance of rescue she might once have deserved, in Susannah's eyes.

For now there was nothing to do, except maybe to turn the LABOR FORCE dial back to 10. She thought she would be allowed that much control.

Before that, though . . . the music. The guitar. It was a song she knew, and knew well. She had sung a version of it to the *folken* the night of their arrival in Calla Bryn Sturgis.

After all she had been through since meeting Roland, hearing "Man of Constant Sorrow" on this New York streetcorner did not strike her as coincidental in the least. And it was a wonderful song, wasn't it? Perhaps the vertex of all the folk songs she had so loved as a younger woman, the ones that had seduced her, step by step, into activism and had led her finally to Oxford, Mississippi. Those days were gone—she felt ever so much older than she had then—but this song's sad simplicity still appealed to her. The Dixie Pig was less than a block from here. Once Mia had transported them through its doors, Susannah would be in the Land of the Crimson King. She had no doubts or illusions about that. She did not expect to return from there, did not expect to see either her friends or her beloved again, and had an idea she might have to die with Mia's cheated howls for company . . . but none of that had to interfere with her enjoyment of this song now. Was it her death-song? If so, fine.

Susannah, daughter of Dan, reckoned there could have been far worse.

THREE

The busker had set up shop in front of a café called Blackstrap Molasses. His guitar case was open in front of him, its purple velvet interior (exactly the same shade as the rug in sai King's Bridgton bedroom, can you say amen) scattered with change and bills, just so any unusually innocent passersby would know the right thing to do. He was sitting on a sturdy wooden cube which looked exactly like the one upon which the Rev. Harrigan stood to preach.

There were signs that he was almost through for the night. He had put on his jacket, which bore a New York Yankees patch on the sleeve, and a hat with **JOHN LENNON LIVES** printed above the bill. There had apparently been a sign in front of him but now it was back in his instrument case, words-side down. Not that Mia would have known what was writ upon it in any case, not she.

He looked at her, smiled, and quit his fingerpicking. She raised one of the remaining bills and said, "I'll give you this if you'll play that song again. All of it, this time."

The young man looked about twenty, and while there was nothing very handsome about him, with his pale, spotty complexion, the gold ring in one of his nostrils, and the cigarette jutting from the corner of his mouth, he had an engaging air. His eyes widened as he realized whose face was on the bit of currency she was holding. "Lady, for fifty bucks I'd play every Ralph Stanley song I know . . . and I know quite a few of em."

"Just this one will do us fine," Mia said, and

tossed the bill. It fluttered into the busker's guitar case. He watched its prankish descent with disbelief. "Hurry," Mia said. Susannah was quiet, but Mia sensed her listening. "My time is short. Play."

And so the guitar-player sitting on the box in front of the café began to play a song Susannah had first heard in The Hungry i, a song she had herself sung at God only knew how many hootenannies, a song she'd once sung behind a motel in Oxford, Mississippi. The night before they had all been thrown in jail, that had been. By then those three young voter-registration boys had been missing almost a month, gone into the black Mississippi earth somewhere in the general vicinity of Philadelphia (they were eventually found in the town of Longdale, can you give me hallelujah, can you please say amen). That fabled White Sledgehammer had begun once more to swing in the redneck toolies, but they had sung anyway. Odetta Holmes—Det, they called her in those days— had begun this particular song and then the rest of them joined in, the boys singing *man* and the girls singing *maid*. Now, rapt within the Dogan which had become her gulag, Susannah listened as this young man, unborn in those terrible old days, sang it again. The cofferdam of her memory broke wide open and it was Mia, unprepared for the violence of these recollections, who was lifted upon the wave.

FOUR

In the Land of Memory, the time is always *Now*.

In the Kingdom of Ago, the clocks tick . . . but their hands never move.

There is an Unfound Door
(O lost)
and memory is the key which opens it.

FIVE

Their names are Cheney, Goodman, Schwerner; these are those who fall beneath the swing of the White Sledgehammer on the 19th of June, 1964.

O Discordia!

SIX

They're staying at a place called the Blue Moon Motor Hotel, on the Negro side of Oxford, Mississippi. The Blue Moon is owned by Lester Bambry, whose brother John is pastor of the First Afro-American Methodist Church of Oxford, can you give me hallelujah, can you say amen.

It is July 19th of 1964, a month to the day after the disappearance of Cheney, Goodman, and Schwerner. Three days after they disappeared somewhere around Philadelphia there was a meeting at John Bambry's church and the local Negro activists told the three dozen or so remaining white northerners that in light of what was now happening, they were of course free to go home. And some of them have gone home, praise God, but Odetta Holmes and eighteen others stay. Yes. They stay at the Blue Moon Motor Hotel. And sometimes at night they go out back, and Delbert Anderson brings his guitar and they sing.

"I Shall Be Released," they sing and

"John Henry," they sing, gonna whop the steel on down (great Gawd, say Gawd-bomb), and they sing

"Blowin in the Wind" and they sing

"Hesitation Blues" by the Rev. Gary Davis, all of them laughing at the amiably risqué verses: a dollar is a dollar and a dime is a dime I got a houseful of chillun ain't none of em mine, and they sing

"I Ain't Marchin Anymore" and they sing

in the Land of Memory and the Kingdom of Ago they sing

in the blood-heat of their youth, in the strength of their bodies, in the confidence of their minds they sing

to deny Discordia

to deny the can toi

in affirmation of Gan the Maker, Gan the Evil-taker

they don't know these names

they know all these names

the heart sings what it must sing

the blood knows what the blood knows

on the Path of the Beam our hearts know all the secrets

and they sing

sing

Odetta begins and Delbert Anderson plays; she sings

"I am a maid of constant sorrow . . . I've seen trouble all my days . . . I bid farewell . . . to old Ken-tucky . . ."

SEVEN

So Mia was ushered through the Unfound Door and into the Land of Memory, transported to the weedy yard behind Lester Bambry's Blue Moon Motor Hotel, and so she heard—

(hears)

EIGHT

Mia hears the woman who will become Susannah as she sings her song. She hears the others join in, one by one, until they are all singing together in a choir, and overhead is the Mississippi moon, raining its radiance down on their faces—some black, some white—and upon the cold steel rails of the tracks which run behind the hotel, tracks which run south from here, which run out to Longdale, the town where on August 5th of 1964 the badly decomposed bodies of their amigos will be found— James Cheney, twenty-one; Andrew Goodman, twenty-one; Michael Schwerner, twenty-four; O Discordia! And to you who favor darkness, give you joy of the red Eye that shines there.

She hears them sing.

All thro' this Earth I'm bound to ramble . . . Thro' storm and wind, thro' sleet and rain . . . I'm bound to ride that Northern railroad . . .

Nothing opens the eye of memory like a song, and it is Odetta's memories that lift Mia and carry her as they sing together, Det and her ka-mates under the silvery moon. Mia sees them walking hence from here with their arms linked, singing

(*oh deep in my heart . . . I do believe . . .*)

another song, the one they feel defines them most clearly. The faces lining the street and watching them are twisted with hate. The fists being shaken at them are callused. The mouths of the women who purse their lips to shoot the spit that will clabber their cheeks dirty their hair stain their shirts are paintless and their legs are without stockings and their shoes are nothing but runover lumps. There are men in overalls (Oshkosh-by-gosh, someone say hallelujah). There are teenage boys in clean white sweaters and flattop haircuts and one of them shouts at Odetta, carefully articulating each word: *We Will Kill! Every! Goddam! Nigger! Who Steps Foot On The Campus Of Ole Miss!*

And the camaraderie in spite of the fear. *Because* of the fear. The feeling that they are doing something incredibly important: something for the ages. They will change America, and if the price is blood, why then they will pay it. Say true, say hallelujah, praise God, give up your loud amen.

Then comes the white boy named Darryl, and at first he couldn't, he was limp and he couldn't, and then later on he could and Odetta's secret other—the screaming, laughing, ugly other—never came near. Darryl and Det lay together until morning, slept spoons until morning beneath the Mississippi moon. Listening to the crickets. Listening to the owls. Listening to the soft smooth hum of the Earth turning on its gimbals, turning and turning ever further into the twentieth century. They are young, their blood runs hot, and they never doubt their ability to change everything.

It's fare you well, my own true lover . . .

This is her song in the weeds behind the Blue Moon Motor Hotel; this is her song beneath the moon.

I'll never see your face again . . .

It's Odetta Holmes at the apotheosis of her life, and Mia is *there!* She sees it, feels it, is lost in its glorious and some would say stupid hope (ah but I say hallelujah, we all say Gawd-bomb). She understands how being afraid all the time makes one's friends more precious; how it makes every bite of every meal sweet; how it stretches time until every day seems to last forever, leading on to velvet night, and they *know* James Cheney is dead

(say true)

they *know* Andrew Goodman is dead

(say hallelujah)

they *know* Michael Schwerner—oldest of them and still just a baby at twenty-four—is dead.

(Give up your loudest amen!)

They know that any of them is also eligible to wind up in the mud of Longdale or Philadelphia. *At any time.* The night after this particular hoot behind the Blue Moon, most of them, Odetta included, will be taken to jail and her time of humiliation will begin. But tonight she's with her friends, with her lover, and they are one, and Discordia has been banished. Tonight they sing swaying with their arms around each other.

The girls sing *maid,* the boys sing *man.*

Mia is overwhelmed by their love for one another; she is exalted by the simplicity of what they believe.

At first, too stunned to laugh or to cry, she can only listen, amazed.

NINE

As the busker began the fourth verse, Susannah joined in, at first tentatively and then—at his encouraging smile—with a will, harmonizing above the young man's voice:

> *For breakfast we had bulldog gravy*
> *For supper we had beans and bread*
> *The miners don't have any dinner*
> *And a tick of straw they call a bed . . .*

TEN

The busker quit after that verse, looking at Susannah-Mia with happy surprise. "I thought I was the only one who knew that one," he said. "It's the way the Freedom Riders used to—"

"No," Susannah said quietly. "Not them. It was the voter-registration people who sang the bulldog-gravy verse. The folks who came down to Oxford in the summer of '64. When those three boys were killed."

"Schwerner and Goodman," he said. "I can't remember the name of the—"

"James Cheney," she said quietly. "He had the most beautiful *hair*."

"You talk as though you knew him," he said, "but you can't be much over . . . thirty?"

Susannah had an idea she looked a good deal

older than thirty, especially tonight, but of course this young man had fifty dollars more in his guitar case now than had been there a single song ago, and it had perhaps affected his eyesight.

"My mother spent the summer of '64 in Neshoba County," Susannah said, and with two spontaneously chosen words—*my mother*—did her captor more damage than she could have imagined. Those words flayed open Mia's heart.

"Cool on Mom!" the young man exclaimed, and smiled. Then the smile faded. He fished the fifty out of the guitar case and held it up to her. "Take it back. It was a pleasure just to sing with you, ma'am."

"I really couldn't," Susannah said, smiling. "Remember the struggle, that'd be enough for me. And remember Jimmy, Andy, and Michael, if it does ya. I know it would do me just fine."

"Please," the young man persisted. He was smiling again but the smile was troubled and he might have been any of those young men from the Land of Ago, singing in the moonlight between the slumped ass-ends of the Blue Moon's shacky little units and the double-hammered heatless moonlight gleam of the railroad tracks; he could have been any in his beauty and the careless flower of his youth and how in that moment Mia loved him. Even her chap seemed secondary in that glow. She knew it was in many ways a false glow, imparted by the memories of her hostess, and yet she suspected that in other ways it might be real. She knew one thing for sure: only a creature such as herself, who'd had immortality and given it up, could appreciate the raw courage it took to stand against the forces of Discordia. To risk that fragile beauty by putting beliefs before personal safety.

Make him happy, take it back, she told Susannah, but would not *come forward* and make Susannah do so. Let it be her choice.

Before Susannah could reply, the alarm in the Dogan went off, flooding their shared mind with noise and red light.

Susannah turned in that direction, but Mia grabbed her shoulder in a grip like a claw before she could go.

What's happening? What's gone wrong?

Let me loose!

Susannah twisted free. And before Mia could grab her again, she was gone.

ELEVEN

Susannah's Dogan pulsed and flared with red panic-light. A Klaxon hammered an audio tattoo from the overhead speakers. All but two of the TV screens—one still showing the busker on the corner of Lex and Sixtieth, the other the sleeping baby—had shorted out. The cracked floor was humming under Susannah's feet and throwing up dust. One of the control panels had gone dark, and another was in flames.

This looked bad.

As if to confirm her assessment, the Blaine-like Voice of the Dogan began to speak again. "WARNING!" it cried. "SYSTEM OVERLOAD! WITHOUT POWER REDUCTION IN SECTION ALPHA, TOTAL SYSTEM SHUTDOWN WILL OCCUR IN 40 SECONDS!"

Susannah couldn't remember any Section Alpha from her previous visits to the Dogan, but wasn't surprised to now see a sign labeled just that. One of the panels near it suddenly erupted in a gaudy shower of orange sparks, setting the seat of a chair on fire. More ceiling panels fell, trailing snarls of wiring.

"WITHOUT POWER REDUCTION IN SECTION ALPHA, TOTAL SYSTEM SHUTDOWN WILL OCCUR IN 30 SECONDS!"

What about the EMOTIONAL TEMP dial?

"Leave it alone," she muttered to herself.

Okay, CHAP? What about that one?

After a moment's thought, Susannah flipped the toggle from ASLEEP to AWAKE and those disconcerting blue eyes opened at once, staring into Susannah's with what looked like fierce curiosity.

Roland's child, she thought with a strange and painful mixture of emotions. *And mine. As for Mia? Girl, you nothing but a ka-mai. I'm sorry for you.*

Ka-mai, yes. Not just a fool, but ka's fool—a fool of destiny.

"WITHOUT POWER REDUCTION IN SECTION ALPHA, TOTAL SYSTEM SHUTDOWN WILL OCCUR IN 25 SECONDS!"

So waking the baby hadn't done any good, at least not in terms of preventing a complete system crash. Time for Plan B.

She reached out for the absurd LABOR FORCE control-knob, the one that looked so much like the oven-dial on her mother's stove. Turning the dial back to 2 had been difficult, and had hurt like a bastard. Turning it the other way was easier, and there was no pain at all. What she felt was an *easing* somewhere deep in her head, as if some network of muscles which had been flexed for hours was now letting go with a little cry of relief.

The blaring pulse of the Klaxon ceased.

Susannah turned LABOR FORCE to 8, paused there, then shrugged. What the hell, it was time to go for broke, get this over with. She turned the dial all the way to 10. The moment it was there, a great glossy pain hardened her stomach and then rolled lower, gripping her pelvis. She had to tighten her lips against a scream.

"POWER REDUCTION IN SECTION ALPHA HAS BEEN ACCOMPLISHED," said the voice, and then it dropped into a John Wayne drawl that Susannah knew all too well. "THANKS A WHOLE HEAP, LI'L COWGIRL."

She had to tighten her lips against another scream—not pain this time but outright terror. It was all very well to remind herself Blaine the Mono was dead and this voice was coming from some nasty practical joker in her own subconscious, but that didn't stop the fear.

"LABOR . . . HAS COMMENCED," said the amplified voice, dropping the John Wayne imitation. "LABOR . . . HAS COMMENCED." Then, in a horrible (and nasal) Bob Dylan drawl that set her teeth on edge, the voice sang: "HAPPY BIRTHDAY TO YOU . . . *BABE!* . . . HAPPY BIRTHDAY . . . TO YOU! HAPPY BIRTHDAY . . . DEAR MORDRED . . . HAPPY BIRTHDAY . . . TO YOU!"

Susannah visualized a fire extinguisher

mounted on the wall behind her, and when she turned it was, of course, right there (she had not imagined the little sign reading ONLY YOU AND SOMBRA CAN HELP PREVENT CONSOLE FIRES, however—that, along with a drawing of Shardik o' the Beam in a Smokey the Bear hat, was some other joker's treat). As she hurried across the cracked and uneven floor to get the extinguisher, skirting the fallen ceiling panels, another pain ripped into her, lighting her belly and thighs on fire, making her want to double over and bear down on the outrageous stone in her womb.

Not going to take long, she thought in a voice that was part Susannah and part Detta. *No ma'am. This chap comin in on the express train!*

But then the pain let up slightly. She snatched the extinguisher off the wall when it did, trained the slim black horn on the flaming control panel, and pressed the trigger. Foam billowed out, coating the flames. There was a baleful hissing sound and a smell like burning hair.

"THE FIRE . . . IS OUT," the Voice of the Dogan proclaimed. "THE FIRE . . . IS OUT." And then changing, quick as a flash, to a plummy British Lord Haw-Haw accent: "I SAY, *JOLLY GOOD SHOW, SEW-ZANNAH, AB-SO-LUTELY BRILLLL-IANT!*"

She lurched across the minefield of the Dogan's floor again, seized the microphone, and pressed the transmit toggle. Above her, on one of the TV screens still operating, she could see that Mia was on the move again, crossing Sixtieth.

Then Susannah saw the green awning with the

cartoon pig, and her heart sank. Not Sixtieth, but Sixty-*first*. The hijacking mommy-bitch had reached her destination.

"Eddie!" she shouted into the microphone. "Eddie or Roland!" And what the hell, she might as well make it a clean sweep. "Jake! Pere Callahan! We've reached the Dixie Pig and we're going to have this damn baby! Come for us if you can, but be careful!"

She looked up at the screen again. Mia was now on the Dixie Pig side of the street, peering at the green awning. Hesitating. Could she read the words DIXIE PIG? Probably not, but she could surely understand the cartoon. The smiling, smoking pig. And she wouldn't hesitate long in any case, now that her labor had started.

"Eddie, I have to go. I love you, sugar! Whatever else happens, you remember that! Never forget it! *I love you!* This is . . ." Her eye fell on the semicircular readout on the panel behind the mike. The needle had fallen out of the red. She thought it would stay in the yellow until the labor was over, then subside into the green.

Unless something went wrong, that was.

She realized she was still gripping the mike.

"This is Susannah-Mio, signing off. God be with you, boys. God and ka."

She put the microphone down and closed her eyes.

TWELVE

Susannah sensed the difference in Mia immediately. Although she'd reached the Dixie Pig and her labor had most emphatically commenced, Mia's mind was for once elsewhere. It had turned to Odetta Holmes, in fact, and to what Michael Schwerner had called the Mississippi Summer Project. (What the Oxford rednecks had called *him* was The Jewboy.) The emotional atmosphere to which Susannah returned was *fraught*, like still air before a violent September storm.

Susannah! Susannah, daughter of Dan!

Yes, Mia.

I agreed to mortality.

So you said.

And certainly Mia had looked mortal in Fedic. Mortal and *terribly* pregnant.

Yet I've missed most of what makes the short-time life worthwhile. Haven't I? The grief in that voice was awful; the surprise was even worse. *And there's no time for you to tell me. Not now.*

Go somewhere else, Susannah said, with no hope at all. *Hail a cab, go to a hospital. We'll have it together, Mia. Maybe we can even raise it toge—*

If I have it anywhere but here, it will die and we'll die with it. She spoke with utter certainty. *And I will have it. I've been cheated of all but my chap, and I will have it. But . . . Susannah . . . before we go in . . . you spoke of your mother.*

I lied. It was me in Oxford. Lying was easier than trying to explain time travel and parallel worlds.

Show me the truth. Show me your mother. Show me, I beg!

There was no time to debate this request pro and

con; it was either do it or refuse on the spur of the moment. Susannah decided to do it.

Look, she said.

THIRTEEN

In the Land of Memory, the time is always *Now.*

There is an Unfound Door

(O lost)

and when Susannah found it and opened it, Mia saw a woman with her dark hair pulled back from her face and startling gray eyes. There is a cameo brooch at the woman's throat. She's sitting at the kitchen table, this woman, in an eternal shaft of sun. In this memory it is always ten minutes past two on an afternoon in October of 1946, the Big War is over, Irene Daye is on the radio, and the smell is always gingerbread.

"Odetta, come and sit with me," says the woman at the table, she who is mother. "Have something sweet. You look *good,* girl."

And she smiles.

O lost, and by the wind grieved, ghost, come back again!

FOURTEEN

Prosaic enough, you would say, so you would. A young girl comes home from school with her book-bag in one hand and her gym-bag in the other, wearing her white blouse and her pleated St. Ann's tartan skirt and the knee-socks with the bows on the side (orange and black, the school colors). Her mother, sitting at the kitchen table, looks up and offers her daughter a piece of the gingerbread that just came out of the oven. It is only one moment in an unmarked million, a single atom of event in a lifetime of them. But it stole Mia's breath

(you look good, *girl)*

and showed her in a concrete way she had previously not understood how rich motherhood could be . . . *if,* that was, it was allowed to run its course uninterrupted.

The rewards?

Immeasurable.

In the end *you* could be the woman sitting in the shaft of sun. *You* could be the one looking at the child sailing bravely out of childhood's harbor. You could be the wind in that child's unfurled sails.

You.

Odetta, come and sit with me.

Mia's breath began to hitch in her chest.

Have something sweet.

Her eyes fogged over, the smiling cartoon pig on the awning first doubling, then quadrupling.

You look good, *girl.*

Some time was better than no time at all. Even five years—or three—was better than no time at all. She couldn't read, hadn't been to Morehouse, hadn't been to *no* house, but she could do that much math with no trouble: three = better than none. Even one = better than none.

Oh . . .

Oh, but . . .

Mia thought of a blue-eyed boy stepping through a door, one that was found instead of lost. She thought of saying to him *You look* good, *son!*

She began to weep.

What have I done was a terrible question. *What else* could *I have done* was perhaps even worse.

O Discordia!

FIFTEEN

This was Susannah's one chance to do something: now, while Mia stood at the foot of the steps leading up to her fate. Susannah reached into the pocket of her jeans and touched the turtle, the *sköldpadda*. Her brown fingers, separated from Mia's white leg by only a thin layer of lining, closed around it.

She pulled it out and flipped it behind her, casting it into the gutter. From her hand into the lap of ka.

Then she was carried up the three steps to the double doors of the Dixie Pig.

SIXTEEN

It was very dim inside and at first Mia could see nothing but murky, reddish-orange lights. Electric *flambeaux* of the sort that still lit some of the rooms in Castle Discordia. Her sense of smell needed no adjusting, however, and even as a fresh labor pain clamped her tight, her stomach reacted to the smell of roasting pork and cried out to be fed. Her *chap* cried out to be fed.

That's not pork, Mia, Susannah said, and was ignored.

As the doors were closed behind her—there was

a man (or a manlike being) standing at each of them—she began to see better. She was at the head of a long, narrow dining room. White napery shone. On each table was a candle in an orange-tinted holder. They glowed like fox-eyes. The floor here in the foyer was black marble, but beyond the *maître d*'s stand there was a rug of darkest crimson.

Beside the stand was a sai of about sixty with white hair combed back from a lean and rather predatory face. It was the face of an intelligent man, but his clothes—the blaring yellow sportcoat, the red shirt, the black tie—were those of a used-car salesman or a gambler who specializes in rook-ing small-town rubes. In the center of his forehead was a red hole about an inch across, as if he had been shot at close range. It swam with blood that never overflowed onto his pallid skin.

At the tables in the dining room stood perhaps fifty men and half again as many women. Most of them were dressed in clothes as loud or louder than those of the white-haired gent. Big rings glared on fleshy fingers, diamond eardrops sparked back orange light from the *flambeaux*.

There were also some dressed in more sober attire—jeans and plain white shirts seemed to be the costume of choice for this minority. These *folken* were pallid and watchful, their eyes seem-ingly all pupil. Around their bodies, swirling so faintly that they sometimes disappeared, were blue auras. To Mia these pallid, aura-enclosed creatures looked quite a bit more human than the low men and women. They were vampires—she didn't have to observe the sharpened fangs which their smiles disclosed to know it—but still they looked more human than Sayre's bunch. Perhaps because they once had *been* human. The others, though . . .

Their faces are only masks, she observed with growing dismay. *Beneath the ones the Wolves wear lie the electric men—the robots—but what is beneath these?*

The dining room was breathlessly silent, but from somewhere nearby came the uninterrupted sounds of conversation, laughter, clinking glasses, and cutlery against china. There was a patter of liquid—wine or water, she supposed—and a louder outburst of laughter.

A low man and a low woman—he in a tuxedo equipped with plaid lapels and a red velvet bow tie, she in a strapless silver lamé evening dress, both of startling obesity—turned to look (with obvious displeasure) toward the source of these sounds, which seemed to be coming from behind some sort of swaggy tapestry depicting knights and their ladies at sup. When the fat couple turned to look, Mia saw their cheeks wrinkle upward like clingy cloth, and for a moment, beneath the soft angle of their jaws, she saw something dark red and tufted with hair.

Susannah, was that skin? Mia asked. *Dear God, was it their* skin?

Susannah made no reply, not even *I told you so* or *Didn't I warn you?* Things had gone past that now. It was too late for exasperation (or any of the milder emotions), and Susannah felt genuinely sorry for the woman who had brought her here. Yes, Mia had lied and betrayed; yes, she had tried her best to get Eddie and Roland killed. But what choice had she ever had? Susannah realized, with dawning bitterness, that she could now give the perfect definition of a ka-mai: one who has been given hope but no choices.

Like giving a motorcycle to a blindman, she thought.

Richard Sayre—slim, middle-aged, handsome in a full-lipped, broad-browed way—began to applaud. The rings on his fingers flashed. His yellow blazer blared in the dim light. "Hile, Mia!" he cried.

"*Hile, Mia!*" the others responded.

"Hile, Mother!"

"*Hile, Mother!*" the vampires and low men and low women cried, and they, too, began to applaud. The sound was certainly enthusiastic enough, but the acoustics of the room dulled it and turned it into the rustle of batwings. A hungry sound, one that made Susannah feel sick to her stomach. At the same time a fresh contraction gripped her and turned her legs to water. She reeled forward, yet almost welcomed the pain, which partially muffled her trepidation. Sayre stepped forward and seized her by the upper arms, steadying her before she could fall. She had thought his touch would be cold, but his fingers were as hot as those of a cholera victim.

Farther back, she saw a tall figure come out of the shadows, something that was neither low man nor vampire. It wore jeans and a plain white shirt, but emerging from the shirt's collar was the head of a bird. It was covered with sleek feathers of dark yellow. Its eyes were black. It patted its hands together in polite applause, and she saw—with ever-growing dismay—that those hands were equipped with talons rather than fingers.

Half a dozen bugs scampered from beneath one of the tables and looked at her with eyes that hung on stalks. Horribly intelligent eyes. Their mandibles clicked in a sound that was like laughter.

Hile, Mia! she heard in her head. An insectile buzzing. *Hile, Mother!* And then they were gone, back into the shadows.

Mia turned to the door and saw the pair of low men who blocked it. And yes, those *were* masks; this close to the door-guards it was impossible not to see how their sleek black hair had been painted on. Mia turned back to Sayre with a sinking heart.

Too late now.

Too late to do anything but go through with it.

SEVENTEEN

Sayre's grip had slipped when she turned. Now he re-established it by taking her left hand. At the same moment her right hand was seized. She turned that way and saw the fat woman in the silver lamé dress. Her huge bust overflowed the top of her gown, which struggled gamely to hold it back. The flesh of her upper arms quivered loosely, giving off a suffocating scent of talcum powder. On her forehead was a red wound that swam but never overflowed.

It's how they breathe, Mia thought. *That's how they breathe when they're wearing their—*

In her growing dismay, she had largely forgotten about Susannah Dean and completely about Detta. So when Detta Walker *came forward*—hell, when she *leaped forward*—there was no way Mia could stop her. She watched her arms shoot out seemingly of their own accord and saw her fingers sink into the plump cheek of the woman in the silver lamé gown. The woman shrieked, but oddly, the others, Sayre included, laughed uproariously, as if this were the funniest thing they'd ever seen in their lives.

The mask of humanity pulled away from the low woman's startled eye, then tore. Susannah thought of her final moments on the castle allure, when everything had frozen and the sky had torn open like paper.

Detta ripped the mask almost entirely away. Tatters of what looked like latex hung from the tips of her fingers. Beneath where the mask had been was the head of a huge red rat, a mutie with yellow teeth growing up the outside of its cheeks in a crust and what looked like white worms dangling from its nose.

"Naughty girl," said the rat, shaking a roguish finger at Susannah-Mio. Its other hand was still holding hers. The thing's mate—the low man in the garish tuxedo—was laughing so hard he had doubled over, and when he did, Mia saw something poking out through the seat of his pants. It was too bony to be a tail, but she supposed it was, all the same.

"Come, Mia," Sayre said, drawing her forward. And then he leaned toward her, peering earnestly into her eyes like a lover. "Or is it you, Odetta? It is, isn't it? It's *you,* you pestering, overeducated, troublesome Negress."

"No, it be *me,* you ratface honky mahfah!" Detta crowed, and then spat into Sayre's face.

Sayre's mouth opened in a gape of astonishment. Then it snapped shut and twisted into a bitter scowl. The room had gone silent again. He wiped the spit from his face—from the mask he wore *over* his face—and looked at it unbelievingly.

"Mia?" he asked. "Mia, you let her do this to *me?* Me, who would stand as your baby's god-father?"

"You ain't jack shit!" Detta cried. "You suck yo' ka-daddy's cock while you diddle yo' fuckfinger up his poop-chute and thass all you good fo'! You—"

"Get RID of her!" Sayre thundered.

And before the watching audience of vampires and low men in the Dixie Pig's front dining room, Mia did just that. The result was extraordinary. Detta's voice began to *dwindle,* as if she were being escorted out of the restaurant (by the bouncer, and by the scruff of the neck). She quit trying to speak and only laughed raucously, but soon enough that, too, was gone.

Sayre stood with his hands clasped before him, looking solemnly at Mia. The others were also star-ing. Somewhere behind the tapestry of the knights and their ladies at feast, the low laughter and con-versation of some other group continued.

"She's gone," Mia said at last. "The bad one is gone." Even in the room's quiet she was hard to hear, for she spoke in little more than a whisper. Her eyes were timidly cast down, and her cheeks had gone deathly white. "Please, Mr. Sayre . . . *sai* Sayre . . . now that I've done as you ask, please say you've told me the truth, and I may have the raising of my chap. Please say so! If you do, you'll never hear from the other one again, I swear it on my father's face and my mother's name, so I do."

"You had neither," Sayre said. He spoke in a tone of distant contempt. The compassion and mercy for which she begged owned no space in his eyes. And above them, the red hole in the center of his forehead filled and filled but never spilled.

Another pain, this one the greatest so far, sank its teeth into her. Mia staggered, and this time Sayre didn't bother steadying her. She went to her knees before him, put her hands on the rough, gleaming surface of his ostrich-skin boots, and looked up into his pale face. It looked back at her from above the violent yellow scream of his sports jacket.

"Please," she said. "Please, I beg you: *keep your promise to me.*"

"I may," he said, "or I may not. Do you know, I have never had my boots licked. Can you imagine? To have lived as long as I have and never to have had a single good old-fashioned boot-licking."

Somewhere a woman tittered.

Mia bent forward.

No, Mia, thee mustn't, Susannah moaned, but Mia made no reply. Nor did the paralyzing pain deep in her vitals stop her. She stuck her tongue out between her lips and began licking the rough surface of Richard Sayre's boots. Susannah could taste them, at a great distance. It was a husky, dusty, leathery taste, full of rue and humiliation.

Sayre let her go on so for a bit, then said: "Stop it. Enough."

He pulled her roughly to her feet and stood with his unsmiling face not three inches from her own. Now that she'd seen them, it was impossible to unsee the masks he and the rest of them wore. The taut cheeks were almost transparent, and whorls of dark scarlet hair were faintly visible beneath.

Or perhaps you called it fur when it covered the whole face.

"Your beggary does you no credit," he said, "although I must admit the sensation was extraordinary."

"You promised!" she cried, attempting to pull back and out of his grip. Then another contraction struck and she doubled over, trying only not to shriek. When it eased a little, she pressed on. "You said five years . . . or maybe seven . . . yes, seven . . . the best of everything for my chap, you said—"

"Yes," Sayre said. "I do seem to recall that, Mia." He frowned as one does when presented with an especially pernicious problem, then brightened. The area of mask around one corner of his mouth wrinkled up for a moment when he smiled, revealing a yellow snag of tooth growing out of the fold where his lower lip met his upper. He let go of her with one hand in order to raise a finger in the gesture pedagogical. "The best of everything, yes. Question is, do you fill that particular bill?"

Appreciative murmurs of laughter greeted this sally. Mia recalled them calling her Mother and saluting her *hile*, but that seemed distant now, like a meaningless fragment of dream.

You was good enough to tote him, though, wasn't you? Detta asked from someplace deep inside—from the brig, in fact. Yas*suh! You 'us good enough to do dat,* sho!

"I was good enough to carry him, wasn't I?" Mia almost spat at him. "Good enough to send the other one into the swamp to eat frogs, her all the time thinking they were caviar . . . I was good enough for *that*, wasn't I?"

Sayre blinked, clearly startled by so brisk a response.

Mia softened again. "Sai, think of all I gave up!"

"Pish, you had *nothing*!" Sayre replied. "What were you but a meaningless spirit whose existence revolved around no more than fucking the occasional saddletramp? Slut of the winds, isn't that what Roland calls your kind?"

"Then think of the other one," Mia said. "She who calls herself Susannah. I have stolen all her life and purpose for my chap, and at your bidding."

Sayre made a dismissive gesture. "Your mouth does you no credit, Mia. Therefore close it."

He nodded to his left. A low man with a wide, bulldoggy face and a luxuriant head of curly gray hair came forward. The red hole in his brow had an oddly slanted Chinese look. Walking behind him was another of the bird-things, this one with a fierce, dark brown hawk's head protruding from the round neck of a tee-shirt with DUKE BLUE DEVILS printed on it. They took hold of her. The bird-thing's grip was repulsive—scaly and alien.

"You have been an excellent custodian," Sayre said, "on that much we can surely agree. But we must also remember that it was Roland of Gilead's jilly who actually bred the child, mustn't we?"

"*That's a lie!*" she screamed. "*Oh, that is a filthy . . . LIE!*"

He went on as if he'd not heard her. "And different jobs require different skills. Different strokes for different folks, as they say."

"*PLEASE!*" Mia shrieked.

The hawkman put its taloned hands to the sides of its head and then rocked from side to side, as if deafened. This witty pantomime drew laughter and even a few cheers.

Susannah dimly felt warmth gush down her legs—*Mia's* legs—and saw her jeans darken at the crotch and thighs. Her water had finally broken.

"Let's *go-ooo-ooo . . . and have a BABY!*" Sayre proclaimed in game-show-host tones of excitement. There were too many teeth in that smile, a double row both top and bottom. "After that, we'll see. I promise you that your request will be taken under consideration. In the meantime . . . Hile, Mia! Hile, Mother!"

"*Hile, Mia! Hile, Mother!*" the rest cried, and Mia suddenly found herself borne toward the back of the room, the bulldog-faced low man gripping her left arm and the hawkman gripping her right. Hawkman made a faint and unpleasant buzzing sound in his throat each time he exhaled. Her feet barely touched the rug as she was carried toward

the bird-thing with the yellow feathers; Canaryman, she thought him.

Sayre brought her to a stop with a single hand-
gesture and spoke to Canaryman, pointing toward
the Dixie Pig's street door as he did. Mia heard
Roland's name, and also Jake's. The Canaryman
nodded. Sayre pointed emphatically at the door
again and shook his head. *Nothing gets in,* that head-
shake said. *Nothing!*

The Canaryman nodded again and then spoke in
buzzing chirps that made Mia feel like screaming.
She looked away, and her gaze happened on the
mural of the knights and their ladies. They were at
a table she recognized—it was the one in the banqueting hall of Castle Discordia. Arthur Eld sat at
the head with his crown on his brow and his lady-
wife at his right hand. And his eyes were a blue she
knew from her dreams.

Ka might have chosen that particular moment to
puff some errant draft across the dining room of
the Dixie Pig and twitch aside the tapestry. It was
only for a second or two, but long enough for Mia
to see there was another dining room—a *private*
dining room—behind it.

Sitting at a long wooden table beneath a blaz-
ing crystal chandelier were perhaps a dozen men
and women, their appledoll faces twisted and
shrunken with age and evil. Their lips had burst
back from great croggled bouquets of teeth; the
days when any of these monstrosities could close
their mouths were long gone. Their eyes were
black and oozing some sort of noisome tarry stuff
from the corners. Their skin was yellow, scaled

with teeth, and covered with patches of diseased-looking fur.

What are they? Mia screamed. *What in the name of the gods are they?*

Mutants, Susannah said. *Or perhaps the word is hybrids. And it doesn't matter, Mia. You saw what matters, didn't you?*

She had, and Susannah knew it. Although the velvet swag had been twitched aside but briefly, it had been long enough for both of them to see the rotisserie which had been set in the middle of that table, and the headless corpse twirling upon it, skin browning and puckering and sizzling fragrant juices. No, the smell in the air hadn't been pork. The thing turning on the spit, brown as a squab, was a human baby. The creatures around it dipped delicate china cups into the drippings beneath, toasted each other . . . and drank.

The draft died. The tapestry settled back into place. And before the laboring woman was once more taken by the arms and hustled away from the dining room and deeper into this building that straddled many worlds along the Beam, she saw the joke of that picture. It wasn't a drumstick Arthur Eld was lifting to his lips, as a first, casual, glance might have suggested; it was a baby's leg. The glass Queen Rowena had raised in toast was not filled with wine but with blood.

"Hile, Mia!" Sayre cried again. Oh, he was in the best of spirits, now that the homing pigeon had come back to the cote.

Hile, Mia! the others screamed back. It was like some sort of crazy football cheer. Those from behind the mural joined in, although their voices were reduced to little more than growls. And their mouths, of course, were stuffed with food.

"Hile, Mother!" This time Sayre offered her a mocking bow to go with the mockery of his respect.

Hile, Mother! the vampires and the low men responded, and on the satiric wave of their applause she was carried away, first into the kitchen, then into the pantry, and then down the stairs beyond.

Ultimately, of course, there was a door.

EIGHTEEN

Susannah knew the kitchen of the Dixie Pig by the smell of obscene cookery: not pork after all, but certainly what the pirates of the eighteenth century had called *long* pork.

For how many years had this outpost served the vampires and low men of New York City? Since Callahan's time, in the seventies and eighties? Since her own, in the sixties? Almost certainly longer. Susannah supposed there might have been a version of the Dixie Pig here since the time of the Dutch, they who had bought off the Indians with sacks of beads and planted their murderous Christian beliefs ever so much more deeply than their flag. A practical folk, the Dutch, with a taste for spareribs and little patience for magic, either white or black.

She saw enough to recognize the kitchen for the twin of the one she had visited in the bowels of Castle Discordia. That was where Mia had killed a rat that had been trying to claim the last remaining food in the place, a pork-roast in the oven.

Except there was no oven and no roast, she thought. *Hell, no kitchen. There was a piglet out behind the barn, one of Tian and Zalia Jaffords's. And I was the one who killed it and drank its hot blood, not she. By then she mostly had me, although I still didn't know it. I wonder if Eddie—*

As Mia took her away for the last time, tearing her free from her thoughts and sending her a-tumble into the dark, Susannah realized how completely the needy, terrible bitch had possessed her life. She knew why Mia had done it—because of the chap. The question was why she, Susannah Dean, had allowed it to happen. Because she'd been possessed before? Because she was as addicted to the stranger inside as Eddie had been to heroin?

She feared it might be true.

Swirling dark. And when she opened her eyes again, it was upon that savage moon hanging above the Discordia, and the flexing red glow

(*forge of the King*)

on the horizon.

"Over here!" cried a woman's voice, just as it had cried before. "Over here, out of the wind!"

Susannah looked down and saw she was legless, and sitting in the same rude dog-cart as on her previous visit to the allure. The same woman, tall and comely, with black hair streaming in the wind, was beckoning to her. Mia, of course, and all this no more real than Susannah's vague dream-memories of the banquet room.

She thought: *Fedic, though, was real. Mia's body*

is there just as mine is at this very moment being hustled through the kitchen behind the Dixie Pig, where unspeakable meals are prepared for inhuman customers. The castle allure is Mia's dreamplace, her refuge, her Dogan.

"To me, Susannah of Mid-World, and away from the Red King's glow! Come out of the wind and into the lee of this merlon!"

Susannah shook her head. "Say what you have to say and be done, Mia. We've got to have a baby—aye, somehow, between us—and once it's out, we're quits. You've poisoned my life, so you have."

Mia looked at her with desperate intensity, her belly blooming beneath the serape, her hair harried backward at the wind's urging. "'Twas you who took the poison, Susannah! 'Twas you who swallowed it! Aye, when the child was still a seed unbloomed in your belly!"

Was it true? And if it was, which of them had invited Mia in, like the vampire she truly was? Had it been Susannah, or Detta?

Susannah thought neither.

She thought it might actually have been Odetta Holmes. Odetta who would never have broken the nasty old blue lady's forspecial plate. Odetta who loved her dolls, even though most of them were as white as her plain cotton panties.

"What do you want with me, Mia, daughter of none? Say and have finished with it!"

"Soon we'll be together—aye, really and truly, lying together in the same childbed. And all I ask is that if a chance comes for me to get away with my chap, you'll help me take it."

Susannah thought it over. In the wilderness of rocks and gaping crevasses, the hyenas cackled. The wind was numbing, but the pain that suddenly clamped her midsection in its jaws was worse. She saw that same pain on Mia's face and thought again how her entire existence seemed to have become a wilderness of mirrors. In any case, what harm could such a promise do? The chance probably wouldn't come, but if it did, was she going to let the thing Mia wanted to call Mordred fall into the hands of the King's men?

"Yes," she said. "All right. If I can help you get away with him, I *will* help you."

"Anywhere!" Mia cried in a harsh whisper. "Even . . ." She stopped. Swallowed. Forced herself to go on. "Even into the todash darkness. For if I had to wander forever with my son by my side, that would be no condemnation."

Maybe not for you, *sister,* Susannah thought, but said nothing. In truth, she was fed up with Mia's megrims.

"And if there's no way for us to be free," Mia said, "kill us."

Although there was no sound up here but the wind and the cackling hyenas, Susannah could sense her physical body still on the move, now being carried down a flight of stairs. All that real-world stuff behind the thinnest of membranes. For Mia to have transported her to this world, especially while in the throes of childbirth, suggested a being of great power. Too bad that power couldn't be harnessed, somehow.

Mia apparently mistook Susannah's continued

silence for reluctance, for she rushed around the allure's circular walkway in her sturdy *huaraches* and almost ran to where Susannah sat in her gawky, balky cart. She seized Susannah's shoulders and shook her.

"*Yar!*" she cried vehemently. "Kill us! Better we be together in death than to . . ." She trailed off, then spoke in a dull and bitter voice: "I've been cozened all along. Haven't I?"

And now that the moment had come, Susannah felt neither vindication nor sympathy nor sorrow. She only nodded.

"Do they mean to eat him? To feed those terrible elders with his corpse?"

"I'm almost sure not," Susannah said. And yet cannibalism was in it somewhere; her heart whispered it was so.

"They don't care about me at all," Mia said. "Just the baby-sitter, isn't that what you called me? And they won't even let me have *that,* will they?"

"I don't think so," Susannah said. "You might get six months to nurse him, but even that . . ." She shook her head, then bit her lip as a fresh contraction gusted into her, turning all the muscles in her belly and thighs to glass. When it eased a little she finished, "I doubt it."

"Then kill us, if it comes to that. Say you will, Susannah, do ya, I beg!"

"And if I do for you, Mia, what will you do for me? Assuming I could believe any word out of your liar's mouth?"

"I'd free you, if chance allows."

Susannah thought it over, and decided that a

poor bargain was better than no bargain at all. She reached up and took the hands which were gripping her shoulders. "All right. I agree."

Then, as at the end of their previous palaver in this place, the sky tore open, and the merlon behind them, and the very air between them. Through the rip, Susannah saw a moving hallway. The image was dim, blurry. She understood she was looking through her own eyes, which were mostly shut. Bulldog and Hawkman still had her. They were bearing her toward the door at the end of the hallway—always, since Roland had come into her life, there was another door—and she guessed they must think she'd passed out, or fainted. She supposed that in a way, she had.

Then she fell back into the hybrid body with the white legs . . . only who knew how much of her previously brown skin was now white? She thought that situation, at least, was about to end, and she was delighted. She would gladly swap those white legs, strong though they might be, for a little peace of mind.

A little peace *in* her mind.

NINETEEN

"She's coming around," someone growled. The one with the bulldog face, Susannah thought. Not that it mattered; underneath they all looked like humanoid rats with fur growing out of their bone-crusty flesh.

"Good deal." That was Sayre, walking behind them. She looked around and saw that her entourage consisted of six low men, Hawkman, and a trio of vampires. The low men wore pistols in docker's clutches . . . only she supposed that in this world you had to call them shoulder holsters. When in Rome, dear, do ya as the Romans do. Two of the vampires had bahs, the crossbow weapon of the Callas. The third was carrying a bitterly buzzing electric sword of the sort the Wolves had wielded.

Ten-to-one odds, Susannah thought coolly. *Not good . . . but it could be worse.*

Can you—Mia's voice, from somewhere inside.

Shut up, Susannah told her. *Talking's done.*

Ahead, on the door they were approaching, she saw this:

NORTH CENTRAL POSITRONICS, LTD.
New York/Fedic

Maximum Security
VERBAL ENTRY CODE REQUIRED

It was familiar, and Susannah instantly knew why. She'd seen a sign similar to this during her one brief visit to Fedic. Fedic, where the real Mia—the being who had assumed mortality in what might be history's worst bargain—was imprisoned.

When they reached it, Sayre pushed past her on Hawkman's side. He leaned toward the door and spoke something guttural deep in his throat, some alien word Susannah never could have pronounced herself. *It doesn't matter,* Mia whispered. *I can say it, and if I need to, I can teach you another that you can say. But now . . . Susannah, I'm sorry for everything. Fare you well.*

The door to the Arc 16 Experimental Station in Fedic came open. Susannah could hear a ragged humming sound and could smell ozone. No magic powered this door between the worlds; this was the work of the old people, and failing. Those who'd made it had lost their faith in magic, had given up their belief in the Tower. In the place of magic was this buzzing, dying thing. This stupid mortal thing. And beyond it she saw a great room filled with beds. Hundreds of them.

It's where they operate on the children. Where they take from them whatever it is the Breakers need.

Now only one of the beds was occupied. Standing at its foot was a woman with one of those terrible rat's heads. A nurse, perhaps. Beside her was a human—Susannah didn't think he was a vampire but couldn't be sure, as the view through the door was as wavery as the air over an incinerator. He looked up and saw them.

"Hurry!" he shouted. "Move your freight! We have to connect them and finish it, or she'll die! They both will!" The doctor—surely no one but a doctor could have mustered such ill-tempered arrogance in the presence of Richard P. Sayre—made impatient beckoning gestures. "Get her in here! You're late, goddam you!"

Sayre pushed her rudely through the door. She heard a humming deep in her head, and a brief jangle of todash chimes: She looked down but was too late; Mia's borrowed legs were already gone and she went sprawling to the floor before Hawkman and Bulldog could come through behind her and catch her.

She braced on her elbows and looked up, aware that, for the first time in God knew how long—probably since she'd been raped in the circle of stones—she belonged only to herself. Mia was gone.

Then, as if to prove this wasn't so, Susannah's troublesome and newly departed guest let out a scream. Susannah added her own cry—the pain was now too huge for silence—and for a moment their voices sang of the baby's imminence in perfect harmony.

"Christ," said one of Susannah's guards—whether vampire or low man she didn't know. "Are my ears bleeding? They *feel* like they must be—"

"Pick her up, Haber!" Sayre snarled. "Jey! Grab hold! Get her off the floor, for your fathers' sakes!"

Bulldog and Hawkman—or Haber and Jey, if you liked that better—grabbed her beneath the arms and quickly carried her down the aisle of the ward that way, past the rows of empty beds.

Mia turned toward Susannah and managed a weak, exhausted smile. Her face was wet with sweat and her hair was plastered to her flushed skin.

"Well-met . . . and ill," she managed.

"Push the next bed over!" the doctor shouted. "Hurry up, gods damn you! Why are you so Christing *slow?*"

Two of the low men who'd accompanied Susannah from the Dixie Pig bent over the nearest empty bed and shoved it next to Mia's while Haber and Jey continued to hold her up between them. There was something on the bed that looked like a

cross between a hair-dryer and the sort of space
helmet you saw in the old *Flash Gordon* serials.
Susannah didn't much care for the look of it. It had
a brain-sucking look.

The rathead nurse, meanwhile, was bending
between her patient's splayed legs and peering
under the hiked-up hospital gown Mia now wore.
She patted Mia's right knee with a plump hand and
made a mewling sound. It was almost surely meant
to comfort, but Susannah shuddered.

"Don't just stand there with your thumbs up
your butts, you idiots!" the doctor cried. He was a
stoutish man with brown eyes, flushed cheeks, and
black hair swept back against his skull, where each
track of the comb seemed as wide as a gutter. He
wore a lab-coat of white nylon over a tweed suit.
His scarlet cravat had an eye figured into it. This
sigul did not surprise Susannah in the slightest.

"We wait your word," said Jey, the Hawkman.
He spoke in a queer, inhuman monotone, as
unpleasant as the rathead nurse's mewl but perfectly understandable.

"You shouldn't *need* my word!" the doctor
snapped. He flapped his hands in a Gallic gesture
of disgust. "Didn't your mothers have any children
that lived?"

"I—" Haber began, but the doc went right over
him. He was on a roll.

"How long have we been waiting for this,
hmmm? How many times have we rehearsed the
procedure? Why must you be so fucking *stupid,* so
Christing *slow?* Put her down on the b—"

Sayre moved with a speed Susannah wasn't sure

even Roland could have equaled. At one moment he was standing beside Haber, the low man with the bulldog face. At the next he'd battened on the doctor, digging his chin into the doc's shoulder and grabbing his arm, twisting it high behind his back.

The doc's expression of petulant fury vanished in a heartbeat, and he began to scream in a childish, breaking treble. Spit spilled over his lower lip and the crotch of his tweed trousers darkened as his urine let go.

"Stop!" he howled. *"I'm no good to you if you break my arm! Oh stop, that HURRRTS!"*

"If I sh'd break your arm, Scowther, I'd just drag some other pill-pusher in off the street to finish this, and kill him later. Why not? It's a woman having a baby, not brain-surgery, for Gan's sake!"

Yet he relaxed his hold a little bit. Scowther sobbed and wriggled and moaned as breathlessly as someone having sexual intercourse in a hot climate.

"And when it was done and you had no part in it," Sayre continued, "I'd feed you to *them*." He gestured with his chin.

Susannah looked that way and saw that the aisle from the door to the bed where Mia lay was now covered with the bugs she'd glimpsed in the Dixie Pig. Their knowing, greedy eyes were fixed on the plump doctor. Their mandibles clicked.

"What . . . sai, what must I do?"

"Cry my pardon."

"C-Cry pardon!"

"And now these others, for ye've insulted them as well, so you have."

"Sirs, I . . . I . . . c-cry—"

"Doctor!" the rathead nurse broke in. Her speaking voice was thick but understandable. She was still bent between Mia's legs. "The baby's crowning!"

Sayre let go of Scowther's arm. "Go on, Dr. Scowther. Do your duty. Deliver the child." Sayre bent forward and stroked Mia's cheek with extra-ordinary solicitude. "Be of good cheer and good hope, lady-sai," he said. "Some of your dreams may yet come true."

She looked up at him with a tired gratitude that wrung Susannah's heart. *Don't believe him, his lies are endless,* she tried to send, but for the nonce their contact was broken.

She was tossed like a sack of grain onto the bed which had been pushed next to Mia's. She was unable to struggle as one of the hoods was fitted over her head; another labor pain had gripped her, and once again the two women shrieked together.

Susannah could hear Sayre and the others murmuring. From below and behind them, she could also hear the unpleasant clittering of the bugs. Inside the helmet, round metal protuberances pressed against her temples, almost hard enough to hurt.

Suddenly a pleasant female voice said, "Welcome to the world of North Central Positronics, part of the Sombra Group! 'Sombra, where progress never stops!' Stand by for up-link."

A loud humming began. At first it was in Susannah's ears, but then she could feel it boring in on both sides. She visualized a pair of glowing bullets moving toward each other.

Dimly, as if from the other side of the room instead of right next to her, she heard Mia scream, *"Oh no, don't, that hurts!"*

The left hum and the right hum joined in the center of Susannah's brain, creating a piercing tele-pathic tone that would destroy her ability to think if it kept up for long. It was excruciating, but she kept her lips shut tight. She would not scream. Let them see the tears oozing out from beneath her closed lids, but she was a gunslinger and they would not make her scream.

After what seemed an eternity, the hum cut out.

Susannah had a moment or two in which to enjoy the blessed silence in her head, and then the next labor pain struck, this one very low down in her belly and with the force of a typhoon. With this pain she *did* allow herself to scream. Because it was different, somehow; to scream with the baby's coming was an honor.

She turned her head and saw a similar steel hood had been fitted over Mia's sweaty black hair. The segmented steel hoses from the two helmets were connected in the middle. These were the gadgets they used on the stolen twins, but now they were being put to some other purpose. What?

Sayre leaned down to her, close enough so she could smell his cologne. Susannah thought it was English Leather.

"To accomplish the final labor and actually push the baby out, we need this physical link," he said. "Bringing you here to Fedic was absolutely vital." He patted her shoulder. "Good luck. It won't be long now." He smiled at her winsomely. The mask he wore wrinkled upward, revealing some of the red horror which lay beneath. "Then we can kill you."

The smile broadened.

"And eat you, of course. Nothing goes to waste at the Dixie Pig, not even such an arrogant bitch as yourself."

Before Susannah could reply, the female voice in her head spoke again. "Please speak your name, slowly and distinctly."

"Fuck you!" Susannah snarled back.

"Fuk Yu does not register as a valid name for a non-Asian," said the pleasant female voice. "We detect hostility, and apologize in advance for the following procedure."

For a moment there was nothing, and then Susannah's mind lit up with pain beyond anything she had ever been called upon to endure. More than she had suspected could exist. Yet her lips remained closed as it raved through her. She thought of the song, and heard it true even through the thunder of the pain: *I am a maid . . . of constant sorrow . . . I've seen trials all my days . . .*

At last the thunder ceased.

"Please speak your name, slowly and distinctly," said the pleasant female voice in the middle of her head, "or this procedure will be intensified by a factor of ten."

No need of that, Susannah sent the female voice. *I'm convinced.*

"Suuuu-zaaaa-nahhh," she said. "Suuu-zannn-ahhh . . ."

They stood watching her, all of them except for Ms. Rathead, who was peering ecstatically up to where the baby's down-covered head had once again appeared between the withdrawing lips of Mia's vagina.

"Miiii-aaaahhhh . . ."

"Suuuu-zaaa . . ."

"Miiii . . ."

"annn-ahhh . . ."

By the time the next contraction began, Dr. Scowther had seized a pair of forceps. The voices of the women became one, uttering a word, a name, that was neither *Susannah* nor *Mia* but some combination of both.

"The link," said the pleasant female voice, "has been established." A faint *click*. "Repeat the link has been established. Thank you for your cooperation."

"This is it, people," Scowther said. His pain and terror appeared forgotten; he sounded excited. He turned to his nurse. "It may cry, Alia. If it does, let it alone, for your father's sake! If it doesn't, swab out its mouth at once!"

"Yes, doctor." The thing's lips quivered back, revealing a double set of fangs. Was that a grimace or a smile?

Scowther looked around at them with a touch of his previous arrogance. "All of you stay exactly where you are until I say you can move," he said. "None of us knows exactly what we've got here. We only know that the child belongs to the Crimson King himself—"

Mia screamed at that. In pain and in protest.

"Oh, you idiot," Sayre said. He drew back a hand and slapped Scowther with enough force to make his hair fly and send blood spraying against the white wall in a pattern of fine droplets.

"No!" Mia cried. She tried to struggle up onto her elbows, failed, fell back. "No, you said I should have the raising of him! Oh, please . . . if only for a little while, I beg . . ."

Then the worst pain yet rolled over Susannah— over both of them, burying them. They screamed in tandem, and Susannah didn't need to hear Scowther, who was commanding her to *push*, to *push NOW!*

"It's coming, doctor!" the nurse cried in nervous ecstasy.

Susannah closed her eyes and bore down, and as she felt the pain begin to flow out of her like water whirlpooling its way down a dark drain, she also felt the deepest sorrow she had ever known. For it was Mia the baby was flowing into; the last few lines of the living message Susannah's body had somehow been made to transmit. It was ending. Whatever happened next, this part was ending, and Susannah Dean let out a cry of mingled relief and regret; a cry that was itself like a song.

And on the wings of that song, Mordred Deschain, son of Roland (and one other, O can you say Discordia), came into the world.

> STAVE: *Commala-come-kass!*
> *The child has come at last!*
> *Sing your song, O sing it well,*
> *The child has come to pass.*

RESPONSE: *Commala-come-kass,*
The worst has come to pass.
The Tower trembles on its ground;
The child has come at last.

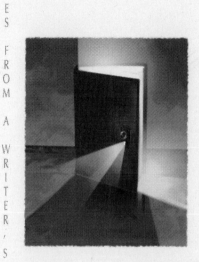

PAGES FROM A WRITER'S JOURNAL

CODA

<u>July 12th, 1977</u>

Man, it's good to be back in Bridgton. They always treat us well in what Joe still calls "Nanatown," but Owen fussed almost nonstop. He's better since we got back home. We only stopped once, in Waterville to grab grub at the Silent Woman (I've had better meals there, I must add).

Anyway, I kept my promise to myself and went on a grand hunt for that <u>Dark Tower</u> story as soon as I got back. I'd almost given up when I found the pages in the farthest corner of the garage, under a box of Tab's old catalogues. There was a lot of "spring thaw drip" over there, and those funny blue pages smell all mildewy, but the copy is perfectly readable. I finished going over it, then sat down and added a small section to the Way Station material (where the gunslinger meets the boy Jake). I thought it would be kind of fun to put in a water pump that runs on an atomic slug, and so I did so without delay. Usually working on an old story is about as appetizing as eating a sandwich made with moldy bread, but this felt perfectly natural . . . like slipping on an old shoe.

What, exactly, was this story supposed to be about?

I can't remember, only that it first came to me a long, long time ago. Driving back from up north, with my entire family snoozing, I got thinking about that time David and I ran away from Aunt Ethelyn's. We were planning to go back to Connecticut, I think. The grups (i.e., grownups) caught us, of course, and put us to work in the barn, sawing wood. Punishment Detail, Uncle Oren called it. It seems to me that something scary happened to me out there, but I'll be damned if I can remember what it was, only that it was <u>red</u>. And I thought up a hero, a magic gunslinger, to keep me safe from it. There was something about magnetism, too, or Beams of Power. I'm pretty sure that was the genesis of this story, but it's strange how blurry it all seems. Oh well, who remembers all the nasty little nooks of their childhood? Who <u>wants</u> to?

Not much else happening. Joe and Naomi made Playground, and Tabby's plans for her trip to England are pretty much complete. Boy, that story about the gunslinger <u>won't</u> get out of my head!

Tell you what ole Roland needs: some friends!

<u>July 19th, 1977</u>

I went to see <u>Star Wars</u> on my motorcycle tonight, and I think it'll be the last time I climb on the bike until things cool off a little. I ate a ton of bugs. Talk about protein!

I kept thinking about Roland, my gunslinger from the Robert Browning poem (with a tip of Hatlo's Hat to Sergio Leone, of course), while I rode. The manuscript is a novel, no doubt—or a piece of one—but it occurs to me that the chapters also stand on their own. Or almost. I wonder if I could sell them to one of the fantasy mags? Maybe even to <u>Fantasy and Science Fiction</u>, which is, of course, the genre's Holy Grail.

Probably a stupid idea.

Otherwise, not much doing but the All-Star Game (National League 7, American League 5). I was pretty hammered before it was over. Tabby <u>not</u> pleased . . .

<u>August 9th, 1978</u>

Kirby McCauley sold the first chapter of that old <u>Dark Tower</u> story of mine to <u>Fantasy and Science Fiction</u>! Man, I can hardly believe it! That is just so cool! Kirby sez he thinks Ed Ferman (the Ed-in-chief there) will probably run everything of the <u>DT</u> story that I've got. He's going to call the first bit ("The man in black fled across the desert, and the gunslinger followed," etc., etc., blah-blah, bang-bang) "The Gunslinger," which makes sense.

Not bad for an old story that was moldering away forgotten in a wet corner of the garage last year. Ferman told Kirby that Roland "has a feel of reality" that's missing in a lot of fantasy fiction, and wanted to know if there might be even more adventures. I'm sure there <u>are</u> even more adventures (or <u>were,</u> or <u>will be</u>—what's the proper tense when you're talking about unwritten tales?), but I have no idea what they might be. Only that John "Jake" Chambers would have to come back into it.

A rainy, muggy day by the lake. No Playground for the kids. Tonight we had Andy Fulcher sit the big kids while Tab & I & Owen went to the Bridgton Drive-In. Tabby thought the film (<u>The Other Side of Midnight</u> . . . from last <u>year</u>, actually) was a piece of shit, but I didn't hear her begging to be taken home. As for me, I found my mind drifting off to that damn Roland guy again. This time to questions of his lost love. "Susan, lovely girl at the window."

Who, pray, be she?

<u>September 9, 1978</u>

Got my first copy of the October issue with "The Gunslinger" in it. Man, this looks fine.

Burt Hatlen called today. He's talking about me maybe doing a year at the University of Maine as writer in residence. Only Burt would be ballsy enough to think of a hack like me in connection w/ a job like that. Sort of an interesting idea, though.

<u>October 29, 1979</u>

Well, shit, drunk again. I can barely see the goddam page, but suppose I better put down <u>something</u> before I go staggering off to bed. Got a letter from Ed Ferman at <u>F&SF</u> today. He's going to do the second chapter of <u>The Dark Tower</u>—the part where Roland meets the kid—as "The Way Station." He really wants to publish the entire run of stories, and I'm agreeable enough. I just wish there was more. Meanwhile, there's <u>The Stand</u> to think about—and, of course, <u>The Dead Zone</u>.

All of this doesn't seem to mean much to me just now. I <u>hate</u> being here in Orrington—hate being on such a busy road, for one thing. Owen damned near got creamed by one of those Cianbro trucks today. Scared the hell out of me. Also gave me an idea for a story, having to do with that odd little pet cemetery out in back of the house. **PET SEMATARY** is what the sign sez, isn't that weird? Funny, but also creepy. Almost a <u>Vault of Horror</u> type of thing.

<u>June 19th, 1980</u>

Just got off the phone with Kirby McCauley. <u>He</u> got a call from Donald Grant, who publishes lots of fantasy stuff under his own imprint (Kirby likes to joke that Don Grant is "the man who made Robert E. Howard infamous"). Anyway, Don would like to publish my gunslinger stories, and under their original title, <u>The Dark Tower</u> (subtitle <u>The Gunslinger</u>). Isn't that neat? My own "limited edition." He'd do 10,000 copies, plus 500 signed and numbered. I told Kirby to go ahead and make the deal.

Anyway, it looks like my teaching career is over, and I got pretty well baked to celebrate. Took out the <u>Pet Sematary</u> ms. and looked it over. Good God, is that grim! Readers would lynch me if I published it, I think. That's one book that'll never see the light of day . . .

<u>July 27th, 1983</u>

<u>Publishers Weekly</u> (our son Owen calls it <u>Pudlishers Weakness,</u> which is actually sorta accurate) reviewed the latest Richard Bachman book . . . and once more, baby, I got <u>roasted.</u> They implied it was

boring, and that, my friend, it ain't. Oh well, thinking about it made it that much easier to go to North Windham and pick up those 2 kegs of beer for the party. Got em at Discount Beverage. I'm smoking again, too, so sue me. I'll quit the day I turn 40 and that's a promise.

Oh, and <u>Pet Sematary</u> is published exactly two months from today. Then my career really <u>will</u> be over (joke . . . at least I hope it's a joke). After some thought, I added <u>The Dark Tower</u> to the author's ad-card at the front of the book. In the end, I thought, why not? Yes, I know it's sold out—there were only 10,000 copies to start with, fa Chrissake—but it was a real book and I'm proud of it. I don't suppose I'll ever go back to ole Roland the Gun-Toting Knight Errant, but yes, I'm proud of that book.

Good thing I remembered the beer run.

<u>February 21st, 1984</u>

Man, I got this <u>crazy</u> call from Sam Vaughn at Doubleday this afternoon (he edited <u>Pet Sem,</u> you will remember). I knew there were some fans who want <u>The Dark Tower</u> and are pissed off they can't get it, because I also get letters. But Sam sez they have gotten over THREE THOUSAND!! letters. And why, you ask? Because I was <u>dumb enough</u> to put <u>The Dark Tower</u> on the <u>Pet Sematary</u> author ad-card. I think Sam's a little pissed at me, and I suppose he's got a point. He says listing a book that fans want & can't get is a little like holding out a piece of meat to a hungry dog and then yanking it back, saying "No, no, you can't have it, har-

har." On the other hand, God & the Man Jesus, people are so fucking <u>spoiled</u>! They just assume that if there's a book anywhere in the world they <u>want</u>, then they have a perfect <u>right</u> to that book. This would be news indeed to those folks in the Middle Ages who might have heard <u>rumors</u> of books but never actually saw one; paper was valuable (which would be a good thing to put in the next "Gunslinger/Dark Tower" novel, if I ever get around to it) and books were treasures you protected with your life. I love being able to make my living writing stories, but anyone who sez there's no dark side to it is full of shit. Someday I'm going to do a novel about a psychotic rare book dealer! (Joke)

Meanwhile, today was Owen's birthday. He's seven! The age of reason! I can hardly believe my youngest is seven and my daughter is thirteen, a lovely young woman.

<u>August 14th, 1984 (NYC)</u>

Just got back from a meeting with Elaine Koster from NAL and my agent, the ole Kirboo. Both of them pitched me on doing <u>The Gunslinger</u> as a trade-sized paperback, but I passed. Maybe someday, but I won't give that many people a chance to read something so unfinished unless/until I go back to work on the story.

Which I probably never will. Meantime, I have this other idea for a <u>long</u> novel about a clown that's really the worst monster in the world. Not a bad idea; clowns are scary. To me, at least. (Clowns & chickens, go figure.)

November 18th, 1984

I had a dream last night that I think breaks the creative logjam on <u>It</u>. Suppose there's a kind of Beam holding the Earth (or even multiple Earths) in place? And that the Beam's generator rests on the shell of a turtle? I could make that part of the book's climax. I know it sounds crazy, but I'm sure I read somewhere that in Hindu mythology there's a great turtle that bears us all on his shell, and that he serves Gan, the creative overforce. Also, I remember an anecdote where some lady sez to some famous scientist, "This evolution stuff is ridiculous. Everyone knows that a turtle holds up the universe." To which the scientist (wish I could remember his name, but I can't) replies, "That may be, madam, but what holds up the turtle?" Scornful laugh from the lady, who says, "Oh, you can't fool me! It's turtles all the way down."

Ha! Take <u>that</u>, ye rational men of science!

Anyway, I keep a blank book by my bed, and have gotten so I write down a lot of dreams and dream elements w/o even fully waking up. This morning I'd written <u>Remember the Turtle</u>! And this: <u>See the TURTLE of enormous girth! On his shell he holds the earth. His thought is slow but always kind; he holds us all within his mind</u>. Not great poetry, I grant you, but not bad for a guy who was three-quarters asleep when he wrote it!

Tabby has been on my case about drinking too much again. I suppose she's right, but . . .

June 10th, 1986 (Lovell/Turtleback Lane)

Man, am I glad we bought this house! I was

scared of the expense to begin with, but I've never written better than I have here. And—this is scary, but it's true—I think I want to go back to work on <u>The Dark Tower</u> story. In my heart, I thought I never would, but last night when I was going to the Center General for beer, I could almost hear Roland saying, "There are many worlds and many tales, but not much time."

I ended up turning around and coming back to the house. Can't remember the last time I spent a totally sober night, but this is one of that dying breed. It actually feels fucked up not to be fucked up. That's pretty sad, I guess.

June 13th, 1986

I woke up in the middle of the night, hung-over and needing to pee. While I was standing at the bowl, it was almost as if I could <u>see</u> Roland of Gilead. Telling me to start with the lobstrosities. I will.

I know just what they are.

June 15th, 1986

Started the new book today. Can't believe I'm actually writing about old long, tall, and ugly again, but it felt right from the first page. Hell, from the first <u>word.</u> I've decided it'll be almost like the classic fairy-tales in structure: Roland walks along the beach of the Western Sea, getting sicker & sicker as he goes, and there's a series of doors to our world. He'll draw a new character from behind each one. The first one will be a stone junkie named Eddie Dean . . .

<u>July 16th, 1986</u>

I can't believe this. I mean, I've got the manuscript on the desk right in front of me so I sorta <u>have</u> to, but I still can't. I have written <u>!!300!! PAGES</u> in the last month, and the copy is so clean it's positively squeaky. I've <u>never</u> felt like one of those writers who can actually take credit for their work, who say they plot every move and incident, but I've also never had a book that seemed to flow through me like this one has. It's pretty much taken over my life from Day One. And do you know, it seems to me that a lot of the other things I've written (especially <u>It</u>) are like "practice shots" for this story. Certainly I've never picked something up after it lay fallow for fifteen years! I mean, sure, I did a <u>little</u> work on the stories Ed Ferman published in <u>F&SF</u>, and I did a little more when Don Grant published <u>The Gunslinger</u>, but nothing like what I'm up to now. I even <u>dream</u> about this story. I have days when I wish I could quit drinking, but I'll tell you something: I'm almost scared to stop. I know inspiration doesn't flow from the neck of a bottle, but there's something . . .

I'm scared, okay? I feel like there's something—<u>Something</u>—that doesn't want me to finish this book. That didn't even want me to start it. Now I know that's crazy ("Like something out of a Stephen King story," har-har), but at the same time it seems very real. Probably a good thing no one'll ever read this diary; very likely they'd put me away if they did. Anyone want to buy a used fruitcake?

I'm going to call it <u>The Drawing of the Three</u>, I think.

September 19th, 1986

It's done. <u>The Drawing of the Three</u> is done. I got drunk to celebrate. Stoned, too. And what's next? Well, <u>It</u> will be published in a month or so, and in two days I'll be thirty-nine. Man, I can hardly believe it. Seems just about a week ago that we were living in Bridgton and the kids were babies.

Ah, fuck. Time to quit. The writer's gettin' maudlin.

June 19th, 1987

Got my first author's copy of <u>Drawing</u> from Donald Grant today. It's a beautiful package. I've also decided to let NAL go ahead and do both <u>Dark Tower</u> books in paperback—give the people what they want. Why the hell not?

Of course, I got drunk to celebrate . . . only these days who needs an excuse?

It's a good book but in many ways it seems like I didn't write the damn thing at all, that it just flowed out of me, like the umbilical cord from a baby's navel. What I'm trying to say is that the wind blows, the cradle rocks, and sometimes it seems to me that <u>none</u> of this stuff is mine, that I'm nothing but Roland of Gilead's fucking secretary. I know that's stupid, but a part of me sort of believes it. Only maybe Roland's got his own boss. Ka?

I <u>do</u> tend to get depressed when I look at my life: the booze, the drugs, the cigarettes. As if I'm actually trying to kill myself. Or something else is . . .

October 19th, 1987

I'm in Lovell tonight, the house on Turtleback Lane. Came down here to think about the way I'm living my life. Something's got to change, man, because otherwise I might as well just cut to the chase and blow my brains out.

Something's got to change.

The following item from the North Conway (N.H.) Mountain Ear *was pasted into the writer's journal, marked April 12th, 1988:*

LOCAL SOCIOLOGIST DISMISSES "WALK-IN" TALES
By Logan Merrill

For at least 10 years, the White Mountains have resounded with tales of "Walk-Ins," creatures who may be aliens from space, time travelers, or even "beings from another dimension." In a lively lecture last night at the North Conway Public Library, local sociologist Henry K. Verdon, author of <u>Peer Groups and Myth-Making</u>, used the Walk-In phenomenon as an illustration of just how myths are created and how they grow. He said that the "Walk-Ins" were probably originally created by teenagers in the border towns between Maine and New Hampshire. He also speculated that sightings of illegal aliens who cross over the northern border from Canada and then into the New England states may have played a part in kindling this myth, which has become

so prevalent. "I think we all know,"
Professor Verdon said, "that there is
no Santa Claus, no Tooth Fairy, and
no actual beings called Walk-Ins. Yet
these tales

(Continued on P. 8)

*The rest of the article is missing. Nor is there any
explanation as to why King may have included it
in his journal.*

<u>June 19th, 1989</u>

I just got back from my one-year Alcoholix
Anonymous "anniversary." An entire year w/o
drugs or booze! I can hardly believe it. No regrets;
sobering up undoubtedly saved my life (and probably my marriage), but I wish it wasn't so hard to
write stories in the aftermath. People in "the Pro-
gram" say don't push it, it'll come, but there's another voice (I think of it as the Voice of the Turtle)
telling me to hurry up and get going, time is short
and I have to sharpen my tools. For what? For <u>The
Dark Tower</u>, of course, and not just because letters
keep coming in from people who read <u>The Drawing of the Three</u> and want to know what happens
next. Something in <u>me</u> wants to go back to work
on the story, but I'll be damned if I know how to
<u>get</u> back.

<u>July 12th, 1989</u>

There are some amazing treasures on the book-
shelves down here in Lovell. Know what I found
this morning, while I was looking for something

to read? <u>Shardik</u>, by Richard Adams. Not the story about the rabbits but the one about the giant mythological bear. I think I'll read it over again.

Am still not writing much of interest . . .

September 21, 1989

Okay, this is relatively weird, so prepare yourself.

Around 10 A.M., while I was writing (while I was staring at the word processor and dreaming about how great it would be to have an ice-cold keg of Bud, at least), the doorbell rang. It was a guy from Bangor House of Flowers, with a dozen roses. Not for Tab, either, but for me. The card read <u>Happy Birthday from the Mansfields—Dave, Sandy, and Megan</u>.

I had totally forgotten, but today I'm the Big Four-Two. Anyway, I took one of the roses out, and I kind of got lost in it. I know how strange that sounds, believe me, but I did. I seemed to hear this sweet humming, and I just went down & down, following the curves of the rose, kind of splashing thru these drops of dew that seemed as big as ponds. And all the time that humming sound got louder & sweeter, and the rose got . . . well, <u>rosier</u>. And I found myself thinking of Jake from the first <u>Dark Tower</u> story, and Eddie Dean, and a bookstore. I even remember the name: The Manhattan Restaurant of the Mind.

Then, boom! I feel a hand on my shoulder, I turn around, and it's Tabby. She wanted to know who sent me the roses. She also wanted to know if I'd fallen asleep. I said no, but I kind of did, right there in the kitchen.

You know what it was like? That scene at the Way Station in <u>The Gunslinger,</u> where Roland hypnotizes Jake with a bullet. I'm immune to hypnosis, myself. A guy got me up on stage at the Topsham Fair when I was a kid and tried it on me, but it didn't work. As I remember, my brother Dave was quite disappointed. He wanted me to cluck like a chicken.

Anyway, I think I want to go back to work on <u>The Dark Tower</u>. I don't know if I'm ready for anything that complex—after some of the failures of the last couple of years let's say I'm dubious—but I want to give it a shot, just the same. I hear those make-believe people calling to me. And who knows? There might even be a place in this one for a giant bear, like Shardik in the Richard Adams novel!

October 7th, 1989

I started the next <u>Dark Tower</u> book today, and—as with <u>The Drawing of the Three</u>—I finished my first session wondering why in God's name I waited so long. Being with Roland, Eddie, and Susannah is like a drink of cool water. Or meeting old friends after a long absence. And, once again, there is a sense that I'm not telling the story but only providing a conduit for it. And you know what? That's okie-fine with me. I sat at the word processor for four hours this morning and did not once think of a drink or any sort of mind-altering drug. I think I'll call this one <u>The Wastelands</u>.

<u>October 9th, 1989</u>

No—<u>Waste Lands</u>. 2 words, as in the T. S. Eliot poem (his is actually "The Waste Land," I think).

<u>January 19th, 1990</u>

Finished <u>The Waste Lands</u> tonight, after a marathon 5-hour session. People are going to hate the way it ends, w/ no conclusion to the riddle contest, and I thought the story would go on longer myself, but I can't help it. I heard a voice speak up clearly in my head (as always it sounds like Roland's) saying, "You're done for now—close thy book, wordslinger."

Cliffhanger ending aside, the story seems fine to me, but, as always, not much like the other ones I write. The manuscript is a <u>brick</u>, over 800 pages long, and I created said brick in just a little over three months.

Un-fucking-real.

Once again, hardly any strike-overs or re-takes. There are a few continuity glitches, but considering the length of the book, I can hardly believe <u>how</u> few. Nor can I believe how, when I needed some sort of inspiration, the right book seemed to fly into my hand time after time. Like <u>The Quincunx</u>, by Charles Palliser, with all the wonderful, growly 17th-century slang: "Aye, so ye do" and "So ye will" and "my cully." That argot sounded perfect coming out of Gasher's mouth (to me, at least). And how cool it was to have Jake come back into the story the way he did!

Only thing that worries me is what's going to happen to Susannah Dean (who used to be Detta/Odetta).

She's pregnant, and I'm afraid of who or what the father might be. Some demon? I don't think so, exactly. Maybe I won't have to deal w/ that until a couple of books further down the line. In any case, my experience is that, in a long book, whenever a woman gets pregnant and nobody knows who the father is, that story is headed down the tubes. Dunno why, but as a plot-thickener, pregnancy just naturally seems to <u>suck</u>!

Oh well, maybe it doesn't matter. For the time being I'm tired of Roland and his ka-tet. I think it may be awhile before I get back to them again, although the fans are going to howl their heads off about that cliffhanger ending on the train out of Lud. Mark my words.

I'm glad I wrote it, tho, and to me the ending seems just right. In many ways <u>Waste Lands</u> feels like the high point of my "make-believe life."

Even better than <u>The Stand</u>, maybe.

<u>November 27th, 1991</u>

Remember me saying that I'd get bitched at about the ending of <u>Waste Lands</u>? Look at this!

Letter follows from John T. Spier, of Lawrence, Kansas:

November 16, 91

Dear Mr. King,

Or should I just cut to the chase and say "Dear Asshole"?

I can't believe I paid such big bucks for a Donald Grant Edition of your GUNSLINGER book <u>The Waste Lands</u> and this is what I got. It had the right title anyway, for it was "a true WASTE."

I mean the story was all right don't get me wrong, great in fact, but how could you "tack on" an ending like that? It wasn't an ending at all but just a case of you getting tired and saying "Oh well, what the fuck, I don't need to strain my brain to write an ending, those slobs who buy my books will swallow anything."

I was going to send it back but will keep it because I at least liked the pictures (especially Oy). But the story was a cheat.

Can you spell CHEAT Mr. King? M-O-O-N, that spells CHEAT.

Sincerely yours in criticism,

John T. Spier
Lawrence, Kansas

March 23, 1992
In a way, this one makes me feel even worse.

Letter follows from Mrs. Coretta Vele, of Stowe, Vermont:

March 6th, 1992

Dear Stephen King,

I don't know if this letter will actually reach you but one can always hope. I have read most of your books and have loved them all. I am a 76-yrs-young "gramma" from your "sister state" of Vermont, and I especially like your Dark Tower stories. Well, to the point. Last month I went to see a team of Oncologists at Mass General, and they tell me that the brain tumor I have looks to be malignant after all (at 1ˢᵗ they said "Don't worry Coretta its benine"). Now I know you have to do what you have to do, Mr. King, and "follow your muse," but what they're saying is that I will be fortunate to see the 4th of July this year. I guess I've read my last "Dark Tower yarn." So what I'm wondering is, Can you tell me how the Dark Tower story comes out, at least if Roland and his "Ka-Tet" actually get to the Dark Tower? And if so what they find there? I promise not to tell a soul and you will be making a dying woman very happy.

                                        Sincerely,

                                        Coretta Vele
                                        Stowe, Vt.

I feel like such a shit when I think of how blithe I was concerning the ending of <u>Waste Lands</u>. I gotta answer Coretta Vele's letter, but I don't know how to. Could I make her believe I don't know any more than she does about how Roland's story finishes? I doubt it, and yet "that is the truth," as Jake sez in his Final Essay. I have no more idea what's inside that damned Tower than . . . well, than <u>Oy</u> does! I didn't even know it was in a field of roses until it came off my fingertips and showed up on the screen of my new Macintosh computer! Would Coretta buy that? What would she say if I told her, "Cory, listen: The wind blows and the story comes. Then it stops blowing, and all I can do is wait, same as you."

They think I'm in charge, every one of them from the smartest of the critics to the most mentally challenged reader. And that's a real hoot.

Because I'm not.

September 22, 1992

The Grant edition of <u>The Waste Lands</u> is sold out, and the paperback edition is doing very well. I should be happy and guess I am, but I'm still getting a ton of letters about the cliffhanger ending. They fall into 3 major categories: People who are pissed off, people who want to know when the next book in the series is coming out, and pissed-off people who want to know when the next book in the series is coming out.

But I'm stuck. The wind from that quarter just isn't blowing. Not just now, anyway.

Meanwhile, I have an idea for a novel about a lady who buys a picture in a pawnshop and then kind of falls into it. Hey, maybe it'll be Mid-World she falls into, and she'll meet Roland!

July 9th, 1994

Tabby and I don't fight much since I quit drinking, but oboy, this morning we had a dilly. We're at the Lovell house, of course, and as I was getting ready to leave on my morning walk, she showed me a story from today's Lewiston <u>Sun</u>. It seems that a Stoneham man, Charles "Chip" McCausland, was struck and killed by a hit-and-run driver while walking on Route 7. Which is the road I walk on, of course. Tabby tried to persuade me to stay on Turtleback Lane, I tried to persuade <u>her</u> that I had as much right to use Route 7 as anyone else (and honest to God, I only do half a mile on the black-top), and things went downhill from there. Finally she asked me to at least stop walking on Slab City Hill, where the sightlines are so short and there's nowhere to jump if someone happens to get off the road and onto the shoulder. I told her I'd think about it (it would have been noon before I got out of the house if we kept on talking), but in truth I'll be damned if I'll live my life in fear that way. Besides, it seems to me that this poor guy from Stoneham has made the odds of me getting hit while out walking about a million to one. I told this to Tabby and she said, "The odds of you ever being as successful at writing as you have been are even higher. You've said so yourself."

To that I'm afraid I had no comeback.

<u>June 19th, 1995 (Bangor)</u>

Tabby and I just got back from the Bangor Auditorium where our youngest (and about four hundred of his classmates) finally got a diploma. He's now officially a high school graduate. Bangor High and the Bangor Rams are behind him. He'll be starting college in the fall and then Tab and I will have to start dealing w/ the ever-popular Empty Nest Syndrome. Everybody sez it all goes by in the wink of an eye and you say <u>yeah yeah yeah</u> . . . and then it does.

Fuck, I'm sad.

Feel lost. What's it all for, anyway? (What's it all about, Alfie, ha-ha?) What, just a big scramble from the cradle to the grave? "The clearing at the end of the path"? Jesus, that's grim.

Meantime, we're headed down to Lovell and the house on Turtleback Lane this afternoon—Owen will join us in a day or two, he sez. Tabby knows I want to write by the lake, and boy, she's so intuitive it's scary. When we were coming back from the graduation exercises, she asked me if the wind was blowing again.

In fact it is, and this time it's blowing a gale. I can't wait to start the next volume of the <u>DT</u> series. Time to find out what happens in the riddling contest (that Eddie blows Blaine's computerized mind with "silly questions"—i.e., riddles—is something I've known for several months now), but I don't think that's the major story I have to tell this time. I want to write about Susan, Roland's first love, and I want to set their "cowboy romance" in a fictional part of Mid-World called Mejis (i.e., Mexico).

Time to saddle up and take another ride w/ the Wild Bunch.

Meantime, the other kids are doing well, although Naomi had some kind of allergic reaction, maybe to shellfish . . .

<u>July 19th, 1995 (Turtleback Lane, Lovell)</u>

As on my previous expeditions to Mid-World, I feel like somebody who's just spent a month on a jet-propelled rocket-sled. While stoned on hallucinatory happygas. I thought this book would be tougher to get into, <u>much</u>, but in fact it was once more as easy as slipping into a pair of comfortable old shoes, or those Western-style short-boots I got from Bally's in New York 3 or 4 years ago and cannot bear to give up.

I've already got over 200 pages, and was delighted to find Roland and his friends investigating the remains of the superflu; seeing evidence of both Randall Flagg and Mother Abagail.

I think Flagg may turn out to be Walter, Roland's old nemesis. His real name is Walter o'Dim, and he was just a country boy to start with. It makes perfect sense, in a way. I can see now how, to a greater or lesser degree, every story I've ever written is about this story. And you know, I don't have a problem with that. Writing this story is the one that always feels like coming home.

Why does it always feel <u>dangerous</u>, as well? Why should I be so convinced that if I'm ever found slumped over my desk, dead of a heart attack (or wiped out on my Harley, probably on Route 7), it will be while working on one of these Weird Westerns? I guess because I know so many people are depending on me to finish the cycle. And <u>I</u> want to finish it! God, yes! No <u>Canterbury Tales</u> or <u>Mystery of Edwin Drood</u> in my portfolio if I can help it, thank you very much. And yet I always feel as if some anti-creative force is looking around for me, and that I am easier to see when I'm working on these stories.

Well, enough w/ the heebie-jeebies. I'm off on my walk.

<u>September 2, 1995</u>

I'm expecting the book to be done in another five weeks. This one has been more challenging, but still the story comes to me in wonderful rich details. Watched Kurosawa's <u>The Seven Samurai</u> last nite, and wonder if that might not be the right direction for Vol. #6, <u>The Werewolves of End-World</u> (or some such). I probably ought to see if any of the little side-o'-the-road video rental places around here have got <u>The Magnificent Seven</u>, which is the Americanized version of the Kurosawa film.

Speaking of side-o'-the-road, I almost had to dive into the ditch this afternoon to avoid a guy in a van—swerving from side to side, pretty obviously drunk—on the last part of Route 7 before I turn back into the relatively sheltered environs of Turtleback Lane. I don't think I'll mention this to Tabby; she'd go nuclear. Anyway, I've had my one "pedestrian scare," and I'm just glad it didn't happen on the Slab City Hill portion of the road.

October 19th, 1995

Took me a little longer than I thought, but I finished <u>Wizard and Glass</u> tonight . . .

August 19th, 1997

Tabby and I just said goodbye to Joe and his good wife; they're on their way back to New York. I was glad I could give them a copy of <u>Wizard and Glass</u>. The first bunch of finished books came today. What looks & smells better than a new book, especially one w/ your name on the title page? This is the world's best job I've got; real people pay me real money to hang out in my imagination. Where, I should add, the only ones who feel completely real to me are Roland and his ka-tet.

I think the CRs* are really going to like this one, and not just because it finishes the story of Blaine the

* Constant Readers

Mono. I wonder if the Vermont Gramma with the brain tumor is still alive? I s'poze not, but if she was, I'd be happy to send her a copy . . .

July 6th, 1998

Tabby, Owen, Joe, and I went to Oxford tonight to see the film <u>Armageddon</u>. I liked it more than I expected, in part because I had my family w/ me. The movie is sfx-driven end-of-the-world stuff. Got me thinking about the Dark Tower and the Crimson King. Probably not surprising.

I wrote for awhile this morning on my Vietnam story, switching over from longhand to my Power-Book, so I guess I'm serious about it. I like the way Sully John reappeared. Question: Will Roland Deschain and his friends ever meet Bobby Garfield's pal, Ted Brautigan? And just who are those low men chasing the old Tedster, anyway? More and more my work feels like a slanted trough where everything eventually drains into Mid-World and End-World.

<u>The Dark Tower</u> is my <u>uber</u>story, no question about that. When it's done, I plan to ease back. Maybe retire completely.

August 7, 1998

Took my usual walk this afternoon, and tonight I took Fred Hauser with me to the AA meeting in Fryeburg. On the way home he asked me to sponsor him and I said yes; I think he's finally getting serious about sobering up. Good for him. Anyhow, he got talking about the so-called "Walk-Ins." He says there are more of them around the Seven

Towns than ever, and all sorts of folks are gossiping about them.

"How come I never hear anything, then?" I asked him. To which I got no answer but an extremely funny look. I kept prodding, and finally Fred sez,

"People don't like to talk about them around you, Steve, because there have been two dozen reported on Turtleback Lane in the last 8 months and you claim not to have seen a single one."

To me this seemed like a non sequitur and I made no reply. It wasn't until after the meeting—and after I'd dropped my new pigeon off—that I realized what he was saying: people don't talk about the "Walk-Ins" around me because they think that in some crazy way I'M RESPONSIBLE. I thought I was pretty well used to being "America's boogeyman," but this is actually sort of outrageous . . .

January 2, 1999 (Boston)

Owen and I are at the Hyatt Harborside tonight, and head off to Florida tomorrow. (Tabby and I are talking about buying a place there but haven't told the kids. I mean, they're only 27, 25 and 21—maybe when they're old enough to understand such things, ha-ha.) Earlier we met Joe and saw a film called Hurlyburly, from the play by David Rabe. Very odd. Speaking of odd, I had some sort of New Year's Night nightmare before leaving Maine. Can't remember exactly what it was, but when I woke up this morning I'd written two things in my dreambook. One was Baby Mordred, like something out of a Chas Addams cartoon. That I sort of understand; it must refer to Susannah's baby in the Dark Tower stories. It's the other thing that puzzles me. It says 6/19/99, O Discordia.

Discordia also sounds like something out of the DT stories, but it's not anything I have invented. As for 6/19/99, that's a date, right? Meaning what? June 19th of this year. Tabby and I should be back at the Turtleback Lane house by then, but so far as I can remember it's not anybody's birthday.

Maybe it's the date I'm going to meet my first walk-in!

June 12, 1999

It's wonderful to be back at the lake!

I've decided to take 10 days off, then finally return to work on the how-to-write book. I'm curious about Hearts in Atlantis; will folks want to know if Bobby Garfield's friend Ted Brautigan plays a part in the Tower saga? The truth is I really don't know the answer to that. In any case, readership of the Tower stories has fallen off a lot lately— the figures are really disappointing, compared to that of my other books (except for Rose Madder, which was a real tank-job, at least in the sales sense). But it doesn't matter, at least to me, and if the series ever gets done, sales may go up.

Tabby and I had another argument about my walking route; she asked me again to quit going out on the main road. Also she asked me "Is the wind blowing yet?" Meaning am I thinking about the next Dark Tower story. I said no, commala-come-come, the tale has not begun. But it will, and there's a dance called the <u>commala</u> in it. That's the one thing I see clearly: Roland dancing. Why, or for whom, I don't know.

Anyway, I asked T. why she wanted to know about the Dark Tower and she said, "You're safer when you're with the gunslingers."

Joking, I suppose, but an <u>odd</u> joke for T. Not much like her.

<u>June 17, 1999</u>

Talked with Rand Holston and Mark Carliner tonight. They both sound excited about moving on from <u>Storm of the Century</u> to <u>Rose Red</u> (or <u>Kingdom Hospital</u>), but either one would fill my plate up again.

I dreamed of my walk last night & woke up crying. <u>The Tower will fall</u>, I thought. <u>O Discordia, the world grows dark</u>.

????

Headline from the Portland Press-Herald, *June 18, 1999:*

"WALK-IN" PHENOMENON IN WESTERN MAINE CONTINUES TO RESIST EXPLANATION

<u>June 19, 1999</u>

This is like one of those times when all the planets line up, except in this case it's my family all lined up here on Turtleback Lane. Joe and his family arrived around noon; their little boy is really cute. Say true! Sometimes I look in the mirror and say, <u>"You are a grandfather."</u> And the Steve in the mirror just laughs, because the idea is so ridiculous. The Steve in the mirror knows I'm still a college sophomore, going to classes and protesting the war in Viet Nam by day, drinking beer down at Pat's Pizza with Flip Thompson and George McLeod by night. As for my grandson, the beautiful Ethan? He just tugs on the balloon tied to his toe and laughs.

Daughter Naomi and son Owen got here late last night. We had a great Father's Day dinner; people saying things to me that were so nice I had to check to make sure I wasn't dead! God, I'm lucky to have family, lucky to have more stories to tell, lucky to still be alive. The worst thing to happen this week, I hope, will be my wife's bed collapsing under the weight of our son and daughter-in-law—the idiots were wrestling on it.

You know what? I've been thinking of going back to Roland's story after all. As soon as I finish the book on writing (<u>On Writing</u> would actually not be a bad title—it's simple and to the point). But right now the sun is shining, the day is beautiful, and what I'm going to do is take a walk.

More later, maybe.

From the Portland Sunday Telegram, *June 20, 1999:*

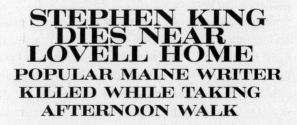

STEPHEN KING DIES NEAR LOVELL HOME
POPULAR MAINE WRITER KILLED WHILE TAKING AFTERNOON WALK

INSIDER CLAIMS MAN DRIVING LETHAL VAN "TOOK EYES OFF THE ROAD" AS HE APPROACHED KING ON ROUTE 7

By Ray Routhier

LOVELL, ME. (Exclusive) Maine's most popular author was struck and killed by a van while walking near his summer home yesterday afternoon. The van was driven by Bryan Smith of Fryeburg. According to sources close to the case, Smith has admitted that he "took his eyes off the road" when one of his Rottweilers got out of the back of the van and began nosing into a cooler behind the driver's seat.

"I never even saw him," Smith is reported to have said shortly after the collision, which took place on what locals call Slab City Hill.

King, author of such popular novels as *It, 'Salem's Lot, The Shining,* and *The Stand,* was taken to Northern Cumberland Memorial Hospital in Bridgton, where he was pronounced dead at 6:02 PM Saturday evening. He was 52 years old.

A hospital source said the cause of death was extensive head injuries. King's family, which had gathered in part to celebrate Father's Day, is in seclusion tonight . . .

Commala-come-come,
The battle's now begun!
And all the foes of men and rose
Rise with the setting sun.

Wordslinger's Note

I'd once more like to acknowledge the invaluable contributions of Robin Furth, who read this novel in manuscript—and those preceding it—with great and sympathetic attention to detail. If this increasingly complex tale hangs together, Robin should get most of the credit. And if you don't believe it, check out her *Dark Tower* concordance, which makes fascinating reading in and of itself.

Thanks are also due to Chuck Verrill, who has edited the final five novels in the Tower cycle, and to the three publishers, two large and one small, who cooperated to make this massive project a reality: Robert Wiener (Donald M. Grant, Publisher), Susan Petersen Kennedy and Pamela Dorman (Viking), Susan Moldow and Nan Graham (Scribner). Special thanks to Agent Moldow, whose irony and bravery have saved many a bleak day. There are others, plenty of them, but I'm not going to annoy you with the whole list. After all, this ain't the fucking Academy Awards, is it?

Certain geographical details in this book and in the concluding novel of the Tower cycle have been fictionalized. The real people mentioned in these pages have been used in a fictional way. And to the best of my knowledge, there were never coin-op storage lockers in the World Trade Center.

As for you, Constant Reader . . .

One more turn of the path, and then we reach the clearing.

Come along with me, will ya not?

Stephen King
May 28, 2003
(Tell God thank ya.)